# I start counting

*Books by Audrey Erskine Lindop*

I START COUNTING

THE WAY TO THE LANTERN

NICOLA

MIST OVER TALLA

THE SINGER NOT THE SONG

FORTUNE MY FOE

SOLDIERS' DAUGHTERS NEVER CRY

THE TALL HEADLINES

OUT OF THE WHIRLWIND

THE OUTER RING

THE JUDAS FIGURES

# *I start counting*

## ❖❖❖❖❖❖❖ AUDREY ERSKINE LINDOP

1966

❖

*Doubleday & Company, Inc.   Garden City, New York*

*All of the characters in this book are fictitious,
and any resemblance to actual persons, living
or dead, is purely coincidental.*

FOR MURIEL

*1* ❖ IT REMINDS ME of Collins Wood in here. I don't know why. This is a mansion compared to Number 3 and it isn't even the same shape. Something in the atmosphere, I suppose, and the way the floors dip away in these old places. Or perhaps it's just because it's in the country and you get the smell of a clean wind blowing through trees.

I still love Number 3. I can think of it without remembering the horrors. After all, it wasn't the house's fault. It was mine.

They let Father Murphy come to see me today. The Home's got its own visiting priest, but they let Father Murphy come specially.

He's super, is Father Murphy. He joked and made fun of the wallpaper, and asked what the food was like, and gave me messages from school. Mother Marie-Adelaide sent me some fudge.

Then, of course, he had to get serious. He pointed out how if I'd never told the first lie I'd never have had to tell any others, and all that sort of thing. He said he knew I'd done what I'd done for the best of motives—he wasn't in any two minds about that—but you couldn't disguise the fact that I'd made a bit of a muck-up of my life before I was even fifteen.

You couldn't disguise that, either.

Not while I was sitting in a Remand Home while the Director of Public Prosecutions decided whether I was to be charged as an accessory after the fact to murder!

I am accused of having "assisted and comforted a murderer." The "comforted" part makes me giggle. It's nerves, I suppose—but somehow it sounds so daft.

If I'm found guilty I could be kept under detention at the Queen's pleasure, whatever and wherever that might be.

The other girls in here are crazy to hear all the details, but I'm not encouraged to talk about it. Only to responsible people.

I told Father Murphy I didn't think I cared what happened. When you've minded so much about one thing, anything except that seems to shrink.

He told me I was wrong to think like that. I owed it to my family. If I had no feelings left, *they* had.

I told him how poor Mother went on and on and on about how ashamed she was that I should have come before the court as being in need of "care or protection."

After all the ghastly things that had happened, she picked on that as the worst.

That *her* daughter!—a member of *her* family!—coming from *her* home!—that the neighbours should hear I was in need of "care or protection!" As if she hadn't cared or protected me herself!

I giggled nervously over that as well. Father Murphy smiled too when I took her off, but he did it sadly. He must have thought it was silly of Mum to be minding what the neighbours thought when she could have minded so much else. But he said it was sometimes people's subconscious defensive mechanism coming to their rescue. They faced only what they could face.

I asked him where he thought I'd go if they found me guilty, and I asked about my cousin Len. He said we must keep our minds and our prayers on the hopeful side of things.

They would keep me in the Remand Home pending the decision of the Director of Public Prosecutions, and we wouldn't think about anything beyond that until we knew the worst.

Then he asked me about George, and if my feelings had changed at all through what had happened. I said "no," and they never would. It wasn't a teenage crush like some of the papers seemed to think. I just loved him and—well, that was that.

It made me a little tearful and scary when Father Murphy got up to leave, like the boarders used to feel at school when their parents had come to visit them and it was time to go.

I kept thinking of little things to ask Father Murphy, to keep him a bit longer. It's not that they aren't kind to you here. They're very strict, but they're not unkind.

At first, when I came before the court, it looked as if I was going to be released into Mother's charge until the D.P.P. (as the police call him) had made up his mind what to do with me.

Then they changed their minds. I suppose it was the protection business, more than the care I was in need of.

In a way I was glad. That they changed their minds, I mean. It would have been awful tied to Mum's apron strings. Never allowed out without her, and meeting people the whole time who knew everything about it and would talk brightly about everything else under the sun.

At least you don't see any people you know in here, and they let you read a lot. They asked me what I wanted to do when I grew up and I said I wanted to teach history, so they got me in some books.

They said I was intelligent and rather advanced for my age. Perhaps that'll stop some of our kind relations sneering at convent educations!

Father Murphy saw my tears. He bent down and peered into my face. Then he gave a little wink and made one of those "click-click" noises out of the side of his mouth like boys do at girls. He did it very expertly and he was right in thinking it would make me laugh.

He told me that by the time I'd got through my *Everyday Life in Roman and Anglo-Saxon Times* it would be the end of the week before I knew it, and he'd be here again next Sunday.

It was lovely having him come on a Sunday. I'd taken a hate to them, Sundays I mean, and I always felt my lowest then. I know it's daft, because things can't be the fault of a certain day so it's ridiculous to blame one. But for me it was a Sunday that started everything. I can still get that shivery feeling inside my head when I think of it. I only have to close my eyes, and there I am back in that Sunday afternoon.

It's very flat and still in my memory—faded and old, as if it was stitched in my mind like a scene in one of those old samplers people used to make. It's even more like a sampler for me because I always count when I am scared—and I was counting a lot that afternoon. One-two-three-four-five-six-seven—in faded old cross-stitching along the bottom, and then we ourselves—clumsy and stiff in old, flannelly-looking wool or whatever they used in those days. There we all were, sewn into our places round the fire. I had Sandy, my big fat ginger cat, in my lap, and we should have been sitting round a real fire in our old house. But that had been condemned to make way for a development scheme, and the new council flat we had found was in a smokeless area. So we were sitting round one of those things with glass coal and a light to make it flicker.

The fire wasn't the only thing I missed about our old house at Collins Wood. You could hear the weather in it. The rain used to hit the tin roof that covered the coal cellar, and the wind used to get caught in the passages and blunder about like a drunk trying to fight its way out. You'd think you'd see more of the weather in these great high flats, but it doesn't seem to belong to you at all. The rain just passes you on its way down and you feel like a whole army under one umbrella. Not even a personal bit of rain to yourself.

Of course they're very well built and everything's shiny inside and warm, except that the door handles fall off, and

when you get a power cut you all sit and freeze; but you
don't get a smell of damp coming from the cupboard under
the stairs like you did at Number 3 Collins Wood, or a bulge
in the bathroom wall which broke into little wet bits if you
stuck your finger in it—but then you don't get the smell of
grass pushing through the cracks, either, and you don't hear
any birds at all.

The birds were wonderful at Number 3. It had quite a
large, wild garden behind. You'd open the big wooden door
at the side, and there you were in the country. It was marvellous when you knew it was so close to town. I often used
to wonder what *the* Mr. Collin was like; he must have
owned a wood at some time—way, way back, George said,
maybe two hundred years ago. I expect his neighbours
were furious with him for selling the wood and letting
houses spring up in it, like the one I minded leaving so
much!

There was another good thing about Number 3 Collins
Wood. You saw more of George—he would never sit in the
living room, even after Mum had changed the carpet and
had it all refurnished. I'll explain why later. He sat in the
kitchen or in his bedroom, and I could often be sure of
getting him to myself.

But in the new flat he sat in the living room and the others
were always there.

I liked it best when we watched television, because then
I could look at him instead without anyone noticing!

It was a pleasant, big room, I suppose, and we'd got it
furnished quite contemporary. Grandad and Mum didn't
care for it much. But the rest of us thought it was nice.
George had made the coffee tables—like slices of a tree on
legs, with the bark still round it and all the notches showing. The carpet was fitted—black needle-loom—and the sofa
was one of those big double-bed put-u-ups. It was scarlet
and had maize-coloured cushions. The curtains were bottle-
green, and so were the other armchairs, and the walls were

a sort of stippled stone that had been done by one of the painters who work for George.

Mum thought it was too bright, and Grandad grumbled that we might just as well have dragged the rainbow in and be done with it.

The only thing wrong with it from my point of view was that it wasn't Number 3 Collins Wood.

It was raining on my Sampler Sunday—not the kind I like—the thin, impersonal, silvery kind, not the stormy country kind.

My cousin Nellie—or Hélène, as she likes to call herself—was normal enough that afternoon, and so were Grandad and Mum. The feeling was between George and Len, as solid as if it were a giant Christmas cracker they were going to pull between them at any moment. And you knew that however long you'd been waiting for it you would jump right out of your skin at the bang.

It was queer, for they get on all right usually. George was a bit tough with Len sometimes because Len was a bit of a tearaway, but Len thought the sun got up with George, much as he tried to hide it.

Now I'll try and explain my family. I've written it out three different ways already, and it still reads muddly—so I've put in a family tree!

Mum wasn't really my mother. She's really my aunt Lucy. I just called her Mother to be like all the rest. My family are a bit confusing, I'm afraid. There was none of that nice straightforward Jacob begat Whatnot, and Whatnot begat Thingumbob, like you get in the Bible. We were very mixed up through marriages.

Aunt Lucy was married before she came into our family to a man called Fred Meakham. They had a son, George. When Fred died of wounds left over from the First World War, and George was still a child, she married my uncle Albert Kinch, Grandad's elder son. My father was Grandad's younger son John, so Lucy Meakham became my aunt

Lucy by marriage. Isn't it awful to try and work out? Aunt Lucy and Uncle Albert had twins—Nellie, or Hélène, and Len.

They did a lot of dying in my family, too—my own mother died when I was five and my father waltzed off with someone else's wife, leaving me with Grandad. When Uncle Albert died from pneumonia, Aunt Lucy asked both Grandad and me to go and live with her and her own son, George Meakham, and my Kinch cousins. There—I've made it as clear as I can. But people still get muddled, because George is so much older than the rest of us.

Here's the tree!

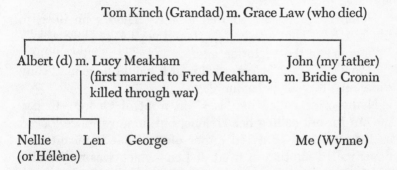

I don't know whether that makes it better or worse. It looks a bit messy. Perhaps it's not quite how they're usually done.

Len and Nellie are my first cousins because Grandad's their grandfather as well—but George was no relation to me. He was Len's and Nellie's half-brother, but no blood connection of mine at all.

When I pointed that out to Nellie, she said, "Who are you kidding, love-sick? It would still be incest with someone as close as that." As I wasn't quite sure what she meant, I looked it up in the dictionary. It said: "sexual commerce of near kindred." Well, that wasn't much help, and when I looked up "commerce" and found it meant: "exchange of merchandise especially on large scale" I was thoroughly confused.

But I understood clearly when Nellie stopped laughing long enough to say to George, "Wynne says it wouldn't be incest if she slept with you—but I say it would."

"*Nellie* Kinch!" I shrieked. "I *never* said that—I'll kill you—I'll—I'll—you *wait!*"

George had one of those quiet voices you can always hear. "Wynne's right," he told Nellie. "It's only incest if you're blood relations."

I thought my face was never going to settle down. It felt as if all the blood in my body was boiling behind my cheeks and charging down my neck.

Nellie laughed and pointed at me. "There's no need to blush, L.S." (That was her shortened version of "love-sick.") "We aren't in the Victorian age."

"More's the pity," George said, "if it would have made any difference to your behaviour."

Nellie often called me "L.S." in front of George, to pay me out for not calling her Hélène, but he never once looked as if he noticed or asked either of us what it meant. She never called me that in front of Len—which was rather nice of her, I suppose, because he would have asked and gone on asking.

Grandad didn't want to go to live with Aunt Lucy at first because she hated the idea of his mice. But George persuaded her to put up with them, and Grandad and I and the mice all moved to Number 3 Collins Wood.

I was too young to remember, but I believe it was a long time before Aunt Lucy stopped squealing whenever she saw the mice! I adored them, of course, and George took an interest in them to cheer up Grandad, and grew fascinated with them himself! It always made people laugh, because George was the last person you'd pick to be a mouse fancier!

It was he who suggested that I called Aunt Lucy Mother. We were all at home that Sampler Sunday. Grandad had broken the television again. He isn't really supposed to touch it round the back, but he gets stubborn at times. He says he was making crystal wireless sets in match-boxes before any of us were thought of. I never quite see what that's got to do with it, really—but he always breaks the television set.

George had taken it off to be mended the Wednesday before, so as there was nothing to look at, we were all reading something. Hélène was learning her part in a play which her amateur dramatic society was putting on. Mum was reading out a letter from Aunt Rene Tindall that no one was listening to, Grandad was reading the *Observer Colour Supplement,* I was pretending to read *Pop Beat,* Len was reading *The Hatter's Ghosts,* and George was reading "The Mouse Fancy" in *Fur and Feather.*

At least, George was supposed to be reading it.

Grandad called across to him, "Read about the two B. E. Whites in the Walsall show, George?"

"Yes," said George.

"Interesting, isn't it? If they really were B. E. Whites it could mean the variety's back, like the fellow said."

"Yes," said George.

But George wasn't reading "The Mouse Fancy" page—I know because I had passed him to get my *Pop Beat* and looked over his shoulder. He was stuck on "News from the Pigeon Lofts" and he hadn't even noticed.

All the time, behind his magazine, he was watching Len, and his magazine was shaking. Not enough to blow your skirts about, I'll admit—just trembling at the edges. Other people might not even have put it as strongly as that, but I was so used to noticing things about George.

Mum crackled her letter. "Your aunt Rene Tindall says she's been badly again. She's annoyed we haven't called on her."

Nobody took any notice, so I said, "Oh dear," which was all I could think of, but it satisfied Mum for the moment.

Hélène was spilt over the sofa. She looked a bit rough to me, with her hair all lank and her jeans all tight round her bottom.

I was six months younger than my school friend Corinne, of whom I was secretly scared. She was a bit of a mixer, was Corinne—she could mix things up for anyone.

I wasn't scared of my cousin Hélène. She was in a different world to ours. She was nineteen, and to my mind much lovelier than some of the film stars we used to see free in the cinema where she worked as an usherette. She wanted to be an actress herself and she was saving to go to a drama school in London. She was going to call herself "Hélène Clancy." The rest of the family shrieked about it. But I was sympathetic—you couldn't expect her to want to make a name like Nellie Kinch famous! But I made sure to call her Nellie whenever I was mad at her.

I was never envious of Hélène as I was of my ten-times-more-ugly friend Corinne—Hélène was way, way out of my class. She was marvellous to look at and knew it, and it was no good trying to make her think she wasn't as long as there were mirrors or men.

Her twin, Len, was plain compared to her. He was small and dark with a nervy little jump in his eye, but he packed an energy I should think they'd have been glad of at Harwell.

On Sampler Sunday I kept on saying to myself, "You're daft, Wynne Kinch, that's your trouble. One, two"—and I started to count in my silly, scared way—"one, two, three, four, five, six—" It was just really something to say to yourself out loud to drown the thought that was scaring you. What was scaring me was why George and Len were acting so queer over that book? There must have been something in it that scared them, too. I made up my mind to get hold of it as soon as Len was out of the way.

Len sat holding the book as if it had been heavy instead of a paperback. I was sure he knew about the looks George was giving him. He seemed to hold the book right where George could see it best, and he cleared his throat every time he turned a page as if to draw attention to it.

George wasn't turning any pages. He hadn't got to "The Mouse Fancy" yet. Len's book was a green and white paperback with "*The Hatter's Ghosts,* Simenon," written on it in black letters. It wasn't a very thick book, but it suddenly seemed to me that Len was either a long time getting through it or he was always reading it. I seemed to have seen his nose in it for weeks.

Mum repeated crossly, "I said your aunt Rene Tindall was poorly again."

Grandad was deep in his paper, so she didn't expect him to answer, but she did expect George to. She was looking at him, waiting, but he was still looking at Len.

I sighed, "What's the matter with her this time, Mum?"

"It's her water-works," I was told. "She caught a chill in them at a friend's funeral."

Now usually anything to do with Aunt Rene Tindall's water-works had the twins rolling all over the place. It was what they liked best if there wasn't anything grisly on the telly. They'd lark about and take the mickey out of Mum and Aunt Rene until George, who was usually eating the sides of his own smile by then, told them to pack it up.

But Len was too deep in that book and Hélène didn't notice. Len was always the ringleader, anyhow.

George put down *Fur and Feather.* "Keen on that book, aren't you, Len?"

"Yep."

George went back to *Fur and Feather,* noticed that he was still on the pigeon lofts, and hurried over to "The Mouse Fancy."

It wasn't like George to be rattled.

Mum said, "They've given her pills, poor thing, but they aren't working—it's so awkward when you're behind a counter and can't keep running off every minute."

That should have sent the twins into fits, but without Len's lead Hélène went on studying, and Len's hands were quite white round the knuckles gripping that book.

Normally Aunt Rene Tindall was one of their favourite forms of mother-baiting. Poor Mum, they always got a rise out of her. You couldn't call their gags very subtle, either. Len once came in to supper dressed like a Chinese coolie in a blue cotton coat and trousers. Heaven knows where he got them from. He told Mum that he had joined the Chinese Communist Party and that he was sure she'd come to love his concubine and that they'd already got a baby called One Flung Cup!

I couldn't stop giggling myself—although Mum was so upset. She said all the things Len knew she'd say, and Hélène anticipated them under her breath too low for her to hear.

"Your Dad would turn in his grave!"

"After all I've done for you!" and "No son of mine . . ." etc.

When she got down to blaming television and Fanny Hill, Len got hiccoughs from laughing.

"How often *have* you read that book?" George fired at Len.

"Couldn't say."

"Try counting."

Hélène looked up from her play. "He's always reading it. Why shouldn't he?" The twins always stuck up for each other.

"No reason," George answered quietly. "But on the other hand, why should he?"

"What book is it?" Grandad asked.

"Simenon," Len replied, his eyes still on the paperback.

When Grandad said, "Eh?" Len shouted, quite unnecessarily loudly, "*Simenon!*"

"The man that wrote about Inspector Maigret. You used to like him on telly, Grandad," I said quickly.

"Your grandad asked what it was called," Mother interrupted. "Not who wrote it."

"No, he didn't," Len answered. "He asked what it *was*—what I should have replied was 'A *book*.'"

"Oh! A detective story." Grandad nodded.

"It's nothing of the sort," said Len.

"Don't argue with your grandad," Mother told him sharply. "He can't say a word but what you have to say the opposite—and don't shout at him. He's not deaf."

Len sat up indignantly. "But it *isn't* a detective story. You know who's done it almost from the start."

"Then why do you have to read right through to the end so often?" George wanted to know.

"Any law against it?" Len enquired.

"Tell your grandad what it's *called*," Mother insisted, tight-lipped. She always fought it out with the twins. I think that was the cause of the war between them. Neither side let anything drop.

Len sent his voice all silly and reeled off: "'*The Hatter's Ghosts* by Simenon—a haunting mystery set in the back streets of La Rochelle. Complete and unabridged. Translated from the French by Nigel Ryan. Penguin Books in association with Hamish Hamilton.' Anybody want any more? —I could start in on the first chapter."

"You still haven't answered my question," George pointed out, and I thought his voice wasn't quite his own. He seemed to be pushing it from somewhere.

I asked, "What's it about, our Len?"

"A town that this hatter lives in, where women get strangled."

Mother said, "What a book to read at a time like this!"

"The right time," Len said.

"Did the hatter see the strangled people's ghosts?" I asked.

"No."

"What, then?"

"I'll read you what's on the cover," said Len. He read out, "'The hatter lives above his old shop in a narrow street of

La Rochelle, and the smelly little tailor opposite can apparently see all that goes on in the dark house.'"

"I don't see what that's got to do with the stranglings in this town," snapped Mother.

"Neither do I," purred Len. "Neither do I, Mother mine."

He could be ever so dramatic. But then he was quite a bit of an actor in his way. He used to play all the parts against Hélène when she was studying for something. They'd be lying over the sitting-room on their stomachs, reading at each other, and they really got quite so as you thought you were getting your money's worth.

Mother shuddered. "I wonder you can read about things like that after what happened to those two poor mites."

"They weren't mites in *The Hatter's Ghosts*," George told her.

"If you've read it," Len snapped at him, "why all the questions?"

"There was only one. *Why* do you read it *so often?*"

"Because I like it."

"When I were young," Grandad put in testily, "we only read good books on Sundays."

"This *is* a good book," Len told him. "The atmosphere is wonderful and so are the characters—you even find you're on the strangler's side."

I noticed that Len had gone the kind of greasy white that he always went before he had one of his awful headaches. Mother took him to a doctor about them when he was seven and he had to take phenobarbitone, but as far as I knew he hadn't had an attack for months and probably for years.

Hélène caught me looking at George and I went plum-coloured as she chanted, "'Georgie-porgie, pudding and pie, kissed the girls and made them cry!'"

"It's a good job they don't want you to sing in that play, Nellie Kinch," I said heatedly. "It'd have the audience walking out."

It was a witless answer and Hélène only grinned at it.

"Is it a dirty book?" Mum wanted to know.

"Not in the least," George told her.

"Then what's all the fuss about?"

"There's no fuss," said George. "Len just doesn't seem able to answer a straight question."

"Oh yes, he can! I—read—it—so—often," Len shouted, separating the words, "be-cause—it—fasc-in-ates—me."

"A good enough reason," George told him. "But you could have said so in the first place."

He went back to *Fur and Feather*.

"If your aunt Rene Tindall gets any more chills," Mum said gloomily, "her kidneys'll give out altogether."

That got our Len going. He gave a shout of laughter and threw down the book as if he was relieved to be able to stop talking about it. He got up, hobbling to the fireplace with his hand on his back and his voice all high and Lancashire.

"It were that bad, Luce," he piped, "I were on the run all through the night. Run! Run! Run!—and as soon as you're back in bed you get that prickly feeling, and run, run, run all over again—"

"Eee! And the *colour!*" Hélène joined in. "Doctor said, 'That's too cloudy for 'ealth, Mrs. Tindall.'"

"*Nellie!*" rapped out Mum.

Grandad grinned, and Len bent over him, still using Aunt Rene Tindall's voice. "It's me kidneys, Mr. Kinch. Doctor says one's as soft as a bit of goose shit."

"*Len!*" shrieked poor Mum.

Grandad chuckled. "Got her voice off pat, hasn't he?"

Hélène had sat up. Even with her thick mahogany-coloured hair and her long dark lashes, she managed to screw her face into something that gave the impression of the little shrivelled apple that was Aunt Rene Tindall. "Doctor said there were pus in me specimen."

"Nellie!" Mother blazed at her. "If you're going to be disgusting, leave the room!"

"Yes, that's quite enough," George said, and then he told Mother, "But it's exactly how she does talk. If you saw her on television you'd laugh yourself."

"I should *not* laugh at your aunt Rene Tindall made sport of on telly!"

"I didn't mean her herself—I meant a character like her— all aches and pains and awful details. No wonder the kids laugh."

"I've never been amused at other people's ailments and I'm surprised to hear you are, George," Mum said stiffly. Then she asked him, "Can you take Wynne back to her school tonight?"

I looked swiftly at him. He shook his head. "I've promised to put up some shelves this evening for old Mrs. Bennett."

"And no charge, I suppose? You'll never make your fortune, George Meakham."

"Old-age pensions don't run to bookshelves," said George.

"Good thing somebody knows it," came bubbling out of Grandad's pipe.

My school had just broken up for the Easter holidays, but on that "Sampler Sunday" it was our yearly one-day conference for teenagers. We had met that morning at the convent at nine-forty-five and then we went to Mass at ten. There was coffee and biscuits afterwards, and then the speakers got started. It was wonderfully interesting. There were so many topics. A folk singer talked and then sang quite a few songs, we had someone suggesting unusual careers, and there was someone from the Catholic Marriage Advisory Council to answer any problems on sex or things to do with it that we didn't understand.

I stayed for the buffet lunch in the hall, and I would have stayed all the afternoon, but Sundays were my best chance of seeing George. He was usually at home until the evening, so I'd arranged to go back for the wind-up of the conference at seven.

"It's the discussion bit I don't want to miss," I explained.

"It's the most interesting part—you can ask about things you've heard in the day."

"Len," Mum called across to him, "can you see Wynne to the convent tonight?"

I was the only Roman Catholic in the family. It came through my real mother, and because of the things that had been happening in our town lately, Aunt Lucy was scared of us girls being out late at night.

"Sorry, Mum," Len told her. "I can't let down the Salvation Army."

"Salvation Army!" she snorted. "You're going to that dreadful pop group. I should have thought your sister's safety was more important than kicking up a noise in someone's cellar."

Mother always called me the twins' sister, and she always referred to me as her own daughter.

"Do you have to go again tonight, Wynne?" George asked me. "You went to Mass this morning and you had the whole morning at the conference."

There was a time when George would take me anywhere. He'd go out of his way when he was driving to work. He'd call for me at the convent and sometimes he'd let me go with him just for the drive and I'd sit outside in the van, or even trot round the site where he was working. But lately he was funny with me. He quite definitely went out of his way to avoid me. And it wasn't my imagination. I don't imagine things about George. He'd walk along a street with me, or stay and talk in a room if Hélène or Corinne were with me, but if I was on my own he seemed to sheer off.

"Cut it out for tonight, Wynne," he advised me.

"All right," I said, and I thought, "A year ago he'd have run me there himself, wherever he was going."

"I'll take her," Hélène offered. "I might see Father Murphy and I think he's gorgeous."

"What's the good of that?" Mum snapped. "That just puts two of you in danger."

Hélène laughed. "I'm old enough to look after myself."

"That last poor little thing was only a month or two younger than you," Mum told her. "I should think you'd want to take care with a maniac on your doorstep."

"Ten miles away is hardly our doorstep, Mum," Len pointed out.

"It's near enough for me."

"Ten miles away isn't *near*, Mum," Len insisted. He was polishing his soft black boots with Mum's silver clothes brush.

She held out her hand for it. "He's got two feet, hasn't he? He could use them to come this way—or do you think it was a mad dog that really did it and the police have all gone daft?"

George said, "There's been nothing to prove he's from this town, Mother. His two feet could very well have brought him from somewhere else and taken him back there."

"Well, he's chosen Dalstead Common to do away with two poor girls and I'm not letting mine give him a chance to make it four."

Hélène was exasperated. "Mum, how often do Wynne and I go out on Dalstead Common since we left Collins Wood?"

I thought what a good thing it was they didn't know how often I crept off there.

"There's nothing to say the brute will keep to the common," Mother answered. "You never know with madmen."

"He's sane enough to keep out of the way of the law—he knows right from wrong. You don't notice him bragging about it in the street," said Grandad. "You're not mad according to the law if you know right from wrong, and he knows that or he wouldn't be keeping out of the law's way."

"Get out, Grandad," snapped Len. "He's steaming bonkers."

"He might just want you to think that, boy."

"It's hardly a sane way to behave, Grandad," George put

in, "to strangle girls and then mangle their bodies and leave them on the roadside to look like a car accident."

"That's what *is* sane about it," Grandad argued. "He knows it's wrong so he tries to make it look like an accident."

"But he'd have to be bonkers to have strangled them in the first place," Len shouted.

"Your Grandad's not deaf," Mother told him, and added tactlessly, "There's enough trouble with real road accidents without him having to make them up."

We were all a bit quiet when she said that, wondering how George would take it because of what happened at Collins Wood, but he didn't seem to mind.

They were discussing the man the papers were calling the "Dalstead Strangler" and sometimes the "Dalstead Mystery Killer."

When the first girl was found, the police sent out a message for a hit-and-run driver. Then the pathologist found she'd been strangled before she was run over. So they were ready for the second one, so to speak. The cars the strangler had used were just found abandoned and the police knew they were the ones he'd used through something to do with the tyre marks.

In each case the car had been stolen. It wasn't very nice for the people they belonged to. One was a woman, so it wasn't so bad for her, but the poor man—even after the police had asked him questions and let him go, quite satisfied he'd had nothing to do with it—still got people staring at him.

"Funny he doesn't rape them," Len said.

"Bit of a waste, I call it," said Hélène.

"*Nellie!*" Mother rapped out.

George ignored her. He always ignored the twins when they were silly and went too far.

He used to lecture us about it at times.

"You rise like no self-respecting trout would ever rise, Mother! Of course they try it on. Don't give them the satisfaction of looking shocked—they'll soon get tired of it if they don't get any fun out of it. Let them 'F' and 'B' as much as they like—just pretend you haven't noticed."

Poor Mother used to try, but she just couldn't ignore them.

She snatched her silver clothes brush out of Len's hand and said to George, "Tell those girls they've got to be careful, or I'll never know a minute's peace."

George stood up. "I've already told Wynne not to go tonight—and I don't think Nellie should go out on her own either."

"Hélène to you, gorgeous," Nellie told him. "And I'm hardly ever out on my own."

"Wynne," said George, "even in the daytime you ought to see you've got Corinne with you, if you're going any distance."

"All right," I said.

He put *Fur and Feather* on the arm of Grandad's chair and left the room. A little later we heard the front door shut behind him. I felt flat, like I always did when I knew George was out.

Mum said to Grandad, "I wish you'd have a word with him—I'm the last one to grudge anything to old folk, but that Mrs. Bennett takes real advantage of him."

"*If* it's Mrs. Bennett he's gone to," said Hélène.

I didn't look up. I knew she'd said it on purpose because of my crack about her singing.

"He *said* Mrs. Bennett," Mother replied. "And she's always been a scrounger."

"Her house must be full of shelves," said Hélène, "if he puts them up every Sunday."

"What are you getting at, Nellie?"

"He goes out every Sunday evening, and it's always Mrs. Bennett."

Grandad picked up *Fur and Feather*. "Perhaps it's a difficult job—and the lad's only got his spare time."

Hélène was looking at me under her eyelashes. "I don't think you'll find it's all spent with Mrs. Bennett."

"If it was all spent with Madame Kosygin, it wouldn't be any of your business, would it?" Grandad snapped. He was quick to catch fire where George was concerned, and that, of course, put me on the old man's side. I did lots of little jobs for Grandad. Not that I wasn't fond of him in any case, but I talked to him more than the others did, because he was always willing to rattle on about George without realising that I was encouraging him.

When the doorbell rang suddenly, I jumped. I wasn't really afraid of the "Dalstead Strangler," although, as Len pointed out, the bodies were found on the edge of Dalstead Common, which was nearly ten miles away from Dalstead Old Town and about fifteen from Dalstead New Town, which is where we'd had to move to, worse luck.

Corinne and I sometimes tried to scare each other over the strangler when we were bored, but it didn't really work and we thought my mum was a bit of a nit to make the fuss she did about him.

But I jumped when I heard that doorbell go. I tell you—everything seemed different, that "Sampler Sunday."

"It's for me," said Hélène, without looking up from her script.

"Psychic, or expecting someone?" Len wanted to know.

"Paul," she told him.

Paul worked in the bank where George and his partner Mr. Wells had their business account. He was twenty-two and absolutely dotty potty over Hélène. She treated him like something not even a starving alley cat would think of bringing in.

"I thought you were going to wash your hair tonight," I fired at her.

"I am."

"Then what did you ask poor Paul for?"

"I didn't. He asked me."

"*Nellie* Kinch!" I said angrily. "You really are the ruddy end."

I ran across the living-room to open the door for poor Paul, with Mother calling after me, "Wynne! What would Father Murphy say about that language?"

Mother was terribly anti-Roman Catholic. I think that somewhere she thought that all Catholics were still up to the Gunpowder Plot, but she always held them up against me if she wanted to tick me off. My poor old religion always got it in the neck. If I did something wrong, it was what you could expect from mumbo jumbo and bobbing about to plaster saints. But if someone wanted me to do something, it was what would that nice Father Murphy think of me if I didn't!

Paul wasn't expecting to see Nellie. She never bothered to open the door to him unless everyone else was out. He had a lovely white smile that wasn't a bit like a tooth-paste ad. I made mine the same size, trying to make things up to him—sometimes I think I must have struck him as a pint-sized aunty, the way I used to try and chat him up so as not to feel bad about Nellie.

"She's in," I told him.

"She should be," he said. "She's expecting me."

"It's her hair night," I warned him as I took his coat. Our hall was tiny, but the built-in cupboards made up for no space—I hung his coat on one of those tin hangers you get back from the cleaners. The whole cupboard smelt of "Tigress by Fabergé," off Hélène's sheepskin jacket.

Paul frowned a little. "We're going out."

"She's forgotten," I said. "Remind her."

In the living-room Mother, Grandad, and Len said "Hello" to Paul. Hélène looked up, said "Hi!" and looked down again.

Paul walked over to her. "You're not coming out in that get-up, are you?"

"I'm not coming out period."

"You said you'd come to Swan's—I've booked a table—"

"Unbook it, sex-mad," she said silkily. I was always wild at her when she was affected like that—it wasn't fair against poor old Paul—like throwing a ball at a blind man.

"Cup of tea, Paul?" Mother offered.

"No, thanks, Mrs. Kinch."

He was still standing over Hélène's long body, which drenched the sofa in Tigress.

"Do you *have* to wash your hair tonight, Hélène?" He never dared to call her Nellie.

"More than that," she said, without looking up at him. "I've got an audition tomorrow—I'm going to have a manicure and a face pack—the lot."

"She has to take trouble at her age," I said stupidly. I do think if you can't be nasty wittily you ought not to try it at all.

Hélène answered, "We haven't all got your gorgeous complexion, Puss Bun"—which made me feel dreadful because she meant it nicely.

My figure needed watching and my hair made me cry at times. It just wouldn't hang straight—but lots of people said my complexion made up for it. My mother was Irish and Grandad said I got my eyes and teeth from her as well.

Len put his head round the door. "Want to come and listen to the group, Paul?"

"No, thanks, Len."

"Okay. Sweat it out, down-trodden!"

Hélène threw him a gleam under her deep brown lashes and Len sent her the same kind back. You might have thought those two were in love with each other.

Grandad peered past *Fur and Feather*. "There's some beer in the fridge, Paul, lad."

"No thanks, Mr. Kinch." To Hélène Paul said, "Where is the audition, then?"

"They're going to let me know."

"Can I take you to it?"

"How the hell do I know?—I *told* you I don't know when it is myself."

"Nellie!" Mother called over to her. "Can't you answer a civil question civilly?"

"Mum," Nellie answered, "would you please take note that my name is Hélène."

"Marie Lloyd was good enough for Marie Lloyd," Mum snapped.

"I dare say, Mother dear—but you'll note that she didn't call herself Nellie Kinch."

"Hélène's very pretty," Paul said loyally.

"Nit!" I thought. "Nit! He'd do better to bash her one."

I'd have been furious if he had, of course, but there was something about him standing there so worshipfully that made me tingle. I expect it was because I was having difficulty in making George remember that I was alive in those days—and Hélène didn't even have to bother to look at people to get them all buzzing round her.

I am always puzzled about that "play-hard-to-get" advice. What's the good of playing hard to get if someone's going out of their way to avoid you in any case? "Be aloof," you get told. "Be distant!" But how are people going to know you're being distant if you can't get near enough for them to notice?

Hélène can do this. She wanted the manager of her cinema once. Just after she started and she was learning the job. Heaven knows why she wanted him. He was *stringy* and went all "in" like the front of a spoon at the chest. He had catarrh and he was thousands of years older than she was (though on that score, of course, I'm very sympathetic). He just laughed at her and called her "Little Nelly Kelly" which Hélène thought was frightfully witty. He had an ulcer and a wife, three children, and dentures, but Hélène cried for him night after night. She read all the books he liked (and he'd got *dreadful* taste). She took up yoga breathing to get slimmer. It was awful at night—I'd

rather have had the sobs, they sound more regular. But I
expect it was because Hélène didn't do it right—yoga
breathing, I mean. She was great on the sobs. I used to sigh
just after one of them at the top of my lungs—if that's what
you'd call it—to let her know I was being kept awake. I was
young and a bit smug in those days, because George was
still spoiling me. She went off her food and Mother got
every tooth in her head looked at in case she was swallow-
ing poison.

Then she got him—the cinema manager, I mean. Goodness
knows how she did it, but it wasn't long before they re-
versed the roles. He was absolutely dotty potty over her,
and she was turning up her nose and saying he smelt of
cough candy!

There was a fearful to-do. Mrs. Cinema Manager called
to see Mother. We were at Collins Wood then. Everyone
started polite and then lost their tempers.

They were all in the living-room. Hélène and Len and I
nearly knocked each other's teeth out trying to spy and
eavesdrop. There was only one keyhole and we simply
weren't patient enough to take it in turns.

Mother kept on saying, "This is a respectable house," until George got quite angry with her.

"For God's sake, Mother, no one's accusing the *house*. It's
Nellie and her husband this lady's worried about."

That set Mum and Mrs. Cinema Manager off. They
started with "your daughter" and "your husband," but they
ended with "that little bitch" and "that dirty old man!"

I had a bruise the size of a plum on my temple where I
collided with Len at the keyhole.

Mrs. Cinema Manager demanded that Hélène should be
taken away from the cinema because she was a corrupting
influence, and Mother threatened to write to the Watch
Committee about the manager, because no innocent
young thing would ever be safe with him.

Mrs. Cinema Manager said Mother ought to be ashamed

of herself bringing up a young Jezebel, and Mother got stuck on the word "disgusting" like one of those breathless old gramophone records. "A man of his age! Chasing a sixteen-year-old girl! It's disgoosting. Disgoosting. Disgoosting. Disgoosting."

That's when I got my bruise, but it was worth it.

George had to get between them and push them away from each other. He said if Mrs. Cinema Manager could deal with her husband he'd see that Hélène was no more trouble. He did, too. She never told me what he said to her, but we didn't hear any more about the cinema manager from Hélène. We heard some more from him, though. Even after his wife's visit he kept on ringing. Once he pretended to be Paul, and George told Hélène to let him think she thought he really was, and make a date. George went on it instead of Hélène, and knocked him flat out.

After that he let her alone, but she certainly had an effect on him.

I asked George, "How did she *get* him? He was laughing at her only a little time ago."

George smiled. "She grew up in that 'little time ago'— that's how she got him."

When the second strangling took place, we raked up the old cinema manager. "I think he's left the district," Hélène said, "or he'd be just the type."

"Get out!" from Len. "He'd be a hundred and eighty-five."

I'm a bit sensitive about men's ages. "It was only three years ago—he'd only be forty-six."

"*Only!*" the twins both shouted at me.

Paul had one more shot at trying to make Hélène go out with him that Sampler Sunday.

"Look, eat for two of us, sweetheart," she suggested.

Mum took shocking advantage of him, as usual. "Paul, love, if you're not doing anything after all, would you see our Wynne to her school tonight?—there's some kind of 'do' on she doesn't want to miss."

"Oh, *Mum!*" I protested. "There's really no need—Father Murphy comes right out on the steps and watches us go."

"He can't see through walls and round corners, can he?"

"No—but there's eight of us coming back this way."

Grandad bent down to turn on another bar of the electric fire. "No one could strangle eight of 'em, more's the pity."

Mother ignored him. "I'm that scared until they catch the brute, Paul, and there's no one I'd feel happier she was with than you."

Paul said, "All right, Mrs. Kinch."

"And you will wait for her and see her back, won't you?"

"Yes, if you like, Mrs. Kinch." He turned to Hélène. "Will you be visible when we get back?"

She looked up, relenting a little. "Yes—you can shout at me through my hair dryer."

"Mind you don't overheat his blood," said Grandad. "Too much excitement's bad for a lad."

"I'll just get my coat," I told Paul, and then something caught my eye in the chair where Len had been sitting. It was *The Hatter's Ghosts*, half slipped behind a cushion. I made an excuse to puff up the cushion, picked up the book, and hid it against me as I went out of the room.

2 ❖ THE NEXT MORNING there was the most fearful kerfuffle. Poor Mother couldn't eat her breakfast and the twins were at their worst long before the poor soul even saw the papers.

There was nothing they loved more than taking off those plays which you get on the telly sometimes, that make the North Country seem all dustbins and sneaky alley cats and drunk men and women going round wearing curlers in a household fog.

Mother and her sister, Aunt Rene Tindall, came from the North, you see. They were born in Newcastle. They are both extremely proud of it and the twins make the best of it. Len had his hair pulled down over his eyes and Hélène was still in her rollers and the goggles she wears to save her false eyelashes in the bath. Every other word they used began with an *f*, and they used it in a really daftly exaggerated North Country accent.

Even though George had told Mum not to hit the roof when they used that word poor Mum was a-tremble with umbrage. She put the marmalade on her toast before the butter.

The play they were acting over breakfast was called *The Black Mirror's Gold Friend*, and it had something to do with the two mirrors on our wall—the black one was Mother's and came from her home in Newcastle, but the gold one was my mother's and Grandad and I brought it with us when we moved from the South, so I expect that was all highly symbolic.

They were a Mr. and Mrs. Drip, and Hélène was apparently stirring a stew in a dustbin.

Len said, "Can't you find anything better than that? The f'ing cat's been at it."

Hélène answered, "F'ing cat's *in* it."

George asked, "When do we get to the funny bits?"

Len turned into a narrator with his voice as lah di dah as he could get it. "Do not adjust your sets, this is not a technical hitch, you're only *supposed* to see the backs of their heads—the back of the head is more expressive than the face—in *The Black Mirror's Gold Friend,* for instance, you will see the back of the head of George Meakham—of Meakham and Wells, Builders and Contractors—now what does it tell us?"

"To shut up?" suggested George.

"It tells us that here we have a very unusual man—the face can hide the self—the back of the head is defenceless against our probing."

Hélène held out a jug to Len. "Get me a drop of typhoid from tap on landing, luv. Queue should be shorter by now."

Mother threw her such a look. But Len was still the narrator.

"We know that Mr. Meakham is calm, unflappable, and unemotional in the front—but at the back—have we a hatter's ghost?" asked Len.

George helped himself to coffee. We all drank tea, but he made himself his coffee.

"We'll 'ave to get new doostbin," wailed Hélène. "How do you expect me to keep stew hot in leakin' pot?"

Mother exploded. "There's more to the North than dustbins and bad language and dirty talk. There's manners in the North, and brains and hard work, and folks with kindness in their hearts and no shame for what they've come from."

Her own accent got thicker as she grew angrier, and Len and Hélène dropped the Drips and took off what they knew she'd be saying next.

"And as for scenery—if there's anywhere to beat West-

morland and Cumberland I'd be glad to be shown it—you
can have your Devonshires and Cornwalls—I'd rather take
what we can find in the Midlands—give me Silverdale and
Grange-over-Sands."

Poor Mother had got to Grange-over-Sands before she
realised they were all saying it with her.

George turned to the twins and said mildly, "Cut that
out." Then he asked me, "Did you say you were going to
the dentist with Corinne, Wynne?"

Corinne wouldn't let her mother take her to the dentist
in case she looked silly, but she was an awful coward, so I
had to go with her.

I laughed. "Yes. Reverend Mother says we ought not
to be ashamed of our faith letting people see us pray, so I
told Corinne I'd go down on my knees for her in the
waiting-room if she wasn't brave."

"Might lessen the faith of the other patients in the dental
surgeon a bit," smiled George.

Then he waved to us all and went out. He and his partner
Mr. Wells had opened a small builder's firm together.
George himself was a joiner. Mr. Wells did all the electrical
things himself and they employed five men.

George was tall and his hair was rusty. The lids of his
eyes were heavy and gave him a lazy look, and his smile
was slow and lazy-looking too. He was a big build of man,
and although he held himself straight he never seemed stiff
or anything. In face he seemed rather loosely bound together. His smile turned down instead of up. His eyes were
not lazy when you really saw into them. They had a rather
violet-y deepness to their blueness which made them a bit
hazy. His voice was a bit hoarse and he didn't have an accent you could really pick on. Just his own kind of George's
voice. There was perhaps something a bit metallic in
George's voice. He used his words so carefully, and not
many of them, and you felt he really meant what he said to
you because he had chosen it. He wore huge horn-rimmed

glasses. The rims were so thick they made a sort of balcony across his face.

He hadn't always been short-sighted. He joined the army when he was very young. I believe he signed on for five years or something, or maybe it was seven. Anyway, he got posted to Korea and then he got invalided out. A booby-trap blew up and gave him a nasty wound in the neck. The scar doesn't show much, but it affected his eyesight. I've never known him without the big glasses.

His father was a joiner, so I suppose it was in his blood.

He called through the letter-box to me, "Papers," and pushed them through on to the mat.

I went to pick them up. I was wondering how long ago it was that George gave up kissing me when he dashed off to work. I could have sworn he used to do it last year. I could never resist an extra glimpse of him, so I opened the front door and called down the passage, "Thanks, George. 'Bye."

"'Bye," he called back. "Get the dentist to drill Corinne's head off." He moved quick enough, for all his lazy looks.

"Will do," I called, and blew him a kiss, but he was already running down the stairs whistling.

I took the papers into the kitchen. We always had our meals in there—there was one end broken off by a screen and Mum refused point-blank to call it a dinette. She said a kitchen was a kitchen if it wasn't a dining-room.

We had the *Mirror* and the *Express* in the week, and the *Observer* and the *Sunday Mirror* at weekends.

I plumped the papers on the table and was just about to pick up my toast when Mum let out a wail.

"He's struck again! Dad! He's struck again!"

"Who has?" snapped Grandad. He'd had a letter from another mouse fancier and he wanted to read it in peace.

Poor Mother held out the paper, her hand really shaking. "The Dalstead killer—he murdered another poor soul last night."

Grandad bent forward to peer at the picture. He was one

of those who push their glasses up on their forehead to see better. "Looks a bit older, this time," he said.

Mum said, "What *are* the police doing? They must be blind, not catching the brute."

"They haven't seen him yet, Mum," said Hélène. "So they haven't had a chance not to catch him."

The "poor soul" had a longish sort of face and a rather fizzy-looking mop of pale hair. The photograph was taken at Hastings, beside a tall black wooden building.

"What's that?" Len wanted to know. "A public convenience for giants?"

"Don't be so disgusting," cried Mother, "when the poor soul's not even cold yet."

"It's a net shop," Grandad told Len. "They're one of the sights at Hastings—great tall, narrow places where they hung the fishing-nets—old as the hills. They've been there for years. No one remembers Hastings without them."

"She was a schoolteacher," said Mother in a shocked voice. "Think of it—a *school*teacher meeting an end like that."

"It's no worse for her than a whore," said Len.

Hélène picked up the paper. "Miss Gwendoline Travert— thirty years old—"

"Thirty!" interrupted Len. "More likely fifty."

"You can't tell from this sort of photograph," Hélène told him.

"Funny picking on an older woman this time," said Len.

Mother pulled at Grandad's arm. "Dad, we ought to get police protection for the girls—"

"Don't be so daft, Lucy," he said. "Our girls are in no more danger than anyone else's."

"Maybe, maybe not," said Len.

"Dad, get George to go to the police," Mother insisted.

"Maybe they won't give him back to us." Len giggled nervously—and when I looked up I saw that he had gone that greasy white.

Mother was crying. Grandad gave me a thump. I had gone off into one of my trances.

"Pour your mother out a cup of tea, Wynne, and get her an aspirin." And then he said to Mother, "Now come on, Lucy, there's no point in taking on like this—the police would think you were daft if you went to them."

I fetched Mother the aspirin and gave it to her with a glass of water.

Mother found another fact to horrify her. "The poor soul was a stranger here, Dad, she only came a month ago. Oh! Whatever will people think of Dalstead!"

Hélène was still studying the paper. "She'd been dead two hours when she was found. They think she was killed at seven o'clock—just after you'd got to your conference, Puss Bun," she flung at me. "What a lucky escape."

"Nellie!" Mother raged at her. "How *can* you make jokes when the honour of the whole town is at stake?"

"Honour of the town!" said Len.

"Yes—well, a *strangler!* Folks won't think it safe to come here."

I was too occupied with my own thoughts to realise that it was Mother's North Country sense of hospitality that was so outraged.

"He didn't try to make this one look like a car accident," Hélène observed. "He made it look like a suicide—'found hanging by her stocking in a 'bus shelter.'"

"Wonder what made him change his tactics," said Len.

"He's not so mad he can't read the papers," Grandad pointed out. "He'd know the police were on to the car business."

"It was our 'bus stop," Hélène squeaked. "Our 'bus stop for Collins Wood!"

"Well, you won't say *that's* not on our doorstep, will you?" Mother wanted to know.

"It's getting nearer," Len agreed, and I could see he had one of his terrible headaches.

But all I could do was think of that 'bus stop. I had waited in it so often.

I didn't realise how long I had been standing with the teapot in my hand until Grandad shouted at me, "Look lively, Wynne. What's the matter with you this morning? Your mother doesn't want it cold."

I poured the tea into Mother's cup so quickly it splashed on to the cloth.

I had been trying to think what time I heard George come in the night before. He was a funny one, was George. You could never hear him walking about, for all he was such a big man. He used to say that he'd make a good burglar. All you'd hear was the door bang. Mum was always asking, "Is that George coming in or going out?"

I hadn't had a chance to look at *The Hatter's Ghosts*. Hélène was ages over her beauty treatment the night before and Grandad was using the bathroom until late, so I couldn't sneak off there. I wanted to read the book right through before Len missed it and wanted it back again. I had it hidden in my school case.

I got up from the table and took my cup and plate to the sink. "Don't worry, Mum," I said. "They'll catch him soon."

"It couldn't be too soon for my liking," she told me.

"Never mind," said Len. "The fact that he's turning to older women's a good sign. He's broken his pattern. He's growing up—any psychiatrist would tell you that."

"And any psychiatrist could tell you you'll be late for work," Grandad answered.

"*Work!*" sniffed Mum.

Len worked at a record shop in the High Street and Mother never could get over it.

Hélène made a face. "Now, Mum, don't give us that 'he's got nothing better to do all day than listen to pop records and read filth.'"

Mother fired at her, "You won't deny, I suppose, that we were the only people in this block of flats with *Fanny Hill* open on the kitchen table when Doctor came to your grandad's knee?"

"Well, I'm sure the doctor would much rather find it on the kitchen table than under the pillow, which is probably where Aunt Rene Tindall keeps her copy."

"*Len!*" said Mother.

Grandad flapped his hands about. "That'll do. That'll do. Now clear out—for God's sake. Go and earn your livings."

"My audition isn't until twelve," said Hélène. She'd had a letter that morning asking her to report to the Jubilee Hall, where she was to read for the Amateur Dramatic Society. Our society was a bit grand in its own eyes because it once had a member who turned into a film star.

Mother began collecting the dishes. "Well, you're not going there without me," she answered.

Hélène whirled round, snatching her goggles off. "Without *you!*" she squeaked unbelievingly.

"Without *me*," said Mum. "I'm taking you there and I'm waiting outside to take you on to the cinema afterwards."

Bedlam broke out.

"Mum, for the love of all that's holy," from Len.

"Lucy, you're being downright daft," from Grandad, and mounting hysterics from Hélène.

"A right nit I'd look! A right, prime nit. Going to an audition with me Mum waiting outside—what would Mr. Preston think? What would all the others think? You'll lose me the *part!*"

"The girl's nineteen, Lucy, and it's broad daylight."

"The other poor soul was *thirty*, Dad."

Hélène flung herself weeping on to the sofa. She was thrashing about, banging the cushions.

"Mind your eyelashes," I warned her. I didn't mean to be nasty. I knew she hadn't got another pair for her audition and they stuck out so far I thought she'd knock them off.

Len flung his hands about as if he'd been one of those

actors that haven't got any words to help and have to make people understand through their fingers.

"Mum, you'll *kill* the girl's chances—they'll think she's a *nit*. Why don't you take her *nappies* with you and do the thing properly? Change them in between the scenes."

Grandad told him, "Save all that wriggling for the pop shop. Now Lucy, you're going too far."

"He'll have come from the South," Mother said doggedly. "That's for certain—you don't get that kind here or up North."

"Then maybe he'll go back there," I suggested quickly. "Turn round and go right back there tonight."

She said, "What time's your appointment with Corinne?"

"Eleven—but I thought I'd start off a bit early because I want to—"

"Want to what?"

"Go to Woolworth's first," I lied, and promised myself that it wouldn't stay a lie because I really would go to Woolworth's.

"I'll take you there, before Hélène."

This time it was me who was indignant. "That's absolutely *daft*, Mum. There are hundreds of people round Woolworth's and Corinne's only five minutes from there."

"Lucy," Grandad told her, "you won't have a minute's peace and you'll never get anything done about the house if you take the girls everywhere they want to go."

Hélène erupted from the sofa, snatched up her glasses, and made for the bedroom. "You've ruined my chances," she threw at Mum. "You've put me right out of the mood."

"You *can* be put right out of a mood," Len said, as we heard her slam our bedroom door.

"And you can be put *into* one," said Grandad, "which is happening to me this minute."

Len went out of the room and we heard Hélène open our bedroom door. Then we heard nothing else until the front door banged.

"Len didn't even say goodbye," said Mum.

When I went to look, I found that Hélène had slipped out with him. Mother was furious, and I was appalled at the idea of her playing nursemaid to me. Corinne would despise me for it.

Besides, I wanted to call on old Mrs. Bennett, and I couldn't do that with Mother around.

3 ❧   I WENT OFF TO THE BEDROOM I shared with Hélène, and got the copy of *The Hatter's Ghosts* out of my school case. I managed to cram it into my handbag by taking everything else out except my money and keys. Then I put on my coat, wound the scarf George gave me for my birthday round my neck, and nipped into the hall.

Mother, in her hat and coat, was standing at the front door.

"We'd better get off now," she said, "if you want to get to Woolworth's first."

I'm afraid I sulked the whole way, and I was mad at having to buy myself a comb. If I'd gone by myself I should only have walked right round.

I sulked all the way to Corinne's too. I really could have strangled Mother. I could hardly answer her civilly, so we didn't speak at all in the end.

Corinne really did despise me. I could see it as soon as my Mum explained why she was there. Corinne was polite enough to my mother, of course. She'd have got a clout if she'd treated mine like she treated her own.

Corinne had a yellowy kind of face with snappy little black eyes. I thought her hair was ghastly, but I spent hours trying to get my springy waves to fall flat and move about in lank pieces when I tossed my head like she did.

I always felt clumsy beside Corinne. She was a little wiry thing as thin as a pencil, and as lively and quick as I was dreamy and a bit too plump. Corinne was already fifteen and wore lipstick and shoes with quite high heels. My mother thought it was dreadful and Corinne's father thought so too. But her mother stuck up for her in everything. There were always rows between her parents, and Corinne's mother quite often threatened to leave her father for "picking on the girl."

George always said he'd pick on her once and for all and sling her in the Dalstead Reservoir.

Corinne's mother opened the door and let us in.

My mother said, "I'm worried about this dreadful business, Mrs. Eldridge—I don't think we should let the girls out alone."

Mrs. Eldridge always reminded me of a plucked chicken. She had one of those pale goose-pimply skins and pinky eyelids. And there was just a streak of red left in her hair, right at the top, which seemed to stand up. Her hands were that sort of pale maize colour which dead chicken's feet go. Perhaps Corinne's sallowness came from her. Anyway, I always saw a label round Mrs. Eldridge's neck saying, "Good Roaster. 14/6."

"Cup of tea, Mrs. Kinch?" she asked.

"No, thanks," said Mother. "I thought I'd go with them both to the dentist."

Mrs. Eldridge sent a nervous look at Corinne. She knew that Corinne wouldn't like it. Behind my mother's back Corinne screwed her face up and made fierce thumbs-down signs at the floor.

"Bill says it's all right in the day-time," said Mrs. Eldridge.

"We're all entitled to our opinions," said my mother firmly.

"There are *hundreds* of people about, Mum," I put in wearily. "He really would be mad if he came out and strangled us in the middle of *that* lot."

Mother ignored me. Corinne went off into faces again.

Theirs was a much smaller flat than ours. There were only the three of them. Theirs was Beldon House and ours was Fairley, after some old alderman.

"Surely you must be so busy, Mrs. Kinch," suggested Mrs.

Eldridge. She was under absolute machine-gun fire from Corinne's faces.

"There's a murdering madman in our midst," said Mother, not meaning to sound melodramatic. "And I'm not too busy to keep *my* girls out of his way."

There was a tune I'd heard somewhere that her first four words fitted into—I began to hum them in my head. "There's a murd-er-ing mad-*man*, a murder-ing mad-man—" My foot was tapping to the rhythm.

Mrs. Eldridge said, "Look here, Mrs. Kinch, I'm just off shopping. I pass the dentist. I'll walk the girls along."

"What about walking them back?"

"Oh," said Mrs. Eldridge, "I've quite a bit to do. I'll call in for them."

Then she winked at Corinne, hoping for a smile to show she'd done right. But Corinne wasn't giving out any "thank you's," even in smiles.

"Right you are, then," my mother said. "So long as somebody's with them." And she left without saying goodbye to me. She was cross because I'd been sulky with her.

As soon as she'd gone I said, "I'm sorry, Mrs. Eldridge, but Mum's really rattled about this thing. We've all been telling her not to be daft—but she's really most terribly scared."

"Well, it's not a nice thing," said Mrs. Eldridge. "Corry darling, I'll just put my coat on—shan't be a minute."

Corinne was wearing her white lace-patterned stockings, a black skirt right above her knees, and a long black leather jacket. She was trying out the steps of a new dance and she stopped to say to her mother, "You're not *really* coming?"

"Oh well, Corry, I must. I promised Mrs. Kinch."

"You never used the word 'promise.'"

"Oh well, I'll just walk along."

Corinne gave in rather easily. "Suit yourself," she said.

Mrs. Eldridge looked pleased, as if she'd expected more trouble. "Have you had your tranquilliser, darling?"

"Yep."

"Well, don't worry, darling—they never hurt these days. They've got such new equipment. Those drills are so quick you hardly feel them."

"Anything you say, Mother mine, relieves my tensions immediately," sang Corinne, and then she winked at me.

"Oh Corry," giggled Mrs. Eldridge delightedly. "You are a silly girl."

Corry was unusually nice to her mother all the way to the dentist. I'd have been suspicious, if I'd been Mrs. Eldridge. But she wasn't. She simply glowed under Corinne's good mood like you see some people light up when their lover comes into the room.

The only time she was a bit acid was when she asked me politely how George was.

"He's fine, thanks," I said.

"That's good," she said, in the way that some people say, "What a pity."

She couldn't stick George, and he didn't love her any either. He said she couldn't have laid an egg she deserved more than the one Corinne came out of.

She said his sleepy look was insolent. But then George once picked Corinne up by her collar when we were both about eight and locked her out in the garden during a tea-party at Collins Wood. He said to Mrs. Eldridge, "Do you mind? But we keep our nuisances outside." She did mind. To this day she'd see George hanged if she had half a chance. I expect that's why I like to think of her as a dead chicken.

I told him once, when things were still so lovely and easy between us, that Mrs. Eldridge had said he looked insolent. He laughed. "The poor old hay-bag's not the only one. I had a reputation for it in the army."

I was a bit shocked. I mean, George is so down on cheek of any kind in the family. "You mean you answered back officers and things?" I asked.

"Not the good ones," he told me. "And you don't have to answer back 'things.' They can see it in your eyes. They used to call it 'dumb insolence.'"

We were just passing the arcade, and I was in the middle of saying something to Mrs. Eldridge, when Corinne suddenly yanked at my hand and pulled me down a side turning. "Run, you twit," she shouted. "Run!"

I was so surprised I ran after her like a tame fool.

Mrs. Eldridge shouted after us. The wind blowing her coat open made a great big red bat of her.

"Corry!" she yelled. "It's no good trying to dodge the dentist—you'll only come down with toothache!" But it wasn't the dentist Corinne was trying to dodge.

"I don't want to run into Frank Smith," she puffed. "And with Mum we'd have had to go the straight way or she'd want to know why—and I might've bumped into him out on his errands."

"But you're crazy about Frank Smith," I reminded her breathily. "So why do you want to avoid him?"

"No make-up," she answered.

"What?"

She turned to me and pushed out her mouth. "No make-up. Dentists won't do you in it."

"Oh," I said. "Well, what about your mother? Won't she be wild when you get home?"

"Yes."

"Then what are you going to say to her?"

"Oh, I'll just say I was too ashamed to let her see how scared I was of going to the dentist, and then she'll call me a 'poor little mite' and say that the right person I should have had at a time like this was my silly old mum."

"Oh," I said for the second time.

Corinne wore a green scarf round her neck. I would have felt awful in it. It was as bright as poster paint in some parts and dirty in others. But the jaunty way Corinne wore it you might have thought it was a mink stole. She sprang along the street pushing out the figure she hadn't got, and both men and boys turned round to look at it!

She'd got the most fearfully thin little legs and her knees didn't sit straight on them, but once when some boys whistled at her and then changed their minds, calling out, "Your gams are too skinny, Liz," she just turned round and made a couple of clicking noises out of the side of her mouth, and they went crazy about her. We all went into a Wimpey bar and they neither looked at me nor talked to me.

I remember going home and bursting into tears; my waist seemed so thick and, oh, everything was wrong with me.

George caught me crying. That was before he seemed scared of being alone with me. He took my chin in his hand and turned my face to him. "What went wrong with the plumbing?"

"Boys think Corinne's marvellous," I sobbed. "We met some she'd never even seen before. They thought she was awful at first, but then she just rubbed their faces in it. They didn't even notice me. I had to slip up to the counter and buy my own Coke in case anyone noticed I'd got left out."

George said, "One—I won't have you going out with boys that Corinne's never even seen before—two, I won't have you going out with boys she *has* seen—and three, if you're not very careful I won't have you going out with Corinne at all!"

"Corinne's with it," I sobbed. "I'll never be with it."

"You'll be with it when Corinne's had it," he told me, and gave his funny little inside chuckle.

"But what's she *got?*" I gulped. "I tell you they were all laughing at her to begin with."

George said, "Look, Corinne's got what she ought to have at twenty-five. When she's twenty-five people will think she's what she ought to be at forty-five. She's a dwarf adult —that's very sad and we should be sorry for her. She's already lost her childhood and she's going to lose her youth—

because by the time she catches up with it she'll be too old to enjoy it."

There was only one trace of his Yorkshire ancestry in George's voice—the way he separated "*en*-joy." But of course I've met Londoners who think that we in the Midlands talk exactly the same. No ear, I suppose. It was George's father, Fred Meakham, who came from Yorkshire.

I sobbed to George on that occasion, "It's all very well, but Corinne gets fun *now*."

"It's nice to know she knows what it is," he said. "That damn fool mother's left her nothing to be pleased with. She can't have a treat any more because she's got nothing to compare it with—people don't understand the verb 'to spoil.' It means 'to destroy.'"

"She's my friend," I said, a little stubbornly. I was braver with George in those days. He hadn't changed to me by then.

"She's your friend," he told me, "because even the other nasty kids find her too nasty, and only a nice one like you would put up with her." And he ruffled my hair and went out.

Corinne really was scared of the dentist. I felt terribly sorry for her. She was a greasy white, like Len went whenever he was scared, and she prattled away to hide it. She flipped the magazine she'd been reading back on to the table as if she'd been throwing a boomerang. One gentleman and one old lady gave her a pair of bumper scowls. Then she arched her back in the chair like someone I'd seen on television dying of cholera, and then flopped her bottom back on it, got out her compact, and dabbed all over her face. "I think I'll give Frank Smith his cards. Once I get a boy interested in me it's a bore, and I want to chuck him in."

She was talking extra loudly so that the people in the waiting-room would be impressed. They were, but not in the way she hoped.

"Corinne, your mother's right," I told her. "It really won't hurt, and if it's going to, he'll give you an injection."

"Who cares?" she said. But she was shaking.

Just before her turn came she whispered, "Will you say a prayer for me, Wynne? Pray I don't look scared when he starts."

"Okay." I nodded quickly. Corinne looked on the verge of being sick.

"Reverend Mother says we ought to say them openly," she suddenly challenged me. "You know, make the sign of the cross and say a prayer where everyone can see you."

"George says it might make other people think the dentist wasn't very good," I whispered.

"Oh! So George knows more than Reverend Mother, does he? George knows better than Our Lord, I expect."

For once I was quick enough to think of a reply on the spot. I said, "You get down on your knees, Corinne, and I'll be right behind you on mine. After all, it's you with the teeth being stopped."

That silenced her.

In point of fact I had asked Father Murphy about what Reverend Mother had said, and he told me she really only meant that where it was possible to say a prayer we shouldn't want to hide it. Obviously if you kept going down on your knees all along the High Street and crossing yourself right up to the Co-operative, you'd be picked up as a nut case.

Corinne tried to get me down. She did our old "stare and don't blink" act. We glared straight into each other's eyes and whoever blinked first was out. I nearly always won because I could go into a day-dream. But Corinne's eyes watered and pricked.

The dentist put his head round the door. He said, "Come along, Corinne."

She smiled and had to pull herself out of her chair as if the seat had been a magnet. She turned round and grinned

at me. "Learn all the jokes in *Punch* to tell me." Then she
tottered to the door. Her ankle turned over on the way. I
knew it was nerves, but the old lady near me "tut-tutted"
because her heels were a bit too high.

She flung her tiny bit of figure up at the dentist as she
went through the door. He was tall and didn't notice. He
called to the old lady near me, "I won't keep you a minute,
Mrs. Sykes."

When the door closed behind Corinne, I was so agitated
I started to pray.

"Please God, don't let Thy servant Corinne suffer—she
may not behave very well, but look at some of Thy other
servants—look at them throughout history—Napoleon and
Louis XV and Henry VIII and some of the modern ones—
and what about Thy servant the Dalstead Strangler?"

There was such a silence in the room I opened my eyes. I
realised that I must have crossed myself openly, but how
much I said aloud I'll never know.

I was getting some very odd looks and the old lady next
to me offered me a peppermint. "I take them to make my
breath nice for the dentist—have one, dear. He's very gentle.
It won't be half as bad as you think."

Corinne came out before I could answer. She was bouncing with life. "Next patient, please, the drill's red-hot."

The dentist's receptionist said, "Be quiet, Corinne. Mrs.
Sykes, please."

When we were outside I said importantly, "I prayed for
you *in front* of people."

"You should have saved your breath," she sang. "It was
only a check-up after all."

I was so mad I could have clouted her one. Instead I
fluttered fingers at her. "'Bye."

"Where are you going?"

"I've got a date."

"Oh! So my fair lady has, has she? Well, don't forget my
fair lady got stood in on my date with Tim Orkins."

"I'll pay you back some other time," I told her, and went off with my head in the air. After all, it doesn't *hurt* anyone to say thank you for praying for them—never mind taking all the credit. For all she knew it might have been my prayers which reduced her appointment to a check-up. I was about to go back and say this—it not having occurred to me before—but I thought it would be undignified. Anyway, I was glad of an excuse to sham mad at Corinne because I certainly didn't want her hanging around when I called on Mrs. Bennett.

So I ducked into the British Home Stores to shake her off.

People in Dalstead make a terrible fuss about this end of the town. It's what they call the Dormitory End. It got flattened in the war, apparently, and it's all been put up newly. Once upon a time it was all old and black and white and hanging over the road, like some of the ancient houses in New Street. But now it's all supermarkets and great high boxes and glass, glass, glass. The only time I like it is at sunset, when all the little square windows catch fire.

I prefer the pokey old black bits in New Street. I'm crazy about anything old. It sets off all my day-dreams. I wonder who lived there and what it was like, and who used this or that thing.

I want to go in for old things when I grow up—have an antique shop or dig in old cities or be one of those people on television who can say, "Ah! Egyptian make-up case—Pharaoh the Something or Other—such and such a dynasty —such and such a date."

A lot of my day-dreams are me on television saying such and such a date right off pat, when experts have thrown their hands up over something so obscure that no one could be expected to know what it was, and it's really only out of courtesy that the compère turns to the glamorous little schoolgirl from Dalstead.

George hated antiques. He says he resents the fact that a

chair he has made himself could survive him for hundreds
of years when it hasn't even got his brain!

I fingered some undies in the British Home Stores and
when I looked down the counter there was Corinne doing
just the same. She copied every single gesture I made. Honestly, how childish can you get?

I kept my eye on Corinne and soon she got her attention
taken off me by the make-up. I took the opportunity to dart
out of the back entrance, which opened on to New Street.

I fairly pelted along to the almshouses where nosey old
Mrs. Bennett lived. She used to be a district nurse and she
attended my mother at the birth of the twins.

There was no need to have an excuse for visiting her,
because we were always taking her little things in spite of
Mum calling her a scrounger.

She was deaf, so I hammered hard on the door and lis-
tened for her to come shuffling up the little narrow passage.
Her breath came heavily, pulling the bolt back. "Wait a minute," she said, as she always did, "it's a very old lady this
side of the door, you know."

"It's only me, Mrs. Bennett," I shouted. "Wynne Kinch."

"Wait a minute," she answered. "You'll need a bit of pa-
tience, Winnie."

She was one of the few people who called me Winnie
and it made me as mad as Hélène got when people called
her Nellie.

Finally Mrs. Bennett managed the door. "Well, Winnie,
there we are—My! What a fine big girl you're growing—
you can make two of your sister Nellie."

Mrs. Bennett always said the things you didn't want to
hear.

I gave a false smile and told her, "I just thought I'd call
and see how you were."

I would much rather have called on the old lady next
door, who was a sweet old thing and talked about the past
in a way that you like to hear about. She made it sound so

gay and interesting, and you knew exactly what kind of people they were when she said that "carriage people" called.

"Well," said Mrs. Bennett. "How am I, then? Well, I suppose I mustn't grumble." But it didn't stop her from doing just that for the next quarter of an hour.

I had meant to slip my question in quite smoothly, but I fairly had to bounce it at her to get it in between her catarrh and her rheumatism.

"When will George be through with the shelves he's making you?"

She said, "What shelves?"

"The—the bookshelves."

She looked fussed for a moment, and then said, "Oh, in the *kitchen?*"

"Bookshelves, I thought they were," I said, puzzled.

"That's right—you know what a lovely cook I am? Everyone says you've never tasted good food until you've tasted Bridget Bennett's." She was never behind in self-praise, but I often thought it was on the surface—a sort of loud shout to drown people's real opinion of her. A lot of folks had fallen out with Mrs. Bennett and left her in no doubt as to what they thought of her.

"It's my recipe books," she said. "You know—I write everything down—when Noel gets married, his wife will bless me for them."

Noel was her godson. She had no one else. She absolutely doted on him. I don't suppose he came to see her once a year. He wrote near Christmas and his own birthday. She was crocheting him and his future bride a pair of giant curtains, just as though they'd use such things. It made me want to cry.

"So I asked George to put up a shelf or two in the kitchen —it doesn't do them any good to have them lying about."

"May I see them?"

"Take yourself in."

Her kitchen smelt sweetly old-fashioned of herbs. I often thought how funny that was. The kitchen of the darling old lady next door smelt rather fusty and not very clean.

To the right of the cooker there was one shelf containing five stiff-backed notebooks—it must have taken George a good ten minutes to put up that shelf.

I went back to the living-room.

"Is that all he put up for you?" I asked. "Isn't he going to put up any more?"

She cackled. "That's not to say I wouldn't say 'yes' if he asked me—I haven't seen him in a twelvemonth."

I muttered something about asking him for her myself, and said "Goodbye."

The wind was getting up. It was April, but the sky had black lumps bobbing about in it and the wind seemed as if it wanted to cut your throat.

Corinne was waiting for me outside, leaning up against the 'bus stopstand eating a Picnic bar.

"Some date!"

"I never said *you'd* enjoy it."

"Where are you going now?"

"Mind your own business."

She crumpled up the paper from the Picnic bar and dropped it in the gutter. "Look, have I *said* something?"

"No," I said truthfully, and she hadn't, either. She'd been no more Corinnish than usual, and it was my fault if I felt foolish for praying aloud without knowing it. Still, I didn't often have Corinne trying to chat me up, so I made the most of it.

"I'll come with you," she said condescendingly, "wherever you're going."

"There'd be conditions," I said.

"Like what?"

"Like leaving me entirely alone for half an hour."

"Where?"

"At Collins Wood."

"Leave you alone?"

"Yes—with no prying, spying, or interruptions."

"Okay," she said.

The truth was, of course, that Corinne was lonely. Except for myself and the odd boy-friend she hadn't anyone to go around with of her own age. George was right and our other school friends steered clear of her.

"Where do you want to be left alone?" she asked me, as we waited for the 'bus that would take us to Collins Wood.

"In Clare's room," I said.

I wanted more than ever to read *The Hatter's Ghosts* and I always liked to go to Collins Wood if ever I was unhappy or scared.

"One, two, three, four, five, six, seven—" I started to count to myself on the 'bus.

4 ❖ COLLINS WOOD WAS MY BEST HOLD over Corinne. She would always come round to anything I wanted if there was a chance to go to Collins Wood. It was shameful of me really, because I knew that the school wanted her rather gruesome imagination played down and not played up. But there were so few things I could do to interest her. I had no boy-friends, and ours wasn't the sort of home she was crazy to visit, with Mother never leaving us alone. "Well, Corinne, how's your grannie?" "Is your daddy's cold better?" "What did Doctor say about your cousin Anne? Did he think she's on the mend?" And "Won't those high heels throw your feet out, dear? Your bones are still soft, you know."

There was George, of course. She pretended she didn't like him, but every time she saw him she threw out her little bit of figure at him. Mine was too big for my age and it made me self-conscious. I held myself in rather than thrust myself out, and it was making me a little round-shouldered. Before he took to ignoring me, George was always tapping me on the back and telling me to stand up straight.

Corinne thought George was super, but whenever she wanted to get a crack at me she'd knock him through his age. "When you're *twenty*," she'd say, as if she was only just working it out in her head and hadn't already got it off pat, "when you're twenty—he'll be forty-one."

"It's my favourite age for men," I told her. "I can't wait for him to get there."

But that was really only when we'd quarrelled—or she'd drawn a square in the air with her finger to describe my mother. That really used to make me mad. Not that I didn't agree with her, but I wasn't going to have her saying it—even in the air.

Although she was scared of George, she was all on fire inside when he was around, and fabulously got up in her most kinky gear. We were friends, but she'd have adored George to take an interest in her, however much it hurt me. Although in a way it was only because she was mad keen for me to think he didn't dislike her and she was in on things with me. We always shared everything.

When Hélène was at work or had a date, I could take Corinne into our bedroom and we got a bit of peace in there. But more often than not Mother came in to us. "Don't you two little girls want to come into the living-room? You're all on your own in here." She meant well, of course, she was only being hospitable, but it was hopeless to try and be private.

Corinne was fascinated and scared by Number 3, Collins Wood. I played up to it, I'm afraid. I loved the place so much I welcomed any opportunity to talk about it.

I'd pass Corinne a note in class saying, "Felt *her* very strongly today," and Corinne would come out of any sulks she might be in, or bad mood, and pass an important note back, "Hadn't we better go to Collins Wood while *the feeling's* still on?"

Corinne simply had to have little dramas in her life that made her feel important. At school she was always claiming to see visions. The school was mad at her, of course, because the Church isn't keen on people seeing visions—and you can see how they wouldn't be. They'd have every nut and hysterical person claiming they were being personally chatted up by Our Lady, or something.

Collins Wood was about twenty minutes' 'bus ride from our school and a quarter of an hour farther on from our flats.

It always used to bother me that the 'bus conductors

might wonder what I was doing, going out there so often. I got to know them all on that route.

The 'bus was only a single-decker, so you couldn't exactly lose yourself in the crowd. The conductor I knew best was quite a nice man, and always said, "How's my little colleen?" So I suppose at some time I must have told him I was half Irish.

Of course it was stupid of me to think he'd wonder what I was doing! He didn't know the family had forbidden me to go to Collins Wood. I was a nit to feel guilty every time I saw him, and even more of a nit to look it, which I'm sure I did.

The reason I knew that particular conductor best was that Corinne had a bit of a crush on him at one time. But he always gave his smile to me, which made old Corry mad. She sauced him once quite badly, and he looked as if he'd like to belt her one.

I was furious. "Fancy letting him notice us like that," I said. "He might find out who we are and report us to Mum. I'm sure he's suspicious already. He thinks it's odd we come out here so often."

"Oh, go and boil your guilt complex," she said.

The air got better as soon as you got to Dalstead Common. Houses and shops had crept up to it and there wasn't a sign of a wood any more, but somehow it was still very much in the country.

Number 3 Collins Wood was in a little clutch of old houses on the west side of the common. They were huddled together in a little hunted corner, as if they were crouching away from the great, towering new buildings which marched nearer and nearer to them.

Once you were in their gardens, the new part of Dalstead seemed a hundred miles away.

Number 3, like Number 5 and Number 7, was scheduled to come down and make way for something. It was a thought I simply couldn't bear, and whenever I could I went back. I was simply unable to believe that one day there wouldn't be a Number 3 Collins Wood any more.

Mother and George sold it to some people called Roberts, and I was always having to go to confession and accuse myself of wishing them ill for living there. I was paid out, too, because they only stayed two years and then sold out to these beastly speculators who're only waiting for Number 1 and Number 9 to give in to pull the whole lot down. Every night I pray for them to hold out.

It belonged to George's father, Fred Meakham, and when he died Mother let it off in rooms until she married Grandad's elder son Albert. Then the twins came and she used the whole house for the family again.

Poor Mother—she couldn't have been very happy. I believe she grieved hard for Fred Meakham, but I think she was heartily relieved when pneumonia took off Uncle Albert Kinch. I once heard George telling Mr. Wells that the only person who missed him was a prostitute in Kensal Rise to whom he owed money. Goodness knows what he can have been doing down there. I suppose he must have been on holiday. I think there was a feeling between George and Grandad that Uncle Albert only married Lucy Meakham because she had Collins Wood and a bit of money behind her. Fred Meakham was a careful man, and you could save in those days. It was his share of the money from the sale of Number 3 that George put in to buy his partnership with Mr. Wells.

Fred's death was caused by a bit of shrapnel, I believe, that had been in his body all those years, that worked round, or something, and caused a thrombosis.

Mother loved him dearly. It's not hard to understand. I've seen his photograph, and there's a look of George in him all right. I didn't mean to write that as if I was saying there was a look of God! But I must admit that's how it reads.

Len's got a bit of a look of him, in a smaller, funny way

you can't explain. But then, of course, they're half related—
and they've all got big feet. Even Hélène. That's because
they've got the same mother, of course, and it comes from
her. Big feet don't come from the Kinches—they come from
Mother's Tindall side. Still, we won't go into my family tree
again! I showed it to the matron here—at the Remand Home
—and she said if anyone could make head or tail of it they
were a better man than she was.

I must have been a bore to George—goodness knows we'd
lived together long enough, but it was still a relief to me
every time he came back from work—and I must've showed
it, however hard I tried not to. What was worse, I got down
in the dumps every time he went out.

He ticked me off about it once. He said if women want
something on a collar and lead they ought to buy a dog.

Of course I was tickled pink to be called a woman. But I
tried to explain I was anxious about him. If he was late I
had him dead and buried and the flowers already wilting
on top of his grave.

He told me I was full of "pissy fears." It's been a joke ever
since. The twins were crazy about that word, of course, and
never let it be for about two weeks. Everything was one of
"Wynne's pissy fears"—including the noises I said the geyser
was making, and which finally blew up!

I don't know why I loved Number 3 so much. Perhaps it
was because it brought George into my life. Perhaps it was
because my own mother's death had left me shy and frightened of things, and Aunt Lucy's big arms were tender and
comforting. She's absolutely wonderful with babies and
small children, or if you're ill. I expect that's what's the matter, really. She's still annoyed inside that we're not still
babies and small, and she's quite pleased if we're ill so long
as it's not serious.

Or perhaps Number 3 was such heaven to me because it
came after the cramped little place Grandad and Mother
and I had shared. I was only five when we left it—four when

Mother died. It was a flat above a shop shaped like a flat iron, on the corner of a London street, and it smelt of firewood and paraffin and nails. I didn't mind that—after all, it was an ironmongers', and I love the smell of paraffin. Number 3 smells of that in my first memory of it. Paraffin—warmth and Christmas.

It was the night that Grandada and I first arrived. That's a funny slip back—I haven't called him Grandada since practically that very day—the twins said it sounded just too daft for words. Mother (or Aunt Lucy, as she was that first day) told them to let Baby say what she liked. George gave me an elephant ride round the room on his shoulders. But it was the twins I took notice of, and I never called Grandad Grandada again. I was scared of those twins. They were ten and much worse than they are now.

The lights were all on at Number 3 that day we arrived. It was winter and late in the evening. There was an old Beatrice stove in the hall which accounted for the cosy smell of paraffin. The fire was piled high in the grate—and there was the Christmas tree. It was only the twelfth of December really, but George got Mum to put it up and dress it early so that it would be the first thing I'd see. They even put presents round it. It was one of the most marvellous things that ever happened to me—that first evening. It's lodged in my head rather like the holy pictures I keep in my prayer book.

Grandad was on edge until he'd settled his mice. They'd come in their travelling boxes, of course, but he had to set them up in his room in their proper quarters and he was scared of draughts and all sorts of things.

Aunt Lucy had been a bit unkeen to have them, as I think I said before—but George had said you couldn't separate the old boy from his lifetime hobby—it would be like leaving half of him behind.

So they fixed him up with his mice in the basement. The basement at Number 3 wasn't like ordinary basements. It was nearly ground level and the sun found it out. There was a bedroom, a living-room, a kitchen, and some back rooms. I can't quite remember what they were used for, but I remember the living-room. It smelt large and light and at the same time safe and cosy. It had an old black fire grate in the middle of two cream-painted chimney cupboards that went right up to the ceiling. Grandad rigged up all his mouse cage paraphernalia against the wall facing the big, deep windows.

"They'll be all right here, Baby," he told me in a relieved kind of voice.

Do you know what my present was, under that Christmas tree in the dim hall passage at Collins Wood? A tiny ginger kitten, six weeks old. George opened the coloured box it was in and gave it to me.

"He's new to this family," George told me. "He may feel a bit odd and lonely. You'll have to make him feel at home."

There was quite a kerfuffle to follow that, because Grandad got scared about his mice. We'd never been allowed to have cats before. But George promised to make a big wire screen to go round the mice until Sandy got used to them.

Sandy's nearly nine now, and he minded leaving Collins Wood every bit as much as I did. It took him ages to get used to a tray in the new flat. I suppose it's daft to keep on talking about the "new" flat when we've been there two years and a bit.

When Corinne and I got off the 'bus at Dalstead Common, it had turned into one of those ragged, stormy days that strew bits all over the place. The trees seemed to be shivering angrily, whipping round at the wind as if they didn't like being pulled about.

Blossom was tossing in the air as if someone was throwing up handfuls of confetti and the sky was all moody and dark.

We had to walk right over the common to get to Number 3. The funny lead-blue lights of the storm that was brewing gave the bracken and scrub quite a shine. Several heavy raindrops began to fall, like someone trying a few out first before they up-ended the bucket!

Corinne shivered—not because of the sudden chill the rain was bringing, but because of the "Dalstead bodies," as the three poor girls who were found near the common were called.

"We might be walking on the *very spot*," she whispered.

"No," I said practically, "they were found on the road-side. That is—the ones he tried to make look like accidents."

She threw me an angry little look. She hated me trampling on things.

Number 3 stood back from the road with a view right over the common. It had only a short garden in front of it—the lovely long one was behind it. I don't want to give the impression that it was a mansion or a very grand place or anything. In the old days it would have been some small business man's house, I expect—someone who wanted their family brought up in the country rather than the stuffy old town of Dalstead.

George thought that with the other ones like it on the same side, it must have been built in about 1760. There were some even older houses on the opposite side—black and white and really tumbling.

Number 3 was white and square and then dipped down at the back into passages and an old conservatory. Fred Meakham got it cheap, I believe, and did quite a bit to it. Being a builder, that sort of thing was in his line, of course.

It was not in a good state now—the upper windows on the right of the porch were boarded over and the front door-step was crumbling away under the little porch like a quar-tered apple that was supported on two thin pillars. A bit of guttering hung down and the paint was scabby. But it was still a lovely chalky white. It never got creamy yellow like town paint. The house had always been a bit lop-sided. George didn't admire the workmanship of those days—he liked the Georgian designs but said they were very bad builders and you got a lot of settlement. He thought the Victorian houses were much better built.

Corinne and I pushed our way through the nettles and American currant bushes all tangled up at the side door. Round the back the conservatory door was hanging off its hinges.

It was in here that we kids used to play—lying on our backs and watching the rain splash down—and it was in here that Grandad was finally persuaded to keep his mice.

From the conservatory we could get into the kitchen. There was a broken pane of glass through which I could just squeeze my hand and pull back the bolt on the inside. I often cut it a bit and for that reason used to take a little packet of sticky plasters in my bag.

Corinne whispered at me as I let us in, "Where did you feel Clare *this* time?"

"Oh," I said, "just generally."

"Are you going to do anything—or say anything special to make her come to you?"

I said, with Father Murphy's and Mother Katherine's faces in mind, "Of course not. You know we're not allowed to invoke the dead."

Corinne sniffed. "Wouldn't be the first time we'd tried it."

She was right. There had been times when I had stood in the living-room calling to Clare while Corinne stood electrically still beside me, her eyes looking into every corner.

It was really because I was sometimes just the tiniest bit afraid of Clare's ghost that I liked to take Corinne with me. Otherwise I preferred to have Number 3 to myself. Except of course that it was also nice to have someone to talk to about it. "This is where we used to have the old blanket chest that the twins put Grandad's mice into—there wasn't a blanket left without a hole in it!"

But if you hadn't got Corinne you could sit comfortably down on the floor with your back against a wall and re-member, "I used to hear George's bath water running in from this room—and I always knew whether it was hot or cold." It was a game we used to play. I went through a spell of being scared of the dark. It was just after I heard about Clare. After that nothing would make me pass the living-room door at bedtime, and even when George carried me I kicked and howled and screamed. A fine help I must've been to him, poor love, reminding him of Clare past the living-room door, of all places.

It was George who started the bath game. When he put me into bed, he said, "What's the betting you couldn't tell whether it's the hot or the cold tap I'm running into my bath?"

And of course by the time I'd waited for him to have it and had lain there trying to work it out, ten to one I had dropped off to sleep.

Even though it had been shut up for so long, the whole house still smelt dry, and light and windy. George said it was a textbook case on dry rot for baby architects.

George was never nice about it. I suppose because of Clare, but the reason he gave for not liking me to go there was that the dry rot made it unsafe. "One day, something's coming down on that job, Wynne, and you might look a bit of a mess underneath it."

I never told him I still went back. He didn't approve of my feelings for it, in any case. "What's the good, when it's coming down? You might as well get the parting over now —why keep on rubbing it in? You want to think about the house you'll have of your own, some day, when you marry and have a family."

I hated talk like that. I just shut my eyes to a day when I might have to leave home or George left it. There wasn't such a day in my calendar.

"This flat's a sight easier to run than the old house," Mother had put in. But George was still on about me.

"You want to take an interest in new things at your age, Wynne, not old out-of-date kind of stuff."

"She'd better stay interested in out-of-date things if she's going to teach history," Grandad chuckled.

"The future'll be history some day," said George. "So she'd better take an interest in that, as well."

I ran quickly round Number 3, sniffing all my favourite smells. The paint on the big push-up windows and the solid doors looked even whiter in the funny light the thunder was spreading.

Ivy was tickling the window in my old room. That was another thing; we all had a room to ourselves. Corinne was tramping round me, sighing. She wanted the "fun" to begin. But she didn't dare upset me, in case she spoilt my "mood."

When I'd breathed up the atmosphere in every room, and gone down into the basement and heard the coming thunder wind bustling about in Grandad's chimney cupboards, I said, "Okay, let's begin," and we went upstairs to the living-room.

This was the room that George wouldn't go into, not even when Mum exchanged the carpet.

I said to Corinne, "Now *don't* interrupt me—I want to be quite, quite alone and *quiet*—otherwise I won't get anything." And I turned the big stout key firmly against her.

I wanted a nice bit of peace and quiet to give me time to find out what there was in *The Hatter's Ghosts* to make Len and George act so queer about it.

Perhaps it might also tell me why George lied about old Mrs. Bennett.

**5** ❖ I PUT MY BAG ON THE FLOOR and took out the book.
I could have done with a torch. You could hardly see out of
the living-room windows. They were big, floor-length ones,
but the ampelopsis, which I hope I'm spelling right, came
down in a great green fall from the balcony above, and the
thunder light made the room even darker.

George had waged war against the ampelopsis, but
Mother liked it. She said it broke up the line of the house.

I stood close to the door so that Corinne could hear me
and called in a sort of hollow, church voice, "Clare! Are you
near me, Clare?"

I could practically hear poor old Corinne go stiff with excitement.

"Clare!" I called. "Clare!" I made my voice all eerie. Then
I sat down with *The Hatter's Ghosts* and a glacier mint. I
took it out of my mouth now and again to call out, "If you
can hear me, Clare, knock three times."

Then I knocked three times. It was an awful thing to do,
of course, and Father Murphy gave me a right stiff penance
when I confessed to it. But I reckoned if Corinne was daft
enough to believe me it wasn't much of a sin. Sometimes she
tried to get me to promise it wasn't me doing the knocking.

"Do you promise by Almighty God that you don't make
all those noises yourself?" Corinne was always dramatic.

"I won't swear by anybody," I told her. "If you don't believe me, that's your look-out, and you don't have to come to
Collins Wood with me, do you?"

She wanted like mad to believe me, of course. It was the
sort of excitement she needed.

I had never met Clare. All I had seen was a photograph

that Mother unearthed when we moved. She was a blond girl with nice shy eyes, and lips pressed together as if she was trying not to laugh.

George had taken it. They were on holiday at Ryde. In three months' time they were going to be married. George was still young and Clare was nineteen.

I've never been jealous of Clare. Corinne's always worrying me about it. "After all, he must've thought the world of her—he's never married. It must mean that it broke his heart so badly that he can't look at anyone else."

"He looks at girls all the time," I said.

"Yes, but he's never had a steady one."

That was the reason I wasn't jealous of Clare. I was grateful to her if her memory kept George's eyes checking up on women's good points and never settling on one for good.

Clare had lived in Dalstead proper. She had worked in the post office. She used to come out to Collins Wood on her motor-scooter.

It happened one Saturday in March, when George was still in the army overseas. Clare came out from Dalstead on her scooter. She and George were going to live at Number 3 to start with. He was going to make them a self-contained flat. She was bringing out some colour cards to go through with Mum.

Nobody seemed to know quite how it happened, but there were a dog and a child involved somewhere. It was a wet, misty sort of day and the roads were greasy. Our grocer was delivering in his little green van. Whether he swerved to avoid the child and its dog—or whether Clare swerved and skidded, or whether they both did, I don't know, but the van caught the side of Number 9's wall and turned over. The child wasn't hurt at all and the driver was only bruised. But Clare and the dog were killed.

The twins were only seven then, but Len's never forgotten it. The goods in the van had all spilt out. There were packets of biscuits, and bacon and tins of peas and things, and what Len never forgot was the sugar. Packet after packet had burst right open, and some of it was white and some of it wasn't. Some of it was red and gritty from Clare's blood and some of it was red from the dog's.

Len says he remembers standing there, watching them both flowing into each other. And he suddenly went down on his knees and tried to keep the two lots of blood separate. Not because he didn't like the dog, which was some kind of little black mongrel, but because he got it into his head that George would want to know which was Clare's. It was after that he started his terrible headaches and was put on phenobarbitone.

She didn't die at once. They carried her into the house, which I didn't think they ought to have done. It would have been better to cover her up where she lay and have waited for the ambulance. But Uncle Albert Kinch insisted. They put her on the sofa in the living-room. She was so badly hurt she kept struggling, and she fell off the sofa and hurt herself more.

I've heard Mother telling Aunt Rene Tindall that the whole time she was trying to help, her lips were moving in a prayer to ask God to let the girl die. She said she thought she would have strangled the girl herself if she'd lasted to suffer much more. She did die before the ambulance got there, calling for her own mother, while Aunt Lucy was trying to stroke the only bit of forehead that wasn't all covered in blood and red sugar.

Her family had her cremated, and her ashes were scattered.

By the time George managed to get home, all that was left of the girl he had laughed and joked with, and planned to make his life with, was a dull stain on the living-room carpet.

Mother had had it cleaned, of course, and moved it round with some furniture over it—but everybody felt it there until she got rid of the carpet.

George sat the whole of one day in the living-room all by himself. Then he never went in it again—at least not to stay. He'd talk in it, and and maybe sit down for a few minutes if somebody called, but he did all his reading upstairs. He turned his own room into a bed-sitter and he spent lots of time in the kitchen.

Mother always thought it would not have been such a shock if Clare had been buried. If he could have come home and gone to see an ordinary grave with her name on it, he might have believed it all more readily. But to come home to nothing—to say goodbye to a warm, living person one moment, and the next to know that no wind in the world could bring you even the scent of her, must be enough to make you think people are kidding you—some terrible kind of sick joke that you'll get explained to you some day, if you keep on trying to see it hard enough. Nothing left of her you could touch, except a rose bush in the Dalstead Crematorium and a stain on the carpet.

People thought he took it very well on the surface. He never spoke about it and he didn't seem to mope—but months afterwards he started to suffer from memory lapses. He just couldn't think where he'd been or what he'd done.

It seemed rather late for delayed shock, and the doctors began to wonder about the wound in his neck that he'd got in Korea. Then something he said made them send him to a psychiatrist. I never knew what it was he said—although I asked him often enough. I could ask him anything in our friendly days.

"I can't remember," he told me, in that funny flat voice with the smile behind it.

"Can't remember?" I said.

"If I could," he said, "I don't suppose I'd have had to go to a head-shrinker."

He was quite amusing about what the head-shrinker had to say. He used to regale Mother and Grandad after he'd had a session.

"I'm like a child," he told them, "when it first finds out that its parents are not made to last forever—I'm suffering from emotional immaturity. I have seen death and known about it, but I have never really believed in it. I have never brought myself to accept it. I am suffering from the shock of discovering that man is not immortal. I'm a right nit, aren't I, if I'm only just catching on to the truth of common platitudes at my age! On the other hand the chap could be right, and I *am* a right nit!"

But I was dead certain it hadn't affected him mentally. What might have caused the blackouts was overwork. He threw himself into an absolute frenzy of work after Clare died, and perhaps that, coming on top of the shock, set him back.

"I'm sure," Mother used to go on rather drearily, "it would have been better if he could have come home and seen a *grave.*"

"What's the difference between decaying bones and a pile of white powder under a rose tree?" Grandad wanted to know. "There's nothing there, if you're one that thinks there's nothing to come—and if you're a believer you shouldn't be bothering about remains in any case."

"It was the coming back to *nothing*," Mother insisted. "One day she was there, and the next—no trace of her— nothing at all—swept bare."

And I remember Mum making a great sweeping movement with her arms.

I think if George and Len had cried like Mother or howled like Hélène, it might have been better for them both. But they bottled it up and Len got headaches and George's memory went funny for a bit. There was nothing surprising in that. You could almost expect it after such a shock. I told myself again "there was nothing surprising in that"—and I found myself counting out loud—"One, two, three, four, five, six—"

Then I stopped thinking about Clare and went back to

reading *The Hatter's Ghosts*. I concentrated so hard I was forming the words with my lips. So far I couldn't see anything that could have made George and Len act so queer. But then you can't expect to tell much from the beginning, can you? The little town that it all took place in seemed a bit like ours, except that it was in France. You know, it was old and it rained a lot, and most people knew each other, like we do. They'd been to the same school, perhaps, and they met in their cafés like we meet in our pubs.

I heard a cough outside the living-room door. I had forgotten poor old Corinne. She hadn't been getting much "fun."

I put down the book and called out, "Give one knock for 'yes,' Clare, and two for 'no.'"

Then I asked Clare some questions and Clare answered me through my own fist on the mantelpiece.

I didn't feel bad about Clare. I was sure she wouldn't mind about me kidding Corinne along with her ghost. Clare would be sure to understand what I felt about George. She had no need to be jealous of me, either. I mean, if she hadn't died and they'd got married, they'd probably have had kids of their own by the time I came along that I'd have been happy to play around with. Then George wouldn't have had to give me a pet kitten to take my mind off coming to a new home and facing the twins, and I wouldn't have become *his* pet kitten, to take *his* mind off things. My feelings would just have gone uncle-ish towards him if Clare hadn't died, and there would have been her to love as well as him. But George spoilt me more than I spoilt Sandy. He was there if I cried. He laughed when I laughed, and he was forever making me toys and inventing games for me. Perhaps he looked on me as the child he might have had with Clare. As for me, I didn't see how the clock could get round without him.

The only trouble is that for me it's lasted, and for him it hasn't. I don't seem to exist for him properly now.

I was sure Clare would understand how I felt about Collins Wood, too. She might not have liked it herself—I don't expect you do care very much for somewhere you've died in great fear and pain, and I didn't expect George to remember it kindly, but for me it represented a time, a time when I had George all to myself and when it never occurred to me that anything could change.

I was just about to give two knocks on the mantelpiece in answer to a question from Clare to myself when my doubled-up fist got stuck in the air.

There were some figures and some writing scribbled on the wall—I didn't know quite what they were, but they looked like measurements. The important thing about them was that they were George's, and an even more important thing was that they hadn't been there when I was at Collins Wood three days ago. I should have noticed it at once. I noticed every tiny change at Number 3—a bit of board loose, mice droppings, a new damp spot, newspaper and dirt that a tramp had brought in.

I should certainly have seen George's little calculations, however tiny they were. And I hadn't, because they hadn't been there three days ago.

Number 3 Collins Wood had only been empty about six months. During the holidays I managed to get out to the house several times a week, and when we were back at the convent I used to come every Thursday. We broke up from school at four every day, and I told Mother I stayed on for extra French on Thursdays because Mère Marie-Adelaide said I was slow at it.

Nobody noticed me going into the house so much. A builder's man saw me once, and a woman cycling her bundle to the launderette in Michael Grove—and once there was a man inside. I was scared blue in the face at first, but he said he was looking over the place. He thought it was still for sale. I told the truth. I said I used to live there and liked to keep coming back.

But mostly I crept in unnoticed. The common was pretty wild in front of the house and it was the woody end—and only Numbers 1 and 9 were still occupied, and they were both on a slant at their corners, so there wasn't anyone to overlook Number 3.

I peered at the figures again—small and neat, they were. George was big and neat. They said 22 by something or other and something else "to scale."

But what was George doing at Collins Wood, and what was he doing in the empty living-room, when he didn't even like to go in when his family were living there?

Corinne called out to me, "Couldn't you get through to her?"

I'd forgotten the ghost of poor Clare. With my eyes still on the little bunch of pencilled figures on the wall, I called out, "Clare, can you tell me whether Corinne's boy-friend Frank Smith's being true to her?"

Corinne always armed me with a list of personal questions for Clare—I was just about to give one loud knock for the answer "no" on the mantelpiece, when I thought my heart had exploded with fright.

Before my fist touched the wood there was a sharp, angry rapping and Corinne screamed. It was a really terrified scream. Yelling, "Corinne! Corinne!" louder than I've ever yelled before, I ran across the room and senselessly hammered against the door myself.

There was another loud rap and then someone said, "Wynne—open this door at once."

It was George's flat voice the other side.

I stood still in the way that a rabbit freezes when a ferret stares it in the eye. George was silent. He always gave you a second chance to obey his first command. We'd all noticed that as kids. Len, who thought the world of him really, said it was to help us to keep our dignity and give in before he had to say it again. Hélène said it was because he was too lazy to repeat himself.

I struggled with the key, but it was rusty and stuck at times. In my panic I got it good and jammed.

George's voice said, "Don't wrench at it—give it a bit of a lift and turn it gently."

I sobbed, "Corinne—what's happened to Corinne?"

He said, "Nothing. She just didn't hear me coming."

People just don't hear George coming, of course—poor Corinne must've thought it was the strangler himself behind her.

I was so silly with the lock I began to get weak and tearful. George gave the door a kick. It must have loosened the key in the lock or something. It opened suddenly and nearly caught me in the face.

George seemed huge. He was wearing a new woollen jacket, and I noticed it wasn't the one that I had knitted him for Christmas. He must have come from work. Way, way above me, his cloudy blue eyes looked down at me behind those thick-sided glasses. His hair wasn't really rusty. It was fair—not really that, either.

Corinne was sort of shrivelled up behind him. She was whiter than Len before one of his awful headaches.

She whimpered, "I didn't know it was him—I thought it was the murderer."

I got a tic in the corner of my eye, which I often do when I'm upset.

George could see the living-room mantelpiece. I watched him closely but he didn't look past me at the wall, or anything. He was standing in the middle of the room with his hands hanging loosely down at his sides as usual, and his shoulders back as if he was still a soldier.

He said, "Right. Go downstairs and get in the car, both of you."

We went downstairs and got into the car. I remembered that I had left *The Hatter's Ghosts* upstairs, but I didn't like to mention it. I thought I'd get it the next time I went to the house.

I'd rather have hanged myself than cheek George in the normal run, but I did feel a bit bad about poor old Corinne. After all, I'd inveigled her out to Collins Wood.

"You should have let her know it was you," I told George reproachfully. "It always upsets her stomach when she gets a scare."

I felt a bit like Aunt Rene Tindall until George said quietly, "She must be used to it doing somersaults with the tricks you play on her."

Then I felt like dying. It meant he'd heard me invoking the name of Clare. He'd heard me making a game out of her ghost with Corinne. He'd heard me rapping his Clare's answers to my own silly questions.

I thought I was going to be sick, but I swallowed it. I couldn't think of anything to say. I just looked at him, pouting a little.

The thunder broke as George put the car into gear. The lightning sent a jazzy nerve right across the dark sky above the common and the rain came down as though it was personally pelting us.

I looked back at the house. I thought, "Tomorrow, I'll pop down and try and make good the damage George must have done to that door when he kicked it."

I always cleaned up Collins Wood. In the garden shed I had Ajax, soap, and a sponge. When they came to knock it down I wanted them to see it was clean and cared-for. Daft, I know. Like somebody trying to make up a loved one's face just before they were executed.

George said, "If I catch either of you in that place again, you're going to know all about it."

I guessed what had happened. Mother had got windy when we didn't get back from the dentist, gone round to Mrs. Eldridge, found we'd run away from her, panicked, and sent for George from work.

I thought, "He'll never forgive me, never" and instead of

being nice I said cheekily, "You can't think so badly of it if you go there and write on the walls yourself."

George asked us, "Did you two hear what I said just now?"

Corinne answered him timidly, "Yes, Mr. Meakham, we won't go there again."

I cleared my throat and looked right out between the spears of rain trying to pierce the bonnet of the Bedford. "Mrs. Bennett asked after you. She said she hadn't seen you for years. She asked me to give you her love."

George said, "Thanks," and at the next traffic lights he said, "Wynne, if you're not careful, you'll be the ghost at Number 3. Not Clare."

*6* ❖ THE TWINS WERE AWFUL when we got back—they were going round the flat with their "grand" voices on. Everything they picked up they sneered at, from a fork to Sandy's saucer.

"Oh, mey word, I really do believe this isn't *sil*vah."

"Good heavens, we carn't eat off anything that isn't *sil*vah!"

They knew that it wouldn't be long before poor Mother broke down and said she came from good, plain folk and she wasn't ashamed of it.

They were paying her out because they were convinced that she had caused Hélène to muff her audition. By insisting on going with her and causing her to run away and get herself into a state Mother had lost her the part. I daresay it was true enough. Your mood can break or make you, and it's daft, but you can't always choose which it does. I know, because of the state I get into with George. In the old days—at Collins Wood, or not long after we'd moved—I was completely relaxed with him. I could say the most cheeky things and ask the most nosey questions, and he'd only give his inside chuckle. Sometimes I think he used to encourage me. That's why I cling so hard to Collins Wood, I suppose. Things were so different there.

Mother was in a right old spin about me going off there with Corinne. "The *common!*" she squeaked. "Dalstead *Common!* Why don't you just put a notice round your neck and ask the strangler to do you next?"

"He'd hardly sit about in the same place," Grandad observed, "in case the police sat about in it too."

"If he's *mad*," Mother retorted, "we've no right to guess *what* he'll do."

"He's *not* mad," said Grandad.

George asked him, "How do you know?"

"He's bright enough to trick things up as suicides and car accidents."

"Not so bright, since the police saw through it at once," said George. "You couldn't be normal and go round doing *that* sort of thing. He's a nut. You can take it from me."

"Friend of yours?" Len wanted to know.

"Maybe," said George, "if he comes from this town."

"I still think it's a waste not to rape them," said Hélène.

"*Nellie!*" poor Mother shrieked at her.

"Are you a virgin, Hélène?" Len wanted to know.

She frowned as if trying to remember. "How many times do you have to do it to stop being a virgin?"

"Only once, you nit."

"Help!" she said. "That's me out."

Mother caught George's slight shake of the head and refused to rise.

"I met someone that knew that last poor thing," mused Mother, "in the supermarket."

"What, someone that knew her in the supermarket or someone in the supermarket who knew her?" Len was just trying to be irritating, of course. He was absolutely wild with Mum for spoiling Hélène's chances at the audition.

Mother ignored him and told George and Grandad, "They say she looked after her people, poor thing."

"Yes, that could be worse than being strangled," said Len.

George's cloudy eyes reached him and George's flat voice said, "Pack it up."

Len snatched up a cushion. "Anyone seen my flaming book?"

I bent down and tickled Sandy. The colour was high in my face.

"Which book?" Mum asked.

"*Hatter's Ghosts.*"

"I should think you could recite it by now," said George. "You shouldn't need to read it any more."

"I'm studying it," said Len.

"What's there to study in it?" Grandad wanted to know.

"Women being strangled."

There was a ring on the doorbell and Mother and I jumped like anything. It was one of Len's friends—a member of the new folk-singing group Len was forming, called the Lolly Burners. His hair was inches long behind his ears and there were little gold rings in them. He had a really dusty beard and a great big phoney amethyst on the middle finger of his right hand. There were pitch-black rims to his nails and he'd bitten most of them.

That was another thing George had briefed us on; never show any surprise at whoever the twins bring home. If Len hoped Mother was going to say she was blessed if she knew whether it was a girl or a boy, he was disappointed. Although she did give him a look when he sat on the sofa. You've never seen anyone so dirty.

Mother and Grandad were marvellous at first. Mother offered Dusty Beard a cup of tea, which he refused, and then Grandad tripped up and asked him if he'd like a cake of soap. George gave him such a look.

"We were just wondering which one of us had done the stranglings," said Len. "It's got to be someone from somebody's family."

"Not from *this* family," Mother corrected.

"He'd still be in somebody's family," Len insisted. "And ten to one they'd never think their little Willie could do such a thing. Now then, Grandad, what were *you* doing at the time this schoolteacher bird got bumped off?"

"Same as I'm trying to do now," snapped Grandad. "Read me blooming paper through a lot of rot."

"And you, Brother George? What were you up to? Visiting old Mrs. Bennett as usual?"

George told him, "Wake me when it gets funny."

"I can't think how you can joke at all," Mother sighed. "This last poor soul was a stranger, certainly, but the other two poor little mites were known to us."

"Get out, Mum, we didn't know them," Len argued.

"Not know Mary Drake and Susan Andrews?" Mother demanded. "Your father was only at school with Frank Andrews and I had the next bed to Jessie Drake when you were born."

"That doesn't mean you know their *children*, Mother," Len told her, and clutched his head in exasperation.

Dusty Beard said, "I knew the Drake bird. I used to date her."

That was when Mother tripped up. "Jessie Drake's daughter went out with you looking like *that?*"

Dusty Beard didn't answer. He was quite nice, really. He just *looked* the sort of person who'd put obstructions on railway lines. "She said she was keen on some chap or other."

George looked up from *Fur and Feather*. "Did the police ask you any questions?"

"Sure, like they thought I was some sort of computer or something that'd slip them the answers all worked out."

He was talking rather carefully. I think he'd have thrown in a lot of beatnik jargon if he wasn't careful, and he didn't think Mother looked the type. In a way it was good of him to mind. ~

"Did they think it was someone she knew?" asked George.

Dusty Beard shrugged. "Couldn't say. They pulled in all the boys they thought she knew. There was a good load of them, from what I heard." Dusty Beard grinned and Len and Hélène laughed.

"Anyway, they got nowhere?" George asked.

Dusty Beard shrugged. "Like I'm saying—I wouldn't know."

"Well, they haven't accused anybody," Hélène reminded him. "If they had they'd be holding him."

"No—he's loose, all right," said Len. "Birds beware! He'll strike again!"

"Len!" Mother remonstrated. "How *can* you! Your father would turn in his grave."

Hélène sighed. "Why do you keep on about Dad, Mum? You never liked him."

"Nellie Kinch, I must ask you to leave the room. Whatever will this young man think?"

"He'll think you're a hypocrite, Mum. Aren't you interested in facing the truth?"

"Decent truth, yes. Not your sort." Mother was simply trembling with rage. "All I can say is, I've never been so ashamed."

"You must have been, Mum, because you've said you haven't about four hundred million times before."

They really were mad at Mum. They were just itching to get their own back.

The doorbell went again.

"Oh!" sang Len to the tune of "The Yeomen of England." "Oh, here is the stran-glah, the stran-glah of Dal-stead!" He and Hélène swooped into the hall.

George looked up at Mother. "Play it cool, Mum." Then he leaned over to Grandad and held out *Fur and Feather*. "Seen the mice news today, Grandad? I'll run you out to the next show if I can work it."

Grandad said, "Ta, lad."

They were trying to breed Dutch Perfects, but Grandad was getting something wrong with the colour in between the saddle and the tail or something.

George said to Dusty Beard, "You interested in mice?"

Dusty Beard said, "*Mice?*"

George gave his inside chuckle.

The twins came in positively beaming. They had Aunt Rene Tindall between them.

Mother got up. "Well, Rene!" she said. "I thought you were badly."

George said, "Hello, Aunt," and pushed forward his chair. He didn't look too pleased. He could have enough of Aunt Rene Tindall, could George. I hoped to goodness he didn't go out. There'd be no check on the twins without him present, and with the anti-Mother mood they were in they needed some kind of check.

Mother indicated Dusty Beard. "This is Mr.—"

"Mike," he said.

"Mike," she repeated. "He's in Len's musical society."

Mother lumped everything to do with what she called "that awful noise they make now instead of singing" under the heading of "Len's musical society."

Her eyes fell on me sitting in my chair. She rapped out, "Well, Wynne, what've you got to say to your aunt?"

I said, "Hello, Aunty."

Aunt Rene Tindall nodded at me. "Hello, dear, you look peeky."

Grandad fluttered his fingers at her and went back to the "Mouse Fancy" in *Fur and Feather*. He could have enough of her too. The twins were busy plumping up cushions on the sofa and fetching footstools.

"There," said Len. "Put your bad kidney against this, Aunty."

She said, "Thank you, Len, you're a right thoughtful lad."

I'd like to say Aunt Rene Tindall was different from what you'd expect, but I can't. She must be *exactly* what you'd expect.

She had fluffy fawn hair which no pins could control, and she'd got one of those vague sort of faces that you wouldn't think she'd be able to see or talk out of, it was so dull. She wore fawn fluffy clothes and her glasses were always smeary. Her only interests were illnesses and chapel. She gaped like a fish on a slab at Dusty Beard.

George passed her, broad and tall with his arms hanging straight. "Sorry, Aunty, I've got a date."

He tapped Hélène on the back. "Pack it up, you two." She said, "Give my love to Mrs. Bennett—if she's sober."

I thought, "What a silly crack." Mrs. Bennett was T.T.—absolutely thunderingly T.T. Whenever she delivered a baby in the old days the first thing she'd do when she'd got it to breathe was to pray over it, "Lord, spare this child from indulgence in the grape." She was a right old nut case over drink.

George called, "Goodbye, Mike," and went out whistling. I longed to catch him in the hall and beg him to forgive me for Clare, but I couldn't move. Oh, for the days when I felt so sure of myself with him.

The twins settled Aunt Rene on the sofa and sat at her feet. Never a good sign. It meant they were going to ask after the health of every single one of her more ailing neighbours in turn.

Mother had a go at them. "Len, Nellie—you don't often stay in of an evening—why don't you take yourselves out?"

Len turned his bright, nervy eyes on her. "But Mum—we don't *often* have the pleasure of seeing Aunt Rene."

"Nor do I," said Mother. "And I'd like a chat with her for once, on me own."

I was sorry for her, really. It was rather like Corinne and me hoping the grown-ups would leave us alone. The twins were all set to get a performance out of Aunt Rene Tindall for Dusty Beard's benefit.

In no time at all Len had her on to her minister's wife's hot sweats—and then Hélène brought up Aunt Rene's oldest friend Mrs. Paxton, and pretended that she couldn't remember how her eldest son had died. "Oh, bless you, luv, yes—why, it must be nigh on—let's see—it'd be twenty-five years ago now, wouldn't it, Luce?"

"Very likely," Mother said. She was eyeing Dusty Beard's

heroic efforts not to snort with laughter. He'd evidently heard about Aunt Rene Tindall before.

"What happened to him?" Hélène asked sweetly. "Did he die in the war?"

"Why, bless you, no—'e never took his first poor breath— Mrs. Bennett tried over and over—slapped and slapped him. But it were no good. He were strangled in 'is little cord."

Dusty Beard popped a quick bit of chewing-gum into his mouth and started to chew violently.

Grandad said, without looking up from his paper, "I can think of two more I could wish had strangled in their little cords."

Len and Hélène ignored him. "He wasn't her only child, was he, Aunty?"

"Oh no, dear—she had six. Every time she and Will came together she were caught."

Poor Dusty Beard blew his bit of chewing-gum right across the room. It hit the mantelpiece and fell in the hearth. Sandy got off my lap to investigate. He has to be in on everything, does Sandy. I picked him up and gave him a playful cuff for drawing attention to it. Poor Dusty Beard was red in the face. Mother glared at Dusty Beard, but didn't say anything. She did her best to get Aunt Rene Tindall and the twins off illness, but of course she hadn't got Aunt Rene on her side, either. Aunt Rene was enjoying it just as much as the twins, in a different way.

"She carried her first for—let's see, Luce—comin' on ten months or so, wasn't it?"

"I don't know," snapped Mother. "And I'm sure no one else wants to either."

"Oh, we do," the twins chanted reproachfully. "We're always interested in Aunt Rene's friends."

"Bless them," said Aunt Rene. "Most young folks are only interested in themselves these days."

Mother rolled her eyes to heaven, and the twins sent

Dusty Beard a look as if to say, "You haven't heard anything yet—she can do much better than that."

"Is ten months too long?" Len asked her.

"Aye, luv—it's usually nine—but I said to her, 'Nora Paxton, if you lie about on that wet grass you'll come down with the running trots.'"

"And did she?" Hélène asked eagerly.

Aunt Rene Tindall's hands flew up.

"She was run, run, run, *run!* All the time. Like I were last week, Luce, after Katie's funeral—I wrote you about it."

"You did," Mother said, with an expression which would have shut me up about it for good, but nothing could stop Aunt Rene Tindall once she got going.

"You could see by his poor little legs he'd never've been any good—"

"You mean even if he hadn't strangled in his little cord?"

Mother stood up and told Dusty Beard, "We won't keep you, Mike, and Len and Nellie will walk along with you."

Dusty Beard got up, and that broke the twins up. It was rather a triumph for Mother, with no George to support her. But I suppose the twins would've got bored with their joke with no Dusty Beard to show off to.

I made up my mind to fetch that book back from Collins Wood first thing in the morning. This time I wouldn't take Corinne and this time I'd finish reading it, even if the real ghost of Clare came and interrupted me.

*7* ❖ I TOLD MOTHER I was going to the cinema with Corinne. "Well, mind you're home before dark," she said. "I don't want to have to send George after you again."

"Shan't be late," I promised, and I took the 'bus to Collins Wood.

It was sort of hazy over the town, but as soon as you got out to the common the air cleared. There was something dewy and shimmering in the lights you got over the common—like you see something magnified through a raindrop on a window-pane.

"Should be nice on the common today," the conductor said as he took my fare, and added, "You want a dog, with all these walks you take."

I had gone out of my way to tell him I just went for walks on the common. I couldn't get rid of that guilt complex about going to the house. Fancy thinking strangers would notice.

He used to give me a bit of a saucy look, did that conductor, and when Corinne noticed it she was as mad as anything, and flung out what Hélène called rudely her two little "gnat bites." But he didn't seem to see her. It was the same when we were out for a walk once, and a boy whistled at me and not her. She was wild.

There were some painters working at Number 9, but the garden at Number 3 was so tangled now they couldn't see me, even from their ladders.

I slipped in quickly and went round the back. I'd brought a Mars bar for my tea, and I put it in my pocket as I slid my hand through the broken pane of glass to open the door. It was dead quiet in the house with not even the wind tickling anything. It smelt the same—dry and woody. Even the bathroom and the basement sitting-room, which had given trouble with damp, never smelt of it. But I suppose I'm so soppy about Number 3 I'd never see anything wrong in it. When I think of it under snow I could cry to be living there again.

I gave a little start when a board creaked under my feet. I was always a tiny bit scarey of Clare's spirit, although they said at the convent there were no such things.

It always made me think of her in the living-room—especially now it was empty. When it was furnished I never thought about her from one month to another.

The living-room looked out on the front garden. There was a katalpa tree on the lawn, and you don't see those very often. You couldn't see the common because of the wall. You got the views across that from upstairs.

*The Hatter's Ghosts* was lying just where I dropped it when George had knocked. I picked it up and then had another look at the figures George had scribbled on the wall. I couldn't see them any more clearly. Just that "22 × 23" and then the word which looked like "scale."

I puzzled and puzzled over it. Nothing could change my mind about them not having been there the week before.

I had come with Corinne for a "Clare séance," just like the one we had yesterday when George found us. I did even more "questioning" and "answering" the week before, because I wasn't trying to read *The Hatter's Ghosts*. The raps on the mantelpiece took me right close to the wall, and those figures were not there then. George had been on one of the five days that separated my two visits, and that made it the week before. I simply couldn't make head nor tail of it.

Taking my Mars bar out of my pocket, I sat and read for a couple of hours. I still couldn't make out what could have made George and Len so odd about that book. The hatter hadn't got a family. It wasn't like us. The town, as I said before, reminded me of ours, but only because it was small and most people knew each other. I'm referring to Dalstead proper, of course—not Dalstead New Town and the factory end.

The description of some of the shops was like ours, particularly the ones under the old arcade that were dark and dripping on rainy days. But as far as I knew we hadn't got a hatter amongst our friends—or a dirty little tailor.

I read it right through and went back over bits, and I was as puzzled as when I started it. The crimes weren't anything like the ones the Dalstead Strangler was doing. There wasn't any resemblance at all. The book was certainly marvellous for atmosphere. You could almost smell the inside of the hatter's house, but it didn't smell like ours, and nobody in it anywhere was at all like any of us.

I thought, "Perhaps our Len's just nuts."

Popping the book back in my bag, I decided to tell Len I'd found it down the side of the sofa. It occurred to me as I closed the living-room door that I was telling a lot of lies lately. It's surprising how one can make you keep on telling more. I confessed the lie I told Mother about extra French lessons on Thursdays, and Father Murphy gave me another heavy penance and told me to put it right. He's terribly anti-lie. I think he'd rather you were rude or cheated.

I didn't exactly put it right. I simply never mentioned it again. If Mum had asked, "Is it still the French lessons that keep you late on Thursdays?" I'd worked it out to say, "No, not now—I do all sorts of things instead." Father hadn't told me to say I went to Collins Wood!

As it was so fresh and nice I thought I'd have a look at the garden. It wasn't possible to take home flowers, of course, because the family would guess where I got them from— but I used to take a bunch every week to school. Mother Katherine thought I knew someone who lived in the country. It was lovely to see them in the chapel. The lilies went on the altar once, and the mixed bunches always went to Our Lady in Big Hall. It was lovely to see them about the place—a touch of home in school. Every time I came I picked single blossoms and pressed them in my missal and my *Lives of the Saints*.

The grass was knee-height in the garden, but the Prunus and the double-flowering cherry were out. Blossom goes to my head like drink does to Aunt Rene Tindall's. I could jump and skip and sing with love of it—blossom I mean, of course! In the overgrown beds grape hyacinths and tulips were out, and the bergenia was lovelier than ever before. The daffs were going off, and I dead-headed them and tied them down. In March I pruned the roses. Grandad used to be so proud of them. He taught me a lot about gardens. That's what I'd like to be if I couldn't be anything to do with history or keep an antique shop—a lady gardener, or work in a flower shop.

There was a daphne near the pond. It wasn't out because it had been caught by an early frost.

When I'd picked all I could carry, I wrapped the convent flowers up in the paper I'd brought—but it wasn't quite enough. I thought I'd have a look in the copper-house—there was a pile of old newspapers there that the Robertses had left behind.

The copper-house was made of brick and whitewashed. It had one rounded end like a beehive. Inside there was an enormous copper built into the wall, with oven-like places underneath where you heated it. There were three steps up to the copper, which had a wooden lid which had warped and let the damp in.

It used to give me a lot of pleasure to think of the young Georgian brides who must have done all their family washing in there. I pictured them in their little mob caps, their faces all bright and fresh, and the country spreading for miles around them, with no horrid old shoe factories carving up the sky-line—or flats like ours going up in the air like a pile of sandwich boxes.

In the very old days when Mother first went there, she

used to use the copper herself. But it hadn't been used for donkey's years, and the fire-places were full of straw and dust.

The roof must have been leaking somewhere, because the newspapers were too wet to use. I was just going to pop down to the cupboard in Grandad's basement, where I knew there were some more, when I smelt something.

I sniffed again. It was coming from right inside the old copper itself. When I took the lid off it was quite strong, and on the stone step at the side there was a little splodgy stain. It was paraffin. It was a bit dark to see inside the copper, but I could smell something charred.

I plunged my arm down and pulled up some of the contents. I brought up a handful of half-burned and soggy wool. It was fawn and little bits of it pulled away as you plucked at it. The bits had been hand-knitted into a sweater. George had a sweater like that. I knew because I'd knitted it for him.

I felt down for some more, and came up with several pieces that hadn't been properly burned. There was blood on some of them—old, hard, and stiff, but blood. It could have been paint, tomato soup, or dark tan boot polish, but I knew it wasn't. It was blood.

For quite a while I stayed very, very still.

Then I sat back on my heels and counted out loud. I got right up to twenty, and then I thought I was going to faint.

I leaned my face against the rough coolness of the copper. "Perhaps," I said sickly, "when the dizziness wears off I'll be able to think properly." I tried, but I had seen George wearing that sweater only the week before. I went down on my knees and tried to pray, but I found myself gabbling senselessly. Perhaps it wasn't blood. Perhaps when he came out to write those figures on the wall he got some paint on it and didn't want to hurt my feelings, so he burned the sweater. But I couldn't believe in that, either.

Then perhaps he had hurt himself and didn't want to let

us know he had been out to Collins Wood. But why? Why
didn't he want us to know, and what was he doing at
Collins Wood anyway? I knew that George had a roving eye
and, as I say, I was glad because I'd rather he had lots of
affairs rather than keep to one he might settle on. So perhaps
he had taken a girl to Number 3.

The word "girl" sent me cold and sick again. I said out
loud, "It's daft—it's daft—people don't have those kind of
people in their families—they come from somewhere else—
from outside."

But I understood then about *The Hatter's Ghosts*. Len
was like the little tailor.

I started to count aloud. "One—two—three—four—five—"

8 ❖ I DON'T KNOW HOW LONG I sat in that old copper-house, thinking about George and his sweater. But I realised that if he had meant to burn it he hadn't done a very good job. Somehow I ought to get rid of it properly for him. I suppose it was damp inside the copper, and he didn't put enough paraffin in it—although it wasn't like George to muck up a job as simple as that. It wasn't like George to muck up a ten times more complicated job.

"Daft!" I yelled at myself through clenched teeth. "Daft! He's not that sort—he wouldn't! *George!* The best—the finest —the—" I said to myself, "Look, it's *you* that's not right in the head. Just because you find a bit of old jumper—because George didn't go and see old Mrs. Bennett when he said he did—because he scribbled some figures on the wall—because he burned an old sweater with some sort of stain on it—doesn't mean that he's . . ."

But it wasn't "some sort of" stain on it. Nothing I could say to myself was going to alter that.

I thought, "Now. Be *sensible*, Wynne Kinch. You haven't got Hélène's beauty—you haven't got Corinne's personality —but you can be *sensible*. Even Mother Katherine said so, and she hates you because you did better in history than her favourite little suck-up Anne." And then I thought, "Say a prayer at once. No nun hates anybody." But I didn't say the prayer.

"Supposing Len was right," I thought. "All right—suppos-ing it's true. He wouldn't be to blame because he couldn't help it—he's still George—" and then my head shook so hard I wonder I didn't break my neck. "I'm raving mad. *George!*

More likely Len, Grandad, me, Hélène, Mum—or Aunt Rene Tindall! But *not* George!"

And then I started laughing. The idea was so daft—so daft, daft, *daft*. I must've got German measles or something —I must be coming down with softening of the brain or meningitis.

Then I thought, "Made to look like car accidents."

After such a shock with Clare . . . "There are *hundreds* of car accidents a year," I told myself. "Hundreds! Even worse than Clare's—those people didn't turn into—turn into—"

I scrabbled to my feet. Anybody seeing me would have been sure I was a lunatic. I just couldn't accept it—I just couldn't. Anybody in the world except George. I was practically on all fours, shaking my head.

But then *why* did he burn the sweater with blood on it? *Why* was there blood on it? And *why* did he lie so often about going to Mrs. Bennett? He came in terribly late nearly every night. He was out until the early hours. I never heard him because you wouldn't hear George's footsteps on carpet. But Len used to rag him about it.

"I must make a better job of that sweater than he did," I thought.

I could get some paraffin and fire lighters at the nearest ironmongers', which was about a quarter of a mile away. But if I set light to the copper in daylight, there'd be the smoke—and smoke coming from the wash-house on an empty property would probably attract attention. Did George take that risk, or did he do his burning at night when the smoke would not be seen? If I was caught, and I'd piled a lot of leaves into the copper, I suppose I could have said that I was terribly fond of Collins Wood and that I couldn't bear to see the garden so untidy and I was having a bonfire. But would they believe me? Would they rake out the boiler and find some remains of George's sweater before I had a chance to burn it right through?

It would be safer, surely, to come at night. The thought of doing that made my heart give a kick like a can-can dancer. I had never been to Collins Wood at night, and I was a right little scarey-cat in the dark. I'd never really got over it since I got the first shock about Clare. But you couldn't burn things in an empty house in the daytime. Not if you didn't want to be discovered.

But I knew there was nothing I wouldn't do for George. So I thought, "Right, my girl. It's Collins Wood at night for you, whether you like it or not." At first I thought of taking Corinne, but she was a darn sight more windy than I was and she might not keep her mouth shut—in fact I knew she wouldn't.

My best bet was to go alone. I'd have just one shot at asking George about the sweater, and if he said, "Oh, I burned it in the copper at Collins Wood" and gave a good reason, I'd say my rosary right through twice running in thanksgiving.

My first action was to run back to the living-room. With spit and my handkerchief I managed to rub the figures off the wall above the mantelpiece. That at least, I felt, would remove any evidence that he had been there.

I still felt shaky when I got on the 'bus for Dalstead.

A lady was going on and on and on about permanganate of potash. "You can use it for anything," she said. "Gargling —cuts—and I know someone who gave it to chickens to drink—it picked them up like anything."

How marvellous it would be, I thought, to be able to give all your emotions to permanganate of potash; to have nothing else in your head crowding it out.

Everything seemed to have changed for me and I couldn't feel young any more. Even the common didn't look misty and luminous in a nice way. The lights over it seemed leaden, yellowy, and threatening. The magnolia trees in the gardens, as the suburbs started to build up, didn't look like fairies in ballet dresses, which is how I used to think

of them. They looked like sinister lamp bulbs, pink and
malignant.

I said to myself, "You're *daft*—you're *daft!* You don't know
yet—it's just an old sweater—it doesn't mean anything—
there could be dozens of reasons for finding it there. Len's
out of his mind. He was always nervy—Clare's accident put
him all wrong—you don't get given phenobarbitone at seven
if you're all right."

I must've started to count out loud, because the
permanganate-of-potash lady turned round to me. "Does
'bus make you sick, luv?" she asked me. "You ought to take
Marsine like our Johnny. He's a real terror for travel—engine's hardly turned before he's heaving—but Marsine set-
tles him down all right."

"I'm not sick, thanks," I told her.

"You look peeky to me—doesn't she, May? Lots of people
get travel sickness."

Closing my eyes, I prayed she'd get off at the next stop.
"I've hit another Aunt Rene Tindall here," I sighed to myself. "In another minute we shall hear about failing kidneys
and people coming down with the running trots."

I remembered queasily one of Aunt Rene's very worst. We
children laughed so much at the time Mother sent us all to
bed. Poor Mother was eating one of those buns with
custardy cream inside and Aunt Rene leant over it and
said, "That's *just* 'ow Willie's toe went before they took it
off."

The twins lay hiccoughing with laughter long after we'd
been sent to bed.

Mrs. Permanganate of Potash *was* another Aunt Rene
Tindall, and she didn't get off at the next stop.

I went to the ironmongers' in Dalstead. I was too well
known at the little one in Collins Wood. I bought a packet
of fire lighters and a small can of paraffin. They made a very
bulky parcel and they reminded me of what I was in for. I
turned quite queasy again. I tried to slide past Mother with

my parcel, but she stopped me in the hall. The colour of my face caught her attention at once.

She said, "Hello, Wynne—you look quite peeky—I hope you're not coming down with something."

"I'm fine, thanks, Mum."

Then her eye lighted on my parcel. "What's that?" she asked.

"Oh, just some books and things for school." The lies! The awful lies that piled up. My God, if I'd known what harm they'd do!

I put my parcel in the bedroom and asked her, "Mum, would you mind if I slept at Corinne's tonight—there's something we want to see together on the telly."

"What is it?" she wanted to know.

That threw me. It had never occurred to me that she might ask a question like that, and my brain went absolutely blank.

"Oh, I'm not quite sure," I said stupidly. "It's just something Corry wants to see with me that comes on rather late."

"Well, if Mrs. Eldridge doesn't mind," Mother conceded. "But you've got to get round there before dark."

I shivered as she said the word "dark."

I knew how scared I would be that night, even in my beloved Collins Wood.

I prayed that George would come in and make everything all right so that I didn't have to go. But if everything wasn't all right I dare not leave that sweater there any longer. The Dalstead police were poking their noses in everywhere because of what had happened, and there were people from Scotland Yard to help them.

I'd just have to risk Mother ringing up Mrs. Eldridge, but if she did she wouldn't get through—I was going to damage their telephone wire!

"My God," I thought, "I'm a criminal—I'm no better than

the Dalstead—" and then I had to sit down because I felt
sick again.

In the bedroom I was just starting to pack up my
"criminal kit" when I heard Mother coming. I shoved the
fire lighters and the paraffin under the bed.

She said, "Wynne, pet, are you sure you're not poorly—
you're the colour of cotton-wool."

"I'm fine, Mum, *fine*," I assured her, but my voice was soft
and squeaky.

"You'd do better to have an early bed," said Mother,
"than go goggling at telly with Corinne."

"It's something *special*, Mum," I said. "We're longing to
see it together."

"All right," she sighed. "But I do hope you haven't eaten
anything."

When she went out, I snatched the B.E.A. bag someone
had given Hélène and crammed in the fire lighters, the
paraffin, and the matches. I put my Woolworth torch in,
and for good measure my rosary. Then I hid the lot under
my nightie and my sponge-bag.

The front door closed behind someone with no sound of
feet. George! I shot out. "'Lo!" I said.

His cloudy blue eyes looked down at me. He saw mighty
well through his glasses. "Feeling all right?" he asked.

"Yes, thanks."

"You're pale."

He was wearing a sports coat and a green sweater under
it.

"You never wear the fawn one I knitted you," I pouted.

"I was wearing it last week," he said, and went into the
bathroom to wash.

Hélène was on the evening shows at the cinema, so she
was going to be late. Poor Paul had promised Mother to
see her home even though he'd already seen the show twice.
Len was getting into his pop-group uniform to go to the
discothèque.

"I'll be glad when they've caught this bloody strangler," Grandad snapped.

"No gladder than I'll be," Mother retorted. "And if you're asking me, hanging and quartering's too good for him. It's stopping the death penalty that encourages them—no one can tell me that violence hasn't increased since they stopped it—the crimes prove it."

"Ever seen a man hanged?" Len wanted to know.

"No—but I've seen the work done by those that should be hanged."

I closed my eyes. I felt dizzy again. When I opened them, George was looking at me—he had come in to sit down with the evening paper.

"Everyone's on the side of the murderer these days," Mother went on. "And the dirtier the crime and the more pain they cause, the more sympathy they get. A man's only got to axe a blind old lady's brains open and the public howls 'poor thing'—and it's not the old lady they're wailing about."

"Not all the public," Grandad said. He was deep in *Fur and Feather*.

"Hanging's not the answer, Mum."

"Then what is, Len Kinch? You're not sitting there to deny that things've got worse and worse since they stopped hanging? What do you want to save your sympathy for people that batter little girls to death for?"

"I'd bring back the death penalty for cruelty," said Grandad, "to children, or people, or even animals. We don't want folks alive that get fun out of chopping up children's pets or cutting off the head of a budgerigar that's probably some old-age pensioner's only friend—"

"What would you do about train vandalism, Grandad? Bring back the death penalty for kids of eleven?"

"Beat them until they didn't think causing other folks pain was quite such a lark."

"But what's that but cruelty to children and violence?" Len wanted to know.

"It's *teaching* children," Grandad said. "And it's to show them that violence can hurt them as well as others. And I didn't suggest killing them—like they've probably bumped off some engine driver, not to mention a few passengers."

"What's the modern murderer got to fear?" Mother demanded. "They'll openly sneer with a gun in your face. They know they'll only go to prison, where it's not all that bad, at public expense. If they behave themselves life's made better for them, and if they're young they'll be out early enough to start again."

"If you're not going to have the death penalty," said Grandad, "it should be ninety-nine years and nothing off."

"Oh, get out, Grandad! That's nothing more than a living death," from Len.

"And what did their victims get?" snapped Grandad. "Not even a *living* death—just *death!*"

"Two blacks don't make a white," sulked Len.

"I'm not interested in colour schemes," Mother argued. "I'm interested in justice."

"Yes—*your* kind—but it depends on the crime."

"Aye," Mother conceded, "I'll give you that, there's crimes and crimes, certainly. If it's something done in anger, or great fright, well, there's a difference. But in most cases I don't see why the hangman should be considered a murderer and the murderer not!"

"What about this chap going round strangling?" Grandad wanted to know.

Mother said heatedly, "Yes, taking him for a start! Not only does he kill the poor little things, and God only knows what they suffered before they died—it doesn't warrant thinking about—but what of the anguish he caused to their folk? Can you just imagine trying to live the rest of your life knowing that sort of end came to one of your own?"

"He's mad," said Len. "He hasn't a clue what he's doing."

"He's not mad," said Grandad. "And he has got a clue. And there's another thing, to my mind, that could do with clearing up. M.P.'s these days seem to think it's their own opinions and beliefs that count. Well, it's *not*—they're supposed to represent the opinions of the people. It's what *we* think they should be putting forward—they're supposed to be acting for *us*. We don't pay them to air bees in their own bonnets. They should go to Hyde Park if they want to speak for themselves."

"That's right," Mother nodded vigorously. "The man in the street wants hanging to stay."

"You've never asked the man in the street," Len flared up. "Now come on—*have* you? Which man in the street have you ever stopped and said, 'Do you want hanging to stay?'"

"I can't understand you, Len Kinch," Mother droned on. "You'd soon change your tune if it came nearer home—how would you feel if it happened to Nellie?"

"That's daft, Mum—of course I'd *feel*. Come to that, how would *you* feel if the strangler himself came nearer home? Suppose it was one of your family? Your husband, or son, or something—you wouldn't be so keen to see him swinging then, would you?"

I fainted. When I came to, Mum was holding Dr. Mackenzie's smelling salts to my nose, Grandad was holding a glass of water, Len was fanning me with *Fur and Feather,* and George was standing in the doorway, looking at me.

Mother was saying, "That's that, then. There'll be no going round to Corinne's tonight."

**9** ❋ THE DOCTOR couldn't find anything wrong with me except that my blood pressure was a bit high for a girl of my age.

"Blood pressure at *her* age!" Mother squeaked.

"I've had babies of two with high blood pressure," the doctor told her.

Mother made me stay in bed two days, which nearly drove me dotty.

Hélène, of course, shared the room with me, and Len and Grandad visited me on their own or together, but George only came in when someone else was there.

I got at him through Mother. Pretending to be sort of petty because I didn't feel well, I snivelled, "Well, I'm not knitting our George Meakham any more sweaters."

"Oh?" Mother asked me. "Why's that, love?"

"I think he's thrown the one I made him for Christmas away."

"Of course he hasn't, dear. He was in it last week—I remember."

"He hasn't been in it since."

I heard Mother say to him when he came in, "She's fussed about your sweater, George. For goodness' sake tell her you set great store by it."

George followed Mother in to see me. "What's this about the sweater, Wynne?"

"You don't like it any more," I said, and felt very silly and childish. He simply towered above me in bed. Hélène and I had particularly low divans.

"Where'd you get an idea like that about the sweater?" George wanted to know.

"You've thrown it away," I challenged him.

"Wynne!" said Mother. "What a daft thing to suggest. Why ever would he do such a thing?"

"That's what I want to know," I replied.

There was no expression on George's face, but he put his head on one side when he looked at me. There wasn't much expression in his voice, either. He liked to guard his feelings, did George.

"It's true, I do seem to've lost it," he said.

"How could you, George?" Mother wanted to know.

Len appeared in the doorway.

"I don't understand it myself," said George. "I put it in my drawer to be cleaned and when I went to get it it wasn't there."

Mother went bustling off to make sure. George stood looking down at me.

"You sure you didn't chuck it away—or—or—chuck it away?" I asked.

George straightened his head. "You tell me why I'd want to do a thing like that?"

My voice stuck in my throat. "You might have—torn it— or something, and didn't want me to see—"

"If I'd torn it," he answered, "I'd have brought it to you to mend."

"Well, spilt something on it, then—that you couldn't get off." It was as far as I dared go.

"If I'd spilt something I'd have taken it to the cleaners, wouldn't I?"

"And you haven't."

"No, Wynne, I haven't. I've already told you, I just can't find it. I'd like an answer to the mystery myself."

Behind him in the doorway Len's face had gone his awful greasy white. I tried to swallow ordinarily. I thought, "Oh God, Len knows he's lying too."

Mother came back. "Well, I've had a good look. It doesn't seem to be anywhere."

George told me, "You'll have to knit me a new one, won't you?—unless you can find the other one for me."

Then he went out of the room. Mother followed him, babbling about had it got into one of Len's or Grandad's drawers by mistake.

To anyone but me there wouldn't have been anything to see in George's face. But I knew him so well. I saw plenty. He didn't look right about that sweater. He didn't look right at all. He knew something about it he wasn't saying.

I glanced up at Len. "You going to have one of your headaches?"

"No."

"You look as if you are."

"Well, I'm not."

He looked terribly skinny in the legs in his tight black jeans. His hands were thin and nervous, but terribly strong. It came from all that twanging on guitars and resting them from doing anything useful, Grandad said.

"You know something about that sweater, don't you, Len?" I accused him.

You've never heard such a noise. It was like a gas main exploding. "Do you think I'd be seen dead in gear like that? It's the kind Noah's wife ran him up to keep his chest warm in the flood."

"You've borrowed it once or twice," I said. "I've seen you in it."

He stood there swearing and shouting at me until Mother came in and went for him. George had gone out. We didn't hear him, of course—but then, as I've said before, nobody ever did hear George walking about. He was proud of it. He often said how useful it could be.

Mother gave Len's shoulder a clout. "What are you thinking of, lad? The girl's not well—never mind what the neighbours will think."

Len stamped off to the room he shared with George and slammed the door.

Mother tweaked my bed into shape, although it was not untidy. "Whatever has got into everybody?"

"Yes," I thought. "Whatever has?"

I may not have been absolutely certain of George's reactions, but I was in no two doubts that Len was lying. That made me even keener to get out to Collins Wood at night, however bad I felt. My heart simply hammered at the thought of it. I had to keep thinking, "It's for George—it's for George." How to do it wasn't going to be easy—I just knew it had to be done. Anything could be done for George. At first I thought of telling the others—not Mother, of course, she'd have died, and I didn't like risking Grandad coming down with a heart attack either. But Hélène was oddly babyish if anything awful happened. She'd go rushing off to Mother, and I didn't know whose side Len was on. As for George—well, I couldn't tell him, of course. No, it all had to be kept to myself and I decided that Corinne should help without knowing anything. I couldn't risk her mixing things up for me.

That night when we put the lights out Hélène asked me, "What's up with George?"

I said with a sleepiness I didn't feel, "Dunno. Is something up?"

"He was about as sweet as a lemon at supper."

"Oh."

"He marched out soon after—gone to see old Mrs. Bennett again, ha! ha! I don't suppose—"

"Who do you think he's gone to see, then?"

"Some bird he doesn't want us to know about—otherwise why the Bennett lies?"

"How do you know they're lies?"

"Saw him at the cinema once with a bird that wasn't old Ma Bennett on a night he'd 'gone to see her'!"

My voice was calm but I could feel the little tic starting up in my eye. "He couldn't have wanted to avoid you much if he took her to your cinema."

"He didn't know I was on that night. I wasn't supposed to be. I'd switched with Margaret."

"Did you know the girl he was with?"

"*Girl!*"

"Well, it wasn't a man, was it?"

"Not quite."

"You mean it was a queer?"

"God, no—just someone much older than him—or looks it—and none too steady on its pins."

"A cripple?"

"A drunk, you bloody fool."

I was silent, as I could think of nothing to say. I heard Hélène turn over to me. "You know, Puss Bun, you'll have to get over this thing."

"What thing?"

"Oh, don't give me that! It was all right to dote on him as a kid. It was funny and sweet—you hadn't got a father and you picked on him. Nothing more natural. But it's not natural now—it's a father complex."

I yawned audibly. "You going to talk all night?"

"You're going to get hurt, Puss Bun. You know what they say about our George, don't you? Any skirt anywhere does him—no matter how young or how old."

"Who's 'they'?"

"People that know him—the town—his friends."

"Some friends!"

"Me myself I don't think he can help it—maybe he's searching for Clare in everyone, or maybe he's just over-sexed."

"Why don't you ask him which it is?"

Hélène sighed. "Don't be *silly,* Puss Bun." She never said "daft." "He's old enough to be your grandad."

"If he were he'd be Grandad's age, wouldn't he?"

"You *can't* look no further away than George. You *must* get used to the idea of finding someone else to dote on. Apart from his age he's a bird-watcher!"

"Doesn't bring many birds home, does he?"

"Well, who could with Mum around? Ours just isn't that sort of home. There's nowhere for them to sit alone. They'd have Mum trying to make out how serious they are with dotty little questions—Grandad on about mice—and probably Aunt Rene Tindall! Catch anyone bringing birds home! Look," she went on, "I'm fond of George—and Len thinks the sun gets up and goes down with him—and they share a room, don't they? Len says he's out until all hours, night after night. I mean, that's all right, good luck to him—but it wouldn't be good luck to you! I mean, supposing you did get him to wait for you and caught him up around forty when you were seventeen—"

"When I'm seventeen he'll be thirty-eight, and that's nothing these days—some people marry people of fifty."

"I said *around* forty, and it *is* something—when *you're* forty, he'll be older than God's uncle!"

"Just a nice difference," I said primly.

"Okay, okay," Hélène sighed. "But what about the sex side?—I tell you, our George is a bird-lover. You wouldn't want a man you couldn't trust. I've seen him with bird after bird at the cinema—sometimes he's seen me, sometimes he hasn't."

"I'd want George," I said.

"Even if he was a sex maniac?"

I shot up in bed with such violence the clothes leapt out from the sides.

"Oh, shut up, you silly little bitch!"

"Wynne!" she squeaked in genuine shock. She and Len could use filthy words in front of Mother, but one bad one from me and it was *"Wynne!"* I suppose it was because they knew they were joking and doing it on purpose, and I *meant* mine.

"Lots of men have birds," I screamed at her. "You'd soon be twittering away about him being queer if he didn't like them—he just can't do any right—you're forever on at him—"

"Oh, for the love of Mike," she wailed, "I didn't mean a *real* sex maniac—I just meant he was keen—enthusiastic—he *likes* it!"

"Then why didn't you *say* he was just keen and enthusiastic and he liked it? According to you, James Bond would be a sex maniac. So would anybody that was interested in girls. Just because he takes a few to the cinema doesn't mean that he's—he's—" and then my nerves broke out. I exploded into loud sobs.

Hélène was dreadfully upset. She sprang out of bed to comfort me, but once I started I couldn't stop. It was rather like a drunk person who knows he's being rude and doesn't want to be, but can't stop.

It brought Mother, Grandad, Len, George, and even Sandy into the room. He must've seen the lights, Sandy I mean, and thought there was something in it for him.

Mother was in a right old flap. She cried, "Grandad, Grandad, send for Doctor!"

George said, "Let's see what's wrong with her first." He spoke perfectly calmly. But he was worried when he bent over me. I knew my George—I got a little kick out of it. I played up even worse. I thought, "Right, so he still minds, does he? Well, we'll give him something to mind about."

He saw through it at once. He said, "Cut that out." And he gave my shoulder a little cuff.

Hélène sobbed, "It was my fault—I told the poor baby you were a sex maniac."

George asked politely, "Why?"

Hélène looked up at him. "I didn't *mean* it, otherwise I wouldn't have *said* it."

"Maybe Wynne didn't catch on to that," George suggested.

I felt bound to defend her. After all, she had only been trying to help.

"She was only joking," I sobbed.

"Doesn't seem to have made you laugh much," George observed.

"It was only a gag, George," Hélène insisted.

"Make it funnier next time," George suggested, and left the room.

"It's all those horror films," Mother said. "Playing daft jokes on each other at this time of the night. What do you expect but to go upsetting each other?"

Hélène settled back, giggling with relief as Mother went on muttering and tweaking my bed.

"What's the good of all this violence? It only leads to things like that terrible brute on the common. They see it on telly and think it's bright to copy it. You're not to talk about it any more, Nellie, it's getting on Baby's mind."

She always called me Baby if I hadn't been well.

*10* ❖ I was allowed up the next day to listen to the Stations of the Cross because it was Good Friday, but Mother made me go to bed straight afterwards.

She wouldn't let me out on Saturday, no matter how I pleaded, so I didn't see Corinne until after Mass on Easter Sunday. I couldn't speak to her then because Mrs. Eldridge was standing over her with her wings out, as George used to put it.

Also, Corry was mad at me because a boy she'd rather got her eye on was looking at me more than her. I couldn't help being pleased but I didn't show it. I thought Corry would bust her ribs trying to thrust her bit of figure out to match mine!

On Easter Monday, when Mum had gone to see Aunt Rene Tindall and all the rest were out except Grandad, who was cleaning his mice, I phoned Corry.

"Can you talk in private?"

She sounded important at once. "Yup. I'll tell Mother I'm not to be interrupted."

When she came back she said, "Shoot."

I shot. "Ring me up, Corry, and ask me to stay the night because there's a programme we want to see on telly together."

"Oke."

"Only I won't really be staying the night."

There was a little dramatic silence. I knew she was intrigued. "I can't tell you why until later," I explained.

"No dice," she answered at once. "I get told all—or there's no sale this end."

I hesitated. Then I offered, "I'll give you my *own* mother's rosary—the mother-of-pearl with the real silver caps on the Our Fathers."

This time it was Corinne who hesitated. She was a terrible snob about things. She had a rosary of her own, of course, but mine really was prayer with class. She'd always been after it. I liked it—but my own mother meant nothing to me sentimentally and I always used the little red one George gave me when I made my first communion. He wasn't a Catholic, but he chose it himself.

"Done!" said Corinne. "But suppose they ring you up and find you're not here?"

"They won't. Because you're going to pick your telephone up and bust it."

"I'm going to *what?*"

"Well, just give it a knock or something, so's it rings unobtainable if the family try to get on to me tonight—"

"You're going to spend *all* night somewhere?"

"Yes—I'll come round to you with my case. You let me in so your mum won't know I've brought one—and she won't know I'm supposed to be staying the night."

Corinne's voice was all choky with excitement. "Is it a boy?"

"Could be."

"Wynne! You're never going to—you're not going to *let* him?"

"Why so shocked?" I wanted to know. "You say you've done it dozens of times." I knew she had only been boasting.

"Yes, but—are you going to a *hotel?*"

"Could be."

"How will you not have a baby?—*Get out!*" she suddenly shouted. "I said this was private!" I presumed she was talking to her mother.

I heard Mrs. Eldridge say, "Sorry, dear, but you won't be too long, will you, because Mother wants to use the phone."

"I said get *out!*" yelled Corinne. When she came back to me she said, "Well, how will you *not* have one?"

"Oh, I'm all fixed up for that," I said carelessly.

"You're going to tell me some*time*?" she insisted.

"Sometime," I said.

"Will you tell me what it's like?"

"I thought you knew—"

"Yes, but I mean, swap notes—"

"Sometime," I said.

"Hey!" she yelled, and I wondered why she'd only just thought of it. "What about George? How come you've suddenly stopped being crazy about him enough to go off with some other boy?"

"You and Hélène are always on at me to shell him—so I've shelled him," I said.

Corinne was always shelling boy-friends like peas from a pod. At least so she said. Sometimes I thought they shelled her.

"It has to be somebody pretty good you're going to, to make you shell George," she went on.

"It *is* someone pretty good."

"Do I know him?"

"No."

She tried me out. "Well, I can't say I'm sorry—I think George is a dope."

I kept my temper. "So will you ring me?" I asked.

"When?"

"Make it lunch time. Then they'll all be back."

"'Kay." And she hung up.

When she rang up I pretended to be surprised. "Corry! What's she want?"

"Strangling," said George. He couldn't bear Corinne, but the word had made me jump.

Mother picked on it at once. "How can you joke, George, after what's happened?"

The phone was in the hall and I spoke loudly. "'Lo, Corry? What? Oh, all right—I'll just tell Mum—"

"Mum," I called out, "I'm going round to Corry's tonight —we want to see that thing on telly you and Grandad don't like."

I'd made sure this time to look up the right programme in the *Radio Times*.

"You couldn't call it singing," Grandad said.

"You'll have to get back before dark," Mother told me.

"Oh, I'll stay the night at Corry's."

"All right, if Mrs. Eldridge doesn't mind."

"I doubt if Mrs. Eldridge will be consulted," George said. He was wearing a blue shirt which he got somewhere down in the South of France. He and Mr. Wells built a boat together once, and then with some other friends they went all the way down to Marseilles and across to Corsica. They sold the boat at Marseilles and came back by train. Mr. Wells gets stomach trouble but George likes everything that's French. He can eat snails and frogs' legs and he simply loves wine. He always says he likes a country where only the teetotaller's breath smells!!

Len found dozens of pictures of girls in George's drawer afterwards. The French girls seemed to go for him. But I didn't mind—safety in numbers again!

George wasn't usually home for lunch. It depended which way his work was taking him. Len usually got back, but it depended on Hélène's performances whether she got back or not. It was the day she would have started rehearsals if she'd got the part with the Amateur Dramatic Society, so poor old Mother was unpopular again—Hélène was sulking because Mother had lost her the part and Len was sulking in sympathy. They really were the end, those twins. They didn't cheer up until Aunt Rene Tindall came in to tell us about a stillbirth in her street. She was wearing a dress of muddy fawns. Len said it looked like "sicked-up sausage," which put Mum off her lunch. George fairly lashed out at them and in the middle of it all I slipped out to get my bag. I slipped my torch into it and then dumped it in the hall. George had to move it out of the way to get his coat. "Going for a week, Wynne?" he enquired.

"There are books in it," I replied.

I went round to Corinne's about five. She met me at the downstairs hall as I had asked, and put my bag in one of the cupboards. Then we went upstairs.

Mrs. Eldridge said, "Hello, Wynne dear," and I said, "Hello—" Corinne never let you talk to Mrs. Eldridge long. She said impatiently, "Oh, c'*mon*," and you had to follow. She wasn't like that with her father. She tried it on but he said, "Any more lip from you, young lady, and you don't watch the telly at all tonight."

"Lip!" muttered Corinne when we got into her room. "Young lady! He must have been born before God."

In the living-room we heard her mother sticking up for her. "You're always at her, Bill. All the time it's pick, pick, pick—it makes my head ache," Mrs. Eldridge whined.

Corinne shut their voices out by slamming her bedroom door. Her father bellowed, "Close the door quietly, can't you?"

"I hate them," said Corinne through the middle of her teeth.

"You can't hate your mother, she's always on your side."

"Oh, there's nothing in her to hate—she's a fool—now then, payment please."

She held out her hand, and I was just about to drop my "prayer with class" rosary into it when I heard the telephone ring.

"You haven't done it," I accused her. "A fat lot of good that is."

"I couldn't," she said sulkily. "Dad was in there."

"Not all the time," I retorted. It was so like Corinne. She was frightfully brave yelling at her mother, and things like that, but when it came to doing something she'd funk it.

"Well, a fat lot of good that is," I sneered. "What happens if someone rings up for me and I'm not there?"

"What time are you meeting him?"

"Who?"

"The boy you shelled George for."

"Oh! Well, after supper sometime—when it's dark."

My stomach turned again at the thought of the dark. It would be dark by about half-past seven or eight and I dreaded the thought of those cold, black hours in an empty house. If I took the seven-thirty 'bus out to the common, it would be dark by the time I reached the house—then, if it only took me about half an hour to complete my mission, I ought to be able to catch the eight-thirty or nine-o'clock 'bus back into Dalstead and tell Mother that I'd quarrelled with Corinne and decided to come home after all. If I hadn't done this, Mum would have insisted upon someone coming to fetch me and then the Eldridges would have wondered where I'd been in between. I was safe from Mother's efforts to save me from the strangler only if she thought I was spending the night with Corinne, and Corinne would think I had spent it with the "boy" for whom I had "shelled George," which would raise me to great and dashing heights in her eyes.

The thought of the strangler wasn't making me any too happy, either. There was quite a wild bit of common to cross before you got to Number 3. "Don't be silly," I told myself. "He's probably hundreds of miles away by now. He's probably not even in the country."

But my mouth went dry and I felt a bit sick. After all, two of the girls had been killed on the common, and the third not far away. The police were keeping a good eye on the common, of course, but I wanted to be out of their sight— not in it. In a way, I supposed it would look even more suspicious if I were caught going to the house at night, but I just couldn't risk smoke being seen in the daytime and having to answer questions about George's sweater.

We had a high tea at the Eldridges', and when Mrs. Eldridge was clearing it away and when Mr. Eldridge went

out to buy his evening paper, I ripped the telephone out of
its socket.

It was terribly hard to do. I was expecting it to come away
as easy as anything, but I had quite a struggle with it. I
made a fearful fuss about being upset about it—and said I'd
tripped over the wire by mistake.

Mrs. Eldridge was sweet about it. "Don't worry, Wynne
dear. We'll get the man out to it tomorrow."

"If we're lucky," Mr. Eldridge grumbled. "And a nice
thing if we want to use it in between."

Mrs. Eldridge sighed. "She's said she's sorry, hasn't she?
She couldn't help it."

"Wants to look where she's going," said Mr. Eldridge.

"I'll pay for it out of my pocket money, Dad," Corinne
offered in her best convent elocution voice.

Her father gave a little snorty laugh. "A fat long way that
would go—you're in the red with your pocket money already, young lady."

Mrs. Eldridge became quite hysterical. It was terribly embarrassing. "Oh, Bill!" she shouted. "It was a sweet little offer, wasn't it? Why can't you thank her for it? There's not
many kids her age would offer to pay—it's a sweet thing to
do and all she gets is a slap in the face for it—she can't do
anything right with you—not even offer to pay."

"I'd like to have seen her face if I'd said 'yes,'" Mr. Eldridge chuckled. "All right, Corinne lass. Let's see the colour
of your money."

He was a small man with kind brown eyes. Mrs. Eldridge
had bright blue ones with lots of white round them, like a
cut-in-half hard-boiled egg. Her voice was going up and up,
louder and louder.

"There you go! Making fun of her! The child does something nice you wouldn't get other kids doing—"

Mr. Eldridge looked older suddenly and bored and tired.
"It was said for the sake of saying," he answered dully.

I knew it was true—Corinne was terribly close with her

money. She only made the offer to sound good. I felt dreadful about causing a row, especially when I knew it hadn't been an accident.

"I'll pay for it, Mr. Eldridge," I piped. "I've got some money in the post office. If you'll just let me know what it is."

He was leaving the room and he ruffled my hair, which annoyed me. I mean, it's all right if you're a child, but when you've spent hours on a shampoo and set it's maddening.

"Thanks, Wynne lass," he said. "But don't trouble. Just look where you're going next time."

That really set Mrs. Eldridge off. She fairly flew at the poor little man. "Oh yes, it's 'thanks and don't trouble' to Wynne Kinch, isn't it? But not to your own daughter! Oh no! That's different, isn't it? *She* doesn't warrant a thank you! *She* only said it for the sake of saying it! Wynne Kinch meant it, but not your own daughter!"

Corinne said, "Oh Mum, shut up. The neighbours will think you've gone bonkers."

Mr. Eldridge jerked back his thumb at her. "There you are, Mother—that's your thanks for sticking up for her. See what you get for spoiling 'em."

She followed him out, simply sobbing with rage. You couldn't blame Corinne for despising her. She really did get daft now and then, although my mother said it was because she was going through a difficult time and couldn't help it. She was so touchy about Corinne she even snapped Father Murphy's head off when he said he thought Corinne dressed too sexy.

We heard her going on and on at poor Mr. Eldridge. "Oh cripes," I said, "I'm sorry, Corinne. It's made things awful for your dad."

"It's his fault," she said. "He should shell her."

The row had helped me to take my mind off my own fears and the pains that they put in my stomach, but when I saw the clock I knew it couldn't be put off any longer.

"Well," I chirruped, "mustn't keep my date waiting."

She blocked my way, holding her hand out. "Rosary, please," she said.

"Get that!" I exploded. "You didn't do your part—I had to fix the telephone myself."

"And made a right muck-up. You've upset Mum and upset Dad. Mum has to have the doctor when she gets upset like that."

"A fat lot you care about that!"

"I *do* so care about that—anyway, you promised."

"I didn't promise to pay you for nothing."

Corinne watched me for a moment and then smiled slowly at me.

"What's to stop me going outside and ringing up your mum and asking if you got home safely?"

"Your conscience ought to stop you."

"Save that for Mother Kathleen."

"You're a lousy friend, Corinne," I said.

"Lousy friends get lousy friends."

My scare pains were making me feel a bit sick. I couldn't stand and argue with her. I dropped the rosary into her hand. "I've only lent it to you," I said. "Only lent—you've got to work for it to keep it."

She made a rude noise with her lips and banged the door after me. But I hadn't gone more than two yards down the passage outside her flat before she popped out of her door again.

"Wynne!"

I kept on walking. She caught me up.

"Wynne, you will promise to let me know what it's like, won't you?"

I kept walking. She tried bribery. "Want to borrow my amber pendant with the real fly inside?"

"No thanks. David doesn't like insects round my neck." He had a name now. Corinne pounced on it.

"*David!* Ho ho! That slipped out, didn't it?"

"Dozens of Davids in the world," I replied expressionlessly. "It won't help you to find out much about mine."

"We'll see what we shall see," she chuckled. But I knew she hated to let me go. She couldn't think whether she'd get further with me by being nice or more bitchy. She got more bitchy.

"Enjoy yourself, my little bride. It hurts the first time, you know." That's what she wanted to find out, of course—whether it hurt.

"I've done it seven times," she said. "I really ought to know."

I was silent. I'd got to the top of the stairs and started to run down them. She shrimped down them beside me. I know there's no such word, but it's how Corry moves! She couldn't quite keep up with me because her heels were too high.

"I told *you* about *mine!*" she shouted down at me.

"Yours were made up," I threw back at her, and grinned because of mine also being completely made up. I didn't grin for long. Something really sharp hit me in the back of the neck and hurt quite badly. Corinne had thrown a shoe at me. I turned and hurled it back at her. She started what I always called her vixen shrieks—like a really young child whose dummy someone's pinched. "At least it's cut down my lies," I thought. "I've certainly quarrelled with Corinne!"

I ran down the last two flights and left her with doors opening all down the passage outside her flat and her mother yelling, "*Look* what you've done to her now, Bill. You put the poor little mite in hysterics."

# 11 ❖ The PERMANGANATE-OF-POTASH LADY was on the

'bus to Collins Wood again. The one that said you couldn't beat it. I felt sorry about her. Her eyes looked so ill in the lights inside the 'bus that I suddenly knew with one of those funny little stabbing feelings you can get about things sometimes that nothing could ever do her any good; not even permanganate of potash. Something else had beaten her already.

The sadness of listening to her bright tinny voice, telling her bored friend how to do everything better than the friend could, took away my own fears for a time. She didn't know. She didn't know that when the friend came to do all these things she wouldn't be here to criticise. But I knew. I get these odd feelings at times and they're nearly always right. George is the only one that doesn't laugh at them— George and to a certain extent Grandad. He always says gloomily, "It's the Irish—your mother had it—and I said to her, 'Well, Bridie, you may have the sixth sense, but you didn't use *any* of them marrying my son!'"

You can imagine what I get from the rest of the family! Mum says, "I wonder your church doesn't put a stop to it." Len said, "Why can't you use it for the Derby or something useful?" and Hélène wanted to know how things would go with her latest boy-friend. I never mentioned my "funny feelings" to them any more, and now I didn't even feel I could talk about them to George.

I don't get them by looking at hands or anything—they just come in and out of my mind in a flash when I'm thinking of something completely different.

Usually I tried to find other reasons for it if it was a feeling with badness attached to it.

On that 'bus there was a feeling of badness all right, and it wasn't just to do with the poor permanganate-of-potash lady. It was all mixed up with George and Corinne and my beloved Collins Wood. How Corinne fitted in I couldn't quite tell then, so I put it down to the fact that we'd quarrelled and that's why I felt upset inside about her.

Of course I wasn't letting myself think about George—not properly—not really letting my mind accept my fears. And it's the greatest pity in the world that I wasn't. I was only taking things step by step. That night I was taking the sweater. There was something wrong about that sweater and both George and Len were hiding something about it. You don't burn a sweater in the old copper of an empty house for nothing, particularly when there's blood on it. Neither George nor Len had had any cuts or grazes that could have bled, because we'd have seen them in bandages or plaster. So it had to be somebody else's blood. Whose?

I wasn't answering any questions. Not even to myself—and I didn't want to ask any, either. When I caught myself at it I started to count. "One, two, three, four, five—why was George's sweater burned? Why did he tell me a lie about it? Six, seven, eight, nine, ten—" I went on raising my voice inside my own head until I was counting out loud again. It wasn't "my" conductor. I was glad, because he might have thought it was a bit late for one of my walks on the common.

It was cold when I got off the 'bus. It was colder still when I started to walk through the lonelier parts of the common. I began all right. I stepped out confidently and once I nearly giggled. If the police stopped me and wanted to know what I had in my bag, they'd think they'd apprehended a nutty firebug. A can of paraffin, fire lighters, and all those boxes of matches! I would have admitted to being one, too. I should have said I had an uncontrollable urge to start fires, and I would have sent the whole of my beloved Number 3 up in flames rather than confess that I had come to burn the remains of George's sweater because I was afraid that—that —no! No, I was afraid of nothing—nothing at all. It was just that for some reason he wanted that sweater burned and he hadn't done it properly—I was going to do it properly. That was all. There were no questions and no answers further than that.

In a way it was much the same way as I argued over the gift of the faith. Len was always at me about it.

"You can't just sit there and accept that something's right, just because they *tell* you it's right."

"Why not?" I asked. "They're brighter people that tell me it's right than what you are who's telling me it's wrong."

"But there are millions of people in the world who are just as convinced that theirs is the only true religion as you are —some people think they come back and live over and over again."

"Some people might," I said.

"Supposing you find when you get up top that everything you've been taught is all wrong?"

"That's the time to start asking questions," I said.

"Or supposing you find there's *no* eternal life, and there's absolutely nothing?"

"Then I shan't have time to worry, shall I?"

I never got openly fussed or lost my temper. Although sometimes I felt like it. I kept everything out of my face, but it went down into my stomach. My feelings always curdled my insides.

So while I was walking through the lonely bits of common I kept a foolish half smile on my face until my stomach did one of those helter-skelter dives. There was something or someone behind me in one of the thickets. When I stopped, it stopped. There was one of those snow-silences. You know how much quieter it seems when everything's white?

I couldn't tell you what it was I heard—whether it was a footstep—or a twig snapping—or a cough or a breath being drawn in—but it was a movement that wasn't mine—loud enough to bring me to a standstill as if my shoes had suddenly filled up with solid ice and become two frozen anchors.

I thought, "It's probably just the police. They must be taking an interest in this common. They'll pounce out on me in a minute in mistake for the strangler."

I didn't really let myself wonder whether it was the strangler. I put it another way to myself. "He'd be a nut-case if he was still hanging about here—he'd have to *want* to be caught."

But another little question got past my mind—"He'd have to be a nut-case anyhow, wouldn't he, to do the things he does?"

Then I lost my nerve and ran. It was a dangerous thing to do, because it gave my position away and I could have run right into the arms of the police or worse. But I didn't think. I just wanted to get out of those thickets. I fairly hurled across the common and crashed through the tangled-up garden of Number 3. I didn't stop until I was leaning up against the old copper with my breath breaking out of my mouth like Aunt Rene Tindall in one of her so-called asthma attacks.

Then I put my torch on. Nothing had been changed in the copper-house and the bunch of flowers I had picked for the convent still lay where I had dropped them. It had started to rain and some of it was coming through the copper-house roof.

I pulled out the paraffin and the fire lighters and took the old wooden top off the copper. It smelt damp and sour. With the aid of the long stick I had found in the garden I began to stir round the contents. Then I poured in the paraffin and dropped in bits of fire lighters. But the matches I lit went out on the way down. You aren't, of course, supposed to light fires in coppers, are you? They're for water and the fire is underneath.

I was clumsy and slipped with the paraffin can. More of it went over me and the floor than into the copper.

There was a bit of water in the bottom of the copper in any case. The big wooden lid had split right open, and just to help matters it started to pour with rain. The kind I liked usually; heavy, clean country rain. But I didn't like it when I was trying to get something to burn and it was coming through the roof on me. All I could get from my firebug activities were a few fizzles and flashes, and then a wet stink.

I had not brought any paper, and I didn't like to risk my torchlight being seen in the garden—so I groped my way through the downpour towards the house, to get the dry newspapers from Grandad's cupboard. All the time I kept telling myself not to be scared. "This is Collins Wood—dear, sweet Collins Wood."

I put on my torch in the passage, because I knew it couldn't be seen from outside.

The cupboards were on each side of Grandad's fireplace— and the torch was safe here, too, because the shutters were closed. The door had warped a bit, and squeaked when I opened it. I jumped like a flea in spite of myself.

I thought, "This is Grandad's room. We used to peel shrimps in front of the fire, and this is where I used to say good-night and good-morning to the mice."

There was a big pile of newspaper that smelt a bit musty. Still, it would help to sop up the moisture in the middle of the copper.

I had just gathered up a big armful when I heard—footsteps.

When my throat unclosed sufficiently for me to swallow properly again, I put down the papers and switched out my torch. Perhaps it was just my fancy. It could have been a rat, or a board shrinking or contracting, or whatever it is they do in old houses. Or maybe one of the shutters was loose upstairs. The wind had got up with the rain.

Then I heard it again. Someone was definitely crossing the room upstairs. The living-room where Clare had lain dying, her blood all sticky and sweet with sugar.

My stomach felt as if it was on fire inside, and I stood as if my feet were nailed to the floor-boards. Then I heard the floor above me vibrate as the footsteps moved across it and the door was opened.

The only way out from Grandad's basement would have led me right into the footsteps, and the windows were Banham-locked—which George had had done after a burglary.

The footsteps began coming downstairs. I scrambled into Grandad's cupboard and pulled the door hard to after me. It was a good thing it was old and full of cracks, because I hadn't remembered the necessity of breathing.

It seemed a month in which I was silently sobbing in fright for George. I hurt inside, longing for George—I would have given anything to have raced into his arms as I used to when I was a child and the dark got hold of me.

He used to comfort me, but never sloppily. He used to say, "What are you scared of the dark for? No one can see you in it!" But his arms were strong and his chest was hard to cuddle against, and he smelt of shaving lotion and tobacco. Frequently of beer, and always of strong, sleepy-smiled, re-assuring George.

Moments of terror really do show you the truth of those silly old sayings you've heard all your life. The kind that make up Aunt Rene Tindall's daily conversation when she's not talking about illnesses. "The darkest hour before dawn" —"the calm before the storm!"—and "too many cooks," etc. I would certainly have given "ten years of my life" to have been able to rush out of that cupboard into George's arms.

Then a thought slid into my mind with such frightening clarity that it deadened the horrible moment of the door of Grandad's living-room squeaking open and the footsteps coming into the room. They were only a couple of yards from me and my cupboard.

The thought said to me, "Supposing the footsteps *are* George's? Supposing it is *him* in the room."

I died a small death in that cupboard. It was the first time I had allowed my fears to get into words. But now they wouldn't stop.

"Well, that's been your nightmare, hasn't it? That's what put your blood pressure up when you found the sweater! That's what you're here for, isn't it—to hide things up in case it's George."

I put my fingers in my ears to muffle those words—and I shouted back at myself so fiercely in my head that I was afraid I might have fallen into my bonkers way of saying things out loud. "It *couldn't* be George," I rowed with myself. "He isn't the type—he'd never hurt anyone—he's a wonderful person."

"Wonderful people go mad like anyone else. He had blackouts after Clare's death. He had to go to a psychiatrist. The shock may have done something to him. The psychiatrist said that he hadn't accepted her death. Maybe he was resentful of other girls being alive. It could be in his subconscious. He might not even know it, and then there was the car accident. Someone had tried to make the murdered girls look as if they'd been run over. Clare had been killed in a car accident."

I tried to laugh at myself, but I was crying. "It couldn't be George—not my George."

"Why did he lie, then, over the sweater? There was blood on it—why was it burned? Len's got this terrible feeling, too. He's like the little tailor in *The Hatter's Ghosts*. He's hit on something that's made him suspicious."

It has to happen to somebody's family. Stranglers have mothers and fathers and sisters and brothers. How often do you read of some poor mother standing up in court and saying, "He's always been a good boy. He's a wonderful son to me. He's never done anything wrong before."

As much as anything else I think I would have gone mad with emotion if I'd stayed in that cupboard. I wanted to lash out at the walls. I had to get out and see if it was George. I simply had to find out. If it was I could get myself into his arms. That's all I was really thinking about.

From the inside of my cupboard I gave the door a hard hit with my fist. It was stuck and not easy to move. I beat against it.

At last the cupboard door flew open so quickly it crashed against the wall behind it. I rolled out to hear the footsteps leaving the room at a run. They were taking the stairs two at a time when I finally struggled with my torch and flashed it round. I rushed out of the room and up the stairs, calling out to George to wait for me.

By the time I reached the landing I heard the back door being pulled open. I ran into the living-room and skidded up to the french windows.

There was a full moon getting up, but the garden was so thick and tangled you couldn't see very much, especially with the windows blurred with rain.

What I did see was very confusing. Someone went crashing through the undergrowth and the high nettles. But a second or two afterwards I thought I saw somebody else. I definitely thought I saw two people.

I ran down to Grandad's basement again. I was going to pick up my things and go—go anywhere. But my torchlight picked up something on the floor. Someone else had been as scared as me, and someone else had come to light a fire at night when the smoke wouldn't show!

A handful of twigs were scattered about. A box of matches had been dropped near the grate, and a battered old tin kettle was standing there.

My visitor must have been a tramp, or some beats making use of an empty house. I could have cried with relief.

When the rain stopped I would go straight out and get on with the sweater.

But I heard footsteps again. They were not the same kind as the first lot, either. My ears were very well trained. I suppose it started by playing those bath-water games with George, and then later straining to hear whether he was going out or coming in at night, so that I could go to sleep in peace. Indulging my "pissy fears," George used to call it.

The first lot of footsteps had been shuffling, and not really bothering about being heard. But the second lot trod very quietly, and you felt that if the house wasn't empty and creaky you might not have heard them at all.

What's more, someone was listening, listening as carefully as I was.

"It must be the tramp again," I thought. "He just got scared and ran off, and now he's come back for his kettle."

But it wasn't the tramp. Those footsteps were absolutely different—they weren't the same person at all.

Then I remembered that when I looked out of the blurred french windows, for a moment I thought I'd seen two figures. Two figures in the garden at once.

I hurled myself into Grandad's cupboard again and slammed the door after me. It had saved me once. It might save me again. I was too frightened even to count out loud. I just sat with my back pressed against the wall, dying to spend a penny. But nothing was getting me out before daylight.

"Oh God," I thought, "I've been a twit—I've been a right, first-class, sea-going twit."

If anything happened to me it would be ages before anyone found out. Mum would be sure I was staying with Corinne. Corinne would think I was with my boy-friend, and wouldn't like to say so—she'd be that loyal—and it would be ages before anyone made enquiries about me.

An owl hooted in the garden, and I hit my head on the cupboard door. I used to love the owls, and hoot back at them from my bed, as a child. But I didn't love any noises in Collins Wood just then. I had left the biscuits and the torch outside. Supposing they gave me away? I prayed that the strangler (for I had convinced myself it was him) would think they belonged to the tramp who ran out.

I was shaking inside that cupboard, and the sweat went all cold under my clothes.

"Well, this isn't one of my pissy fears," I thought. And suddenly I got crazily angry against George. Me and my pissy fears, indeed! How would he like to be shut up in a cupboard with a strangler the other side of the door? And all because of his wretched sweater. I convinced myself that I hated him—and he was far too old for me! And then I cried because it was such a silly thing to think—and I never knew your heart could beat at the bottom of your throat, but it can.

Mine did when I heard the footsteps again. They were creaking down the stairs.

Even when there was carpet on them, George used to be heard on those stairs. He had to use them when he came in late at night, because Mother insisted on putting the chain up on the front door, and he had to use the back way in from Grandad's basement.

They always caught him out, however quiet he tried to be. He used to get really mad at them.

I started to count out loud again, "—five, six, seven—" and then I clapped my hand over my mouth, to stop giving my position away.

The footsteps got nearer and nearer. They'd stop if a board squeaked too loudly, as if they were trying to find another place to tread. I heard them in Grandad's old bedroom next door to me, but I don't know if they actually came into the room I was in. I think I must have fainted away. I went all warm and muzzy—and I felt sicker than when George took us all to the Scilly Isles in his friend's boat.

When I came round again from whatever had happened to me, everything was silent. I sat there, tucked into myself, for hours and hours.

It must have been about five in the morning when I saw the light creep into the room, through the cracks in the cupboard.

*12* ❖ THE FIRST THING I NOTICED was that my torch and biscuits had gone, so I knew I hadn't been imagining anything.

I hadn't been imagining the footsteps, either—or the fact that there were two different lots.

They were there in the dust and the mud marks, for any-one to see. One lot was not quite distinct—rather like they had sounded. Shuffly and old, and not very large. The other footprints you could see clearly. They belonged to a man with much bigger feet, and who wore the same kind of rub-ber soles as George. They showed up most on the stairs from Grandad's basement. That's where they'd have come in from the wet outside, of course. My own footsteps were visible too.

I stood listening very carefully. But there wasn't a sound. Nothing had moved for hours. He must have gone out when I fainted, or whatever I did. Unless he was still hiding in the house, waiting for me to move first.

I went back into Grandad's cupboard, but after a while I came out. I should have to make a move some day.

It was my instinct to go crashing out of the house scream-ing for people—*any* people—police, strangers, anyone. But I couldn't. I had to wipe up those footsteps. George had got big feet.

I knew it was daft. I knew it was dangerous, but I couldn't leave them about for anyone to see. The newspapers lay where I'd dropped them. I screwed some pages up into a ball and started to clean up the ones with the rubber soles like George's.

The footsteps in Grandad's basement came off all right, but the ones on the stairs seemed sticky.

"He's been into the copper-house," I thought, "and trodden in the paraffin."

I buy George bedroom slippers every Christmas. He treads down the backs and trips up. So I'm always trying to find kinds which might not be so dangerous. I know his size all right. It's twelve—and those footsteps were not far off a twelve.

The footsteps had crossed the hall and were all round the living-room. But they hadn't gone anywhere else. Just round the room that Clare died in. Just round the room where someone had written figures on the wall in George's handwriting. It took me a long time to clean up the marks.

When I came out of the house I was always careful to wipe the blue sort of whitewash off my sleeves and shoulder. It came off the walls of the passage that led to the conservatory and the garden. The children of the people before us had done it, and we thought they must have used a sort of blue bag. It was in the war, when apparently you couldn't get things. We had always been meaning to paint it properly. But somehow we never got round to it, and neither did the Robertses.

I was only worried about the blue mark from our family's point of view. They'd be the only ones to recognise it. I wasn't worried about the police at that moment—except about the newspapers. I didn't know what to do with the newspapers. The police are so clever these days. You've got to be very careful of them. They would probably have been able to trace the footsteps I had wiped up on the pieces of newspaper! There's hardly anything they can't do in those laboratory places. My first idea was to burn them up in the grate. But then what about the smoke?

Finally I decided to bury the newspaper. And then I thought—what a fool I had been—if I could bury the newspaper, I could bury the sweater and I needn't have bothered to terrify myself by coming back in the dark at all.

"Oh! What a nit! What a *nit!*" I wailed inwardly. "How could *anyone* be such a nit?"

I went to the copper-house and peered in the copper again. There was a tremendous amount of un-burned and soggy sweater left. I got my long stick and raked up the remains of the sweater. I put them into my B.E.A. bag and dug a big hole in the bed where the peonies used to be. It was all covered in weeds and layers of old leaves.

I didn't smell any too good either. The combination of the sour bits of wool, the stagnant water, the paraffin and the earth gave off a whiff fit to have people turning round to stare at you.

"Whatever will they think on the 'bus?" I wondered. Particularly as I was still a bit wet from the rain the night before, and thoroughly crumpled from being squeezed in the cupboard.

I trod the earth down firmly over the mess I had buried, to be sure it was good and deep. Then I raked it over with a stick and put little pebbles and leaves all over it, to make it look like the rest of the neglected flower-bed. The weeds were a bit disturbed, of course. But I didn't think anyone would notice that. After all, no one would have counted them before.

After I'd made the flower-bed look as normal as I could again, I went back to see about the copper-house. There didn't seem to be any bits lying about—at least, if there were they didn't show up to me, but the whole place reeked of paraffin. Oh well, I thought. That shouldn't upset anybody. Lots of people could have used paraffin for lots of things.

Then I picked up my B.E.A. bag and set off for the 'bus. While I was waiting I spotted a streak of blue distemper on my shoulder. I scrubbed it off like mad. As I say, everyone at home knew the "mark of Collins Wood." We had cursed about it coming off on our clothes for years.

When the 'bus came I jumped on quickly and went on top.

It was the conductor I knew, and the look he gave me worried me. He sort of opened his eyes, as if I'd made him jump, and as I felt so guilty I was sure he was suspicious of me.

"Bit early for walking, isn't it?" he asked.

"I—I've been spending the night with friends," I explained.

"Don't they run to giving you a bit of breakfast?"

"He *is* suspicious of me," I thought, a panic rising in me. "He knows I've been out all night and he's guessed that my parents don't know."

I must have thought he was psychic, or a mind-reader or something. But you know how it is when you have a knowledge of something—you're sure other people have caught on to it too, and probably give yourself away to them.

Hard as I tried to hide it, he spotted my dress.

"Hullo," he said, "taken a toss in the pond too, haven't you?"

"There was a duck," I told him. "I thought it had hurt its wing and I tried to wade out to it—that far pond—the one tucked away from the houses."

Me and my lies! I wasn't even bothering about them any more. They just peeled off me like the skin of an orange you're trying not to break—more and more twisted and curly.

A gentleman tapped me on the back. "You want to ring up the R.S.P.C.A. when you get home, love—they'll get after him soon enough."

"That's right," said the lady in front. "They were out to a pigeon that got hurt in our garden like lightning—much quicker than Doctor came out to our Beryl."

"They do that for swans," a child piped up. "I saw it on

the telly—they were covered in grease and wriggling about like anything."

"They can break your legs with their wings," a gloomy-looking soul offered from the back seat.

"Ee—not if you treat 'em right!" said the gentleman who had tapped me, and opened a diary. "I never go out without animal ambulance number on me, just in case—and I reckon other folks could do worse than carry it as well."

Several people agreed that it was a good thing to have, and I scribbled it down myself on the back of the holy picture Corinne had given me on my feast day, and which I always carried. I put it down in pencil, very lightly so that I could rub it out and transfer it to my diary. I mean, you never know when you might see some poor little cat or dog in agony from a car injury, and not be able to do anything. George would call it one of my "pissy fears," but I call it taking *precautions*. After all, I was a Guide, and "Be prepared" was our motto.

An argument was jiggling backwards and forwards in the 'bus.

"It's R.S.P.C.A. you want for duck's wing—animal ambulance doesn't do that!"

"They do anything, so I've heard."

"Well, it's usually R.S.P.C.A.—like lad said here—they do the swans. But you won't get ambulance coming out to duck —they're for road trouble."

"They're for *anything*," Tap-on-the-Back insisted.

Then Gloomy Back Seat said loudly, "I've 'eard a lot of fuss about a duck's wing. But girl were murdered last night, and I've 'eard no fuss about that."

I did one of those old Aunt Rene Tindall clichés. I froze in my seat. I really did. It burned into me like very cold water and ice can do. The 'bus started to buzz again, but not nearly so interested, of course.

"Nineteen, weren't she?" somebody asked.

Clare's age! The first one was nineteen, so was the second

—but the next was thirty. And now this one was nineteen again. So the murderer hadn't grown up psychiatrically, as Len thought. He hadn't grown up by sticking to older women.

Someone was asking where they'd found her, and someone else was saying she'd been dragged by her legs. There were bits of bracken and earth in her hair, and they'd found bits of it in the thickets. But she'd been killed on the common all right.

If it was George, I told myself, I wouldn't have heard his footsteps. He always walks so silently. But not in an empty house, with uncarpeted floors, I argued back. Even George would be heard in a room above your head. Well, Corry and I didn't hear him that time we were trying to get in touch with the ghost of Clare. No, because you were talking and anyhow he didn't have to use the basement stairs. I reminded myself that they were the ones that always caught him out. He used to be mad when we lived there. Whenever he came in late by the back way, he'd have to climb those stairs and they always scrunched and gave him away, even when we had carpet on them. Whoever it was had used them last night to get down from the living-room.

Old Front-Seat-of-the-'Bus was still nattering on. "I reckon they ask for it, these young things—all tight trousers and not a brush put to their hair for weeks on end."

Tap-on-the-Back agreed. "Thump, thump, bang, bang, woe-woe-woe! That's not music, and that's not singing. Time was when you had to make right kind of noise, to get it called singing."

"Didn't come from these parts this time, did she?"

"No, from London, I think. She was a waitress at The Swan, out Norton way. Not been there long."

"I reckon they ask for it," Front Seat repeated. "What time did they find her?"

"They think she was done in last night."

So it could have been him I heard—him in the thickets

and him in the house. It would fit in about right. Just after the tramp. I snapped off my mind like a light switch. I didn't want to faint on the 'bus.

When I got off it, I was thinking about school. "It's Mother Marie-Adelaide's feast day just after term starts. I mustn't forget some flowers for her." The last time she put all our flowers on the altar and asked each girl what she'd like her particular bunch to whisper to God! Just as if we were babies. Corinne said she was going to ask Him to make her a good girl and forgive her all her sins, and Mother Marie-Adelaide was so pleased she spoilt Corinne all day. Most of us had asked for something nice for ourselves!

When I put my key in the door, I heard George talking to the cat. He and Sandy were dotty potty about each other, but they didn't like the other one to know it. If George went away Sandy didn't speak to him for days after his return. He'd stalk past George and rub himself against Grandad or one of us, and then sit bolt upright with his back to George and his tail just flicking at the tip. And George pretended he hadn't noticed Sandy taking no notice of him! They made a really daft pair. The battle went on for days, but Sandy always won because in the end George always laughed. The minute he heard that chuckle Sandy knew he was on top, and a few hours later he'd turn and glance at George, and then yawn as if to say, "Oh! You're back, are you?—I didn't notice." Then a bit after that he'd be up on George's lap.

It made things difficult, George being in the kitchen, because I had to pass the open door. Hélène would still be asleep, and if she had her motor-scooter goggles on to protect her eyelashes, she'd never see the mess I was in.

"Pack it up!" George was telling Sandy. "Not so much of the ruddy dignity, and a little more common courtesy—what the hell's wrong with tin salmon, anyway?"

His glasses were on the draining-board, so he couldn't see what a state I was in. If I crept past I might be able to change and stop him asking questions.

But he heard me and looked up. I'd just be a dim shape to him without his glasses—but he'd know it was me, of course.

"Home rather early, aren't you?" he asked.

"I quarrelled with Corinne," I explained.

"Congratulations!" he said.

*13* ❖ THEN HE SMELT ME. He put on his glasses and looked at me. "Did you pick the quarrel in a pig-sty?"

"She threw a shoe at me," I said. "And I threw one back and then I slipped—it was outside, you see, and the ground was wet." It was nearly true, anyway.

"You smell of paraffin," George accused me.

"Yes—well, there was a can of it outside Corinne's block and I must've knocked it over when I fell."

"What was it doing there?"

"Oh, I don't know—it was just somebody's."

He grunted. "Well, you'd better have a bath."

Sandy had taken the chance of gobbling up his tin salmon while we were talking so that George wouldn't know how crazy he was about it. He liked George to think he had to be coaxed. But I'd heard his greedy sucking noises all the time I was staring at George.

I was staring because I knew he'd been up half the night if not all of it. There wasn't much about George I didn't know—his eyes always got red and puffed up when he hadn't had much sleep. My heart got a painful little dig in it. He was shaved and in his shirt-sleeves. His jacket was hanging over the back of a chair.

"Up early yourself, weren't you?" I said. "Or didn't you go to bed at all?"

George's thumb jerked towards the bathroom, meaning I was to wash. There's nothing George hates more than being asked questions. He's always been secretive, has George. Any sign of nosiness and you've lost him for good.

I was just making for the bathroom when the phone went.

George went to answer it and suddenly yelled for me. "Wynne! Come here a minute."

He had his hand over the mouthpiece. "It's Mrs. Eldridge. She wants to tell Mum that you upset her little pet."

"Corry threw the shoe at me first," I stammered. My heart seemed to be beating at the bottom of my neck again. What if Mum found out I hadn't spent the night there? George must have seen how pale I went.

"Relax!" he said. "You didn't kill her, did you?"

Through the earpiece I could hear Mrs. Eldridge babbling away like those voices you get when a tape-recorder goes wrong. He turned to me.

"Did you break their telephone?"

"Yes—I—I tripped over the wire—I did offer to pay."

He turned back to Mrs. Eldridge. "When did you say? When?" Then he told her, "All right. Send the bill to us." And he put down the receiver.

"I can't understand it," I told him. "She said it was quite all right. In fact she even stuck up for me against Mr. Eldridge. He was quite cross but she said it was all right and not to worry."

"That was before you chucked a shoe at her treasure."

He started to grind the beans for the coffee. He couldn't stick the stuff Mum or I made. He said it was like being offered a drop of flood water. He put pinches of salt and knobs of butter in his and made a rare old fuss if anyone let it come to the boil in the saucepan.

"She got it mended very quickly," I said.

"She was phoning from a call-box."

"Oh."

"Wynne," said George quietly. "She said you broke their telephone before you went home last night."

He poured the hot water carefully into the Plain Jane percolator.

I stood very still. "She must've meant after I left this morning."

He shook his head. "I checked. She repeated it. She said after you left *last night.*"

I looked at Sandy. Why, oh why couldn't he do something to *help?* He did. He gave that funny hollow little noise which means that he's going to be sick. He'd gobbled his salmon too fast. I swooped on him. "Oh, Sandy darling, not in here!" I rushed him out to the balcony and stayed with him, stroking his head. Then I got some Kleenex and cleared up the mess.

When I got back the coffee was just beginning to bubble through the holes of the china bit at the top. George was bending seriously over it.

"Where were you last night, Wynne?" he asked.

"Look, George, I told you—she just got muddled. She didn't mean I went home *last night*—she must have been talking about the *fight* that Corry and I had—she must've said, 'after the fight last night'—"

"What time was the fight?"

"About seven, I suppose."

"Then don't suppose—give me a straight answer."

"About seven."

The corner of my eye was beginning to tic. I could have scratched it out. George knew as much about me as I knew about him, and he'd realise I was nervous.

Then he suddenly shot a bit of French at me. It was so quick and I was so surprised I didn't get one word of it. Anyway, my French was hopeless.

George certainly didn't sound like a Frenchman speaking. His accent was so flat and English. But he could get himself along all right.

I gaped at him, not knowing what he was up to.

"Not making much progress, are you, Wynne? You've been having extra lessons on Thursday evenings for months now, and you don't even recognise an old gag like 'the pen of my aunt is in the garden.'"

"I might if you spoke it better," I sauced him.

"Where have you been going on Thursdays instead of staying behind at school to learn French?" he wanted to know.

"I—I—I *have* been staying behind at—"

"And where did you go last night?"

The coffee was ready. He took the milk off the ring and got out two cups. "Want some?"

"Please."

He turned to me. "I still want to know," he said.

"My friends don't get asked where *they've* been," I answered. "Maybe I did go to a discothèque—maybe I was at a coffee bar or two—"

"I don't care what your friends do. That's their parents' look-out. If they want to bring up their kids so they can't get their feet on the ground, it's not my look-out. You are, and you're fourteen and you've been out all night."

"Suppose I ask you where *you* were last night! Would I get the truth out of you?"

His sleepy eyes exploded. I hadn't seen George so angry for years, not since I was about ten or eleven. The expression on his face that morning reminded me of what happened all those years ago. Corinne and I had had a row when we came out of school—one of those silly kids' rows like you go in for at that age. She was bonkers over some type in the supermarket who hands out baskets and tells you where things are. He wasn't bad. His eyes were a bit squinty but Corry didn't care about that. Anyway, I got sick to death of trailing round the supermarket to buy a Picnic bar and a couple of tubes of Smarties just so that Corry could bump into old Hairy Hands, as I called him. I told Corry old Hairy Hands would soon wear off and I was going to buy my sweets at our usual shop. I mean, we used to have to queue for ages at the paying place to get out of that supermarket, and it only took a couple of ticks in our old shop.

"It's only sex," I told her primly. "You've no idea what real love is."

"Ha! ha!" she said, putting an *r* into it. "Look who says I don't! I love him far more than you love that stuck-up George of yours."

"Don't be daft," I said.

"Him and his 'holidays abroad,' and his coffee and his French wines."

"He drinks beer as well."

"If anything happened to Charlie Krantz I'd *kill* myself," she repeated.

Charlie Krantz! It wasn't even his right name. He was Dennis Porter, but Corry had asked one of the girls what he was called and the girl had mistaken the man she was pointing at.

Her eyes were all bright and starting to be starry, a sign we could be in for one of her scenes. She was a great one for dramatics, was Corry.

"Well," she challenged me, "would *you* kill yourself if anything happened to that tired old George?"

"Sure," I said, ignoring the insult. "Look, Corry, let's go into Wheeler's and have a Coke and listen to the juke-box."

I don't like to think of what happened after that because I know it was a sin and I'm not even sure that it happened. That sounds daft, I know, but I was in such a panic my head wasn't working and I don't remember much.

Corry wouldn't have the Coke. She went off in a huff about Hairy Hands. So I went into Wheeler's. I had a couple of Cokes and when I'd used up the rest of my money in the juke-box I went home.

Mum had an afternoon job then, so she was out. Hélène was at her cinema and at that time Len was apprenticed to George's firm. He didn't last long. Len hated it and George said the building trade was in enough difficulties without having Len apprenticed to it.

Grandad was cleaning out his mice. I was wondering what I could do to avoid my homework when the note came through the door with "Urgent" printed on it. It was addressed to Mum, so I took it to Grandad.

He opened it, and for a second or two he went the colour of his champion white mouse and felt behind him with his hand to grip the mantelpiece. Then he said, "Wait a minute! Wait a minute! There's something fishy about this—" and he hurried into the living-room.

I followed. "What is it, Grandad?" He waved me to be quiet and started to dial the police station.

I grabbed the note. It was printed and it read, "Mr. George Meakham has met with a fatal accident at his work. Please come at once." And it was signed "The Police."

Of course, if I'd been older or even if I'd kept my head and thought about it, I'd have realised there was something phoney about it, as Grandad had done. The police don't just sign themselves "Police" and put "come at once" without telling you where. They don't put notes through the door at all. What would have been wrong with the telephone or a policeman coming in person?

But I didn't think and I did lose my head—and how! Suddenly I believed I was in a world with no George in it.

I never uttered a peep. My throat had dried up, so I couldn't. While Grandad was making enquiries at the police station, I fled to the bathroom. I yanked open the medicine cupboard so hard the mirror came off its hinges with a big crunch and caught the side of my hand. It poured with blood. It was a big mirror and I suppose that's what Grandad heard crashing to the floor. I snatched out every bottle I could find and dropped them on the floor. I suppose I was trying to find something to take. Mum's sleeping pills, Len's phenobarbitone—iodine or something. Anything would have done so that I could just black out forever the thought that there was no George in the world any more. I don't even know if I did take anything or not.

But poor old Grandad came in for a right old mess. Me in sort of silent hysterics—not even crying—just grabbing bottle after bottle and crashing them on the floor. Absolutely *everything* covered in blood, and all George's razor blades spilt round me—Grandad thought I'd not only swallowed every possible bit of poison in the place, but cut my wrist as well. My hand simply pumping out blood couldn't have helped him to toss out that theory.

The next time I opened my eyes I was in bed and the doctor was wiping my arm with a bit of cotton wool. I'd had an injection or something and my hand was bound up.

I felt much calmer when I came round after the injection. But I was still at it. In a sort of jelly daze I thought, "They needn't think I've given in. I'm not going to live without George. I'll hold my breath until I die."

Then I saw him. George, I mean. He came to the side of the bed and sat down on it. He peered down at me out of those huge glasses. "The frames are the colour of Grandad's Guinness," I thought.

"Well?" said George. "What have you got to say for yourself?"

"I thought you were dead," I explained.

"Did you think it would bring me back for you to be dead too?"

I slipped into his arms. He held me very close and steady for a long time.

He was quite calm outside but I knew he was churned up inside. I could feel his heart going at a fine old rate, and he was nearly as pale as Len with one of his headaches coming on.

Apparently I hadn't actually taken anything and I was only suffering from shock. I lay curled round George with my face pressed hard into his chest.

"Wynne, I didn't try anything like that when Clare died."

I said nothing. He bent down and kissed my hair. "Will you promise me never to try anything like that again, Wynne?"

I was silent. It wasn't possible to promise. I just didn't feel that I could be left behind without George.

"Did you hear me?" he asked. I nodded against him. "Then let's hear your promise."

"I can't," I told him. "Not if something really did happen to you."

He altered my position in his arms, and lifted my face so that he could look into it. I turned away. I was shy of him.

"Something's got to happen to me sometime," he said. "And as I'm so much older than you I'm likely to go first, aren't I? So you'd better get used to the idea of being left behind sometime, hadn't you?"

He was talking a bit sing-songy, as if I'd been a baby. I wriggled my face round against him again. "It's not that I don't appreciate your friendship, Wynne—we've always been great friends, haven't we? Ever since you first came. But there is this big difference between us—I'm middle-aged and you're—"

I rapped out at him. "Being middle-aged is when you've had half your life—*fifty's* middle-aged."

"People don't always live to a hundred, love," he reminded me. "Besides, there are other things that could happen to me—I might want to get married and live somewhere else. Are we going to have you drinking up the bathroom cupboard if anything like that happens?"

I shook my head against him. "Not if I knew you were happy and—well, it's just—just—" and then I broke down and sobbed. "I thought you were dead. I thought I'd never see you again."

He sat there for ages cuddling and quieting me, and telling me how wrong what I'd tried to do was, and against the laws of God and man and all that sort of thing, but he couldn't get a promise out of me not to do it again.

He tried being more cross and stern with me. "It's a terrible responsibility, having someone who might do something like you tried to do, Wynne."

I just hugged him fiercely and made no reply. He tried everything from jokes and threats to appeals—he reminded me about all the poor women who had lost their husbands and sons in the war, and if they could be brave why couldn't I? And he told me what a cowardly thing suicide is. He tried the works. But I just went on hugging him, not really listening. All I could think about was that he was alive and I hadn't lost him.

"Look, if it's me you're so keen on preserving, why won't you do something to please me? Can't really think much of me if you won't put my mind at rest, can you?"

But nothing was going to make me promise. I thought it would make him take better care of himself if he thought I'd do it again.

Mother came in with the note. The police had asked if any of us recognised the handwriting on it. George prised my arms from round his waist and sat me up against the pillows. Even then I clung to his hand. I felt I just couldn't ever let go of him again.

"Who would *do* such a terrible thing?" Mother wailed. "It's made poor Grandad really queer."

"I should think so, with this young lady's little effort on top of it," George said sternly. "But she's going to promise me never to do anything like that again, aren't you?" he asked me.

I tried to hide away in his arms again, but he shook me off and said firmly, "Now come along, Wynne, you're not a baby any longer."

"Poor little mite," said Mother. "It's enough to turn her mind."

"If I don't get a promise out of her soon," said George, "I'm going to her school to tell the nuns about it."

"I'll have to confess it to Father Murphy in any case," I replied.

"Well, he'll make you promise soon enough."

To change the subject, I looked at the note in Mother's

hand. "Oh," I said, "it's Corry! I ought to have known her *s*. But I didn't really look at it—I just read it and saw what it said."

"Corinne!" cried Mother, aghast. "You mean little Corinne Eldridge?"

"Yes. I should have known it was her. She was mad at me about something and she asked me would I kill myself if George had died—I suppose she just thought she'd test me out."

It was then that I saw the sleepiness explode in George's eyes.

"She wouldn't have thought I'd really do it," I added hastily. "She'd have done it as a sort of joke—"

But George had already left the room and was on his way round to the Eldridges'.

There was a worse shindig than we ever had over Mr. Cinema Manager with Mrs. Cinema Manager.

Corry tried to lie at first, but George was a walking lie detector. He broke her down in no time and demanded that poor Mr. Eldridge thrash her. Mrs. Eldridge ordered him out of the flat (George, I mean) and told Mr. Eldridge she'd leave him if he so much as laid a finger on the child.

So George picked up Corinne, put her over his knee and walloped her. George always said Mr. Eldridge let him get on with it because it was something he'd longed to do himself—but *Mrs. Eldridge!* The noise she made brought the neighbours in.

She called the police to arrest George for assault. But Mr. Eldridge told them there was no charge. He didn't want what Corinne had done to come out in the paper, and he thought it served Corinne right.

Mrs. Eldridge screamed that George was no better than a murderer, and that Mr. Eldridge was no better for not lifting a hand to defend his own flesh and blood. Then she came storming round to our flat and shrieked at Mother and Grandad.

Grandad said if Corinne had had more wallops before, George could have been saved making his hands sore this time.

Mother said Corinne was a wicked, wicked little girl to play such a cruel trick, and as Aunt Rene Tindall had arrived by then she was able to bring out that bit about the spoilt child being sharper than the serpent's tooth.

Mrs. Eldridge shouted that anyway the affection of a girl of my age for a man of George's age was unnatural and unhealthy and he obviously encouraged me, and she thought the police ought to know about *that,* too!

Mother was so enraged she didn't even go for Len for calling Mrs. Eldridge a foul-minded old cow. She said if those were the thoughts Mrs. Eldridge could think she wasn't surprised that she had a daughter who could do the terrible things that Corinne had done.

Mrs. Eldridge yelled that she'd rather have a daughter like Corinne than one like me whose mind was between her legs at my age!

That set them all off. Grandad choked on his heartburn pills, Hélène shouted that I was driven snow compared to Corinne, and that Len was right and Mrs. Eldridge was nothing but a dirty old cow, and Mother shrieked that I was only a baby and I only loved George so much because I'd never had a father and he made such a fuss of me when I first came.

Then Mrs. Eldridge said maybe it was George with his ideas in the wrong place—it wasn't right and you couldn't tell her that it was.

That set George off. He thumped Grandad on the back and shut the others up. Then he suggested very quietly to Mrs. Eldridge that she should go home. Perhaps she didn't realise it, but Corinne might easily have been responsible for sending me to my death. If Mrs. Eldridge still wanted to charge him for assaulting Corinne, that was fine by him, but if she wasn't out of the house in three minutes flat he'd give her good cause to charge him twice.

She fled.

It's a wonder any of them ever spoke to each other again. They didn't, for months. George and Mrs. Eldridge still can't stick each other. If it wasn't for Corinne and me remaining friends I don't suppose either of our two families would ever have been in contact.

Grandad went out of the room to "have a look at the mice" whenever Mrs. Eldridge called, Hélène and Len ignored her, and poor Mum was terribly on edge and a bit too polite.

George never really forgave Corinne, either. But I did. I would have forgiven the devil himself for writing the note, out of sheer joy that it wasn't true. Besides, she was dreadfully upset about it—and I was very fond of her really. We had our rows but we did have fun together, and I honestly think it was all Mrs. Eldridge's fault, the way she played up so much. I mean, you can't expect people to behave unless you teach them how to.

Funnily enough, Corry never complained about the thrashing. She was genuinely horrified at what she'd done to me. She never thought I'd take it seriously. She was sure I'd realise it was her. In fact, she really didn't think at all.

George wasn't going to let her see me, but Mother thought she ought to be given the chance to apologise. She cried and cried beside my bed, and not just because of what she'd made me try to do, but because of what I must have suffered believing that I'd really lost George. I'll always remember that about Corinne. That she was sorry about what mattered to me more than what might have happened to me. It showed she could feel things about people—in the right way.

She couldn't sit down very well because her bottom was so sore, even when I put my pillow under it, and she did some very powerful crying.

We didn't cheer up until Aunt Rene Tindall came to visit me and told Corry to be careful or she'd rupture herself. Then she told me what a terrible sin I'd committed and how all the Hosts of Heaven would be ranged against me. "There shall be wailing and gnashing of teeth," she warned me.

"Let 'em gnash 'em as 'as 'em," snapped Grandad, who happened to have his out at the moment.

Then, of course, a friend of a friend of Aunt Rene Tindall's had just committed suicide and she spared us none of the ghastly details.

I know it was wrong of us, but Corry and I were rolling about with laughter over the poor thing's terrible end. We had quite got over my effort.

But Mother hadn't.

She mopped me with eau de cologne when Corry had gone, and told me that what I had tried to do was very terrible and she didn't think much of my church for not putting a stop to such things.

Grandad staggered into my room in his dressing-gown and said that he reckoned George should have given me a hiding as well as Corinne.

Hélène told me *no* man was worth doing *that* for. There were plenty of pebbles on the beach and when I was a bit older I'd find that out. But she looked a bit off colour and shaken, and she was the one that had a nightmare half an hour after she'd fallen asleep. Not me! But then of course the doctor had left me something to take. Mother gave me two pills when she mopped me up after Corinne had gone, and said she couldn't think what good those nuns were if they couldn't stop one of their pupils behaving like me. As if they had been there all the time and just let me go on snatching things out of the bathroom cupboard!

Len was the most sympathetic. He'd gone that greasy white and taken some of the phenobarb I couldn't find. He sat beside me, holding his head.

"I keep thinking what it would be like if it had been true.

What would we have been feeling like? What would we have been doing? Christ!" he said, "old George is hell to work for, but you'd miss him about the home."

"Yes," I said. "You would."

"And an effing help you'd have been," he rounded on me, "adding your corpse to the list."

He seemed so friendly and upset himself I tried to explain to him, but there really are some feelings that won't fit into words.

"Len, it's not that I wouldn't have minded if it had been one of the rest of you—"

"Look," he said. "We caught on ages ago that George isn't exactly your pet hate—and so's he by now, I should think, poor bastard. He won't dare send you a Christmas card after this, never mind a friendly smile, in case he 'encourages' you and the police get to hear of it!"

I wriggled down the bed until I landed up where he was sitting.

"You don't think Mrs. Eldridge is right, Len? It isn't wrong, is it—the way I feel? For George, I mean. It's not unhealthy and unnatural, is it?"

Len patted me on the head. "Nothing that bitchy old nit says is right. My God, if I could get hold of her—" He clenched his teeth and twisted his fists round so tightly together that I thought his knuckle bones were going to push up through his skin. He could say what he liked about George, but let anyone else take a crack at him! I was quite frightened of him, sitting there. He looked so eaten-up and violent. "If I could get hold of that silly old cow I'd screw her bloody head off. I'd jump on her dead face—and if he had any sense so would that dim little bugger Eldridge. Christ! How I hate females like her. Hysterical nit! I could wring her neck."

He made his hands all red, squeezing them together so hard, and he got so worked up George sent him off to lie down.

George was my next visitor. He sat on the bed again. "Well?" he asked.

I mumbled something, and then perked up to tell him, "I'm not so scared of you when I'm doped. Isn't that nice?"

"There's been a lot of fuss about how you'd feel if anything happened to me, but I haven't heard much about what I'd be supposed to feel like if I'd come home and found you'd bumped yourself off because of me."

"I don't suppose you'd have been as put out as I should," I replied politely.

"I'd have been put out," he said. "Would you like to think I'd bump myself off if you died?"

"Oh, *no*," I said, shocked. I was finding it hard to keep my eyes open, the dope was working.

"Then if I promise not to do myself in if anything happens to you—will you do the same for me?"

"All right," I agreed. "I promise."

He bent down and kissed me good-night.

Like I said, I'd never seen him so angry over anything before as he was with Corry about that note. But I've seen him just as angry since—that day in the kitchen, after I'd spent the night in the cupboard at Collins Wood!

14 ❖ "WHERE WERE YOU last night, Wynne?" he wanted to know again.

"I was at Collins Wood," I said, and I looked hard at him to see how he took it. He rocked back on his heels a bit, and then he snapped out, "Why?"

I couldn't tell him. At first I thought I'd try to, but I was too scared of him, standing there so stiffly with his arms hanging straight at his sides.

"I—I wanted Corinne to think I was with a boy."

"Why?"

"I—she's—she's always boasting about her boys, and I—I haven't got one, so I—I let her think I was spending the night with one. I couldn't just tell her and stay at home. She'd have rung up to check."

"Is that why you broke the telephone—so that we couldn't ring up and check on you there?"

"Yes."

"It didn't occur to you that Corinne might respect you more if you *didn't* spend the night with a boy?"

I shook my head. "She darn well wouldn't. I'd go up in her estimation if she thought I had."

"Did you spend the night alone at Collins Wood?"

I hesitated just the tiniest bit—I had been far from alone all the time, but that wasn't what George meant. So I answered him carefully and sat down on the dinette end. He followed me, standing over me.

"I didn't really go there with a boy."

"Have you ever slept with anyone, Wynne?"

"Good heavens, no." I was glad to be able to laugh. "As if I would!"

He looked at me for a long time with his eyes narrowed. He decided I was telling the truth, which I was of course. He didn't ask me any more questions on that point.

"You didn't seem quite sure just now whether you were altogether alone at Collins Wood."

I thought I'd try him out a bit. It might be possible to tell things from his face. "Well—"

"Go on," he ordered me.

I bent to lift Sandy on to my lap.

"Put the cat down, please, and answer me."

I put the cat down and answered him. "Well—it was just that—I *went* there by myself all right. But—"

"You met someone there?"

"No—not exactly—"

"Well, what *exactly* did happen, then?"

"After I'd been there a bit—could I have my coffee, please?" He nodded at the saucepan and I filled myself a cup and sat down. "After I'd been there a bit, I—I thought I heard someone come in."

Even then I hadn't got the nerve to tell him I thought it was him and that I crashed out of my cupboard to see if it was.

"It was a tramp the first time," I explained. "But I thought I saw two people. And later on someone did come back. Someone different."

"Someone different?"

"He had different feet. Big feet—like—like yours and Len's."

He was just going to take a sip of his own coffee. He held it in front of him for a moment and then put it steadily down in his saucer. He'd gone Len's kind of white.

"What time would that be? When you heard this different person come back?"

"I couldn't see my watch very well." I still could not bring myself to tell him that I was destroying evidence of his having been there. Besides, I wanted to try and find out if he really had. "I was only tidying up a few things, anyway. I had lots of time on my hands, you see."

"What things?"

"Well, bits of old newspaper, and rags and—people do go into empty houses and make a mess. That tramp probably sleeps there every night."

"So what time was it you thought you heard this—other person?"

"I didn't *think* I heard him. I did."

"How did you know it was a 'him'?"

"Footsteps in the morning. They belonged to a 'him.'"

He tried his coffee again. But this time his hand was shaky. "Wynne, did you know a girl was murdered last night?"

"Yes."

"How did you hear about it?"

"On the 'bus this morning. How did *you* know?"

"On the early morning news. You realise, I suppose, that this latest victim wasn't found too far away from Collins Wood?"

"They all were, weren't they? Must've been someone with a grudge against the place."

"Did you get a look at him?" he asked throatily, and he kept his eyes away from me.

I thought I'd see how he reacted. "Sort of," I told him.

He looked at me, then swivelled right round in his chair. "What do you mean, 'sort of'?"

"It was a bit dark."

"See enough to recognise him again?"

"Maybe."

"What did he look like?"

I held my breath and then dared it. "A bit like you," I gulped out.

He got up and walked towards me. He stood over me. I was scared out of the few wits I was trying to use. I tried to change my tune.

"Well—not really—just, well, like Len looks like you—not really *like* you—but just a look of you—like Len's got."

"Like Len's got? What the hell do you mean?"

I backed away from him. "It could have been my fancy—"

"You could hardly have 'fancied' someone with a 'look' of me, could you?"

I wished to God I'd never started the thing. I'd never seen him look like that before. His face had no expression except a soapy kind of fixed look that nearly scared me blind. I thought he was going to bash me one, but he spoke quietly. "Wynne, you know something, don't you? Something you're not telling me. Out with it. Come on, let's have it!"

When I opened my mouth he said, "It won't help, keeping things to yourself. It could be very wrong of you."

I said, "Look, George, I didn't *really* see anyone. I couldn't. I was just—just—I was in a cupboard—"

"You were just what?"

"Well—piling it on—I only *heard* someone—I didn't *see* anyone I could describe properly."

He stepped forward and shook me by the shoulders and nearly had the head off me. "If you saw nothing why did you say you did? It's a damn fool thing to do, isn't it? Why 'pile it on'? Come on, you saw him! Let's have it!"

"I didn't! I didn't!" I sobbed. "I was lying—"

George let me go and I fell back against the wrought-iron bit of the dinette.

He spoke quietly again. "I'm sorry I shook you. But I must have the truth. Tell me anything you know and then keep quiet about it. Let *me* decide when to tell anyone else."

I felt bonkers. I thought, "Is he *admitting* it? Is he telling me he knows I know? Is he threatening me to keep quiet?"

Feeling much sicker than Sandy, I managed to gulp out, "Oh, I'd leave it to you all right to tell the—to tell anyone."

Grandad appeared in the doorway in his mulberry-coloured dressing-gown. "What the hell's happening?"

"It's nothing, Grandad," George told him.

"It's the noisiest nothing I've ever heard—and what's 'appened to 'er?"

Grandad's aitches always went if he was fussed. "She looks as if she'd been 'atched out in a deep litter pen, and smells like it, too."

"Wynne quarrelled with Corinne, Grandad, they had a fight and Wynne got a bit mucked up, and she's very upset."

"Aye, well, she's not the only one—'er mother's very upset too. She's not slept a wink because of this new murder, so for God's sake give her a chance now."

George said, "Sorry, Grandad."

"I didn't do too well myself," Grandad grumbled, "what with Len coming home in the early hours. He's not got the soft feet you've got, hasn't Len."

"I'll speak to him, Grandad," said George.

Grandad went off muttering and George sat for what seemed three days looking at me. Then he got up and tipped the contents of our coffee cups back into the saucepan and lit the gas under it. He pushed a hot cupful at me.

"Drink that."

I drank it.

"Wynne, I shouldn't have scared you like that. I'd no right to be rough with you—but you see, you scared the goddam wits out of me. The thought of you in that house—" He sat down and rubbed his hand over his face like people do when they want to get the water off them when they've been swimming. His face was certainly as wet as if he had been diving into something. "This man's mad, Wynne. He has to be. He doesn't know what he's doing. He might be perfectly all right at times, but at others he might not be able to help himself. He might loathe himself for what he does and not be able to stop it."

"Is he telling me?" I thought weakly. "Is he telling me it's him?"

I felt like fainting dead away, but I managed to ask quite ordinarily, "Isn't there anything he could do about it?"

George shook his head. "You don't go on doing that sort of thing if there's anything you can do about it."

My throat felt as if someone had got hold of me and squeezed a tube of glue down it. My words seemed to stick together as they came out.

"Wouldn't—wouldn't it be better if he—he gave himself up? I mean, if he couldn't help it no one would blame him."

He sat right in front of me and talked steadily into my eyes.

"He might have to be sure it was him first, Wynne."

"Sure it was *him!*" I gasped out, and didn't mean to make it sound funny. "You'd have to be a bit absent-minded not to notice that you were going around strangling people."

"If he was mad he might suspect it was him and not be able to sort out whether he'd done it or dreamed it. There could be a blank in his head that made him afraid of himself —so you see, it could be a help if you told me what you'd really seen."

I felt as if my veins had been in a deep freeze for about a year, and I thought, "I don't care if he has done it—I'm terribly sorry for those poor girls—but I don't care if he has done it."

"George," I whispered, "I didn't see anything—honest to God. I was lying about that bit."

"Why?"

I wondered how fast your heart had to beat before it killed you. "I wanted to—to test you," I told him.

His eyebrows went up. "*Test* me?"

"I thought it might be you."

"I see. What made you think that?"

I went to take a gulp of coffee but there wasn't anything left except the sugary bit in the bottom. I said a quick little prayer. "Please, Jesus, if he goes to strangle me let the others come out to stop it in time, for his sake not for mine, amen."

Then I looked full at him and said, "Your sweater. It was burned in the copper at Collins Wood—but not quite enough —there was still blood on it."

He was silent a good long, terrible minute, while Sandy mewed at both of us hoping to make us think he hadn't had his salmon. I suppose to his mind he hadn't, having sicked it up.

"*My* sweater, Wynne?" George asked gently.

I nodded, and was surprised how heavy my head felt. I could hardly get it up again. I thought it was going to hang there. "The one I knitted you. It had blood on it and—and someone had tried to burn it in the copper at Collins Wood —with paraffin."

George went to the stove and fiddled with the saucepan. But there wasn't any more coffee in that either. We'd had it all and there was nothing in the Plain Jane except dregs. He started to whistle and got Sandy's plate out.

"He's already been fed and been sick," I reminded George.

"Oh, oh yes." It wasn't like George to get confused, but he was confused all right.

He said, "It couldn't have been my sweater, Wynne. Not the one you knitted me. You must have made a mistake. It was probably something that belonged to the Robertses or someone coming into the house when it was empty."

"It was your sweater," I told him. As if you didn't know your own knitting!

"It can't be," he argued. "I've still got mine."

"Where?"

"It's around."

"Last week you said you'd lost it."

"Yes, well, I thought young Len had borrowed it."

"Young Len couldn't have done, unless it was him that burned it up in the copper—bit of a daft thing to do to something you've borrowed, isn't it?"

How I managed to talk so tough to George I really never

shall know, and this time I didn't stop him bending down to feed Sandy again. He gave him the rest of the tin of salmon.

"Too daft," George answered me, and his smile wasn't right. His voice was all sort of kidding you along and not like him. "Look, Wynne, I've got a confession to make about that sweater."

My tongue went round my lips and back the other way again. "Fat lot of good the central heating is in these new flats," I told myself, "if you shiver to death in your own kitchen. It was warmer at Collins Wood without it." Then, of course, I remembered they turned it off at that time of year.

"You know Jimmie Wells?" George asked me.

Of course I knew Jimmie Wells. They'd been in partnership for years.

"Well, Jimmie took such a fancy to that sweater—he went on and on about it. He really did badger me about it and in the end I let him have it."

"Oh," I said. I could just see Jimmie Wells wanting that particular garment. He was a bit of a sharp dresser and it was right badly knitted, was that sweater. I remembered what Len had said about it, too. He said he wouldn't be seen dead in it, never mind borrow it.

George washed up Sandy's plate and put it in the rack. Even then Sandy sat up asking after it.

I was too full of panic to play tough any more. I sprang up from my chair and pushed myself into George's arms. "George," I sobbed—the kind like a cough that gets caught in your breath—"George, it wasn't you, was it?" I couldn't have thought what I was doing. I began to kiss him. I missed his face and got his throat, but I didn't mind. "George, say it wasn't you—you're *lying* about that sweater."

He hugged me and kissed me too and his voice was back to normal. He didn't answer the bit about the sweater. He said quite gaily, "No, sweetheart, it wasn't me. I'm too busy to do much strangling at the moment. We're behind on the Way Hill job. Architect's fault, of course. He chose the bloody sub-contractors."

My sobs got mixed up with a bit of hiccough. "I tried to burn the rest of the sweater, but it's damp in that copper. So I buried it."

George patted me on the back rather like someone trying to bring up a baby's wind. "Where?"

"Where we used to have the peonies and the Robertses just had weeds." I couldn't have resisted a crack at the Robertses even if I'd been dying.

George rubbed his lips against my forehead without kissing me. "Oh, Wynne, you went out there to that empty house—you went out at night when you're scared of the dark—"

I looked up because his voice broke off. He had tears in his eyes.

"I thought I'd better cover up your tracks," I explained. "I wiped up your footsteps, too—the footsteps, I mean."

He held me against him so tightly I squeaked. I was a right old bag of tricks as far as noises went—sobs, coughs, hiccoughs, squeaks. What you might call a really attractive armful. Not to mention the way I smelt. But George didn't seem to notice.

"Why did you have to go at night?" he asked me. "Why the *hell* did you have to go at night?"

"Couldn't very well go in the daytime, could I? I mean, if you want to burn something in secret the thing to do isn't to have a blooming great bonfire in the daytime, is it?"

George asked me very quietly, "Were you really lying, Wynne, when you said you hadn't seen anyone?"

"Yes," I said. "I was in the cupboard."

"In that case you'd better try and put it out of your mind."

"George, I'd never go to the—I'd never tell anyone else, George. Not unless you wanted me to."

"That's my girl. Just forget all about it. It was probably

two tramps—or some beat wanting shelter for the night. It happens all the time in empty houses—we had quite a little colony on that conversion job we did at Shiphampton. It didn't have to be the strangler—in fact it's ten to one it wasn't."

I thought numbly, "You're very anxious all of a sudden to prove it wasn't," and I pointed out, "Last night's girl was found quite near there."

"Yes, but the strangler wouldn't take time to traipse round an empty house, Wynne. He'd make off, not hang around."

"Unless he was following me and thought he'd have another go."

He said, "Wynne, bless you for being so sweet and so brave—I'll never forget it, don't think I will. But promise me never to go to that house again. You see, you had a lucky escape last night. It wasn't the strangler—we're certain of that—but it might have been. You took a ghastly risk—for my sake, I know—but you see, supposing it had been me? I'd have had to be mad, wouldn't I? And madness doesn't acknowledge friends or people it loves. If this man turned out to be someone you know it wouldn't save you—however much he thought of you."

"Yes," I said.

Len came in. I might not know our Len as well as Hélène knows him or as well as I know our George, but the local sweep could have seen that he hadn't had much sleep that night. He hadn't gone his greasy white, but he had the rash on his neck which he gets when he's very upset.

"Morning," he said. "Nothing like a nice bit of emotion over the kitchen table before breakfast."

I suppose we must have looked a proper pair of charlies with me sitting in George's lap, caked in mud and paraffin, and my face all red and blotchy as if someone had thrown a tomato at it, and George still with tears in his eyes.

George thundered at him, "Where were you last night? Grandad said you woke him up in the early hours."

It certainly was a bit of a bark. But then again George could hardly have said, "Pardon my nerves, but Wynne's just accused me of being the strangler and I'm trying to kid her out of it."

Len fairly whirled on him. Talk about nerves! But then of course, he was the king of them, was our Len. The way he shrieked out in the night sometimes could stop the blood in your veins.

"Okay, Casanova," Len said into his face. "So I came in late, but I was earlier than you, wasn't I? Not having been born with no soles to my feet, Grandad heard me and not you."

"Where were you?" George insisted. I thought it was silly of him really. After all, Len was nineteen.

"At the discothèque," said Len.

"What time's it close?"

"Find out."

Honestly, you'd have thought those two loathed each other, but they didn't.

For something to do with his hands, I suppose, Len took down Sandy's dish.

"He's been fed twice already, has that cat," I said. I didn't want to be mean to Sandy. I just wanted him to live.

Len paid no attention to me and George was too bothered to back me up. Len opened a tin of Paws and put it down. Sandy tucked into it with a look as if to say, "See! *Some* people understand a cat needs food." Honestly, how crooked can you get?

George slid me off his lap. I'd mucked up his shirt good and proper.

"Pity we haven't got shares in a dry cleaner's," said our Len. "Every time you two canoodled we'd make a packet. What happened, did you spend the night in a ditch?"

"Wynne and Corinne had a fight," George told him as if he'd learned it off by heart. "Wynne pitched into a tin of paraffin."

"If I'd written that script for telly myself," Len said, "I wouldn't have bitched if the critics had said it was lousy."

George said, "That's what happened."

Len picked up Sandy's dish, washed it, and put it back in the rack.

"Well," said George, "I'd better go and change my shirt."

He touched my cheek with his hand and left it there a few moments. "All right, Wynne?"

"All right," I answered, smiling.

Mother came in. She looked dazed and really wretched. She had also heard the news.

To me she said, "Wynne—I hope you didn't come home alone with that monster on the prowl again. Oh, isn't it *dreadful*. How can they let such things happen—just think of the poor little thing's mother."

She didn't seem to notice the state I was in. Imagine it! I mean, you'd think you'd notice your daughter sitting there smelling of paraffin so early in the morning! But she was so fussed up she didn't. That made me smile quite a bit until George picked up his jacket from the back of the chair. He threw it over his arm and, as plain as a pikestaff, on the left shoulder there was a blue mark from the passage at Collins Wood.

Mother blinked wearily round at us. "Has anyone fed poor Pussy?"

# 15 ❖

I JUST SAT THERE like a great big dead lump of something. Len went off to shave and when Mother noticed the state I was in I trotted out the Corinne story.

Mother fed Sandy again and took Grandad a tray in bed. His knee was bad.

I was counting out loud when Hélène came in and said, "Hello, Baby Soeur, gone bonkers?"

We were on a French jag that week. The twins were saving up to go to St. Maxime for their holidays with some chums. They had bought some Linguaphone records—so everything was "*quel*" this and "*quel*" that, and "*Toi* are telling *moi!*" They get fads and crazes all the time. They might not last long, but they certainly went all out for them. They got so interested in hypnotism once that Mum was quite glad when they put all their fervour into Len's pop group again. Hélène was sure Len would get to the top of the charts one day, and Sarah Bernhardt had got nothing on Hélène in Len's eyes. They were going to be quite generous to the rest of us when they made their first million, but I didn't think they'd have much left after a flat in Mayfair—a suite at the Hilton for "visiting friends"—and a villa in Spain.

Hélène was wearing her goggles that kept her eyelashes safe in the night. When she took them off she squeaked at the terrible state I was in.

I trotted out the Corinne story automatically.

"You look like hell," she said.

I thought, "Maybe George got that blue mark the day he caught Corry and me out at Collins Wood whistling up Clare's ghost. Maybe he hasn't worn that suit since then."

Hélène put on the kettle.

"There's one thing I could do," I told myself. "I could give him time and then go back and see if he's taken a look at the peony bed and checked up if I buried the sweater."

"Did I hear Frère George's voice raised in alarm or anger?" asked Hélène.

"He thought I looked a mess," I said dully, and I told myself, "If that flower-bed's been interfered with I'll know it's him—checking up on the sweater all right."

"Well, you do look awful, Puss Bun," chirruped Hélène. "*Quel* mess!" She held her head and groaned. "I had some drinks last night and *ma tête* is *malade* something wicked."

When I didn't answer she looked my way. "Have you had a row with Frère George? What's the matter, found out he's being unfaithful?" Before I could answer she suddenly turned round, the kettle snorting steam in her hand. "Here! He's not—he hasn't told *you* anything, has he?"

I glared up nervously. "What could he tell?"

She came across to me. "Come to think of it you look more than a mess, you look—rummy. You look like you've had bad news. He's never going to marry that creature, is he?"

I felt dazed and my head ached. "What creature?"

"What! What! What! Can't you answer a question without asking one back? The current girl-friend, I mean. The one that's lasted nearly ten minutes."

"Has he got a steady one, then?"

Hélène gave a sharp, rude little laugh. "I wouldn't call her exactly *steady*—at least not on her feet—but she's been around some time."

"Have you met her?"

"No—I've seen her at the cinema. She looks good from a distance and Len says she lives in a classy district."

"How's Len know?"

"Well, *cette ville* isn't all that enormous, is it? I suppose he just runs into them or something."

"Or followed George like the little tailor," I thought. "The little tailor in *The Hatter's Ghosts*."

"It's none of Len's business," I said out loud. "He'd no right to follow them about."

Hélène snapped at me, "Who said anything about following? I gather she isn't all that *hard* to follow! You might tell Frère George if he asks you to be his bridesmaid that he isn't the only pebble on *her* beach, either."

The door in the hall closed quietly. George going out.

"I keep my nose out of other people's affairs," I said stiffly.

"*This* affair will be yours as well if it turns itself into a marriage," Hélène said. "Quelle soeur-in-law! Ker-ripes!"

Len called out, "I'm off now, Hélène."

"Okay, 'bye!" she yelled.

They never said goodbye to anyone else, those twins, only to each other.

Mum came wandering back for a little knife. "I haven't given your Grandad anything for his butter! Wynne," she said to me, "haven't you cleaned yourself up yet?"

"Len was in the bathroom," I explained.

"Well, he's not now," from Hélène, "and he wasn't there above five minutes either this morning."

"It's that poor thing's mother that I can't forget," said Mum. "What *must* she be feeling this morning! If I ever got the brute I'd reckon hanging and drawing and quartering too good for him."

Hélène held out a small knife. "Here!"

"Eh?" said Mother absently.

"Grandad's butter."

"Oh yes. Ta." Mother wandered off, muttering, "You just *can't* put it out of your head."

"So," said Hélène, "*ma petite soeur*—if you have your Frère George's welfare at *coeur* I'd put him off little Miss B.P."

"Is that her initials?"

Hélène chuckled. "Practically."

I disdained to ask too many questions about George's affairs. I liked people to think I was in his complete confidence. So I said casually, "Oh, *that* one. I don't think there's much danger there. He's through with her."

"Thank God."

She left the kitchen with some tea and a Ryvita on a tray. No butter. We were watching our figure. Every time her hand hovered over anything fattening Len said, *"Attention la ligne!"* He didn't speak his little bits of French too badly, either. I knew from Mother Marie-Adelaide at school. His accent was much better than George's and so was Hélène's —maybe it was the Linguaphone. You had to admire those twins. They may have been scatty and switched from fad to fad, but they did learn a bit from everything before they threw it up.

I was still sitting there like a gook when Grandad hobbled in with his tray.

"Get cleaned up. You're stinking the place out."

He washed up his cup and plate and put them on the rack next to Sandy's saucer. "Has anyone given—?"

"Yes," I shouted. "Hundreds of times—*everyone's* been feeding Sandy every ten minutes."

Grandad turned to look at me as if I'd gone mad. "I wasn't enquiring after the cat. I was wondering if anyone had had the courtesy to give your mother a cup of tea, seeing the state she's in."

"Oh—I don't know."

"Well, I suspect that I do and the answer's no. Now get cleaned up, Wynne—the smell of you's getting on my stomach."

I went into the bathroom, ran the water and borrowed some of Hélène's bath salts. It always made her mad. I think she counted the crystals, but I needed a bit of sweetening that morning.

My stockings and underclothes could be washed, but my dress and my coat would have to go to the cleaner's.

It was a relief to relax in hot water. I've heard it called a dirty habit and that a shower is the only clean way to get washed, but I'm afraid that I prefer the dirty way.

What might be important, I thought, was to find out if the victims were just picked at random, or if it was more like *The Hatter's Ghosts*—with a reason.

What I thought I'd do, if I found I could prove it was George, was to get him to come away with me somewhere lonely, remote, and wild. Of course, those places are easier to dream up in a bath than find on a map. But there must be some old fallen-down cottage up in the Lakes or the Welsh mountains or the farthest bits of Scotland or even Ireland. George, being a builder, could put it right. There were other things easier to arrange in a bath, like earning our living and having to eat, and the family not letting me go with him, and George not wanting me himself. But I could blackmail George. Either he took me with him and I kept an eye on him day and night, or I went to the police and he went into a nut-house. I was quite ruthless. "Broadmoor or a cottage with me, George. Just make up your mind." Come to that I could blackmail the family too, and maybe Grandad could join us for a bit, just so things looked all right.

George had a bit of a pension from the neck wound he got in Korea, and we could live a long time in the wilds on our own produce and the money he'd get from selling out to Mr. Wells.

Oh yes, it was simple enough in the bath—in fact, I quite enjoyed planning it all. Tucked on a mountainside together, caring for all the spring lambs—reading in front of great log fires by oil lamps while the winter winds thumped to get in from outside. We had a whale of a time, George and me. The small matter of George being a strangler—since it would have been due to that little habit of his that we found ourselves in our haven together—didn't bother me much. If he strangled me, well, I'd have done my best for him—and besides, such things wouldn't occur in our mountainside haven.

I'd have talked him out of his little failing. Of course, in the deepest corner of my heart I still couldn't believe it could ever be George, or I couldn't have made such fun of it.

We were just celebrating our first Christmas in the mountain haven when there was a ring at the door. In the flat at Dalstead, I mean, not the haven on the fells.

It was Aunt Rene Tindall. She'd seen the light. Whenever her kidneys were all right for the moment, or people really had had enough of her other ills, she saw the light.

She used to say "it came" to those who had "sooffered."

Mother opened the door and I heard, by the way she said "Oh, Rene, how nice," that she could have done without Aunt so early in the morning.

I slid farther down into my "dirty habit." My hair got wet but I didn't mind. It was so comforting and warm. It was all such nonsense. There would be a perfectly good explanation for all the funny things that scared me so—the sweater, George's lies, the figures on the wall and the marks on his coat, and the queer way he acted about *The Hatter's Ghosts*.

Oh yes. There'd be reasons for everything. I began to feel a real silly-billy about all those fears. I even hummed a little tune, but I frowned when I remembered what Hélène had said about his girl.

There must've been something to it if she was scared he was going to marry her. But George had had so many girls and he wasn't acting as if he was going to marry someone. I would have sensed something different about him if he had. He wasn't acting any different about this one to any of the others—and he *had* kissed me and hugged me that morning. It felt good to have been made a fuss of by George again, whatever the reason. I was laughing weakly at myself for being such a goof as to ever have been suspicious of him —George of *all* people—when a rap on the door nearly sent me under the water, head and all.

"Wynne!" Mother wanted to know. "Have you drowned in that bath?"

"Not until now," I grumbled.

It took some while to clean the bath—the paraffin just moved the dirt along it.

When I got out Mum was trapped in the kitchen. Grandad had disappeared to clean out his mice and Hélène was "studying a part" in our bedroom.

I was about to creep past the kitchen door, but Mum spotted me and called out, thankful to pounce on an ally, "Here's your aunty Rene Tindall. She feels she's seen the light."

"Oh," I said. "That's nice."

Aunt Rene Tindall was sitting bolt upright at the kitchen table. "It were in chapel," she said. "Right over the minister's head. It were a faint white light with a voice inside. 'Rene Tindall,' it seemed to be telling me, 'there is eternal life.'"

I thought it could've done a bit better than tell her something the rest of us knew already, and I felt a fit of the laughs coming on. I suppose it was from relief in a sort of way, really. George could so easily have got the mark that day he found Corry and me at Collins Wood and he just hadn't worn the suit since.

"There's noorishment of vipers in the bosom of your religion, Wynne," Aunt Rene told me. I had a vision of the Pope and all the most important cardinals rushing round nourishing vipers in religious bosoms. I turned my splutter of laughter into a cough.

"Wynne!" said Mother warningly.

Aunt Rene turned to me solemnly. She was wearing her muddy fawns again and a giddy little hard felt hat with a feather and one of those stiff veils that stand out. Her glasses looked huge behind it.

"Aye," she said, "I were singled out. Singled out for message and I'm off to 'elp others to see the light."

Mother jumped up a bit too fast for real politeness. "That's right, dear, you get off and tell them all. I daresay it'll bring comfort to some—"

"Singled out!" nodded Aunt Rene. "Singled out above Minister's head!"

"Very nice, dear," Mother agreed vaguely. "And I'm sure it's only the deserving that are."

"Singled out!" Aunt Rene repeated, and I think if she'd said it again I'd have burst.

As it was she got to the door, which Mother opened a shade too quickly, and said loudly, "Make no mistake on it, Lucy Kinch, make no mistake at all. The Lord is round the corner this instant."

In spite of herself poor Mother looked right past her up the passage, as if she expected to see Him stepping out of the lift.

*16* ❖ IT WASN'T NECESSARY for me to go to Collins
Wood. I could tell that George had been out there to find
out about the sweater himself. He came back about six
o'clock that evening. The blue mark had disappeared from
his shoulder. One of the men or Mr. Wells had spotted it,
I suppose.

He was very jaunty with me. Oh, he hadn't been so jaunty
for years. He called me Wynnikins. That's something he'd
never done before. He wasn't the "kins" kind.

"I've been round to see Mrs. Eldridge," he told me. "My
God, what a fool she is."

"That's no way to talk, George," Mother scolded him.
"She's going through a very difficult time. She had Corinne
much too late. They were married ten years before they got
Corinne. That's what made her turn to Wynne's faith."

"That's pretty bad propaganda for Wynne's faith," George
pointed out, and to me he said, "To give your unlovable
little friend her due, she did at least stick up for you in front
of her mother. She admitted she threw the shoe at you first."

"Good old Corry," I said dully. It was *George's* shoes that
were troubling me. They were his heavy ones. There was a
stain on one of them. I knew what it was because I'd got
the same stain on mine. It was paraffin oil.

"I think you'd better go round and apologise," he told
me. "If only for poor Mr. Eldridge's sake."

"Yes, George, I will."

"Corinne sent you her love."

"Thanks."

He showed signs of dandying himself up. I knew the
symptoms—asking Mother about his washing, etc., and ac-

cusing Len of taking his ties. Then he went off to have a
bath.

While he was in the bathroom I nipped into his bedroom
and had a look at his shoes. It was paraffin all right—the
shoes reeked of it. He'd had a good tramp round that old
copper at Collins Wood, had George.

Still, that didn't prove anything. He might have gone back
there to see if I was telling the truth—I cheered up at that.
On the other hand, if he'd dug up the sweater and moved
it somewhere else, or tried to destroy it again, he would have
to mind very much about it for some reason. If he had done
that, there might be signs of it in the back of his car. Bits of
the sweater itself, perhaps, or more paraffin.

He parked the Bedford near the bicycle sheds just behind
our flats.

I leapt up and said to Mother, "I'm just going round to say
sorry to Mrs. Eldridge and make it up with Corinne."

"Wait till I've time to come round with you, dear, you
can't be too careful these days."

"Oh, Lucy, she won't come to any harm," said Grandad.

"Well, don't linger," Mother called after me. "You know
how I get if you're out after dark."

George was still in the bath. I slipped into his bedroom
again. The car keys were in his handkerchief drawer where
he always kept them. One of Len's drawers was open. He
was always terribly untidy. His socks were all over the place
and one was hanging out of the drawer. When I went to put
it back I felt something in the toe—like aspirins. I tipped
them into my hand. They were little heart-shaped breath
cachous. At least, so I thought, and I imagined he must keep
them for when he came in smelling of drink.

George was as fond of a nice hot "dirty habit" as I was,
and he always took a long time over it, so I knew I'd have
a goodish time to inspect the van and get the keys back in
time.

It was getting dark when I nipped out. The lift was in use, so I ran downstairs.

The Bedford was covered in raindrops. The back was always a shambles because George kept sacks in it and a pile of old blankets for stopping fittings from scratching on their way to a site, or to stop Mr. Wells's retriever Jenny from dirtying up the front seats. In order not to lose the keys I put them in the dashboard. It would be ghastly if I dropped them and couldn't find them. There was quite a heap to search through for any telltale bits of sweater he might have taken off and hidden again.

I searched each blanket very thoroughly—and that's what made me forget the time, I suppose.

George must have been searching for the keys upstairs for some while. He and Grandad were talking about them as they came out of the entrance to our flats.

I did the daftest thing I had ever done in my life. I dived under the pile of blankets, because in my panic I simply could not think what to say I was doing there. George got so wild about any nosey-parkerness.

Under the blankets I smelt a lot of what must have been a very wet Jenny at some time, and some of her hairs got over my face, making me long to sneeze.

When they reached the car Grandad said, "There you are, lad, what did I tell you? You left 'em inside all the time."

George sounded truly baffled. "I must be going off my rocker then. I distinctly remember taking them up." Then to my horror they both got into the car.

George must've leaned across Grandad. "Okay, I'll do the door."

He shoved it to, and something fell with a plop on my head—George's raincoat chucked in the back. He started up the engine and off we went.

"Oh no!" I thought. "It's not true—it's just not true."

Grandad said, "No need to take me right up if it makes you late. Just drop me on the corner."

"It's all right," George told him. "It's wet and you want to be careful with that bad knee."

Grandfather was going to see a friend who had just taken up mice and wanted some advice. He was thinking of going in for Cinnamons and Agoutis.

Grandad and George agreed that the secretary of the Mouse Fancy was right that it was better to cull down the litters to four at birth and dispense with surplus bucks, but only in the case of "selfs." If you kept tans or AOV's or "markeds," the bucks exhibited best. They chattered mice all the way to Grandad's friend's, and I devoutly hoped that George and I were going straight home after that. George and I were not.

Unless I raised my head, which I didn't dare do in case he saw me in the mirror, I couldn't see where we were going. What I did manage to see nearly stopped me breathing altogether; George's hand creeping through the break in the seats and floundering about behind him—floundering very near my face. I strained away. He was groping for his raincoat. I tried to edge it nearer his hand but I dare not go too far. He couldn't get it and still drive at the same time, so he said "Bugger!" and stopped the car.

My teeth took hold of my bottom lip and fairly minced it up. If he got out and came rummaging about in the back any part of me might be showing.

He didn't. He only leaned over the back seat, picked up the raincoat, and dropped it down on my air hole, which hardly improved my breathing situation. Then I heard a match strike. He had wanted a cigarette out of his pocket.

Off we drove again. We must have been going out of town. The other traffic got quieter and quieter. Where were we going—Collins Wood?

It seemed a long time that we kept driving. Much too long for my liking. I didn't dare make a movement or a squeak in case it made him jump and drive into a tree.

At last we turned into somewhere and came to a stop. George got out, locked the car, and I could hear his feet crackling over gravel.

Then a doorbell rang and a door opened. Someone said, "Oh, good evening Mr. Meakham, we're all ready for you."

The door shut again and I worked my way out of my blankets as carefully as a chrysalis coming out of its cocoon.

When I sat up I saw that we were outside a rather grand-looking house in some sort of park.

There was a large notice outside which read "Brinkhill Clinic."

Brinkhill! That was miles away from Dalstead, and what was George doing in a clinic?

"Oh my God," I thought suddenly. "It *is* him, and he knows he's kinky and he's having treatment. He must be going to a psychiatrist again."

I flipped back under my pile as soon as I heard voices.

There were more of them this time, and goodbyes were being said. George opened the back of the car and thumped a great suitcase down which fell over against my hip.

Then he opened the front door and said to someone, "Mind your skirt—it's that dog of Jimmie's."

Whoever it was had a light, lacy kind of voice and she simply reeked of perfume. She must have had a bath in it. Fortunately it was a lovely kind of smell and made a nice change from Jenny. She flipped a fur coat into the back to join George's raincoat and a handkerchief fell out of the pocket. I couldn't get it back without disarranging my blanket, so I tucked it down the front of my dress. I didn't want her rummaging about for it.

"How am I looking?" she asked George.

"Great," he told her.

"Well, I suppose that's one compensation. Did you do anything about finding another job for me?"

"Not until I'm sure you can keep one."

"I'll keep it."

She had a rather smart sort of accent. She didn't sound like someone that needed a job, and the next thing George said rather proved that it wasn't money she was after.

"The council want volunteers to visit the blind. You know —personal interest, listen to their problems, cheer them up, provide transport and run errands. But we'll see how you go first."

"Things are going to be different all round," she said.

"That's great too," from George.

"Any trouble from my lousy little landlord?"

"Nothing that's come my way."

"I'm certainly not going to sleep with him again. Christ! Why did I?"

"You managed."

"I could kick myself for feeding his stinking little ego."

"His wasn't the only stinking little ego you fed that week," said George.

"Well, really!" I thought. "This conversation! No wonder Hélène said she'd make a dreadful sister-in-law."

"Oh, to hell with him! You know what I remember about him? His snobbishness. It was ghastly. The others—well, I don't remember anything much about the others—but him! Right in the middle of everything—did I tell you he was impotent?"

"I didn't ask you."

"Oh yes, I remember now. You're the one that's not interested. What makes you bother with me, then?"

"Maybe I'm sorry for you."

"Yeah. But you still like to sleep with me?"

"Yeah," he copied her.

"But not when I'm pissed."

"When aren't you?"

"Now. I don't know why, considering you're such a bastard, but I'm not sure that I don't love you."

George said, "Balls!"

"*Really!*" I thought. "Well, *really!*"

"I was telling you," she said, "about my landlord. In the middle of everything, or rather nothing, he suddenly told me he came from a much better home than I thought and that there were two titles in his family."

"Everybody likes to show off something," said George. "If they haven't got looks or charm and their money does nothing for them, they take to snobbery."

"Yes. I suppose. You know there weren't *really* all those many men in my 'on the house' week. Some of them were invented for your benefit."

"Really?"

"I thought I saw centipedes around the place as well."

"You mentioned them."

"You know something else? I think you're crazy about that kid sister of yours who's so crazy about you."

I felt the blood burning my face.

"She's only fourteen," George told her.

"They get pregnant at thirteen these days."

"Wynne didn't."

"You didn't answer my question."

"She's a child," George replied, and I could have clocked him.

"I meant that," she repeated. "There weren't all those many men in my 'open house' week."

"There couldn't have been," said George. "You were too sloshed."

Hélène's remarks came back to me then. "None too steady on her feet" and "Miss B.P." was short for "Booze Pot." She must have been in the Brinkhill Clinic for drink. But what could George be thinking about, going around with someone like that? And putting up with her being drunk and messing about with other men?

I was afraid she must be one of the most attractive people he'd ever met, and although I was dying to get a glimpse of her in a way I was afraid to. George didn't put up with nuisances gladly and it couldn't have been very easy to have a girl-friend that saw centipedes about the place. She must have something pretty terrific to keep him, and from the way I heard them speaking to him at the clinic—"We're all ready for you, Mr. Meakham"—he seemed pretty well connected with her. It was like somebody going to collect his wife.

"So how do I solve my problem?" she asked him.

"Don't start on the stuff again," he advised.

"Not *that* problem. My main problem—you. I wasn't kidding when I said I loved you."

"Oh, that'll solve itself. It won't last."

"The other men meant nothing to me."

"You said that, too. Every time."

"I only sleep with them when I'm pissed, George. And I only get pissed because I haven't got you."

George made a very rude noise. I really would have clouted him if I'd been her. He didn't seem to bother about her feelings at all.

"It's true," she insisted. "I get lonely for you."

"You were as pissed as a newt the first time I ever set eyes on you."

"I've taken the cure, haven't I?"

"Don't get sorry for yourself," he warned.

"Look," she suddenly shouted at him, "if I'm such a pain in the neck why the hell do you stick around?"

"I don't have to."

She climbed down, too quickly I thought. "George, you *know* how I feel about you—I swear I wouldn't drink if I had you with me—I get scared without you."

"Who were you scared without before me?"

"I *told* you. Bob drove me up the wall."

"I shouldn't have thought he had time. You weren't married long enough."

"It seemed long."

George said quietly, "Look, Leonie, you told me you were both so drunk on your wedding-day you could hardly answer the registrar. It was you who put Bob on the bottle, not the other way round. He had the good sense to give both of you up before he dropped dead, and you've fooled yourself ever since that you drink to forget him."

"Will you remind me to recommend you for the job of principal of the local charm school?" she asked him.

"I'll remind you."

"I don't think you'd pass the test. The charm test, I mean. You have to have one, to be the principal."

"I'm like Bob. I've had the lot. The tears, the rows, the scares—the scenes in public—the lot. You're a compulsive drinker, a compulsive sexer and a compulsive suicider."

"Bob *did* drink before he met me."

"He drank, but he wasn't a drunk. You were. I don't say it's your fault. It was something in you. Better than being diabetic, maybe, but more noisy."

"George, it just so happens I do love you."

"You're great when you're sober, Leonie."

He stopped the car.

I could hear him turn to her and give her long, deep kisses. There were lots of cooings and mewings and smoochy murmurings.

"Well, really!" I thought. "To do it right in front of me like that!" Then I thought, panic-stricken, "Heavens! Supposing they're coming to make love in the back of the van! They'll do it on top of me!"

But they didn't get out. They just sat talking in low voices and I only caught snatches of it. There were lots of "honeys" and "babys" and "I already told you you had my promise" from her, and from him that he'd been let down too many times to trust her, and if it happened once again—just *once* again . . .

She'd started moaning more than talking. "Baby, you won't leave me alone tonight, not tonight—just ease me in— I might not make it if you left me alone tonight."

"That's the test," George said. "You've got to make it."

I thought how surprised she'd be if I suddenly sat up, tapped her on the shoulder, and said, "You want to be careful he's in the right mood—if he's in the wrong one he could strangle you."

The van started up rather violently and Leonie's suitcase wobbled over and gave me another great thump on the bottom.

Heavy rain began to fall. When we next stopped they did get out. George came round to the back and lugged out the suitcase, and the fur jacket. I was still clutching the handkerchief. I just had to pray that he hadn't disturbed the blankets and exposed any part of me.

He shouted at Leonie, "Make a dash for it." I heard her clamber out and run up some steps. Then he banged the doors and followed.

After what I thought was a safe amount of time I popped up and peered out of the windows through the bouncing rain.

He must have brought her home. Hélène said she lived in a classy district. We were out at Harrowvane—opposite Number 9 Cecil Avenue. That was classy all right. Harrowvane was a good fifteen miles from us. I had no money on me, and if I had tried to walk I'd have arrived back soaked, and several weeks late. I wasn't even wearing a coat and I thought that even I couldn't turn up wet and dirty twice in one day in front of the family.

So I settled under the blankets and was relieved when George came out almost immediately.

I decided that I would give him about half an hour after we got home and then wander in myself, full of my reconciliation with Corinne.

But the next time we stopped it was outside The Red Lion at Shipham.

"I hope," I thought to myself, "that the love of my life isn't starting off on a nice, long pub crawl."

That's just what the love of my life was starting off on.

We visited The King's Arms, The Black Swan and The Case Is Altered.

George drove very fast from one to the other. Sometimes he whistled to himself in between and sometimes he was silent. He smoked plenty. I kept hearing matches being struck.

I was stiff and uncomfortable and terrified on two scores. One was that I was sure Mother would start ringing up Mrs. Eldridge soon and find out I wasn't there, and the second was what should I do if I wanted to spend a penny? For a start I was locked in. That wouldn't matter because I could always undo the door and nip out. But supposing I nipped out at the wrong moment? Either just when George was coming back or, worse still, supposing he came back before I was back!

I scared myself into wanting to go, of course. I'd have been all right otherwise.

I knew that the longer I left it the worse it would be, because he would be more likely to come out of the pub.

Finally I couldn't wait any longer. I scrambled over into the front seats, unlocked the door and just got out in time.

Someone on a motorcycle picked that moment to ride up and floodlight me as if I was being filmed or something.

I couldn't see who it was, but a man's voice asked, "Run out of pennies?"

I felt like *dying*. I believe you can be had up for fouling the pavement. Not that it was a pavement. It was just a gravel verge off the road. Still, I couldn't see Mum minding very much whether it was pavement or gravel just so long as I was had up for fouling it.

It wasn't until I scrambled back into the van that I saw a whopping great neon-light notice sticking out of the side of the pub. It said "Ladies," with an arrow flicking off and on at it. On the other side there was an arrow doing just the same at "Gents." It really wanted you to know where to go, did that pub.

When George came out he was singing. Not loudly, or drunkenly or anything. He was just singing to himself. But he was blowing little raspberries in between the words.

"If you were the only girl in the world—phooooh!"

I really don't know how you put down a raspberry on paper. But it was the rude kind all right.

"—And I was the only boy— Phupp! Phupp! Phupp!— Phooo—*ooh!*"

"He can't be right in the head," I thought. Then I thought, "My God! Suppose he isn't? He can't be if he's done what I think— No, of *course* he didn't. But drink would make it worse."

I had to clap my hand over my mouth to stop myself counting out loud. I was sweating with terror in the back of that van—Leonie's little lace handkerchief was a small wet ball in my hand. I now smelt almost as good as she did.

When he was in The Case Is Altered I managed to get a look at the clock. In a few minutes it would be closing time, so we couldn't go visiting any more pubs, but Mother was sure to have rung Mrs. Eldridge by now.

George didn't seem any the worse for his "crawl." He was whistling quite cheerily when we stopped once more.

"Now," I thought, "I'll give him five minutes, that's enough. Then I'll try and creep in and pretend I've been at home all the time."

But we weren't at home. We were outside Number 9 Cecil Avenue, Harrowvane, once more, and this time George didn't emerge until half-past two in the morning.

*17* ❖ By the time he did emerge I was nearly too drunk and sleepy to bother to hide any more. Amongst the blankets and muck in the back of the van there was a quart of beer with very little out of it. It must have been left from George's or Mr. Wells's lunch. By the time George came out it was empty. I had had practically nothing to eat at all over the last twenty-four hours, and the beer stopped both my hunger and thirst.

The hoo-hah at home was quite something when we got back. I let George get in first and then, trembling with tiredness and none too steady from the beer, I managed to slink into my room, undress quickly, and skip into bed. I simply reeked of Leonie's scent.

They were all in the living-room, and so were the police. There was a young detective sergeant and a young detective constable. I didn't know what they were then, of course, but I've had plenty of time to know about policemen since. They were not in uniform.

They hadn't heard George's silent footsteps, so he must have made them jump when he appeared. I nipped out of bed to spy through the doorway. I had a nasty feeling that their presence must have something to do with my absence.

I suddenly remembered Len's breath cachous. My breath must have smelt awful after all that beer, and there wouldn't half have been a row if Mum discovered that I'd been on the bottle as well as everything else.

I went into George's and Len's room and opened the drawer Len kept the cachous in. They were hidden in his sock again. I popped several into my mouth and went back to do my spying. I might just as well know what I was up against.

Mother was fanning herself with *Fur and Feather* and she was whiter than any shirt advertisement on television. Grandad had smoked the room into a black fog, Hélène was in noisy tears and Len was absolutely sloshed.

He'd been at the gin from the sideboard and I suppose Mother was too upset to notice or stop him. He kept waving the bottle about at the police. It was only half full. I think it was the one we'd had from our grocer's Christmas Club. You know, where you pay all the year and then you can take out goods at Christmas. Nobody drank at home very much except Len on the quiet.

He said to the sergeant, "Wan shum? Makekewhumana-veshum."

The sergeant said thanks very much but they'd rather not.

When George came in the whole family except Len leaped at him to say that I was missing. Len meant to leap but he fell over. The young policeman picked him up, saying something like, "Steady does it, lad."

Mum squeaked, "Len! Have you been drinking?"

"Of course not," said Grandad bitterly. "He's been play-ing the harmonica at the neck of that bottle for the last half hour."

"Oh, leave him alone!" snapped Hélène. "He was wor-ried there wasn't much in it, anyway."

The sergeant said something about fumes and Mother tugged at George's coat.

All of them, except the police, yelled at George that I was missing.

"I rang Mrs. Eldridge," Mother wept. "Wynne's not been there at all."

"She never *got* to Corinne's," Hélène emphasised unnec-essarily.

The sergeant came up to introduce himself to George, since nobody else was in a fit state to do it.

George shook hands with him and the sergeant told George that they would do their best to find me. I was much more likely to be out enjoying myself somewhere, he said kindly for Mother's benefit, than be in any danger, although of course with what had been going on he wasn't surprised she was worried. They had my description and my photograph and did George know any other friends I might have visited?

Before George could answer Len stepped up. He spoke very slowly to try and cover his drunkenness.

"Yeah, any idea where she could have been, Brother George?"

I don't expect anyone except me noticed the sergeant sniff as he stood next to George. I had a strong vantage point peering through the crack. I expect the heat of the fire they were standing in front of brought out the scent of Leonie's perfume. After all, the lucky girl had been rolling about in his arms. The sergeant sniffed once or twice.

George must have thought I'd gone out to Collins Wood again. He was standing very straight, but I could see he was more than upset.

George didn't answer Len's question. He asked one himself. "There wasn't enough gin left in that cupboard for you to get sloshed on. Where else have you been drinking? When did you get in?"

"The usual time," Grandad grumbled. "In time to spoil other folks' rest."

The young sergeant was rather good-looking, so perhaps that's why I was watching him. I saw him sniff again, but this time not near George. Then he suddenly stepped backwards and pulled open the door. I nearly fell into the room. I suppose he must have caught another whiff of Leonie's perfume coming off me through the crack of the door.

So there I was in me nightgown confronted by everybody in the room.

There was a very dead silence. George got over it first. His voice was icily grim. "Where were you?"

"We were worried about you," the sergeant explained nicely, while the young constable, still looking at me, bent down to tickle Sandy, who had just walked majestically in.

"I've been here all the time," I said.

"You *can't* have been!" Hélène squeaked at me. "It was my early night and why wouldn't I have noticed you in bed?"

I was beginning to feel a bit clever and bold. "I was under it," I told her, and had a bit of difficulty not to hiccough.

"*Under* it!" Grandad thundered.

Mother got up and put her arm round me. "She looks washed out. I always said your aunty Rene Tindall was right about keeping a drop of brandy in the house for emergencies."

"Have shome gin," Len suggested, and slopped some into a glass. I drank it down before Mother could stop me.

"Where *have* you been, Wynne?" Mother wailed, and burst into tears of relief.

"Under the bed," I repeated. "I got under it for a joke and I must have dropped off to sleep."

"Dropped off to sleep!" Hélène howled. "And you never woke up with the lot of us tramping about and telephoning everyone?"

"I've never been a light sleeper," I answered with dignity.

I was beginning to feel a bit funny. Sort of very clear-headed and bright. "I needn't have bothered to take those breath cachous," I thought, "if I'd known I was going to be given a gin."

I was very excited. Not happy excited really, just sort of on edge and cocksure of myself, but a bit scared just the same. I tried to tell myself that it wasn't surprising. After all, I'd had about a pint and a half of beer and a gin and no food for a long time, not to mention the strain of having spent the whole of the night before in a cupboard in Collins

Wood, so perhaps it wasn't surprising that I felt a bit light-headed and above myself.

"What bed would that have been that you were under, miss?" the young policeman wanted to know. He was in a tweed jacket and looked rather nice. All the boys were looking good to me that night.

"My bed," I said, and smiled a bit coyly at him. I thought he'd be nice to dance with, but then I looked at George and I realised that I'd never be more attracted to anyone than him. It was a terrible tie to be so devoted to one person. I was thinking of bursting into tears about it when the young policeman said, "That's funny. I took a peep under there when we were looking round." He seemed very taken with Sandy. He bent down to tickle him again.

"Routine," the sergeant smiled at me.

"I did come in a bit late," I admitted.

"A bit!" shouted Hélène. "I haven't been to sleep at all, thanks to there being *no sign* of you in the other bed—or *under* it. You haven't been here at all."

"What time *did* you get in?" the sergeant asked, as if it was just a matter of personal interest—like someone asking about the end of a film he'd missed.

"I'm not quite sure," I said. "I didn't have my watch on." And then I felt as if my wrist had caught fire. My watch was fairly gleaming on it and both the policemen glanced at it. "I mean, I didn't have it on then," I explained.

The sergeant picked up his hat. "You've given your family a bit of a fright," he said firmly.

"A *bit* of a fright!" poor Mother wailed. "Wynne, where *did* you go—if it wasn't to Corinne's? We've all been half out of our minds about you."

"I went for a bit of a walk," I said.

"You kept very dry in it," the sergeant observed pleasantly.

"Been pouring all evening," the young policeman nodded.

"I took shelter," I retorted.

"Where?" exploded Grandad. "You've had your mother half demented."

"Oh, under things," I replied.

I was beginning to feel very clever and knowing—a fine match for a couple of fool policemen, I thought I was. If they hoped I was going to tell them anything about George and that sweater and Collins Wood, they'd got another think coming. I winked at George conspiratorially, which both the policemen saw and George didn't.

Had I been thinking straight, of course, I would have realised that the police wouldn't have been a bit interested in anything to do with George. Not at that moment, anyhow.

"What's all the fuss about?" I wanted to know. "I'm fourteen and a half. Some kids stay out *all* night."

"Kids in this house come home when they're told," snapped George.

I nearly had a laugh at that. I thought, "Then you should have brought me home a bit earlier, shouldn't you, my love?"

But I only said to him, "I'll tell you where I was. No one else."

"Will it be the truth?" George wanted to know.

"I'll give you a chance to check it," I giggled.

"He's been a father to her," Mother explained to the police officers, quite unnecessarily, I thought. It always annoyed me when people tried to explain away my feelings for George in that dull old way.

"Well," said the sergeant kindly. "All's well that ends well. But it's usually two-year-olds we find have been under the bed all the time, isn't it John?"

The young policeman said yes, it was usually around that age that they found people had been under the bed all the time.

"It was *ever* so nice of you to come," gushed poor Mother. "Just the sight of you made me feel better."

"She was in a right old state," Grandad confirmed. "I

couldn't have left her to come round to you. Hélène here
was in much the same state. I reckon young Wynne needs
flogging. And if you ask me she'd been drinking before she
got given a gin."

He was very observant, was Grandad. He always noticed
things. I suppose it came from peering at mice for so long
to see if they were turning out right.

I made a saucy clicking noise at him out of the side of my
mouth.

"She 'AS been drinking," he said. "She's drunk."

"Ish the gin," said Len. "I gave her shome gin."

"As for you," Grandad rounded on him, "a nice help
you've been to your mother, hiccoughing in the corner that
a family's got to stand together no matter 'ow 'ard tragedy
strikes! You can't even stand up yourself, never mind stand
by anyone else."

"Ish relief," said Len. "Ish relief that my baby shister
hashn' been shtrangled."

"It's his nerves," Mother told the police. "They've been
bad ever since he was small. He had a shock when he was
very young and Doctor said you couldn't tell what way it
might take. I just feel so bad pulling you out for nothing."

"We're glad it *was* nothing, Mrs. Kinch," the sergeant
said. "With what's going on at the moment you can't be too
careful. And it's no time," he said to me, in a light but sort
of stern voice, "to take little walks or shelter under things
late at night, even if you are fourteen and a half."

He waved his hat all round and the young policeman
waved his hand and it was George who saw them out.

But the sergeant beckoned Mum. She went into the hall
with him and Len tiptoed after her to listen. He put his ear
right up to the crack of the door.

"Come here!" ordered Grandad. "Mind your manners!"

He couldn't get up after him because his knee was so bad.
The bone was a bit out and the arthritis seemed worse if he
was upset or tired.

Len doubled up with laughing. He reported in drunken whispers, "Does Mum want Wynne innerviewed by a polishewoman! Or hasn't she indulged in carnal knowledge!" He dropped down on the floor, still laughing. "He doesn't mean the polishewoman. He meansh Wynne!"

Hélène ran up to him. "Len! You *couldn't* have got drunk on that drop of gin. I know what was left."

"You 'eard the police," said Grandad. "Fumes!"

When they heard the front door bang behind the police, the three of them fairly jumped down me.

"Wynne, how *could* you! Mother was nearly dead with worry."

"You shilly little nit," Len spoke right into my face, smelling terribly of booze. "Don't you realise there's a SHTRANGLER about?"

"You ought to have the hide tanned off you," from Grandad. "Speak up at once and say where you've been."

"Was it a boy?" asked Hélène. "Everywhere's closed at this time of night."

Mother rushed in and asked violently, "You haven't done anything *wrong?* Wynne! I want to talk to you alone."

"There's no need," I said. "I haven't done anything wrong. I've returned to you a virgin."

"*Wynne!*" Mother shrieked.

"You've got perfume on!" Hélène accused me. "Have you been at my—" She sniffed up close to me. "No, you haven't— but what *is* it?"

"Something somebody gave me."

"Who?"

"Questions! Questions!" I squeaked. "I said I'd tell *George*. Only *George*."

"I'll give you questions questions! George ought to tan the hide off you." That was Grandad again.

They all took it for granted that George would deal with me. He had taken the police officers to the lift. The rest of the family filed balefully past me, Grandad still threatening

hidings, Mother still asking if I was *sure* I was all right and
I hadn't done anything wrong, and there wasn't anything
I wanted to tell her in secret. Hélène sniffed me again. "It's
Sortilège—who the hell gave you Sortilège?" Then she
turned to see Len taking a quick swig from the neck of the
gin bottle. She sprang at him like a young tigress, wrenching
it out of his hands.

"Len Kinch! Do you want to be a B.P. at your age? You're
as high as a kite."

George came back. He looked very stern. He went up to
Hélène struggling with Len.

"Okay," he said. "I'll fix it. You get off to bed."

Hélène let go of the bottle and George took it out of
Len's hand. Hélène went past me again. "And *you* come to
bed," she said crossly. "I've had enough of being kept up.
I'm going to read a part tomorrow and I don't want to look
like hell."

George forced Len to sit down on the sofa. He held out
his hand. "C'mon," he said. "C'mon—let's have 'em."

Len opened an eye and looked blearily up at him.
"Whashoo want?"

I suddenly started to sing. No one was more surprised
than me. "Tiddle iddle 'orses, 'orses, 'orses!" I can't think
where I got the tune from, either. George turned and gave
me a quick, worried look. Then he got hold of Len and
shook him. "If you've given that child—if she's been out with
you and you started her off on—"

"No child me—" I trilled. "I've been a-wooing too—"

George glanced at me again and shook Len harder.

Len slopped against him. "Worduvhonour—donknow
where she's been—"

George snapped his fingers. "Come on, Len boy, or do you
want me to tell Hélène?"

Len's head wobbled. "No—no—be a sport—don' tell
Hélène—"

Len fumbled in his pocket and handed him some sort of

little bottle which George slipped into his own pocket. But I had time to see that it contained the breath cachous.

"I've had some of those," I chirruped. "They don't taste very nice."

George whirled round to look at me and then whirled back on Len. I thought he'd shake the poor boy's head off.

"You little basket," he said. "You dirty little basket."

Len's voice was all wobbly from the shaking. "Washn' me," he kept saying.

"It wasn't him," I agreed indignantly. "I got them myself from his drawer."

"How did you know they were there?"

"Saw them."

"Why did you take them?"

"I had had occasion to resort to a drop of beer and I did not want the fact apparent upon my breath."

"What did you think they'd do for you?"

"Well, they're breath cachous, aren't they? Isn't that why Len takes them, so no one will know he's been boozing?"

George seemed to sigh with relief and then turned back to Len again.

"Shnot me," Len slobbered. "Honest ta God, George, shnot me—I owe my preshent shtate entirely to worry— worry and relief—I was *sho* pleased to see the pair of you come in—sho pleased to see the *pair* of you—"

With that he passed straight out. George stood looking at him a second or two, then humped him over his shoulder. "I'll be back for you," he said to me, over Len's lolloping head.

I snatched up Sandy on to my lap and cuddled him into my tummy. I was feeling most unlike myself.

George was quite a time. He must have undressed Len and put him to bed.

When he came into the living-room again he closed the door behind him and lit a cigarette.

He looked up at me when he was lighting it. "Collins Wood again?" he asked.

I shook my head. "If you really want to know—I've been to The Red Lion, The King's Arms, The Black Swan and The Case Is Altered."

He opened his mouth and shut it, and then I could practically hear him telling himself to play it cool. "Did Len take you there?"

"Len! Of course not. You did."

That had him flummoxed. That really did it. George wasn't easily thrown, either. "And when they closed," I told him, "we paid a little visit to Harrowvane—*and*," I added primly, "I don't know whether we had anything more to drink there—but we were certainly rather a long time."

His tongue licked his lips. He said, "Wynne—did Len see me at any of these places and pass it on? Is that how you know?"

"Len had nothing to do with it," I snapped. "I was taken for a little ride—by *you*." And I told him exactly what had happened. I'd never have dared if I had not felt so odd. But I was feeling odder and odder. George didn't explode as I thought he would. In a way he seemed very relieved. As for me, I prattled on. It seemed as if I just couldn't stop talking. "She dropped her handkerchief," I said, taking it out of my pocket and handing it to him. "I brought it back because I thought Mr. Wells or one of the men might find it and take the micky out of you. But it made a nice change from Jenny's smell."

George took it and put it in his pocket. "Thanks." He never asked me to keep my Leonie discovery to myself or anything. He knew I'd never tell the others a thing about him.

"You must've taken the car keys."

"That's right," I agreed.

His cigarette had gone out. He lit it again. "May I ask why, Wynne?"

"Sure. I was searching the back of the van for clues."

"Clues? To Leonie?"

"No. She came as a surprise to me. For bits of burnt sweater. I thought you might have dug it up and tried to burn it again."

"Oh God," he said softly. "You still think I'm the strangler!"

"Not really," I said politely. "But if you were I shouldn't blame you. You'd be out of your mind, as you pointed out yourself."

"You took an awful risk," he said. "Not only of being strangled, but *crushed*. I was thinking of taking a sink unit out to the barn conversion job tonight. I might have walloped it down on top of you."

"That wasn't all I was afraid might wallop down on top of me!" I replied tartly.

He was chewing the sides of his smile like he did when the twins really got going on Aunt Rene Tindall. "You'd better have something to eat."

"I'm not hungry."

"Well, you'd better go to bed."

"I'm not tired. And what's more, it isn't because you were a father to me."

He looked puzzled. "What isn't?"

"The way I feel about you, like Mum told the police. It's the perfectly normal reaction of a full-blooded female to a full-blooded male."

George said, "Oh!" He pressed his lips very hard together and then covered them with his hand.

"I should like to take this opportunity of telling you," I said, "that at the moment your peccadillos don't alarm me. When I'm older I'll have a chance to combat them, in a normal female manner."

George sat down. His face crumpled up in astonishment. "Where on earth did you get hold of a word like peccadillo?"

"Grandad's crossword. Hélène thought it was a bird. And Mother thought it was something you took to make you sick. But it isn't. It means committing little sins, which could certainly apply to *some* of us sitting not too far off from me."

"Wynne," George told me, "you're over-tired, and those things you took weren't breath cachous. They were—er—some things the doctor gave Len and they could have made you a bit—over-excited. I'm going to make you some hot milk and push you off to bed."

At that time I didn't know that Len took purple hearts and that that was what I had taken. Nobody knew except George, and he was trying to get Len off them by threatening to expose him to Hélène. Len couldn't bear her to know anything bad about him. It was the best tactic George could have tried.

He went into the kitchen and put on some milk to boil. We had a little glass disc to go in the bottom of the saucepan to stop the milk overboiling. Mother was sick to death of the stove getting mucked up. George didn't need the glass thing. He was careful.

I ballet-danced into the kitchen after him. My nightgown was rather fabulous. Hélène had given it to me for Christmas. Fortunately it was lined, so I didn't show any of me.

Aunt Rene Tindall always used to call anything below a man's waist his "rude parts." A woman had two lots of "rude parts"—above and below the waist. It used to make me mad. It seemed an insult to the human body.

I put my arms round George's waist and my cheek against his back.

"Juliet was only fourteen, might I remind you, Romeo Meakham."

"Yes, and didn't get past it, might I remind you, Juliet Kinch. Pack it up, Wynne, and get me the Ovaltine."

"I think I'd rather have gin."

"Get the Ovaltine."

I got it and put it roguishly behind my back when he held out his hand for it.

He managed to grab it from me and make the Ovaltine. Then he knocked me up a Marmite sandwich, plonked me on a chair, and fed me like you do a baby. You know, "One mouthful for God, one for Mum, one for Dad—" It must have been about half-past four in the morning.

I had the sandwich but wouldn't touch the Ovaltine. He was wonderfully patient. Only when I tried to wriggle on his knee did he snap, "Bit free with a strangler, aren't you?"

I wagged my finger in his face. "Ah! I haven't made up my mind yet. But you know something about it. Oh, there's something *very*, very fishy about you and that strangler—is it Mr. Wells?"

"Yes. Now get to bed."

"That means it isn't you, then—ha! ha! Gave ourselves away then, didn't we?"

"Mr. Wells and I take it in turns to do the strangling. Get to bed."

"I think I'll come in with you tonight."

"You'll do nothing of the ruddy sort. You're a big girl now—you'll go in your own bed. Under it or on it, I don't give a damn, but you'll go to your own."

"Oh! I don't mean for peccadillo purposes. You'd go to prison. I'm under age. But there's an awful lot I've got to say to you, many, many things. I want to *declare* myself to you."

He fairly frog-marched me down the passage. He snapped on the light in our bedroom, jerked me through the door to Hélène and appealed to her quite desperately. "For God's sake sit on it, or something. It's high."

Hélène had shot up in bed when the light went on, and George closed the door as if the cops were after him. "For crying out loud!" said Hélène. "Wher*ever* did you go this evening?"

"To The Red Lion, The King's Arms—and—The Case Is Altered."

"Good heavens! No wonder you're sloshed, you poor baby! Did Len take you?" she asked in a horrified voice.

"No, no, everybody blames Len—it wasn't him, poor blameless lad."

But I wasn't going to give George away. I was far too cunning for that.

"I'm not without admirers, you know," I told her. "You wouldn't think I was attractive, but some people would."

"You're darned right they would, and that's when you want to look out, at your age."

She got out of bed and shepherded me into mine. "Now, look, get to sleep, honey, and give us a break. We really can't take any more."

Lying down immediately, I pretended to fall straight off to sleep. But as soon as I heard Hélène breathing heavily I sneaked out of bed, felt for my old red dressing-gown behind the door, and slipped out of the room.

I snapped on the light in George's room, just as he had done to Hélène in ours. He wriggled on to his elbow, blinking in the light.

"For the love of Chri—get back to your room at once."

Poor old Len was flat on his back, his mouth gaping open and Sandy asleep on his chest in a little orange mountain.

George sprang out of bed. He was wearing his light blue pyjamas.

"There are some things I have to discuss with you," I explained.

"Tomorrow," he said, and propelled me sharply to the door.

Len was always a good one for noises in his sleep. He let out a terrible, wobbly, ghostly howl right down poor old Sandy's ear. Sandy never was a pussy for the bogies, even in the daytime. He jumped at his own shadow and he was terrified of Grandad's mice.

He might have been catapulted off Len's chest. He shot through the door with his tail like a flue-brush, and tripped up Mum as she came running down the passage to see what was the matter.

"Oh, Sandy cat!" she burst out. "You'll be the death of someone some day."

George shoved me behind him and I clung happily to him. He put his head round the door. "It's all right, Mum, just Len with one of his nightmares."

"Does he want a phenobarb?"

"He's had enough pills," said George firmly. "Pop back to bed and try and get some rest, Mother."

"It's not a very restful household," Mum said plaintively. "And that cat'll have somebody over some day."

But she went quietly back to bed.

"Now," said George, turning me round, "I've had about enough of you tonight to last me a flipping lifetime."

"I want to *talk* to you," I pleaded. "You've been avoiding me for *years*."

"Showed good sense then, didn't I?" he said with feeling. "Look, Wynne, those pills you took are quite strong and they've had an effect on you. You aren't yourself."

Len gave another long, shuddering howl.

George pleaded with me. "Wynne, I don't want that boy woken up. We'll have a hell of a time with him if he doesn't sleep it off."

"Then don't wake him," I advised sensibly.

Hélène had heard the howl and found me missing. She came running in without a dressing-gown.

She went straight up to Len's bed and knelt beside it. She looked wildly round at George and me. "What's the matter? Is he ill?"

"*He's* fine!" George said wearily. "*He's* asleep."

Hélène got up. "Look," George begged her, "take Wynne back, will you?"

Hélène stroked Len's forehead. "He'll feel like hell tomorrow, poor lamb. Come on, Puss Bun," she yawned at me.

"I want to talk to George," I said.

"It's late, honey. Talk tomorrow."

"Tomorrow never comes."

"What do you mean it never comes?" snapped George. "It's here already."

All my gaiety suddenly fizzed away like those Alka-Seltzers that George took some mornings. I sat on his bed and howled. Hélène put her hands on my shoulders but I shook them off. George tried to pull me up, but I squirmed away from him and lay taut across his bed.

"You can't sleep with George, honey," Hélène cooed, a little shocked. "You're too old now."

"I don't want to *sleep* with him," I wailed. "I want to *talk* to him."

"Oh my God!" groaned George, and turned round in a circle slapping his forehead. I set up my howling again. George and Hélène consulted each other's eyes.

"It's a rotten shame," said Hélène, "whoever got her tight."

George didn't say it was the pills. I suppose he didn't want to give Len away. He just agreed, "She's certainly good and high."

"There's only one thing to do," said Hélène. "Put her in Len's place—then she can prattle the rest of the night."

"*Thanks!*" George exploded. "Thanks a *lot!*"

"Oh, she'll drop off herself soon—she's flat out on her feet as it is. We can't have her waking Mum up again."

Hélène pulled the bedclothes off the still-stupefied Len. "You take his top and I'll take his feet—I'll have him in with me."

As if he was too exhausted to resist any more, George put his hands under Len's shoulders and humped him off the bed. Hélène took his feet and they carried him, sagging between them, across the hall to our bedroom.

I gave a whoop of victory joy, skipped ahead of him, and started directing the traffic.

Grandad came out of his room just as they were negotiating the rather difficult turn into our bedroom. "What the *'ell* is going—?" He broke off to point at the practically unconscious form of Len swinging between them. "Whatsa matter with 'im?"

"Nothing. He's going into Wynne's bed."

"Why?"

"Because she's going into his."

"Belt up, oldster!" I said amiably.

Grandad turned to me with his mouth open.

"She's a bit goofy tonight," George mumbled.

"Have you let her get at the bottle again?"

Len gave out another of his dreadful howls. Grandad leapt inches into the air and Hélène let go of Len's legs. His heels made quite a thud hitting the carpet. George scooped him up over his shoulder and dumped him on my bed in our room.

Hélène asked, "Grandad, can I have a pair of your ear bungs so poor George can get some sleep?"

"Ear bungs! You want a wooden 'ead to keep out the sound of this lot, and what's so special about George getting any sleep?"

Hélène slipped past him into his room. Grandad went to bed with wax ear muffles every night, so as not to hear Len's pop records.

Mother came out. "Grandad, whatever *is* going on—we've got the neighbours roused. I can hear them moving about."

Grandad pointed at Len reclining on my bed through the open doorway, and then jerked his thumb at each of us in turn. "*He's* going in with *'er,* and *she's* going in with *'im.*"

"Whatever for?" poor Mother wanted to know.

"Wynne wants to talk to George," Hélène explained, and handed George the ear muffles.

"Can't she do that in the morning?" Mother asked.

"We have *tried*," George said wearily, and gave me quite a hard cuff. "Come on, get a move on if you're coming with me."

"George!" squeaked Mother. "She's too old for that. Oh, Grandad, it isn't nice."

"Oh, do stop fussing, Mother," Hélène said crossly. "There's nothing to worry about. Wynne's pissed to the eyeballs, that's all, and so is Len."

Mother gave a little horrified yelp and Grandad put the flat of his hand against her and pushed her along to her room. "Look, let them get *on* with it. Let them get *on* with it. If the neighbours call the police, so much the better. The sooner the whole lot end up in cells the sooner we'll get to sleep."

Back in his room, George pointed at Len's rumpled bed. "All right," he told me sternly. "In there."

I suppose he was scared I might try to get in with him. I saw him busily softening up the wax ear muffles between his hands. He was going to cut out the sound of my voice just as soon as he could. Then he jumped into bed, walloped the clothes over him and snapped off the bedside lamp before I had got my dressing-gown off.

He needn't have bothered with the ear muffles. I was suddenly so exhausted I couldn't have gone on talking if he'd been patting my hand and begging me to speak to him.

For a few minutes he said "Yes" and "No" and "Go to sleep" at intervals, in case I was still prattling. Then it got down to "Mm," but I think I was asleep before him.

*18* ❧ We were a real sorry lot the next morning. I felt dreadful over my performance. I simply couldn't look at George. At least, not when he was looking at me. His eyes were all swollen and puffed-up and his voice was hoarse. His breakfast was just Alka-Seltzers and coffee.

Len couldn't get up at all. He was lying in bed with some ice on his head and a chamber-pot in the crook of his arm.

Sandy had spent the night under the kitchen dresser and wouldn't come out.

Poor Mother was really ill and Grandad made her stay in bed, and it seemed that he never once stopped saying that I ought to have the hide tanned off me.

Hélène had little cotton wool pads soaked in witch hazel strapped under her eyes with band-aids. She was going to read her part and she was convinced she looked older than God's aunty.

Grandad smelt violently of embrocation, which he always rubbed into his knee when it was extra bad. His temper was awful. He said to George, "For God's sake get this lot out of the house today. Take them into the country. Take them to the sea. Take 'em anywhere to give your mother a bit of peace and quiet."

"I'm too weak to contemplate such horrors," said George.

"Then I'll contemplate it for you. Wynne! Nellie! Pack up some sandwiches."

"Len's not well enough to go," Hélène protested. "And I can't come—I've got an audition. The producer's coming into town specially for it.

"Then you can take yourself off to see friends after it. If there's one thing I've made up me mind to it's that your

mother's getting the house to herself today. I'll take her a
bite of lunch in bed. As for you, George lad," he said when
he thought Hélène and I were out of earshot, "a nice exam-
ple you are, coming in at all hours reeking of beer and
whores."

"I'm out of nappies, Grandad, and my girl-friends aren't
whores."

"You owe it to your mother to get her some rest. Up half
the night larking about changing beds. The least you can do
is to get the lot of them out of her way and keep them out
of it as long as you can."

"Have a heart, Grandad! The roads are hell at this time
of year—no one but fools try to get to the sea."

"Then take 'em to Sleydon."

"Sleydon! At a holiday time!"

"Take 'em *somewhere*," Grandad shouted, and he
sounded really tough.

"Len's not fit enough. He'll only be sick," argued George.

"'e'll revive in fresh air." There was a ring at the bell. "If
that's Rene Tindall—" Grandad began.

"No," breathed George. "Oh no—because that would
prove there wasn't a God."

I went to the door. It was Corinne. She was agog with
excitement, dying to hear all about it. "I guessed it was
David again," she whispered, "when your mum rang up and
thought you were with us. What time did you get in?"

"Half-past two in the morning."

"You never! Wasn't everyone mad?"

"Everyone still is."

She was wearing a bright orange sheath dress that shone
like poster paint, and her hair was caught into a pony tail.
She wore lace stockings and little patent shoes with baby
heels and sling-backs. She'd been to Mass, which was more
than I had. She'd got foundation cream on her lips and a
suggestion of some kind of sparkly eye-shadow on her lids.

She tripped into the kitchen. "Good morning, Mr. Meakham," she said sexily.

George looked at her dress, took a pull at his coffee, and winced.

"Corinne, lass," said Grandad firmly, "I'm afraid it's not very convenient to visit this morning. We've all had a rather poor night."

Corinne was throwing her bit of figure out at George, but he had his eyes closed, drinking his coffee.

She'd have been bonkers over George if I'd let her, although she knew that would be the end of our friendship.

"Get the sandwiches, Wynne," ordered Grandad.

"There's nothing to make them from."

"There's bully-beef. It kept better than you going in the First World War."

"Are you going on a picnic?" Corinne asked.

"Yes," said Grandad.

"No," said George.

"Can I come too?"

"No," said George.

"Yes," said Grandad.

"Goody-goody," clapped Corinne. "I'll help with the sandwiches."

She pulled open the fridge. "Gosh, you haven't got nearly as much as we have—is cold stew nice in sandwiches, Mr. Meakham?"

George shuddered. "Get in the fridge and shut the door behind you, will you, Corinne?"

She gave the tinkling laugh which always got people looking at her because it was so noisy and which she thought was because it was so attractive. I suppose I'm being bitchy about poor Corinne, which is twice the sin the way things are—but there is no good kidding yourself about people and she really was dreadful that day.

She was also absolutely determined that George was going to take more notice of her than of me. She sat at the table in the dinette end and fairly ramming her little knees at George.

The bread wasn't right for sandwiches. It crumbled and the butter wouldn't spread. Corinne hissed at me, "They can't be all that wild at you if they take you for a picnic. Did they *know* you were out with David?"

Before I could answer Len groaned.

"Grandad," Mother called weakly, "is our Len all right?"

"I 'ope not," Grandad shouted back.

Corinne skipped into the passage and saw Len through the open door of Hélène's and my room.

"What's Len doing in your bed?"

Again before I could answer, the doorbell rang once more. Corinne darted to open it.

Aunt Rene Tindall stood there. Her flat was in a neighbouring block, but she'd popped out without a coat, pink with excitement. "Milkman says you'd police half the night!"

Oh, those neighbours of ours! They say you could die in a flat and no one would notice, but our block was worse than a tiny village. You couldn't *live* without them knowing absolutely everything about it.

George sat in front of his empty coffee cup. "Aunty," he said, "I've just seen the light. There is *no* God."

Aunt Rene Tindall advanced upon him. "You'd do better, George Meakham, to keep an eye on your kith and kin than sit and blaspheme on the Lord."

You wouldn't think they'd make them these days, would you? Aunt Rene Tindalls, I mean. You'd have thought they'd have died out when the dodo was still a fledgling, but it's surprising how many are left. George had a theory that they still get born just to keep the numbers up.

"Well?" she snapped. "Everyone lost their tongues?"

Corinne's little black eyes were popping in between us like a puppy that sees biscuits in different people's hands. She loved anything wrong between everybody, or a scene or a row. You could almost hear her blood boil with excitement.

George's sleepy eyes really did look insolent, peering at Aunt Rene Tindall. He'd taken off his glasses so as not to see her too well.

"Wynne got lost," he told her flatly.

"'ow?"

"By losing herself."

"Where's Lucy?"

"In bed and not to be disturbed," said Grandad. "George, that van of yours can hold a lot. You'll have room enough on the picnic for your aunt Rene Tindall."

George's hand clasped and unclasped itself over the handle of the bread-knife. "Grandad," he said. "Any regard I ever had for you is slowly dying."

Grandad cackled happily. "Your aunt Rene loves a picnic —but if I recall rightly, ants, wasps, and other picnickers always make a set at her and the wounds always turn nasty."

George picked up the bread-knife and threw it like a dart past Grandad, under the sink where we kept the sani-bin.

"Next time I throw it," he threatened, "it'll skewer every mouse you've ever bred." But he was smiling in spite of himself. Grandad looked so determined.

"Hard-boiled eggs, Corinne girl," Grandad ordered gleefully. "Get going on hard-boiled eggs. Mrs. Tindall can't resist one of them, for all they 'come back on her' all the afternoon."

Mother appeared in the doorway. "Oh, Rene!" she said, defeated, and then, even more depressed, "Hello, Corinne dear."

"Rene and young Corinne are just off on day's outing with George," Grandad reported happily. "So get back, 'ave a bit of a sleep, and I'll wake you up with a bite of lunch at one. Better start getting Len up, 'adn't you, George?"

Aunt Rene Tindall turned on Mother. "See what church abstinence does for you, Lucy? You and your family practically godless and Wynne in the arms of Rome! No wonder she stays out all night. No *wonder!* Where was she, I'd like to know?"

"So would we," breathed Grandad, "so would we. But George here is keeping that bit of news to himself."

He pushed a glass of milk into Mother's hand and eased her on to a stool. "If you won't lie down, Lucy, sit."

It seemed funny in a way that Grandad was so much fonder of a daughter-in-law than he ever was of the son whom she married, or his second son, my father.

George asked him about it once, and Grandad had answered, "Albert was always a mean-minded bugger. Lucy was worth ten of him, and John went off so I never knew him that well. Why shouldn't I like Lucy best? She's all I've got."

Aunt Rene Tindall plonked herself opposite Mother. "Where *was* Wynne?"

"She wasn't *that* late, Rene," Mother hedged. "I mean, not how you look at it nowadays."

Len weaved into the kitchen, clutching his head. "Blood!" he said. "Ber-loody hell and blood!"

Aunt Rene Tindall sprang up. "I'll not stay here another minute and listen to language like that!"

George sprang up and opened the kitchen door for her.

"George!" said Mother, shocked.

"Why," Len demanded dramatically, "why did I wake up in Wynne's bed?"

"Because you were too drunk to get into your own," snapped Grandad.

"That's not fair," said Hélène, who was just passing on her way from the bathroom. "He *was* in his own, and we dragged him out of it and put him into Wynne's. He was unconscious, poor lamb, he didn't know."

"Where did Wynne go?" Aunt Rene asked.

"She wanted to sleep with George," Hélène explained, and carried on into our bedroom.

"Sleep wi' *George!*" Aunt Rene exploded.

"*Talk* to him, Rene," Mother said fussily. "She wanted to talk to him all night. He had to borrow some of Grandad's ear bungs."

The eggs Corinne had put on to boil were bobbing about in the saucepan, sounding like a waterfall rushing on to hard pebbles.

She moved so close to me she almost lay on me. "Thought it was *David* you were out with last night!"

"George *is* David," I told her stupidly. I never really thought what I was saying. I could never have believed how you'd suffer for not thinking what you were saying, in the way that I was going to.

"You mean a great big girl like Wynne slept in with *George?*"

"Only to talk to him," Mother insisted.

"Well, all I can say—"

"We'll spare you the trouble, Aunt Rene," George told her.

"Whatever are those eggs dancing about for?" Mother wanted to know.

"They're off on a picnic," Grandad reminded her.

"Off to church would be best," Aunt Rene answered. "I can't think how you can let them be so godless, Lucy."

Grandad propelled Mother towards the door. "I've said she was poorly, Rene. She needs no interference from anyone."

"She'll get it from Watch Committee if you ask me," said Aunt Rene. "Letting a big girl like Wynne go in with George."

"We didn't ask you anything," said Grandad. "Not even to visit us so early in the morning, or to stay now you 'ave."

"*Very* well," snorted Aunt Rene. "I can take a hint as well as the next person—and I know when I'm not wanted."

"Oh Grandad!" said Mother reproachfully. "He didn't mean it like that."

"Yes he did," said Grandad cheerfully, and got Mother out of the room.

Aunt Rene left, slamming the door, but not before saying that if I'd been *her* daughter and George had been *her* son, *she* wouldn't have given countenance to such blatant sinfulness; and I think she also added something about it being the likes of us that brought down the walls of Jericho.

Corinne was looking at me as if I was wearing a diamond tiara. Her little black eyes were on fire with a greedy sort of mixture of excitement and curiosity.

When the door went behind Aunt Rene, George said to Grandad, "I nearly forgive you everything for that."

Len sat down and gulped black coffee, but Grandad wouldn't let him sit long. He meant what he said all right, about wanting Mum to have the place to herself for a bit. He didn't rest until he'd got us all on the road to Sleydon in George's van.

We certainly weren't the only ones off to Sleydon. Half Dalstead seemed to have the same idea, and George grumbled the whole way about other drivers.

Len sat beside him clutching his head and moaning, "God, I hate Grandad. I'll let all his mice out—I'll put the wrong buck in with the wrong does or whatever they are. I'll get all his self-coloured things muddled up with whatever they are."

"I'll help you drown yourself if we ever get to Sleydon," George promised him.

Sleydon was a pretty place. There was a lake with nice sandy shores and trees right down to the water. But all you could see of it was the winking of the sunlight on different-coloured cars.

I don't remember much about Sleydon that day. I was too taken up with the way Corinne behaved. She was really at her daftest and it made me simply mad. The way she flirted with George was absolutely absurd, and what was worse he seemed to like it. He laughed at all her scatty jokes and he didn't tick her off, however far she went. Like I said, he seemed to enjoy watching her make a spectacle of herself, and she certainly did that. She lay about as if she was one of those starlets you see trying to catch a producer's eye at a film festival. She was on her back with one of her legs over a knee, and her padded brassiere pulled so tight that her own little figure couldn't fill up the space and the padding made popping sounds as she moved.

I know I shouldn't be talking like this, but I was so wild with her that day I still get annoyed in my mind—just the same as I did at the police station later. That's one of the things I feel most miserable about. It hurts nearly more than anything. But it's too late now to stop it. I should have done it then. I shouldn't have let myself get jealous of her, then I wouldn't be left with angry memories.

I suppose we both tried to make each other jealous that day.

I knew that Corinne couldn't bear the drama I'd been the centre of; me missing until the early hours of the morning, Mother ringing the police, all the neighbours talking, and no one except George and me really knowing where I'd been.

She was boggling with all that talk about me sleeping in with George. She was dying to hear every detail, but she was so furious that it wasn't her that had been the centre of attention that she was determined to make George take more notice of her than of me.

I don't know why he did. Usually he hadn't two good words to put together about her, but that day he seemed to find it a relief to kid her along and make a fuss of her. Maybe he was embarrassed with me because of the night before and Leonie. Or maybe he was just fed up and found her a counter-irritant.

She was blessed if she was going to ask me any questions about that night. I hadn't even confided in her, and that, on top of my being mixed up seriously with an attractive man while she was still only clicking with second-year teen-agers or fantasy lovers, set her dead on showing no interest in me and my carryings-on.

It set me dead on convincing her I'd had a real old romp with George.

Sometimes I feel like jabbing my fingers in my ears to shut out those lies I told, but it only boxes them up in your head and you can't get away from them at all then.

When George took Len off for a hair of the dog and told Corinne and me to get the picnic ready, "such as it was," she whipped out her mirror and smeared some more founda-tion cream over her lips.

It was difficult to tell her anything, since she wasn't going to ask anything. But I had to lead into the subject somehow, and I chose the daftest way in the world.

I had put out the sandwiches and blew an ant off them. "I hope George doesn't go to prison over last night. After all, I'm under age."

I must say Corry was absolutely marvellous. Not "Did you really sleep with him?"—"What was it like?" Not any of the questions I knew she was dying to ask.

She was fiddling with her stringy little bits of hair.

"Couldn't get into much trouble," she said, "if you didn't have any sex with him—"

I sent her a glance of pure hatred. "I wouldn't say that," I hedged.

"Your family kept on about you only *talking* to him."

"Well, what else did you think they'd keep on about? They didn't want Aunt Rene Tindall thinking the worst!"

Corry didn't answer. It was like ringing up someone on the telephone and saying cheerily, "Hello, this is me!" and then just hearing the other person say, "Yes?"

"We didn't get in till half-past two," I told Corinne.

"You said that once already." She yawned into her mirror and then turned it into an inspection of her teeth.

I knew I was doing the wrong thing and being undignified

and silly, but I hammered away at it. "He took me to The Red Lion, The King's Arms, The Black Swan and The Case Is Altered."

Corinne nipped out a tissue and took some foundation cream off her top teeth. "*That's* the only thing he could go to prison for," she sneered at me. "You've got to be *sixteen* to go in a pub and *eighteen* to have a proper drink in it. I should know. Frank once tried to take me in and we got a right old spiel from the landlord. If George took you into a public house he's a nit."

"He didn't," I admitted quickly. "I had my beer in the back of the van."

"I can see it," Corinne answered. "George taking his baby sister beer from a pub. He'd more likely feed you strained carrots."

She was so pleased with herself, and so cocksure that nothing had happened, I could have murdered her. Well, I did really, didn't I? In spite of what Father Murphy says. She wouldn't be dead if it wasn't for me, no matter how much they tell you you can't trace fate in little steps and blame yourself for the path it took. I pushed her on her path and tripped her up on it. Father Murphy says that it's sometimes as bad to have too much conscience as to have too little. He says the over-developed kind can become anything from self-pity and self-indulgence to a masked desire for praise and approval.

Well, I'm not clever enough and I'm still too shocked to take in all that. All I feel is that my best friend, however much I disliked her, would be alive today if it wasn't for me, and what's more I miss her. You can be very fond of people without liking them.

Let the psychiatrise and religiousise themselves round that!

At Sleydon, that day, I must have gone bonkers. Usually I was so careful of George's "good name," as Mum, Grandad, and Aunt Rene Tindall would have put it, and yet here I was trying to convince Corinne that he was taking an unhealthy interest in me. Me of all people, and to Corinne of all people! I knew what a mixer she was, and I knew she was not capable of keeping a secret to herself. I also knew what her mother was like, and yet I went on and on and on about it. I felt compelled to convince her that George was my lover.

I became Leonie when I spoke of George and myself. I was Leonie in the front of the van and not me in the back.

"We've got a friend with a flat in Harrowvane," I told Corinne. "She lets us borrow it to meet without the family knowing. It's not so much sex between us. You're right about that. It's more real love. We're going to get married when I'm sixteen. George says he won't find it difficult to be faithful to me between then and now, because he doesn't want anyone but me. But we've got to wait because of the law."

Corinne was beginning to listen to me without making monkey faces to prove she wasn't.

"This friend of ours is lovely," I said. "And she quite understands. She's for us all the way. Sometimes I wonder why George goes for me and not for her. She's got everything. She's marvellous to look at and she mixes with top people. She's got plenty of money—you can tell by her voice there's no one she doesn't know. All our circle, that's hers and mine and George's—they're chiefly her friends, of course—sort of top people—but they've become mine and George's, they know all about us. They know we're in a difficult position and they're helping us to wait. It isn't easy waiting, but they're helping us to wait." I liked that bit so much I repeated it: "They're helping us to wait."

I went off into a thing that held poor old Corry spellbound. "You see, we have to be secretive, Corry. It's George that I meet at Collins Wood."

"What about the time he caught us whistling up Clare's ghost? He didn't look as if he was expecting you then."

"Oh," I laughed, "all those things were just a blind. I made that an excuse so it wouldn't look bad if I was ever caught going to Collins Wood. I could tell Mum that you and I went there. Just a couple of foolish kids."

"Thanks," said Corry, and I ought to have seen the danger in her eyes, but I was in the middle of my romance with George and I missed it.

"We're not going abroad for our honeymoon," I told her. "I expect when it finally does happen we shall hardly be able to believe it—you know, when you've been waiting so long. We're just going to hurry off to our own home and stay in it."

"Where's that?" she snapped.

"In the Lakes. It's terribly isolated, but what do we care?"

Corry was slowly opening up the cushioned end of a Kirby grip between her teeth. She pinned back a piece of hair, staring at me. She was beginning to believe me—I knew my Corry.

I laughed, "Thank goodness my old dutch is a joiner. He fixed the place up himself. It was just an old derelict cottage —right on a mountainside. But it's fabulous now—pine panels and stone fireplaces and—well, we haven't got electricity, just oil lamps, but we don't mind those. We're miles and miles from anywhere—but like I said, why should we care? We only need each other, you see. George's mates pull his leg about it—oh yes, most of them know. You can't hide a thing like that. They laugh when I have to stay outside a pub and have a bitter lemon because I'm too young to go in with George."

That used to happen when I was a kid. Either George or Grandad brought me a bitter lemon out from a pub.

"He buys me grown-up perfume, though. Smell!" And I held out the sleeve of my jumper to Corry. It was the one I had worn in the back of the van and it still smelt of Leonie's Sortilège. Corinne sniffed and eyed me narrowly. "It's real French stuff," I told her, and then I went rattling on again. I wondered afterwards if I hadn't properly got over my purple hearts. I certainly felt that I couldn't stop talking again. "George's mates say, 'It's just as well the future Mrs. Meakham isn't a booze pot!'" I laughed like George's mates were supposed to, and added, "You'd love our little cottage. You can hear the wind fairly bumping about outside and we can have a whole log on the fireplace. George is going to retire and live on the pension from his Korea wound. That's so he can be with me all the time, you see. He says he's very greedy for my company."

Corinne was about to say something. What it was I shall never know, but George and Len came back and stopped her.

George's hair of the dog had done him good, but Len's had made him gloomy. He couldn't come out from his sunglasses and he called George ruddy hearty. George grinned and chivvied Corinne and me about not getting the picnic ready.

"What have you been doing?" he asked. "Visiting a rival pub?"

"Oh no, Mr. Meakham," said Corinne sweetly. "We're not allowed to do that, are we? It's illegal at our age, isn't it?"

"I'm glad you're so law-abiding," George told her. But I shot her a frightened look. Was she going to mix things for me, to pay me out for trying to put one over on her? Corry would do anything if she was in the mood.

I unpacked the picnic nervously. It was certainly none too nice.

"How is it," George wanted to know, "that all English sandwiches taste of sand on a picnic, even if you're nowhere near a beach?"

"Have you always been fond of the Lakes, Mr. Meakham?" Corinne wanted to know.

I felt my face tingle and pushed the packet of sandwiches at her.

"I like anywhere better than Sleydon," George told her. He pushed the packet of sandwiches on to Len. "Think of these as a direct punishment for your outbreak, Len, and you'll never want to break out again!"

Len shuddered and took an apple instead.

"Would you live in the Lakes altogether when you're married, Mr. Meakham?" Corinne wanted to know. I tried to kick her foot and knocked over the thermos of tea instead. It spilt over Len's foot. He got up, fairly leaping about, yelling he was burned to the bone.

"Put it in the water," George advised him.

I leaned across the table and said fiercely to Corinne behind the screen of the picnic-basket lid, "Corry Eldridge, if you don't give over I'll *kill* you."

"Why?" she asked me innocently. "If most of his mates know, why shouldn't I?"

Len pulled off his sock and started blowing on his ankle.

"Apart from anything else," said George, "that means the end of the tea, doesn't it?"

"There's a weeny drop left," I muttered. "But we ought to save some to put on Len's foot when it's cold."

"Well, I hope Grandad's blown himself up in the oven while getting Mother's lunch," said George amiably. "We'll be about twenty-four hours on the road going home."

"It's made a great red mark," grumbled Len. "I'll be all out in blisters tomorrow."

"Try and look upon it as a counter-irritant to the pain in your head," George suggested.

I put some tea in a saucer and blew on it.

"This drop of tea's cold now, Len," I told him. "It's a good way to stop burns blistering." Mother Jennifer taught us first aid at school.

I soaked my handkerchief in the remains of the tea and dabbed Len's ankle with it.

"Would you, Mr. Meakham?" Corinne persisted.

"Would I what?"

"Live up in the Lakes altogether if you ever got married?"

"Why should I live in the Lakes at all?"

"Oh!" Corinne acted taken aback. "I thought Wynne told me—" She clapped her hand over her mouth and looked helplessly at me. "Sorry, Wynne, have I said something?" My heart was hammering with agitation.

George lay back and put a newspaper over his face. "If any of you drown in the Sleydon lake, don't call me, please."

Corinne may not have been doing it just to spite me. It might just have been her way of finding out if there was anything true in the tale I told her. She went and stretched beside him. She did. She'd got the devil's nerve. She was touching him all along his leg and she saw that her hair fell across his arm. When she leant over him she managed to touch him with her bit of figure. I couldn't believe my eyes. Even Len took off his sun-glasses to goggle at her.

She was like a sexy star in an Italian film. Except of course that you don't have to work so hard to have someone aware of a full-grown bosom. Corinne was practically lying along George.

"I wouldn't like Wynne to go too far away," she said. "Couldn't you take a flat in Harrowvane? I mean, if you've got friends they could find you one."

I went blood red right over my face and neck.

George suddenly shot the newspaper off his face and sat up. He dusted Corry off him as if she'd been some kind of insect. He said, "I've had enough of this picnic. We're going home."

He didn't even look at me as he went off to the car. I sat there absolutely horrified. He'd be sure I'd told Corry all about the evening before, about him and Leonie and everything. He'd think I'd told Corinne his private business —a thing he trusted me not to do.

Yet how could I possibly tell him the absurd tale I'd strung her along with? About us and our cottage and the "future little Mrs. Meakham."

My face began to sting again and I felt tears in my eyes. But I decided that *how* I told him didn't matter—the great thing was to tell him. Anything was better than letting him think I'd given away his secrets.

I got up and scampered after him.

He was lighting a cigarette at the wheel of the car. "George," I gulped out, "I didn't tell her anything—I promise I didn't—"

"Then how did she hit on Harrowvane?"

"I told her—it was daft, I know, but she made me so mad flinging herself at you like that I tried to make her jealous. I told her that—that we were going to get married when I'm sixteen and live in the Lake District."

He must have taken pity on my steaming hot face and my painful embarrassment. He turned and looked rather kindly at me. "That still doesn't account for Harrowvane."

"I said we'd got a friend with a flat who let us meet there sometimes. I never mentioned Leonie or let Corry get any ideas about her and you. I promise, George, really promise—"

"Okay," he said. "I believe you. But you didn't let her think there was anything between you and me, did you, Wynne? That mother of hers is pretty neurotic. It wouldn't be too good for her to get the wrong ideas about us."

I was finding it hard to keep the tears back. I felt I could choke from embarrassment. "I told Corry we were waiting until I was sixteen. I said there wasn't any sex between us— but I did tell her you were in love with me."

I thought, "I'm not going to wait for the earth to swallow me up. I'm going to dig a hole and sink down it."

George's hand caught hold of my chin. "Bit of a nit, aren't you?"

I nodded, trying to keep the tears in. "I'm terribly, terribly sorry, George. I'll go back and say it's all lies."

"Well, just say the Lakeland dwelling's fallen through and we've got to hang on a bit longer, and then get that pathetic little mini-tart into the car. I'm obsessed with the desire to return her to her doting mum."

*19* ❧ LEN WAS BATHING HIS FOOT in the Sleydon lake again when I ran back. Corry was lying with her skirt right up to the elastic in her briefs. Her dress was pulled off her shoulders and she was holding the neck down to get more sun.

She sat up, smiled slyly at me and lay down again. "I thought your fiancé looked a bit off about the life you'd planned together."

"Of course he did," I said. "I was having you on."

"You were?"

"I was."

I began to collect up the picnic things. "Len," I called. "We're off."

"What, no cottage in the mountains?" Corry jeered.

"No cottage in the mountains."

"And he's not 'greedy for your company'?"

"No, of course he's not. There couldn't be anything between us at my age."

"What about Lolita?"

"Lolita's a book. Come on, Corry—George wants to get going."

Corinne sat up again. "What about the perfume? The fabulous Sorti—Sorti—"

"—lège. Yes, well, that's not really mine."

"Whose is it, then?"

"A friend's."

"Whose friend's?"

"George's. Len!" I called again.

"Coming, coming, coming!" he called back grumpily.

"The friend who lives in Harrowvane?"

"Yes, well—"

"Oh, so *some* of it's true."

I said patiently, "It's true he's got a friend in Harrowvane —and I got her hanky by mistake. That's why I smell of Sortilège."

"Yeah!"

"Yeah. Now do hurry up, Corry."

She put her head back, her little black eyes snapping. "I think the whole of it's true."

"Don't be daft."

"You slept in his room last night, didn't you?"

"Yes, but—"

"Your own aunty told your mum she thought it was terrible."

"Aunty didn't know what really happened."

"Just as well, you can get into trouble with girls under age."

"George has never laid a finger on me in that way."

"Tell that to the marines!"

"You didn't believe me before," I said angrily, "and now when I admit it's not true you think it is!"

"Your boy-friend—if you can call him a boy—was mad at you for letting it out. You've just had a little conference and he's told you to come back and tell me you were just trying to joke."

"I told *him* I was lying too, Corry."

"He's just the Lolita type. Old and done for and after something too young to know how bad he is! I'll tell *you* something—he's the dirtiest old man out. If we'd been alone this afternoon I'd have had to watch my step!"

I shrieked with explosive laughter and then lost my temper completely. "You're off your rocker! Do you know what he called you just now? A pathetic little mini-tart!"

"He never!"

"He did. He thinks you stink!"

She jumped up and brushed herself down furiously.

Len came limping back. "It'll turn septic and then I'll have to have it amputated, and that'll be the end of my career. Whoever heard of a one-legged pop star?"

"George wants us all in the car," I puffed. Losing my temper always made me out of breath.

"George wants! George wants!" Corinne shrieked. "Who cares what George wants?"

"We do and you'll have to," I told her. "Unless you want to walk all the way home."

"Who says I have to do what Mr. Big-head Meakham wants?" she yelled. "Who says!" And she snatched up her handbag and raced into the woods.

"What's eating her?" demanded Len.

"I shouldn't have told her what George said about her," I replied, and I went running after her. "Corry! Corry! Come back, don't be silly!"

Whether she really got lost or whether it was all done to scare us, I'll never know. I hardly had any conversation with her afterwards and I was too angry with her to have much to do with her again that day. We were over an hour searching for her. We asked everyone we met and at last a lady said she'd seen a little girl answering to her description go off with a man in a green car. She thought it took the main road to Dalstead.

We drove off in that direction. I was crying, George was grim-lipped and Len sat beside George, cursing Corinne.

I was counting out loud in the back of the van to stop myself from thinking what Mrs. Eldridge would say if we got home without Corinne, and of how she'd go for George.

I had reached one hundred and fifty-six when we saw her. She was walking back along the main road towards Sleydon, as jaunty and cocksure as anything in that shrieking orange dress. Her head was thrown back and her hips were swinging, and she was throwing her little figure out at every car that passed.

George pulled across the road and hooted at her. She stopped, tossed her head back, and then stalked on.

George said, "Hop out, Len, and get her in."

Len nipped out of the car and ran after Corinne. He wasn't too gentle swinging her round or lugging her back. He opened the door and fairly shoved her into the back of the van.

She fell up against me and spat at George, "I don't have to go back with people who call me dirty names. You wait till my mother hears the names you called me."

George said, "Shut up!" and put the car in gear again.

"Corinne!" I said. "Whoever did you get a lift with? You shouldn't go off with strangers in cars."

"I didn't like him," she said. "He made passes at me, so I got him to put me down."

"More likely you did the pass-making and *he* put *you* down," Len flung at her. "You'll get what you ask for one of these days!"

And afterwards we found out that Len was right. She'd been so saucy with the gentleman who had given her a lift that he got windy and turned her out on the road.

I knew, of course, that if a man had made a real pass at Corry she'd have been good and scared. She was all bull and show-off. It was talk for the sake of being smart. She wasn't really a "wanton," as Aunt Rene Tindall called her. I know that there are fifteen-year-olds who sleep with boys and are really immoral, but Corry just liked you to think badly of her. It was nice to be able to say that for her afterwards.

George spoke to her without any emotion in his voice, not even crossness. He said, "Corinne, from today I don't want Wynne to see you any more. Please keep away from her."

"Not good enough for your precious bride, I suppose."

"Oh, Corinne!" I said, starting to blush up. "I told you all that was a bunch of lies."

George spoke to Corinne. "One more peep out of you and you'll regret it."

She was silent until we got to Dalstead. But she kept putting her tongue out at me and making faces at me. I took no notice, staring ahead of me. I didn't like to see Corry in those moods. Even though I reminded myself over and over again that it was all her mother's fault for letting her do what she liked, it still made poor Corry seem ugly and horrid. That was what was so unfair, I thought. Most people saw Mrs. Eldridge as a sweet and loving mother and they were sorry for her for having a daughter like Corry.

But after all, if you don't train a puppy and it wets all over the place and bites people, it's your fault and not the puppy's, but it's the puppy people are going to hate and one day someone might hurt it.

I was mad enough at Corry, coming home in the van. She'd mixed things too much for my liking. But even so I hoped George didn't mean that we couldn't see each other again. I'd got so used to Corry, and I should miss her whatever she was like.

"Say you're sorry to George, Corinne," I whispered. "Then maybe things will turn out all right."

She blew a raspberry at the back of George's head.

When we drew up outside her block of flats George said, "Out you get, Corinne."

She got out daintily enough, but she gave the door such a vicious slam that the whole van rattled. Her teeth were clenched in fury.

I don't know how George got out of his seat so quickly, but he managed to catch her as she was belting towards the flats. He marched her back by the collar of her shift dress and jerked her towards the van. He pulled open the door for her and ordered, "Close that door properly."

She squirmed and kicked out at the paintwork. George shifted his grip and caught her by the arm. His lips had

practically disappeared, they were so tightly pressed together. He held her still this time, his fingers closed round
her forearm. He separated his words carefully: "Close—that
—door—properly."

She leant out and closed the door gently.

George said, "Thank you," and released her. She waited
until she was well out of his reach and then set up a fine
old hysterical screaming as she rushed towards her block
of flats. "Mum, Mum! He hurt my arm! He called me rude
names—he made a pass at me and called me rude names—I
had to run off and hide in the woods. Mum, Mum, I'm
frightened of him!"

Windows all up the block of flats opened and heads
popped out. "Oh, George!" I cried, near to hysterics myself.
"Whatever will Mrs. Eldridge say!"

"Mrs. Eldridge," he replied tartly, "is lucky her child is
still alive."

When we got home Mrs. Eldridge was already on the
phone to Mum.

If her day in bed with Grandad's little bite of lunch had
done poor old Mum any good, Mrs. Eldridge's call had certainly put paid to it. She looked white and tired and frightened. Poor Mum so hated scenes and she seemed to get so
many of them. She was frightened of Mrs. Eldridge. But
then she was always put out by a stronger personality or
anyone who shouted.

Mrs. Eldridge was fairly shrieking. She sounded like a
dozen trapped blow-flies caught in the earpiece.

When Mum could get a word in edgeways she said,
". . . had to run off in the woods? But Mrs. Eldridge, that's
daft—Wynne and Len were there."

Len, passing her, said, "Even if we hadn't been there she
wouldn't have had to run away from George."

Mother was too harassed to do anything but ignore him.
"Mrs. Eldridge!" she said. "He couldn't have left a bruise on
her arm—he's not like that. He wouldn't do it."

George said, in passing her, "She was lucky it wasn't round her neck!"

Grandad was in a fine old rage and absolutely mad at George. "Great 'eavens, lad, you can't even take 'em on a picnic without getting your mother bothered to death."

I flew at Grandad. "It wasn't George's fault! It was Corinne's. She ran off and got a lift with some man and we searched for her for hours. He didn't hurt her arm. He just held it to make her close the door properly. It was my fault, I upset her and then she played up."

"She'd have played up in any case," said George. "And it was Grandad who sent her on the picnic."

Mother sat down and burst into tears. "Mrs. Eldridge thinks there's something wrong between you and Wynne, George."

"Well, as there isn't," said Len, "what the hell's it matter what that old bitch thinks."

"Len!" snapped Grandad. "How's that sort of language going to help your mother?"

"It'll be all over the town," poor Mother wailed. "Mrs. Eldridge is such a dreadful gossip."

"If any of it gets to my ears," said George, "I'll sue her for slander, and you can tell her that from me."

"She says she's not going to let Corinne be friendly with Wynne any more because she doesn't think George is safe with young girls. Oh, whatever will the neighbours say!"

"You care too much about the neighbours, Lucy," Grandad scolded her. "There isn't anything wrong between George and Wynne, and that's all that should matter to us— and no one's going to miss young Corinne anyway."

"George got it in about stopping them being friendly first," said Len. "Mrs. Eldridge is shutting the door after the horse has bolted."

It took quite a bit of time to calm Mother down. Hélène was off duty and very depressed because she hadn't got the part she went to read for. I couldn't understand how she kept not getting parts. You'd think any amateur dramatic society would jump at looks like hers. I only hoped that it wasn't because she was a bad actress. That would be so frustrating for her.

After supper she went off with Len to his pop group and George started dandying himself up. I supposed he was off to see Leonie. We weren't catching each other's eye.

Grandad had a mouse ill. He was always at war with wheezing troubles. I did my best to help him, but about ten o'clock the poor little thing died. Grandad parcelled it up to send it off for a post mortem.

Aunt Rene Tindall called, on the excuse that she wanted to see if Mother felt better after her rest, but her twitchy old nose poked into all our bedrooms to see who was sleeping with who!

I'm glad to say Mother was really tough with her. She snapped, "Rene Tindall, if that's the way your mind works you can take it out of my kitchen."

So Aunt Rene went off in a huff twice in one day.

Hélène came in about half-past twelve. When I asked, "Where's our Len?" she said, "Am I my brother's keeper?"

I woke up when Len came in at two, but I didn't hear George, who must have been later.

The next morning Corinne's photograph was on the front page of our newspaper and everybody else's.

It was a studio portrait Mrs. Eldridge had had done of her on her twelfth birthday. She looked very demure and madonna-ish with the row of pearls her granny had given her.

Our headlines said, "Dalstead Girl Sees Strangler," but some of the papers which Len went out to buy said, "Convent Girl Fights Strangler." They all said that Corinne Theresa Eldridge, aged fourteen, of 26 Beldon House, Dalstead, had gone out the night before to post a letter for her mother. The time was about ten o'clock and on her way back past the Church of St. Luke-in-the-Fields a man had sprung out and attempted to strangle her. Corinne fought him off and returned to her home in a state of great shock. But she was able to give the police a description of a man whom they felt might be able to help them in their enquiries.

The man she described was George.

# 20 ❖ He was asked to go down to the police station to answer a few questions.

At home Mother, Grandad, and Hélène were loudly indignant. Hélène said it was as plain as a pikestaff that the little bitch was just getting her own back. Grandad said he wished it had been the strangler she met and that he'd made a good job of her. Mother went on and on about the letter George had had from Mrs. Eldridge that morning. It was the one Corinne had been out to post.

It was a dangerous letter to write and George had said before the police came that it was typical of the sort of letter a stupid neurotic woman like that would write. She accused him of manhandling Corinne, pressing his attentions on her at the picnic, and calling her lewd and insulting names. She threatened to take the matter to her solicitors if George didn't apologise personally to Corinne, and she was going to ask the Reverend Mother to get me expelled from the convent because of "certain things happening in my home which made me an unfit companion for decent girls."

Mother was in far more of a tizzy about that letter than she was about George being taken to the police station. The police had asked George to take the letter with him down to the station. Mrs. Eldridge had told them she'd written it and also, we learned later, confided that she'd always suspected that the strangler was George.

Hélène, Mother, and Grandad were too busy with their own noisy indignation to notice that Len and I were keeping ours quiet. I felt as if I had a lump of ice inside me and Len had gone his awful greasy white.

He'd slipped out of the kitchen and locked himself in his bedroom. I tapped on the door.

"Len," I said. "It's Wynne. Can I see you?"

"What for?" His voice sounded stiff and far away.

"I want to tell you something."

"Let it wait."

"It's about George."

He turned the key and pulled the door open. The top drawer in his chest where he kept his socks was open.

"Oh, Len!" I said. "You haven't been taking those things again? Those things that I took by mistake?"

"Mind your own bloody business," he told me.

I went into the room and locked the door behind me. "Len, it's about George's sweater."

"What sweater?"

"The one I knitted him for Christmas."

Len's eyes were like some little wide-eyed animal that's had a scare inside its cage. "Can't say I recall it," he said stickily.

"You borrowed it more than once," I snapped at him. "For all you said it was gear you wouldn't be seen dead in."

"You're joking!" he sneered. "I don't go out in knitted nightshirts."

But he *had* been out in it. Like I said before, George had once made a joke about it. "Who did Wynne knit that sweater for, I should like to know?"

As I've also said before, it was right badly knitted and sloppy and hanging. I was trying to watch television at the same time and I didn't get it right. George only wore it out of politeness. He liked to be tidy and smart. Len liked it because it made him look more beat than ever. But why was he lying about it? Why?

I sat on the edge of George's bed and burst into tears. "Len, they've taken him down to the police station! Corinne's given a description of him! He's suspected, Len— and I found his sweater at Collins Wood."

He took a step towards me at first. Then he stepped back and pulled open his sock drawer again. From the toe of a blue sock he took out a small bottle and shook some purple hearts into his hand. He held them out to me. "Here! Take a couple."

"No, *thanks!* They made me dreadful last time, and you shouldn't have them either."

He said, "Shut up," and slapped some into his mouth.

Sandy mewed and scratched at the door. He couldn't bear people to be shut in together somewhere. He had to find out what they were talking about.

"Let him in," I advised. "He'll only create and then Mother will want to know what we're up to."

Len opened the door, let in Sandy, and locked the door again behind him. Sandy stepped in all stately, like one of those people who lead a procession. But then he became fussed and restless. He sniffed round the cover of George's bed and then just sat there, mewing at us.

Len looked down at him. "It's like he knows something's wrong. They say they do."

"People always think that about their own animals."

But it certainly looked as if Sandy was troubled all right—and he was definitely crying for George.

I wiped my eyes and blew my nose. I had seen by Len's eyes that I wasn't talking to the wrong person. "Len," I repeated, "I found his sweater down at Collins Wood."

"So what were you doing down at Collins Wood?"

"I love the place. You know I do. I was happy there with George."

"You sound like some old divorced woman."

"You know what I mean. He's a bit off with me now. Well, not off—but sort of different."

Len was lighting a cigarette. He blew down it instead of sucking up it. The flame went high like you sometimes see happening in a pipe. His eyebrows were raised in the light of it. "God Almighty!" he said. "What do you expect? You're a big girl now. You've got a wobble up top. He can't bounce you on his knee any more. What would Mrs. Eldridge say!"

"Never mind that," I snapped. "He doesn't want to bounce me, anyway. He's fixed up elsewhere. *Listen*—I found that sweater in the old copper. Someone had been trying to burn it."

Len wheeled on me, laughing. Those things he had taken were working already. His eyes were all lively and dancing and his nerves were fairly jerking about. I suppose he'd been at them all day. The purple hearts, I mean.

His laugh was sort of, well, it's hard to explain. Sort of sophisticated. How you might hear someone laugh in a play. You know, they go to the soda syphon and put a squirt into their glass and snort some sour remark over their shoulder.

"*Trying* to burn it!" Len snorted. "I thought I *had* burned it!"

I stood up slowly. "*You* burned it?"

His voice was certainly soda-squirt light. "Sure! I went to a lot of trouble, too. D'you mean to say the bloody thing didn't catch?"

He poked at the back of his sock drawer and brought out a half bottle of whisky. It had a funny little bakelite cup-top screwed on it. Len filled it up and swilled it down. "Hélène and most of our friends detest drink. But I'm a square for it. Every evening," he said, "every evening about the same time the hatter went out for his drink in the café. Only he didn't take the hard stuff, of course, just wine. And every evening the little tailor followed him. He didn't have the hard stuff, of course, only wine."

I tried to take the bottle off him, but he fought me off like he fought off Hélène.

"Len!" I dared not shout, but I sort of hissed at him. "Len, there was *blood* on the sweater. I'm sure there was—it had gone all hard and brown. But it was blood."

"Yeah!" Len laughed. "That's right. There was blood on it."

"But—"

He stood over me and took another swig of whisky.

"How did you know there was blood on it?" I asked.

"Saw it."

"Where?"

"Tucked away in his drawer."

"What—wet and sticky and—and covered in blood?"

"No, gone a bit brown by then. But it was blood all right. Like you said."

I leapt up from the bed, very near to hysterics. The ice in my stomach felt like a waterfall inside, crashing down on to rocks.

"George is in trouble. George is in trouble. *Can't* you stop gagging? Why was there blood on it? Didn't he say?"

Len went all dramatic and silly, like he could sometimes. He was looking wild and kinky. "No, Baby Soeur," he said, and his voice could have been Hélène's, only deeper. "No, Baby Soeur. Big Brother didn't. Big Brother said it was paint from a building site."

"That's not what he said to me. He said he'd lost it first, and then that he'd given it to Mr. Wells, and then when I shot through that he went back to saying he couldn't find it."

"He certainly couldn't do that," said Len. "I nicked it and burned it at Collins Wood."

"Why?"

"Don't like the sight of blood. Did you tell him you'd found it at Collins Wood, Wynne?"

"Yes."

"What'd he say?"

"Well, he couldn't understand it. And he was telling the truth if *you* burned it."

"He tried all sorts of things on me first. Told me the thing had got messed up when I borrowed it," said Len.

Then he did a sudden sort of snakey dance and clicked his fingers to some rhythm in his own head.

"When did you find the blood on it first, Len?"

I waited until he slowed down a bit and then I asked him the same question. Then he answered me, half-whistling: "Day the second girl was murdered."

"When? Whenabouts?"

"The girl was murdered in the night and I found brother boy's sweater stowed away the next day. Lemme see. Be about four o'clock in the afternoon. Brother boy tried to say I'd been out in the sweater that day."

"And had you?"

He suddenly came out of his dance and swooped down on me. He caught me round the throat and squeezed and shook until my eyes quite hurt trying not to pop out of my head.

"You'd try to pin it on me, would you?" he shouted. "You'd try to pin it on me too. Nice pair, aren't you, you and George. Both trying to say it was me."

"Len," I shrieked. "Len, you're hurting me!"

Mum, Grandad, and Hélène were all hammering against the door and rattling the handle. "What is it? Len!" "Wynne!" "Why the 'ell's this door shut?" "What are you doing in there?"

Len let me go and I rushed to the door and pulled it open.

"She's trying to pin it on *me*," Len shouted before I could speak. "She's trying to pin it on *me*."

Hélène hurried in and took his arm. "Come on, Puss Bun. You've got upset about Big Brother."

"I'll fetch his phenobarbitone," said Mum, and ran off to the bathroom.

"He's been drinking," said Grandad, sniffing suspiciously.

Hélène rounded on him. "You're always *on* at him, Grandad. Can't you see he's upset about George? He's very fond of George."

"None of us 'ate him," Grandad snapped in reply. "I tell you the boy's been at the bottle."

"He tried to strangle me," I sobbed.

"Don't be a nit, Wynne," said Hélène.

"If you ask me it's Wynne that's upset about George. Come in the kitchen, lass. I'll make you some tea."

I was holding my throat. It really hurt. Len's hands were so terribly strong. Hélène saw me as she was turning back Len's divan cover. "Oh, for God's sake, Wynne, stop trying to draw attention to yourself. Haven't we got enough trouble without you piling it on?"

I went into the kitchen and swallowed down the tea Grandad made me. It wasn't easy. As I said, those hands of Len's were really strong.

"He *did* try to choke me, Grandad," I gulped.

"Then you shouldn't have upset 'im," Grandad said. "You know what he's like with his nerves."

I tried to get down some more tea. All I could really think of was George. But I did find time to wonder if I ought to tell Hélène about the purple hearts and the whisky before she gave Len his phenobarbitone. "Better leave well alone," I thought. "She wouldn't believe me in any case."

I was so stupid with fright my brain just didn't seem to help me with anything. George hadn't burned that sweater. Len had. But George had definitely been back to Collins Wood to check if I was telling the truth about burying that sweater. He couldn't have got paraffin on his shoes from anywhere else. Suddenly I choked up the tea and was sick.

"I don't know!" poor Grandad sighed. He'd been washing up the tea things and he'd flipped the cloth over his shoulder. "Why the 'ell I didn't stay down south and open the door to no one but me mice, I'll never know." He flicked the tea-cloth down and started to mop me up with it. "Surely to 'eavens, child, you're not so daft as to take this serious? You're not *really* daft enough to think our George is the Dalstead Strangler? The police'll know that in two ticks, if you don't."

"He's been with them more than two ticks."

"He's been with them no more than the best part of half an hour. It takes a bit of time to get down there, you know. They've got to ask a few questions. After all, that noisome little pestilence accused him. They'll have to ask him where he was and what he was doing."

"Yes," I thought, panic-stricken, "they will, and where was he and what was he doing."

"There's about as much truth in it as there was in him making love to her all the afternoon at Sleydon, and you were there to see how true that was, weren't you? If the police were as daft as to charge George on that little beast's evidence, they'd have been too daft to get out of the way of traffic when they were coppers on the beat."

My throat stabbed sharply from where Len had grabbed it. "How daft would they be if they questioned Len?" I thought, and was sick again.

"That's it," said Grandad. "That's the lot. Into bed with you. I don't know, I'm sure. I reckon Mother's right. It's all that telly and pop singing. How can you expect kids to grow into sensible folks with proper grey matter when they listen to all that howling? It's enough to send anyone off—most of the words sound as if they come out of a loony bin."

I don't know why, considering I was in such a state, but I bothered to snap out, "I don't think much of some of the old ones. What was so bright about 'Let's all go down the Strand, have a banana'?"

"I'll send you down the Strand," Grandad threatened, "and you won't get no banana at the end of it. Look at you, all of a shake about a bit of nonsense caused by a rotten little brat and her fool of a mother."

He bundled me into my bedroom and made me lie down on the bed. "Now, just you stay there until George gets back, which should be any minute now, and think what he's going to say when he hears you've decided he's the strangler without so much as asking him."

Grandad didn't know that I had asked him, of course, and that I hadn't liked some of his answers. I thought the police might not like them either.

He had definitely been out at the time that Corinne described her meeting with the strangler. But then so had Len. Len, who had burned George's sweater because there was blood on it. George had accused Len of borrowing it the day the second girl was strangled. But George pretended the blood was paint and to me he practically gave a baker's dozen different explanations.

When Grandad closed the door, I knew what I was going to do. I was going out to see Miss Leonie Sortilège at Number 9 Cecil Avenue, Harrowvane. There wasn't anybody I could find out her real surname from, but I was just going to stand on her doorstep and ring her bell until she answered it. If she said George had been with her the night before it would put my mind at rest. Then, when he came back from the police station I should go straight to George about Len. I should tell him about the sweater and show him the bruise on my neck.

But first I had to know about George.

In one of my drawers I had a "film fund." I was saving up for a camera so that I could take colour films of Collins Wood before it was pulled down. I knew it was an expensive hobby, but I wanted a whole album of Collins Wood from every angle, and if possible inside snaps as well. So I put all my pocket money into my money-box and saved. I had thirty shillings.

I tucked it into my bag, put on my blue Dannimac and crept out of the house.

At the edge of the shopping centre I got a taxi.

The last time I saw Number 9 Cecil Avenue was through the fold of a blanket and then I only got a peep at the hedges surrounding it. It was one of those old white mansions standing far back from the road, and it had been converted into three flats. It had a round lawn in front of it and a circular gravel drive.

The front door was a great big oak thing with a brass dolphin for a knocker. There were three name plates reading "Inglis," "Lucas," and "Protheroe." I tried to think which one suited Leonie and I picked the middle one for luck. I rang the bell twice but nothing happened. If she was called Lucas, she was out.

Then I tried Inglis and nearly fell down the steps with surprise. A voice which seemed to come from absolutely nowhere asked me what I wanted. I looked up and down and round about and there wasn't a human soul in sight. It was one of those loudspeaker things that I'd never seen before.

"Speak into the left-hand side of the porch," said the voice, which was a lady's and sounded like an elderly one.

"Please," I said, shouting into the wall and feeling a perfect fool. "Does Miss—Miss Leonie live here?"

"I think you want Protheroe. Press the Protheroe bell."

"Oh, thank you," I murmured, to what I still considered nothing, and pressed the bell marked "Protheroe."

A cross-sounding voice said, "Yes? What is it?"

"Is that Miss Leonie Protheroe?"

"Mrs."

I'd forgotten the "Mrs." She'd spoken about a husband in the van. I still felt a twit talking into a brick porch with no one in sight. "Mrs.," I corrected myself. "Mrs. Leonie Protheroe?"

"Yes."

"May I talk to you, please?"

"What about?"

The voice seemed much deeper than I remembered. It had none of the light summer sounds it had conjured up for me in the back of the van. It sounded rather thick and mannish.

"I'm George Meakham's sister, Wynne," I shouted. "Please let me speak to you, Mrs. Protheroe."

She said, as if she was tired, "Okay, come up. Top flat."

Something buzzed and the front door opened by itself. I walked nervously into a hall with a big marble star on the floor and one of those staircases twisting up, like you see in films. It curled round an enormous iron lantern hanging down into the well. The carpet was dark red and I wondered how they got it to spiral round like that without making clumsy tucks.

At the top there was a pale blue door with the figure "3" painted on it in sapphire blue. Neatly printed under the white bell-push was the name "Mrs. Protheroe."

I rang. My mouth felt all sticky and I didn't seem to have anything to moisten it with. I waited for what seemed ages. Then I rang again. There was movement inside, and then someone crashed into something and that deep voice said, "Bugger the bloody thing."

Then the door pulled open. She nearly fell backwards and some of the drink slopped out of the glass she held in her free hand. "Impatient little bitch, aren't you?" she enquired. "You ought to pay for that vase."

"I'm sorry," I stammered. "I thought you hadn't heard."

"What do you think I travel on, roller skates?"

She would have been beautiful if she hadn't looked so ghastly. It's a silly way to describe her, but it's the only way I can do it. She would have been much lovelier than Hélène if she'd looked clean. She had eyes like Mother Marie-Adelaide's Siamese cat and you could see that her hair was real blond—the honey kind. It didn't look as if she'd brushed it for weeks. Her face seemed to have almost perfectly shaped features, but it looked tired to death and sort of stained with discontent. She was in a white towel dressing-gown and there was nothing on her feet.

"Did big brother send you down to spy on me?" she asked.

"He doesn't know I'm here."

"Oh yes. He's in the nick or something, isn't he? He's been laying his hands on the young."

"He *hasn't*," I shouted foolishly. "Corinne just made it all up to spite him because he ticked her off. She lied about the picnic, too."

"Oh yes," she said. "There's a *tie*, isn't there? You're the little sister who's so superior to other people's little sisters."

"I'm *not* his sister," I snapped. "I'm no relation at all." But I had time to be pleased that he spoke well of me.

"Well, what do you want? I'm finding big brother a trifle too pompous lately."

I went robin red-breast in the face. I realised that I was going to have to ask her if George had spent the night with her. "Could I come in, please?" I asked. "It's a little bit private—but terribly important."

She stepped back very unsteadily. "Enter."

I went into her hall, which seemed all duck-egg blue and gold. There was a gold wooden table with one leg curving down to the wall, and there was a vase on it—a lovely peacock blue filled with ripe corn. Its twin from a table opposite was lying shattered on the floor.

"This way," she said.

Her bathrobe stopped above the knees. She had the loveliest legs I had ever seen.

I felt all feet and elbows in her sitting-room. I hardly dared sit down. It was the sort of room I dreamed about. Full of antiques and ornaments. I wondered what George thought of it. His taste was far plainer and more contemporary. He'd have called all those lovely things knick-knacks.

She slopped to the big marble-topped table. Bottles and glasses and jugs stood on it. She was helping herself to something. Over her shoulder she said, "I can't stand cocktail cabinets and bars."

I couldn't think what to say.

"Want anything?" she asked me.

"No, thank you very much."

"Don't drink yet?"

"No, thank you."

"Want a soft one?"

"No, thank you."

"Well, what do you want, 'thank you'?"

I clasped my hands and pressed them tightly between my knees. "Miss Protheroe . . ."

"*Mrs.!*"

It was so stupid of me to keep on forgetting that.

"Mrs. Protheroe, did—was—did George—was George here last night, please?"

"Oh, for Christ's sake!"

I jumped up and went towards her. Tears fell in spite of my trying to stop them. I felt such a fool, but I just went on crying.

"It's terribly important, Mrs. Protheroe. You see, Corinne's accused him of being the strangler—the Dalstead Strangler! But if he was with you, he couldn't have been."

She lit a cigarette from one that wasn't even smoked half through. "Look, I've already *told* the police he was here last night."

I stopped crying. "Oh, how wonderful! I didn't know— I'm so sorry."

"Sit down. You worry me, bobbing about."

I sat. "I'm so sorry," I repeated. "I wasn't sure—I mean—"

"Don't be sorry." She suddenly laughed. "I wasn't sure either!" And she went on laughing. A deep, unhappy kind of laugh that made you think she could never find anything funny.

My comfort left me. "You weren't sure?"

She lolled towards the table again and poured out more drink. "Sure you won't?"

"No. Yes—I mean, no thank you. *Why* weren't you sure?"

She turned and faced me. The bathrobe fell open, showing the whole of her front. She didn't bother to do it up. She laughed again. "Your brother George doesn't approve of my habits. He can be a pompous sod sometimes, can't he?"

"Why aren't you sure?" I hammered dully. "You said you told the police he was here."

"Well, *he* said he was. That was why."

"Well, *was* he?" I shouted. "Was he? Or wasn't he? For goodness' sake, you ought to know."

"I ought!" She nodded, tipped back her drink and said, "He's right. You're nice."

I was getting tearful again. "Mrs. Protheroe, please! It's so important. It's terribly, terribly, *terribly* important. The police are asking him questions now."

"Look, honey. I had a bit of a party last night. I can't remember things too clearly. But I told the police George was here. They asked me, so I told them."

"But was he?" I asked. "Was he really?"

"He said he was, sweetie."

"But *was* he?" I almost shrieked.

She got up to fill up her glass again. She held up a bottle. "Change your mind?"

This time I did shriek. "*Was* he here? Was he here, or did he just say he was?"

She left very little room in her glass for any sort of water or anything. I think it was gin she was drinking.

"God knows, baby. I don't. He said he was here, so maybe he was. Somebody was. Somebody had to be."

The inside of my mouth had gone funny again.

"I get depressed, my love," she said. "But your brother's been very kind to me." She lifted both her arms up at me and flapped her hands. But I didn't get the reason just then. I couldn't think of anything but the lonely fact that she couldn't be sure George had been with her that night.

I said, "Could I please go to the bathroom? I'm afraid that I'm going to be sick."

I couldn't wait for her to answer. A hot and cold wave had enveloped me and there was a wet band round my head. I got up and rushed for the nearest door. She just let her glass drop flat on the carpet. Fortunately it didn't break. But she didn't bother about the mess.

"Not that one!" she yelled. "Not that one!" She gripped me by the shoulders quite heavily. "Not on your life, you don't go in there. Big brother would *never* forgive me for that. Bathroom and loo to your right."

I felt so ill that what she'd said didn't really drum into me at that point. All I could think of was being sick in the right place. The bathroom was my idea of paradise. All full of wiggly Victorian bamboo mirrors and trailing plants and shells and gold rings for the towels, and marvellous bottles, and what George would have called "general mess."

I did, as I clutched my head over the lavatory pan, wonder what was in the room she was so sure George wouldn't want me to see, but I supposed it was just his clothes or some kind of give-away like that.

When I got out she seemed much more sober, although her glass was full again. She was certainly very kind.

"Vera," she said, "I've been a cow." She must've seen my face. "It *is* Vera, isn't it?"

"Wynne."

"My God, yes! What the hell made me think it was Vera? Look, sweetie, I've been my usual gorgeous selfish self. It's something your brother's always complaining about. You're really worried, aren't you? And who wouldn't be, with big brother facing strangling charges! I'm a cow. A straightforward, insensitive cow. You come here for help and I treat you like a bailiff. Poor sweetie. But you see, I wouldn't have been like that if I'd thought there was the slightest possibility of his being a strangler. He's just not the type. Be a good girl and drink this up." She handed me a glass of something.

"Excuse me, please," I said, "but it isn't drink, is it? I mustn't have that. It makes me sing and keep people awake all night."

"You can't have had a lot of experience!"

"Well, only that night you—we—I mean George and you . . ."

She pointed to the glass in my hand. "It's brandy. Good for sickness. The night you—we—George what?"

"Oh, nothing," I said, my face the colour of robins' breasts again, and sipped nervously from the glass she'd given me.

"Come on, honey," she said. "What night? Where and when? We've never met before, have we? Don't tell me I've forgotten you visiting me as well!"

I told her. I told her all about that night I lay hidden in the back of the van. You've never seen anyone laugh so much. I was afraid she was going to hurt herself. The bathrobe thing fell open again, but this time she closed it quickly up. "Darling," she gasped. "Do you realise—do you realise that it could have been possible that your brother and I might have parked somewhere and—"

"Yes," I said primly. "I did."

She fairly fell over again. Then she pulled herself together. "Look, my sweet, we're going to the police."

"But you've already—"

"Yes. Well, I'll say it again."

"Oh no!" I said. *Please!* They'll think it's not true!"

I was scared out of my wits and I felt a bit drunk again. "Goodness," I thought, "I'm a right old booze pot too!"

"Why won't they think it's true if I say it twice?" she wanted to know. She tripped on her way into the bedroom. She left the door open, shouting through to me. "We'll get down to those police and we'll give them hell for holding our George. You don't mind the 'our' bit, do you?"

I was scared. I thought it might do much more harm than good if we went to the police, particularly with her in that state. They'd want to know why I'd contacted her, and when they heard I'd gone hoping she could prove he couldn't have been near Corinne they might want to know why I was so suspicious in the first place.

"Mrs. Protheroe," I said, and had a bit of difficulty in getting it out.

"Leonie!" she shouted from the bedroom. She had climbed into black slacks and a lilac mohair jumper.

I went to the door. I had a bit of hiccoughs. I thought, "I must never, never drink again. I must give it up. I must be like Aunty Rene except for bad turns."

"Please, Miss Leonie," I said, "I don't think it's a good idea. I think that we'll make them suspicious."

"We'll *un*-suspicious them," she laughed.

I wished more than anything in the world that I'd never come. She was brushing her hair and it lay over her back like a veil.

"You see, baby," she told me, "as you're so worried I'll confess something. I'm a bit pissed now and again—do you know what that is?"

I didn't know what to say.

"It means drunk—someone who's sloshed, stoned, bottled —get it?"

"Yes."

"Well, when you're like that you don't remember things. Someone was here with me last night—I'm buggered if I know who it was—but George told the police it was him and I daresay it was. Baby, I honestly can't remember. I know it makes me stink but I can't. When I'm sober he likes me a lot—but when I'm drunk your brother can't do with me, and I passed out flat last night."

"He drinks a bit himself," I said. "And he's not my brother."

"Well, brother, sister, grandfather, or grandmother, whatever relation the hell he is to you, I can tell you one thing. He isn't the strangling type. He's the saving type. The goddamn saviour type. Now come on, kitten, let's go and see London's wonderful policemen. They've sent someone up from Scotland Yard, as if Dalstead couldn't manage things."

I bent to pick up the glass from the floor. When I straightened up she was looking at me with a bottle of whisky poised over a second glass.

"You were drinking gin before," I told her.

"Runs in the family, doesn't it. Goddamn bossy, both of you. You're a real little chip off the brotherly block—just can't help interfering."

"It's just that I don't think we ought to go down to the police station with you—I mean—well, we've both been drinking."

"You don't think I'm pissed now, do you? Good God, no— I said I get pissed *at times*—but this isn't one of them."

She was pouring the whisky all over her hand. "I'm as sober as a judge now. I'll get out the car and we'll go down to that station and give them all hell." She stared at me again. "He didn't tell me how attractive you were."

"Mrs. Protheroe," I begged, "I don't think you should drive—"

"For Christ's sake leave me alone," she snapped. "I can't stand the two of you at it. He sold my goddamn record-player. He said it made me drink too much, sitting and soaking to music at night. Bloody nerve, when you come to think of it. It's not as if I was married to the guy."

She was terribly drunk and falling about, but she didn't sound slurry like Len. Her voice wasn't really slurry. It was thick and loud, and she shouted certain words.

"Please," I begged. "Please, please, Leonie. We'll only make things worse for him. They're sure to wonder why I didn't believe him when he said he was here last night."

"Come to that, why didn't you?" She lost her balance and fell back against the marble-topped table. It was a horrid, slow kind of fall. She seemed ages slipping, but she couldn't have been because I jumped forward quickly enough and she was already on the floor.

She was quite a small person, but hard to get up. Her arm had knocked one decanter over and it had smashed on the marble top of the table. "Oh, bugger!" she said. "The ring neck. They're not easy to find anywhere."

I wedged her up against a chair. "I'll get a cloth," I said. "Where's the kitchen?"

"My goodness! You masterful Meakhams!"

"My name's Kinch."

I started for the hall, and she shouted after me, "First on the left, Vera—not the right. You mustn't go there or he'll never forgive me."

The kitchen was in a lovely old mess. It didn't look as if she'd washed up for days.

I came back and mopped the carpet up. She was lying on her back, her arms under her head and her hair over her face. She was humming. She might have been sun-bathing on some beach. The drink was still dripping down not far from her head.

"Sweetheart, know what you could do for me?"

"What?"

"Pop out and buy us some booze. There's nothing so embarrassing as running out when you've got unexpected guests."

"I haven't any money."

"Darling, my credit's fabulous."

"I've got to go home when I've helped you to bed. You can't walk about. You'll fall over again. Please, where can I find the dustpan and brush?"

"What for?"

"To sweep up the glass. You'll tread on it."

"He's right. You really are an enchanting child. Pour me a drink, will you, baby?"

"I don't think you should have any more. You might hurt yourself."

"Oh God, like brother like sister. Look, I'm a big girl now. Pour me a drink at once, you little bitch."

"No," I said. "Where's the dustpan and brush? I really *must* get home. My family will get the police."

"Oh yes," she said. "So must I. The car keys are in the Dutch chest, honey."

"You can't drive, you can't even stand," I protested. "You'd have a shocking accident and hurt other people as well."

"Could be brother talking, couldn't we? Pompous baskets."

She was struggling to get up, but while her speech was perfectly clear her legs were absolutely useless to her. She lay back again, quite unperturbed. "I hope I'm not coming down with anything. They say polio goes to your legs."

"You've already *come* down, with too much to drink."

We both heard the key turn in the lock.

"Well, well, well," she said. "Quite a family gathering!"

It was George letting himself into the flat.

# 21 ❖ I WAS COUNTING ALOUD when he came in.

". . . five, six, seven, eight, nine, ten, eleven . . ."

He said, "What are you doing here, please, Wynne?"

I didn't answer. I ran to him with questions of my own. "What happened? Have they let you go? What did they say to you?"

George put his arms under Leonie's shoulders and heaved her up on to the big white sofa. He didn't address her and he didn't reply when she said, "Good evening."

To me he said, "It took them about ten minutes to find out that your dear little friend was telling a pack of lies."

Feeling quite weak with relief, I flopped into a chair. "Oh George, they know it wasn't you, then? They're sure it wasn't you?"

"They're sure it wasn't anybody. At least three people saw the little pest on her way to post her letter and a good few more spotted her on the way back. She was her usual perky self and quite unmolested."

He was picking up the decanters and the bottles from Leonie's marble-topped table and taking them into the bathroom. I suppose he was pouring their contents one by one down the lavatory.

Leonie on the sofa sat up. She spoke through her teeth, her voice ice-cold and clear. "I'll kill you, you bugger. I'll kill you."

George took no notice. He was pulling out drawers and opening cupboards and looking under furniture. Sometimes he'd hand me out a half-empty bottle, and sometimes he found a glass tucked away with the contents quite mouldy in it.

"Did you hear me, you arrogant bastard? What right have you to go round chucking out my belongings?"

George handed me a bottle of whisky. "Pour this down the lavatory, Wynne."

When I came back I said, "George, are you *sure* it's all right? Mrs. Protheroe couldn't remember if you were here last night."

"Yes," he said. "Her doubts made my alibi look pretty shaky for a minute. It's just as well they broke Corinne down."

He picked up Leonie's telephone without asking her and got through to our flat. "Hallo," he said. "Mum? Wynne's with me. We'll be home soon."

When he put down the phone, he picked up Leonie just as if she'd been some kind of doll or something. She looked up, smiled at him, and then spat in his face. He gave her a cuff on the side of the head, carried her into the bedroom, and dropped her into her bed. He rolled back the bed-clothes, bundled her under them, clothes and all, and flung them up again so that they covered her face. She folded them back again very deliberately. Honestly, you'd never have thought there was anything wrong with her if you hadn't seen her reeling about. She was as cool as a mountain brook, but she looked vicious. Her eyes and her mouth were in two straight lines.

George was rustling through her bedside table taking possession of bottles of pills. She suddenly shied her pillow at him. It hit his shoulder and knocked a bottle of pills out of his hand. It skidded across the floor without breaking. George recaptured it and threw her pillow back.

"You can sleep flat if you chuck it again," George told her.

She put it behind her head and beckoned me. "While your nauseating brother is destroying my property, Vera, do you think you could get me a glass of water?"

"Not a glass," said George. "There's an enamel mug in the kitchen. Bring her that."

"If I could get at you," Leonie said to George. "If I could get at you, you sod—"

"You have in the past," George told her. "That's why I'm taking precautions."

He moved everything as far from her bed as possible. When I came back with the mug I handed it to her and she threw the contents in George's face.

"All right," he said. "Go thirsty. Come along, Wynne."

"Will she be all right?" I asked anxiously. "Supposing she wants anything?"

"She can't have it."

I looked back as we let ourselves out of the flat. I felt awful leaving her like that, but it seemed to have happened to George before.

"Supposing she gets out of bed and hurts herself?"

"She can't get out of bed at this stage. That's the only good thing about it. It takes hours sometimes for her to get the use of her legs back, and by that time she's sleeping it off."

We passed a lady on the stairs coming up to the second flat. George said, "Good evening." The lady just sniffed.

The van was parked outside. We climbed into it and George drove off.

"Mum will want to know where I've been," I said.

"We'll say you were trying to prove my alibi. Which you were, weren't you?"

"Yes."

"Was it proved to you satisfactorily?"

There were little wet beads on my forehead when I thought of the desolate fear I felt when Leonie admitted she couldn't remember. I don't think I'd ever have been able to ask him, even if Corinne hadn't been found to have been making things up.

"What was in the room she wouldn't let me see into because you wouldn't like it?"

"Wouldn't she let you see into it?"

"No."

For anyone else I suppose he would have been relaxed—
considering he'd been suspected of being the Dalstead
Strangler and then had to put his drunken girl-friend to bed.
But for George he was not relaxed and there was a terrible
tiredness in its place.

"Isn't it sad?" I asked. "For someone so young and so
pretty to get so drunk?"

"Very."

"You took her to a home for it once, didn't you? That
Brinkhill Clinic place."

"Her doctor took her."

"Oh, he knows, does he?"

"He knows—he's got the other key to the flat."

"Do you—mind very much about her, George?"

He changed the subject. "Wynne, I meant what I said
about not wanting you to see Corinne again."

"Heavens!" I squeaked. "As if I would, after what she
tried to do to you! I'd strangle her myself if she came near
me. I'd strangle her and jump on her face."

The things you say! The dreadful, dreadful things you say
without thinking about them—and then how are you going
to stop thinking about them for the rest of your life? That's
what they tell me in here. In the Remand Home, I mean.
Particularly Matron and Father Murphy when he visits me.
He says it's the sort of thing that anyone could say. The
sort of thing not to think about. But try. Just try not to think
about something like that, when it's your best friend—no
matter what she was like. And Mrs. Eldridge! Poor, poor
Mrs. Eldridge! I usually start to think of her at night. If
only I hadn't told Corry those lies on the picnic at Sleydon.
If only I hadn't tried to "put one over on her" because I was
jealous of her flirting with George. Those ridiculous lies I
told about him being in love with me and him waiting to
marry me and take me off to the cottage on the mountainside! If only I hadn't got back at her when she told me he'd

been making passes at her all the afternoon, and let her know he'd called her a mini-tart, she might never have been so bitchy about him. She might never have tried to get her own back, and that could have meant that she might still have been here.

Matron makes a pot of tea quite late at night and lets me go and have a cup with her if I get the jitters. She told the doctor she'd rather do that than get me on to sleeping draughts. She asks me the same old questions again and again, and I tell her the same old story, but I always feel better for it. I'm saving up to buy her a big expensive book on birds. She's always interested in anything that flies into the garden. We had a nuthatch last Friday, and you'd think she'd won the pools.

I said to George that night in the van, "If Corinne Eldridge went down on her bended knees I'd never speak to her again." That's another thing I feel so desolate about. She practically did go down on her knees and I didn't speak to her.

Mother Marie-Adelaide says that of all Corry's sufferings she thinks her remorse must have made her suffer most. What a thing to say to try and cheer me up! As though I'd have wanted Corry to suffer anything else. You soon get to know the people who understand. They say the things that really do cheer you up. Like Matron and Doctor and Father Murphy. Poor Mother Marie-Adelaide just meant well.

George told me in the van that night, "The fellow that gave Corinne a lift in his car at Sleydon rang up the police. He'd seen her photograph in the paper, and he rang up to say that if that was the kid that was accusing someone of strangling her, they ought to know that she'd hitch-hiked a lift in his car and that no street woman he'd ever met had got a bigger bag of sexy little tricks."

"Poor Mrs. Eldridge," I said.

"Poor Mrs. Eldridge! Serve her bloody well right. Poor

little Corinne—what on earth's the poor little brat going to turn into."

At home George stopped them asking me any questions, although Grandad smelt drink on my breath again.

"Your aunt Rene Tindall's right," he declared. "Sodom and Gomorrah had a better crowd than you lot."

"Leave her alone," George snapped. "She tried to help."

All over supper the talk was of what action should be taken against Mrs. Eldridge.

George, looking down at Sandy, said, "This cat's ravenous —did anyone remember to feed him?"

Hélène got his plate. "We've had quite a bit on our minds, what with you being politely questioned as to whether or not you're a murderer. We actually forgot Sandy's food— yes, we actually forgot it."

"Wickedness like Corinne's ought to be punished," said Mother. "Mud sticks. Your Grandad thinks we ought to go to a solicitor about Mrs. Eldridge, George."

"Mud sticks much harder if you hug it to you," said George. "We'll forget all about the wretched business."

"But what about that dreadful letter she wrote you?"

"Burn it."

Aunt Rene Tindall was there, full of advice and explanation about how it was all because Corinne was a child of the change of life.

Len, who had been acting very edgy with me, lost his temper and shouted at her, "Oh for God's sake, Aunty, go and drown yourself and take your drearies with you."

Mother said, "Don't be so rude, Len." But she didn't put much feeling in it.

Grandad snapped, "'e's right, Rene. We've got enough trouble without you adding pus and phlegm and all the other 'orrors you treat us to every time you open your mouth."

"Well," she said, getting up and sniffing, "I'm sure I know when I'm not wanted, so I'll take myself off."

George opened the door for her. She went out with her shoulders all hunched and her head high, and what we called her "nose-pinched" look.

"Oh dear," said Grandad. "Now the neighbours *will* hear everything."

"There's nothing to hear," George told him. "Except a hysterical child encouraged by a neurotic mother telling a pack of lies."

"They'll do all right with that," snapped Grandad.

"No, they won't," said George. "They're sensible people round here."

There was a ring at the front door. Len said wickedly, "What about sending the strangler an appeal through the papers to start on Aunt Rene Tindall?"

Mother said dutifully, "Len!" and added wearily, "She's come back to have it out, I suppose. We shouldn't have been so rude to her."

But it wasn't Aunt Rene Tindall come back to "have it out." It was poor little Mr. Eldridge. He was the colour of putty and looked as if he needed the kiss of life.

It was Len who had let him in.

"It's Mr. Eldridge," he called, as though the name ought to scare us to death.

George went out to meet him, his hand outstretched. I was looking through the kitchen doorway, and to me it seemed as if Mr. Eldridge hung on to George's hand as if it was all that was keeping him upright.

"Len!" called George. "Get some beer out of the fridge. Come in, Mr. Eldridge."

But he kept him in the hall and didn't bring him into the kitchen, where the rest of us were. Len brought the beer and George poured Mr. Eldridge out a glass. "You must've had quite a day," he said.

"I don't suppose you enjoyed yours," Mr. Eldridge's voice sounded as grey as his face looked.

Mother made things worse for him. "It's not as if it's the first time Corinne's made trouble, Mr. Eldridge."

"I know, I know," Mr. Eldridge sighed.

George put a hand on Mr. Eldridge's shoulder and guided him towards the sitting-room. He didn't say anything, but somehow the rest of us knew that he'd rather we didn't follow.

I don't know what they talked about, but somehow George cheered Mr. Eldridge up. When he went he'd lost the awful defeated look in his eyes.

It made things seem even more terrible later.

George said he didn't want any more trouble stirred up, and he'd accepted Mr. Eldridge's apology and he didn't want to hear any more about the matter.

Corinne rang up the next morning and I refused to speak to her. She tried again three times in the afternoon, and in the evening Mrs. Eldridge rang up and raged at Mum. She said all poor little Corry wanted to do was to tell me she was sorry, and she considered it sinful that I was too stuck-up to speak to her.

Mother said I wasn't stuck-up, and George had forbidden me to have anything more to do with Corinne because she was an unsuitable companion for me. Mrs. Eldridge said she liked that when you thought what was going on between George and me, and with others who were no better than they ought to be if you liked to listen to the stories. George wasn't a fit companion for anyone.

Mum said at least she didn't get men who had given me a lift in a car ringing up the police to say that I had behaved like a prostitute.

Mrs. Eldridge said she'd have Mother know that even at the police station Corinne chose to be interviewed by a lady detective because she was so shy of men.

Mother gave a snort of laughter and Mrs. Eldridge gave a great shriek of rage down the phone, and Grandad took it out of her hand, put it back on the hook, and cut Mrs. Eldridge off.

"You'll have to do the same, Lucy, whenever that woman rings up."

Mrs. Eldridge didn't ring again, but Corinne just wouldn't give up. She rang while we were all watching television and I took the call outside in the passage where we had the phone.

It was the last time I spoke to her. I'll never forget what I said. I said, "Listen, Corinne, after what you did to us I'd like to strangle you myself, and that's flat. I never want to see you again!"

I know now that she was sorry for hurting us all, and if I'd let her see me I expect she would have been able to say so. But it all went wrong and we both got on our high horses and couldn't get off them.

She started off all right. "Wynne, I've got to see you. Can I come round now?"

"No, you can't. George has forbidden you the house."

That narked her. She got a bit hysterical. Remembering his snubs at Sleydon, I suppose. "Oh, he has, has he? Well, he'd better be careful how he treats me, had Mr. Big Head Meakham. Perhaps he'd like me to go back to the police and say I didn't make it up after all."

"Fat chance you've got of making them believe you."

"Yeah? You wait. How do you know it wasn't true? Didn't think I might just have said I made it up out of friendship for you, did you?"

"No, I didn't, because you didn't either."

She was definitely getting hysterical again. She just wasn't used to being crossed. If her father ticked her off she despised him. She used to say, "The silly nit can try it on, but I've only got to let Mum catch me crying and she's ready to take an axe to him."

"George says you're a spoilt little pest."

"Who cares what he thinks?" she sneered at me over the

phone. "You and your corny story about George going to marry you and live up in the Lakes! Well, I'll tell you something. I really *am* going to be married, just the minute I'm old enough."

"It's rather sudden, isn't it?" I asked bitingly. "I don't seem to have heard of any boy wanting to marry you before."

"He's not a boy," she said. "He's a man. A grown man with a good job, and he *does* want to marry me. He said so. Which is more than your tired old George ever did. My man's only twelve years older than me. When I'm forty he'll only be fifty-two. Which is nothing. Anyway, we don't notice the difference in our ages. We've got so much in common."

I was intrigued in spite of myself, but I kept my voice disinterested. "How long have you known this person?"

"Well, quite a time really. But we never clicked before. You know him, too."

"What's his name?"

"Wouldn't you like to know!"

"Not much."

"Then why ask?"

"Because I don't believe you."

"No? If I came round to you now I could show you my engagement ring."

"What kind is it?"

"Well, it's only a token one really. We're having a diamond later when I can wear it openly. This is an elephant hair one, but it's lucky. I wear it round my neck. It's someone you know," she taunted me again. "Someone you thought liked you better than me. If you don't believe me, come to Number 3 Collins Wood and see!"

"Number 3 Collins Wood!" I stuttered. "What right have you to go there?"

"It's not your house any more," she retorted. "I'm not trespassing any more than you are, me Lady Kinch. You know him awfully well," she taunted again. "But he says you're too lumpy for him."

"I don't believe he exists," I repeated.

"Okay. Come and see for yourself. I'm meeting him at Number 3 tomorrow night."

"I'd be more likely to see the ghost of Clare than anyone wanting to marry *you*," I said.

She gave her maddening tinkle laugh. "Suit yourself, but he'll be there, all right. He hasn't stood me up yet and we've had quite a few dates. I'm catching the six-o'clock 'bus. Hop on it if you want to meet him, but don't let anyone see you come into the house, and don't stay too long. We've got other things to do than talk to you."

I hung up in an absolute fury that she should even have dared to pretend that she had dates at my beloved Collins Wood. It made me wild that I couldn't order her off the place.

It was a Tuesday when Corinne had rung me. The next day at about half-past nine Mr. Eldridge called. He wanted to know if Corinne was with us.

We were all at home except Hélène and Len, who were both at her cinema.

Grandad was on edge because one of his does was going to have a litter, and Mr. Wells had called on George, so everyone was in the sitting-room.

George and Mr. Wells were discussing some kind of trouble they were having with impregnated flax for a roof on one of their bungalows. I remember it because Grandad was always terribly nervous when he was expecting a litter and he kept interrupting their conversation. There was a mixture of technical building talk and technical mouse talk. George in between them both was like someone speaking two languages.

The talk had just got on to something about "indented joints" and "mating notches," which tickled me because it brought Grandad's mind round to his mice again and he said something very mousey to Mr. Wells. Mr. Wells didn't catch on, and explained to Grandad about wooden fish plates and main timbers being cut with mating notches which could be wedged, but Grandad didn't hear and was going on about mouse mating!

I was giggling to myself when Mr. Eldridge rang the doorbell, and I suppose that it was the last laughing I did for a very long time.

He asked us if we'd seen Corinne. Mum was awful. She said, "No, Mr. Eldridge, and not sorry for it either. I'll have to be frank with you. If that girl of yours comes here worrying our Wynne I'll not be above marching her down to the police station."

George moved her gently out of the way and spoke to Mr. Eldridge. "What's the matter? Hasn't she come home?"

"No," said Mr. Eldridge. "She went out after tea. Said she was going to a cinema with a friend. But her mother's looked up the film she was going to see, and it's not showing anywhere in Dalstead."

George turned to me. "You haven't seen her, have you, Wynne?"

I was just about to say no, I hadn't, but she had asked me to meet her at Collins Wood. Then George moved. He offered Mr. Eldridge a glass of beer, and as he went to get it I noticed his right shoulder. He was wearing his sports coat and on the right shoulder was a brand-new "blue mark" of Collins Wood.

Passing me, he asked again, "Haven't seen her, have you, Wynne?"

I felt as if my tongue had been in a deep freeze and hadn't thawed out yet. So did my lips and the whole of my inside.

"Er—no," I replied. "Not since the picnic at Sleydon."

"Did she say anything to you on the phone?" Mr. Eldridge asked.

"No," I lied. "She was just trying to make things up with me."

The mark on George's shoulder was new. I was sure of that. You could tell the old ones. They looked flattened and pushed into the cloth, but the new ones looked dusty and on top of the weave. I was an expert on "blue marks of Collins Wood"—I had spent so much time getting them off my own clothes!

Mum said, "If you ask me, Mr. Eldridge, she's playing up. She's a right little madam, that one, and I don't care who hears me say so."

Mr. Wells's voice was always tired. "She must have a bit of a fancy imagination to make up the tale that she did about George."

"Yes," said George. "She's probably trying to scare everyone to pay them out for not taking her strangling seriously."

"That's what I told her mother," said poor little Mr. Eldridge. "But I'm afraid that she's still in a state." He blew his nose and stood up. "Yes. Well, thank you very much. I expect the naughty young miss will come back in her own good time."

I could imagine Corry making fun of him. " 'Naughty young miss!' He'd have sounded a square in the ark."

George saw him out, and when he came back his right shoulder was nearest to me again. Suddenly my mind went to sleep or something, and I forgot where I was or who I was with. I had no idea that I was counting aloud until I felt George shaking me.

"Wynne! What the hell's the matter? Wynne!"

I saw Mother's anxious face and the startled expressions on the faces of Grandad and Mr. Wells, but I couldn't stop.

". . . Four, five, six, seven, eight, nine, ten, eleven . . ."

**22** ❖ Mrs. Eldridge called at seven-thirty the next morning. Corinne hadn't been home all night.

George had gone off to work, thank goodness in view of some of the things that Mrs. Eldridge had to say.

It was George that Corinne was hiding from, according to Mrs. Eldridge, because she was so afraid of him. We all reminded her again and again that the police had broken down Corinne's story completely and that she had admitted she was lying.

Mrs. Eldridge would have it that the police had bullied the poor little mite into an admission of lying. It was only natural that all of us would stick together. We had worked out all our lies. She didn't care what we said. George had forced his attentions on that poor innocent child at the Sleydon picnic, and that's why the child had had to go home in another car.

Grandad said, poor little mite nothing. The man that gave her a lift told the police she'd done her best to seduce him. Mrs. Eldridge said that's what she thought we'd do. All stick together and lie.

I put on a coat and caught the 'bus to Collins Wood. I couldn't think of anything else to do. There were hundreds of thoughts tearing round in my head. Had Corry spent the night at Collins Wood because I did? Was she trying to prove to me that her romance was true? Or was it that she'd been made to look a fool over the strangling story and, like George said, wanted to give us all a good scare?

Surely she wouldn't have dared to spend the night out with a man, even if he really existed, and I couldn't see her having the guts to stay there by herself. She always was a scare-pot. Something must have been wrong if she really had taken herself to Collins Wood. George had warned me that the dry rot was dangerous. Maybe she'd fallen and hurt herself. Or maybe she'd been too frightened to come back. If she really had gone there and had seen someone, like I saw the tramp, it would be enough to send her into fits.

Perhaps, I thought, she'd stayed with friends or relations, just to prove it to me that she was conducting an "affair of the heart," as Aunt Rene Tindall still called it. But except for myself there really weren't any friends, and surely relations would have sent her home.

It was "my" conductor on the 'bus. By mine I mean the one that made me feel grown-up by the looks he gave me, and the one I always chatted to.

"How's my little colleen?" he wanted to know.

"Fine," I said. "You didn't see my friend, did you? You know, the one I sometimes come out to the common with? She said she'd meet me on the six-o'clock yesterday evening, but I missed her."

"I wasn't on the six-o'clock, love," he told me. "You must know every inch of that common by now. I never knew such a girl for walking. Still, I suppose it's better than having your nose glued to the telly the whole time."

"Yes," I said uneasily. "I love walking."

I always had the feeling that he knew I was doing something I wasn't supposed to, in going back to Collins Wood. It was daft of me, because how could he? But he lived in one of the new houses on the other side of the common, and I was sure he must have seen me going into Number 3 at times and had wondered what I was doing. It may have been my imagination, but he always seemed a bit suspicious and sarcastic about my great love of exercise on the common.

"It's a wonder you don't have a dog, with all the amount of walking you do," he chuckled.

It was raining when I got to Collins Wood. For once the house looked uninviting. It looked old in a tired sort of way, instead of an exciting way. The rain made the front of it seem slippery and dreary, like an old gravestone in a neglected cemetery.

Or maybe I was just seeing it differently. I was blaming it for the blue mark on George's shoulder, and I was frightened of going in.

The overgrown path to the back was dripping and clinging, and the evergreens that I had always thought so Christmassy looked sinister.

But it was only the outside. Once I was inside, it all felt just the same again. Light, and woody-smelling as if a log fire had only just gone out, and the rain that could be heard on the coal cellar roof made me feel cosy like it used to on winter nights.

"Corry!" I called. "Corry, are you here? It's Wynne."

That gave me the shivers a bit because it reminded me of how we used to "invoke" Clare.

There was no answer, so I called again, and then I started to search. I went right through the house and the old copper-house, but there was no sign of Corinne anywhere.

I caught a 'bus back to Dalstead and told Mother I'd been to church to look up the notices.

That evening Mrs. Eldridge called again. This time George was at home.

It was one of the nastiest scenes I can ever remember. She wasn't screaming and shouting any more. She was quiet and sort of dead, which was much more awful.

She said that she was quite aware that George was spreading wicked rumours about Corinne's character, and that he'd bribed the man who gave her a lift in his car to ring up the police and blacken her character, but perhaps he would agree that her own mother knew her best. It wasn't as if they were an ordinary mother and daughter. They had always been particularly close, and if George thought that she was spoilt he was very mistaken. She was devoted to her mother, and had never been known to tell her a lie. If George doubted the affection that Corinne felt for her mother, perhaps he would care to read the letter that Corinne had been writing to her just before she disappeared. The little love must have meant to put it under her mother's pillow, or something. No child writing a letter such as that would be capable of running away and hiding, at the risk of worrying the mother she obviously adored. She handed George an unfinished letter. "Read it out, please," she said, with a proud little smile on her face, "so that they can all hear it."

George read it out. I couldn't bear to watch poor Mrs. Eldridge's glowing face. George kept clearing his throat with embarrassment.

The letter started, "My beloved heart," and it went on:

This is to tell you what you mean to me. You're the *only* thing in my life, however much I made you think I'd got plenty of boys around. I'm sorry if I've ever been cheeky to you. I didn't see what we meant to each other. Silly me, when right under my nose is you. When I'm older and done with lousy old school, we'll be together always. There isn't anything I wouldn't do for you. You know what I mean. You can have your way, any time. I'll never want to leave you, in spite of the difference in our ages, and I promise I'll be good and never look at boys again. . . .

The letter ended there. George folded it up and handed it back to her. None of us were meeting each other's eyes.

"Well?" asked Mrs. Eldridge, with that silly little prinky smile on her face. "Have either of *your* daughters offered to stay with you forever, Mrs. Kinch, and never to look at boys?"

"I should think they was ill," said Mum, "if they wrote me a letter like that."

George said, "Don't you think it might have been meant for a boy-friend, Mrs. Eldridge—someone she had a crush on?"

Mrs. Eldridge exploded. "There you are! You're so down on the child you can't even use the sense you were born with. Whoever else could she possibly stay with for always when she left school? A child of that age!"

"It sounds like a boy to me," said Mother.

"Course it's a boy," Grandad snorted.

"You don't write letters like that to your *mother*," protested Len.

"You're all down on her!" Mrs. Eldridge shrieked.

I was just about to say that I believed that the letter could have been written to a grown-up man, when I thought maybe I wouldn't. Silence is golden, as Mother Marie-Adelaide never stopped saying until after everything happened, when she said that *naturally* she hadn't expected me to apply it to the *police*.

Len was giving George a queer look. Like he did when he was reading *The Hatter's Ghosts*. George noticed it, too, and looked worried.

I was telling myself not to be daft. The mere fact that it was Corinne who was missing, and had written a letter like that to the man who was interested in her, ought to have brought me to my senses. George dating Corinne at Collins Wood!—Corinne, whom he couldn't stick at any price. George offering Corinne "romance" and marriage!

She must've been in the middle of that letter when something stopped her from finishing it. Maybe she had a date with whoever it was, or maybe she was never going to post the letter. She wrote one like that to Charlie Krantz at the supermarket.

Mrs. Eldridge put it back in her bag. "No matter what you say, Mr. Meakham, I'm positive my daughter is hiding from you. I don't care what the police say, she was frightened by a man that night, and she came home and told me that it was you. Out of friendship to Wynne she didn't want to go to the police, and I had to drag her there."

I could see what had happened then. Old Corry, furious with George, and knowing what a state her mother would be in if she knew she'd got in a car with a strange man, makes up a tale about George attacking her, and then she can't get out of it and has to tell the same one to the police.

"I'm going to the police now," said Mrs. Eldridge. "I'm going to tell them that until they've arrested you and put you under lock and key, my little girl will be afraid to come out of her hiding place."

When she went, Mother said, "Poor soul."

"It seems unfair that so much stupidity should be piled up in one person," said George.

I decided that I ought to tell George about what Corinne had said about Collins Wood. It wasn't going to be easy, but I simply felt I had to know about that blue mark on his shoulder that he must have got the very day Corinne said she was going out to meet someone at Collins Wood.

I was just getting up my courage after taking as long as I could over the washing-up and feeding Sandy, when the doorbell went.

It was the police. The same two that came when I was missing in the back of George's van. The young constable and Detective Sergeant Dowley.

Mother sent me along to fetch George. I was so nervous I forgot to knock on the door. He rammed something quickly back into his top drawer and said to me, "Don't you get taught any manners at school? Knock before you burst into somebody's bedroom."

He was angry because he was frightened that I might have seen what he was stowing away with such speed.

"I'm sorry," I said, "but the police want to see you."

George went into the sitting-room and I heard him asking them if they'd like a glass of beer. They said they would.

They were very friendly and understanding. Mrs. Eldridge had shown them Corinne's letter.

I took the opportunity of creeping back into George's room. I wanted to know what he was so anxious to hide away in his drawer. It was one of his drip-dry shirts, and there was blood on it.

I was still staring at it when I heard the sitting-room door open. George was coming to fetch me. I only just got out of his room in time.

Sergeant Dowley didn't seem quite so friendly to me. He said the last time he'd spoken to me he didn't exactly come away with the impression that I was very truthful, and this time it would save everybody a lot of trouble if I answered his questions straight. No more "sheltering under things" and not answering.

"I told your mother you needed a good hiding the night you were missing, didn't I, Mrs. Kinch?"

"Yes," said Mum. "But Wynne's so truthful, really."

"You'd have got it if you'd been my daughter," the sergeant told me.

"She'd have got it if she'd been mine," said Grandad.

"Well, now," said the sergeant cheerfully. "What about this friend of yours? Have you any idea who this letter was meant for?"

"Her mother thinks it was meant for her."

"We know what her mother thinks," the sergeant said. "We want to know who you think it was meant for."

"You've upset the child," my mother said indignantly. "She's as white as a little ghost."

I said, "It's all right, Mum." But I felt as white as a ghost. George's drip-dry shirt, and the blood on it, seemed to be filling the whole of my head.

"Never spoke to you about anyone?" the sergeant wanted to know. "Like girls do when they get a crush on someone?"

"No," I said firmly. "She never spoke about *this* one."

"Did she have a lot, then?"

"No."

"Then who were the others she spoke to you about?"

"She didn't."

"Well look, love, you said she didn't speak about *this* one, as if she had spoken about others."

"Well, I mean she didn't tell me about the one who wanted to marry her."

"*Marry* her? Someone wanted to marry her? A kid of that age?"

"Well . . ." I could have snapped my tongue off. I felt all tangled up, and afraid of that face in front of me. It was pleasant, and good-looking, but you could see in it that he knew I was lying. I made it worse. I was being a nit and laying traps for myself, never mind falling into theirs.

"Oh, she was just making it up," I said. "She was often like that."

"Then she did speak to you about someone special."

"No, she didn't."

"Then how did you get the marriage idea?"

"Well, from that letter she wrote. Mrs. Eldridge made George read it out to us."

"There was nothing in it about marriage."

The sergeant's voice reminded me of the noise a dog's teeth make, wearing down a bone.

The young policeman was tickling Sandy, but he was listening just the same.

"Now," said the sergeant quietly, but still with the bone in his voice, "we've come round to agreeing that she did talk to you about someone. Did she say who it was?"

"No." I was scarlet in the face.

"Hallo, old whiskers," the young policeman said to Sandy. "Hallo, old whiskers."

Glad to change the subject, I warned him, "You have to watch out. He bites when he likes you."

"I've got one at home," the young policeman said, and added, "Did she tell you what he was like?"

"No," I said.

"Well, what did she say?" the sergeant snapped. "She said something. We've admitted that. He wanted to marry her. That's not all that usual with a girl of fifteen, even in these days."

"She was making him up."

"What makes you think that?"

"Because I made up something about—about someone. I think she was getting her own back."

"When did she try getting her own back?"

"On the phone, the last time she rang up."

"Now what exactly did she say, that last time she rang up?"

"Oh, nothing really—"

"If she wanted to get her own back, she couldn't have rung up and said nothing. She'd have said plenty. What was it? Look, love," the sergeant said, and the "love" didn't sound all that cosy—it sounded a bit menacing. I think he'd have liked to jump up then and there and give me the belting he said he would have given his own daughter if she'd been me. "Your friend might be in danger. We hope she isn't, but we can't be too careful, can we, when you think what's been happening lately? Now, if you're not going to help us, we might be too late to help her. *What did she say to you when she rang up?*"

All I could think of was George's shirt. "I've told you," I whispered. "She made him up. I know when Corry's making things up. He doesn't exist."

"Would she write a letter to someone that didn't exist?"

That took the blood out of my burning face. She wouldn't, of course. Not even Corry.

My brain, which felt stuffed with George's shirt, wasn't helping me much. I said, "Well, she did go on about meeting someone. But it's true I thought she'd made him up."

"Did she say who he was?"

"No. She just said he was a man."

"What was he like?"

"Small," I lied. "Small and thin—and a bit like Frank Sinatra."

That should do it, I thought. George was tall and broad, and not a bit like Frank Sinatra.

"Why couldn't you have told us that in the first place?"

"I told you! I thought she was making it up," and I burst into tears.

"Be'ave yourself, Wynne," said Grandad.

But Mother rounded on the police. "Look how you've upset her. If you did more about keeping the traffic out of a muddle, so that decent folk can cross the road . . ." George put a hand on her shoulder. She tailed off, mumbling, "Do more good to get after the people that commit crimes than come bothering an innocent child."

"Anything else you can remember?" the sergeant asked. "We'd be very grateful to hear."

When they left I sat hugging Sandy tight into my stomach.

It was George who showed the police out. Mother fussed over me, asking me if I'd like a cup of tea, and wouldn't it be nice to have a hot bath and go to bed. Len collected the beer glasses and took them to the kitchen. He wasn't usually so helpful. I guessed he wanted something to do. He looked really queer, did Len.

Grandad said to me, "Why you couldn't have answered up in the first place, instead of keeping them hanging about trying to get the truth out of you like a penny from a moneybox, I'll never know."

"I don't think it's right," said Mother. "Coming here frightening the child to death."

"It's young Corinne that could have been frightened to death," said Grandad. "And Wynne here did nothing to help them to find her."

"When he comes back," I told myself, "I'll tell George I

knew he'd been to Collins Wood the day that Corinne said
she was going to meet someone there."

But George didn't come back. He went out with the police, and didn't come back until the early hours of the morning, smelling of Leonie. I knew because I crept out of bed
and saw that so as not to wake Len he'd undressed in
the passage and put his clothes on the chair. They reeked
of Sortilège.

He'd gone to work before I woke up in the morning.

When Len was in the bathroom I had another look at that
shirt. It was blood all right. I got a pair of scissors, took the
shirt and went down into the courtyard. There was a completely hidden space between the bicycle sheds and the
wall which divided us from the Comprehensive School.

It took me what seemed hours and hours, but I snipped
the shirt into hundreds of small pieces. I stuffed them all
inside a plastic food bag and soaked all the pieces to make
them heavy. In the grounds of the convent there was a dis-
used well. That was where my bits of shirt were going.

Until I could get to the well, I put the plastic bag under
my school hat on my part of the wardrobe shelf.

Hélène never touched my part of the shelf. She was so
busy going for me if I moved anything on hers that she had
to be very careful about mine, so as not to get a "What
about you?"

The next day's papers were full of Corinne. Her photograph was on the front pages and there was a big search
being organised. Anyone who had seen her was asked to
contact the police, and her description was given, and a
list of the clothes she was wearing.

"My hat!" said Hélène. "If the little bitch is anywhere she
can read all this, she'll be tickled pink."

Hélène always regretted that remark.

It came out later that somebody had seen Corinne.
Several people, in fact. She had been on the six-o'clock
'bus to Collins Wood the day she asked me to join her.

After that it was quick, of course. The police went to the common, with tracker dogs and goodness knows what. I suppose it was a natural thing to do, to search an empty house.

They made a much better search than I did. She was under the floor boards in Grandad's basement, and she was wrapped in a pile of old newspapers.

She was wearing a ring made of elephant hair on the third finger of her left hand.

**23** ❖ I FELT LIKE SOMEONE WHO HAD DIED inside his own head. Something moved my arms and legs, and opened my mouth and let out noises, but none of that made me feel alive.

Mother kept wiping her eyes and saying, "Oh poor Mrs. Eldridge! What must she be feeling like? The poor soul. It doesn't bear dwelling on."

But the first time I found that I could cry was when I thought of that ring made of elephant hair. Corry must have believed all those lies that her murderer told her. She must have believed that he was really fond of her. She wasn't just boasting to get her own back on me.

He must have gone on kidding her pretty well to the last, to keep her in that empty house with him. It was thinking about the moment when she found out that released my tears, and then I thought they would never stop. She wouldn't have believed he could harm her. At least, not at first. She would have thought it was some kind of joke, that he was just trying to frighten her. She would have been puzzled and perhaps even a little bit angry before it dawned on her—and then—no, it didn't bear thinking about. It didn't.

Nor did it help to wonder if I could have saved her if I'd gone down to meet him like she asked. Somebody coming might have put him off, or if he'd gone for both of us one of us might have got free and brought help. But I didn't believe her. I didn't go down. That's when my crying fits started again.

In some strange way it almost comforted me at the time to think that I too might be in danger. If by any chance she'd told him she'd asked me to join them that night, and he thought that I knew who he was, he might want me out of the way for that reason alone.

In the papers it said something about police waiting by Mrs. Eldridge's bedside, and doctors saying she wasn't well enough to answer questions. She had been taken to hospital and treated for shock.

There was a picture of Mr. Eldridge, which made him look happy and blown as if he was at the sea-side. His tie was flying in the wind, and his hair was all untidy. His face was turned so you couldn't really see it. It was just that he looked so untidy that made him look carefree.

George was asked to go down to the police station, and this time so was I.

Mum came with me, and like Corinne I was asked if I would rather talk to a lady detective. Mum said tartly that *her* daughter could be trusted with a man.

I saw a Detective Superintendent Ranville from Scotland Yard, and he reminded me of one of Sandy's whitings. He was sort of cold and smoothly long, and I simply couldn't stop seeing him curled round in a saucepan like a fish. But he wasn't curled round dead. He was alive, all right.

He was nice. It was Sergeant Dowley that was having trouble keeping his hands off me. He told the superintendent that I was the young lady who he wasn't all that sure had too good an idea of the truth.

The superintendent looked as if he'd got a face that hadn't kept up with the age of his body. It was shiny and rather babyish, with its great marble eyes.

They gave Mum a cup of tea and offered me one, but I couldn't swallow, or at least I felt as if I couldn't.

They were awfully nice to Mum. They jollied her along, and told her not to worry. They gave me some sort of warning that anything I said could be given in evidence, just like the telly police, and I didn't need to say anything if I didn't want to, but I was dying to say anything I could think of that would muddle them up and put them off thinking that George might be able to "help with their enquiries."

I should think that poor Corry and her story against George probably did him less harm than me trying to protect him.

I've never done so much wriggling about in words. Not ever in the whole of my life. But every time I set off down one track, there were the police at the end of it, before I even got there.

There was no bullying. Sergeant Dowley kept his dislike of me as private as he could. He thought I was an "out on the tiles" type of teenager, and he didn't hold with my kind. I could see him longing to tell me again what would have happened to me if I'd been his daughter.

Sandy's Whiting was much calmer. He didn't give away what he thought of you at all, or whether your answers had gone home, or whether he believed you, or anything. A right old poker-face, was Sandy's Whiting.

But there was a lot of kidding, and more cups of tea, and inside a quarter of an hour at the very most they had me strangling in all the untied ends of my own lies.

George was being questioned in another room, but people kept popping in between us. Even Sandy's Whiting got up now and again and left us, presumably to see how they were getting on with George. Whenever he went out of the room, Sergeant Dowley warned me not to play him up, because he was a devil, was Sandy's Whiting. Ooh, don't go by that quiet sort of look! Get the wrong side of him, and my word! I'd do much better to make a clean breast of anything I knew to Sandy's Whiting. My word, if I realised what had happened to people who hadn't made a clean breast of it to Sandy's Whiting, I wouldn't be sitting there looking so pleased with myself! The sergeant thought it only fair to warn me.

Every time someone popped in and heard what I'd had to say, he looked sort of surprised or sorrowful, and said, well, it was a bit of a worry because that wasn't what George had just said.

Mum never left off saying, if they spent more time getting the traffic out of a muddle . . .

I never shall understand Mum. She wasn't a bit worried about George being asked questions, and you'd think anyone would jump from knowing he was being questioned to wondering if he was suspected, and then to whether they were right to suspect him. But not Mum. What was more extraordinary to me, she wasn't really put out about Corinne. All her tears were for Mrs. Eldridge. When you think how upset she was about the poor souls the strangler murdered before Corinne—people she didn't even know— and people she defended against the daft charge that they probably asked for it—you'd have thought that Corinne would have been just about the end for her. But she said Corinne *did* "ask" for it, and pray to God her poor mother never realised it was her own fault.

Mum was just annoyed, at that police station. Not terrified, or sick with worry, or—well, she was just annoyed. She drank the tea, and said I'd always been on the anaemic side, and didn't they realise I'd had a shock about my friend, and couldn't they just go out and find the murderer, and stop bothering ordinary folks, when you thought of the rates they paid.

Sandy's Whiting popped back to tell us again that my brother George wasn't saying at all the sort of things that I was saying, which was very confusing for everybody. Sandy's Whiting didn't want to be rude, but he thought if anyone was telling the truth between my brother George and me, he thought it was my brother George!

Mum opened her mouth, and Sandy's Whiting said yes, dear, as soon as she persuaded me to help them out of this muddle they'd have more time to go back and get the traffic out of a muddle, wouldn't they?

Then Sandy's Whiting looked me cold in the face, and

there were no dears or duckies or loves. He said to remember something. The man who killed my friend Corinne had probably heard about me through her. He may have known that she rang me up and told me about him. He wouldn't be feeling very friendly to me, would he? Didn't I think I ought to cut out all the silly lies and tell them what I knew?

Mother said it was no better than the Gestapo, worrying a young girl.

I was in such a state of numbed shock that I couldn't really think about Corinne as Corinne. Not the Corry I'd been friends with for so many years. Just as well, I suppose, because I was scared and ill enough as it was. I was just floundering about, trying to help George and damaging him.

George's alibi for the night Corinne was killed was Leonie again. But the police knew she was a booze pot, and not at all reliable.

My mind was going round like a hamster on its wheel, what with trying to remember my old lies, and thinking up new ones to cover the ones I'd forgotten. If they hadn't been suspicious of George in the first place, they were good and suspicious of him by the time I'd finished trying to protect him.

They'd found the fragments of the sweater I'd buried at Collins Wood. The bits were being analysed. I denied knowing anything about it, but of course it wasn't going to take them long to know it was George's, if they didn't know already, and then they were going to want to know what made me so suspicious of George. They'd be a flat ten minutes hooking all my reasons out of me, judging from the way they'd tripped me up so far.

They knew George had visited Collins Wood, and they knew he'd been there the day Corinne died. Whether they knew it from him or they'd got it out of me, I was too muddled to tell.

Why was I so fond of the house at Collins Wood, they wanted to know, and why had I gone there on a certain date, etc., etc. I wasn't with them very long, but it seemed to me that every time I opened my mouth I convicted George in their eyes.

After all, you don't try and get rid of somebody's blood-stained sweater unless you're sure he's done something pretty awful in it.

I kept answering questions they didn't ask, or didn't seem to have asked, and then they'd look surprised, as if they hadn't meant it, but it was what they wanted to know in any case!

They got out of me that Corinne really had told me quite a bit about this man she was so crazy about, and that she'd actually told me she was going to Number 3 to meet him, and asked me to go too. Then, of course, they wanted to know why I'd kept such an important thing to myself. After all, there was my best friend missing, and a fearful flap on about it, and everyone looking for her, and I'm asked if I'd got any idea where she might have gone, and I say no. Why?

What could I say? That I didn't dare tell them because I knew that George had been out to the house the day Corinne died, and that my constant nightmare was that he might be out of his mind, and have done her in like all the rest? It's not the best thing to say, if you're trying to protect someone.

It didn't seem the best thing, either, to confess that George had lied to me about the sweater, and that I knew how often he'd been to Collins Wood because of the paraffin on his shoes and the blue marks. I couldn't say that I knew perfectly well that Len was just as suspicious of him as I was, and I was determined not to say that I'd spent the whole night alone at Number 3—if you could call "alone" sharing the place with a tramp and someone else who took exactly the same size of shoes as George. And it might be wise not to mention that the footsteps led to the cupboard that I was hiding in. Or that I'd cleaned the footsteps up.

I *didn't* say anything of the sort. I said the opposite. But somehow they found it all out.

Then Sandy's Whiting said Mum could take me home, but of course for me not to go off anywhere, because they might want to talk to me again. They had still some more questions that they wanted to ask George. So he didn't come home with us. There must have been quite a bit they wanted to ask him. He was with them twelve hours on that occasion.

As soon as Mum and I got home, I went to see Len. He was lying on his bed, and he smelt of vinegar. It was one of Aunt Rene Tindall's recipes for headaches.

Hélène had put the rag on his head before she went off to her cinema.

I leaned over him. "Len," I said. "Len, it's time to tell me. What do you know? They've got George there still. They're keeping him. You think it's him, don't you?"

He sat up, snatching off his vinegar rag. "Like I told you," he snapped. "The day after that second bird had her neck screwed, there was that sweater of brother boy's, caked in blood. *That* bird was made to look like a car accident, if you remember—a bloody one!"

"He could have hurt himself at work."

"He didn't, did he? Or we'd have seen it."

"Maybe one of the men hurt themselves, or Mr. Wells."

"Then why didn't brother boy say so? I gave him the chance. I asked him about it. He acted real queer. He lied. He twisted all over the place. I got the wind up. Then he was so peculiar about the book I was reading."

"*The Hatter's Ghosts!* Yes! That's what I noticed. But why? The crimes weren't even the same that took place in the hatter's town."

"No. But they were stranglings, and I wondered if I read it often enough, I'd get some kind of clue as to what was happening in our town. I mean what made stranglers tick. George noticed how often I was reading it, and acted queer about it. He asked so many questions about it, it gave me

the willies. I thought something must make him so interested in stranglers. I got so scared I took that sweater out
to the old house and burned it. At least, I thought I had.
He's been acting queer ever since our stranglings started,
has George."

"Len, do you know someone called Leonie Protheroe? A
friend of George's?"

"Who doesn't? The bottle-punisher. She's the daughter
of some bloody rich contractor or something, who won't
have anything to do with her, and she married another
bloody rich contractor who won't have anything to do with
her. But she's a dish. When she's sober she's as sweet as hell.
I know. I've spoken to her on the phone now and again.
She's surely after Brother George."

"How do you know what she looks like?"

"She's around a lot. When she's pissed she looks like a bit
of gristle out of a leftover stew, but when she's been playing
it holy—Ker-rist! There's no dishier dish. You can't blame
Brother George. If that's laid on a plate you'd have to be a
misfit not to say thank you."

"Have you met her?"

"No. I've followed them. I wanted to know what brother
boy was up to. Maybe we're wrong. When she's pissed the
biggest saint would want to strangle her, but George hasn't
—yet."

"Oh, Len! Don't joke."

"Who's joking? He'd been to the old house the evening
he was wearing the sweater. He took the van out, and I
followed on my scooter. I reckoned I was rather a good
detective. But I couldn't have been. He spotted me. Wanted
to know what I was doing there. You see, he'd found out
about me being on the pills. A pal of mine in the group
started me on them—the amount I take, says this pal,
wouldn't give a baby the burps, but of course Brother
George has always been a bit conventional. Also, of course,
I take a bit of liquid, and maybe they squeal at each other.

Anyway, I said why shouldn't I be out at Collins Wood? I'd always loved the old dump. Brotherly love was a bit low, on account of the pills, and brother boy didn't go for my jaunty air. Especially when I said, Anyhow, come to think of it, what the bloody hell was he doing there? He said he'd tell me if he could trust me to keep my mouth shut, but you couldn't trust people who mixed drink and drugs. They got themselves and other people into trouble. We had quite a ding-dong, and I drove off. But it was that night that scared the pants off me.

"He didn't come in until about three o'clock that morning. I pretended to be asleep when he peeped into the room. But I was looking through slits. Brother boy even had blood in his hair. He was a hell of a long time in the bathroom. You learn a lot when you share a room with someone. There was blood on his jacket. He nipped that off in a brown paper parcel. Must have taken it to the cleaner's, because it's back again and it's all right. He looked a bit of a sight that night— or that morning, rather. His back was a sadist's dream. Looked like claw marks. Scratched to bits, he was. A proper railway track. I heard him getting the ice out, in the kitchen. Maybe he wanted it for his eye. It was good and swollen. Someone had fought with him pretty hard, and I know enough about things to know you don't get those sort of scratches from a man. There was a blooming great bite in his neck. His collar hid it in the daytime. Some bird had been up against him, and it was the very next day that this other bird was found at Collins Wood. One of the faked car accident ones."

"I wonder why he didn't take the sweater to the cleaner's," I said.

"Too bloody, maybe. He might not want questions asked. The next morning I was just getting my scooter out of the sheds, to get off to work, when down he comes with a brown paper parcel and dumps it in the dustbin. He didn't see me, but when he'd got into the van and driven off, I had a look-see at that parcel. It was the sweater. I thought it was the daftest thing he could have done. I mean, it could start any nosey cop off thinking things. I mean, with birds being found trussed-up all over the place, you can't be too careful. I remembered the old copper at the old house. So I took a run out there and burned the sweater. At least, I thought I did. Like I said, you see things, sharing rooms with people, and that wasn't the first time that our George had come back with a bit of blood on him."

"Oh, Len!" I said. "Len!"

"Yeah, and he got mighty funny with me after that. He lied himself sick over that sweater, and it turned into him playing detective on me! Everywhere little Leonard went, Brother George was sure to be. I wonder we didn't trip over and break each other's necks."

"But *why* did he follow you, *why*, Len?"

"Make sure I wasn't following him, I suppose. It got as daft as that. He told me he was afraid I was keeping bad company."

"Oh, Len," I said, "it's terrible, but I feel so much better for talking to you. I've nearly been out of my mind about this."

"Me too. I kept telling myself that it couldn't be him, and if he was nuts surely I'd have seen it, in the bedroom. But then he *did* go a bit bonkers when Clare died."

"He *didn't* go bonkers. He suffered from delayed shock, and so did you, only yours wasn't delayed. You had to have phenobarb, even at seven, because the accident made your nerves so bad."

"I didn't have blackouts and go to head-shrinkers."

Len sat nervously biting his nails.

"I wondered if I should go to the doctor about him. But then I thought, 'No, supposing it wasn't him, and I went and got him suspected, and he couldn't get himself unsuspected.' I can tell you it played hell with my nerves."

I put my face in my hands. "Oh, it *couldn't* be him, Len, it couldn't. He's *not* nuts. He's the sanest person out."

"That's how they all are. They'd seem no different to you and me. He could talk about it all quite normally, and say the fellow who's done it must be nuts, and all the time he's nuts himself. But he certainly wouldn't seem it, or he'd be inside already. A girl's not going to go out with a chap that looks gaga, or says he's going to kill her. He might not even know he's done it, or he might not be able to stop it."

"He told me that about the strangler once, himself. He said that the man might not be able to stop it."

Len went to his drawer, and took out the half bottle of whisky he hid in his socks with the purple hearts. There was some whisky left in the bottle, and he took a swig as well as some pills.

"Talk about old Protheroe! This little do has turned me into a boozer myself."

"Does Hélène know you suspect George?"

"Good lord in heavens, no! 'Sensible Annie' would have asked him outright, and if she didn't get the answer she liked, she'd have gone to the police for his own sake! Then he might have added her to his list for his own sake! Killer-nuts don't have much chivalry, even to the family."

"I asked him outright, or as good as that, and he didn't lay a finger on me."

"Oh well, he thinks the world of you."

"Not any more."

"Oh, doesn't he! Anyway, he knows wild horses wouldn't get you to the cops. I knew you were safe enough. But he doesn't think so much of Hélène. I didn't want her under the floor boards at Collins Wood."

"Len," I said, "you didn't go spying on George in the middle of the night at Collins Wood, did you?"

I told him about my little stay in the cupboard, and how I had seen the tramp, and then heard someone else. I thought he was going to faint. He had to sit down on the bed.

He said, "Wynne, you *nit!* You little bloody *nit.* Don't you realise the guy's flat steaming bonkers? Whoever he is, he's steaming bonkers! Don't you *ever* go out to the place again, not *ever—*" Then he broke off. "Oh well, I suppose it doesn't matter now. They've got him."

"Len, it couldn't be him, it couldn't," I sobbed. "Not really! We're just imagining it."

"Well, if it's not him it's someone he's fond of. Some mate of his he's trying to protect. I've even spied on old Jimmie Wells. He seems sane enough, but you never know."

"I thought it was you once, Len, you acted so queer."

He swung round on me. "You'd rather it was me, wouldn't you? You wouldn't go round burning up my sweater, would you?"

"Yes, I would, of course I would. Oh Len, what are we going to do?"

"Well, there's not much we can do. They've got him now."

"We could make Leonie swear she was with him the night Corinne died. We could make her sign a statement."

"What happens if he bumps someone else off? They can't stop, you know, once they get started. Like drink."

He took another swig from his bottle.

"We'll tell him we know," I said desperately. "We'll both confront him, and say we've found out, and we'll act as private gaolers. One of us will always be watching him, and we'll keep threatening to go to the police."

"You're as crazy as him, if he is crazy," said Len, and finished what was left in the bottle.

"Len," I said, "keep Mum and Grandad talking. I'm going to ring Leonie Protheroe."

We needn't have bothered, really. Mum and Grandad were too busy discussing things themselves, and Aunt Rene Tindall had called. Everyone knew that George was "helping the police with their enquiries," of course.

No one stopped me from ringing up. Leonie answered. Oh, goodness, she was drunk! There was nothing clear in her voice this time. I've never heard anyone so drunk. She could hardly get her words out. But she knew who I was.

"Leonie, George is down with the police again."

"Has he got a crush on them, or something?"

I shan't try and write like she spoke. No one would be able to read it. I'll just put it down straight.

"Blast them," she said. "They've been here. The whole damn police force. Everyone's been here except George. I warned him. I said, 'I'll stand anything but neglect. Where's my record-player?' Well, tell him—it's too late. He's done it for good and all. I've had it and him and everything. Tell him I'm one less to strangle."

She gave an awful loud laugh, and she choked on it.

"Leonie, I'm coming to see you. I've got to see you urgently."

"Can't let you in, baby. Legs have gone." And she hung up on me.

I rushed back to Len. "We've *got* to get in to her somehow. She's *got* to say George was there the night that Corinne died."

I pulled open George's top drawer. His car keys were in the little cardboard box where he always kept them, and under it was a Yale front-door key, and a goldy-looking one. They were tied together on a bit of red twine. Of course, they could have belonged to lots of places. George used plenty of keys in his job. But I guessed he'd mostly keep those at the office. With any luck these might be the two that had let him into Leonie's flat, the time he found me there.

I chucked the car keys at Len. "Come on, Len. We'll see what we can do. She'll sign a statement he was with her, if I have to hold a knife to her throat."

Len was a good driver. Even George said so. But Hélène was always scared with him, in case his nerves gave out.

In the van I said the most terrible thing. "I wish there'd be another murder right this minute, while George is still with the police. Then everyone would know he couldn't have done it."

**24** ❖ NOBODY STOPPED US ON THE WAY UP to Leonie's flat. When we let ourselves in, all the lights were on. I called, "Leonie! It's George's sister, Wynne!"

"Ker-rist!" said Len, looking round the place. "I gather she's not on National Assistance."

"We'll have to go into the bedroom," I said. "She can't get out of bed when she's like this."

I went to the bedroom. At first I thought she was asleep, with a red scarf or something wrapped round her. Then I went forward. It was her sheets that were red. I screamed.

I could think only of what I'd said in the van. That I hoped someone else would get murdered. Long before I found time to be sorry for poor Leonie, I was thinking that it was God's way of showing me George was innocent. She'd been murdered while he was still down at the station. I was saying a prayer of thanksgiving in my head. Father Murphy felt very strongly about that bit. You can quite see his point in a way.

"Oh Len!" I bubbled. "It isn't George! Somebody's killed her when he couldn't have done it."

It was really terrible, the way I was taking it. Looking back on it, I can't believe it was me. Me, who could cry myself to sleep if I saw a dog run over. I suppose I'd had so many shocks at that time I was getting used to them. Still, it didn't alter the fact that what I was practically doing was clapping my hands and saying, "Isn't it marvellous, someone's been murdered!"

Len came in behind me, and gave me one of the biggest surprises of my life. It just proves the old saying that you never know. I thought his nerves would explode at the sight of blood. He'd never got over Clare's accident, and I thought he'd collapse, or go absolutely berserk.

He looked over my shoulder and said, "She hasn't been murdered. She's done herself in. Look, she's holding what she did it with!"

I simply stood back and stared at him. "Cut her throat," he explained, as if he'd been a gardener telling me how someone had pruned a rose. "Cut her throat with that bit of china from the bedside lamp."

The lamp had been made of china cupids, with little ribbons and flowers round them. She'd smashed it, and there was a jagged half of a cupid lying near her hand. The blood had collected in the petals of the little rope of flowers.

"It could have been someone else," I said. "Someone could have broken the lamp and gone for her."

"No," Len said, "it's ringing a bell. Listen. It's coming back to me. This bird is a 'compulsive suicide.' I heard George call her that once. I overheard a conversation one night. George'd come back about three in the morning, and she rang just as he got in the door. The phone only ponked once, and he snatched it up. But I heard what he said. He said, okay for her to go ahead and cut her blessed throat, cut her blessed wrists, swallow anything she liked, as long as she did it and stopped trying to scare him about it. He hung up on her. My guess is that it was a booze threat—you know, just the same way that some old ducks get their children hanging round them through throwing heart attacks. She did scare him, though, because about an hour later he got up and went out. I suppose he thought she might have taken his advice."

Len left me sitting on the floor and went to the bed. He picked up Leonie's wrist. "Ha! Ha!" he said, as if he'd been at a darts match and scored a bull's-eye. "I'm right! Scars! She's had a go before. They don't always mean it, you know. They just try it on to scare people into their power."

Later I remembered, of course, how Leonie had flapped

her wrists at me. She wanted to show me what she was capable of. My thoughts were absolutely scrambled. There were so many things I couldn't take in. I couldn't take in Leonie, dead in her pretty-shaped bed with the red scarf round her. I couldn't take in the extraordinary calm of Len; Len, who could get so worked up over nothing at all that Mother fetched his phenobarb.

Now I know, of course, that it's sometimes the most placid people that break into a thousand pieces, and the nervy ones that you'd think would mushroom up like the Bomb who stay calm on the ground.

It suddenly occurred to me that Leonie might not be dead. We hadn't even bothered to try and help her.

I ran forward and pulled back the bedclothes. Before I fainted I had just time to see what the odd, soaked square was, on her chest. It was a packet of cigarettes. Some were loose—little red squashy rolls, with the tobacco spreading out. There was ash in the blood as well. She'd been smoking a lot before she died.

When I came to, Len was trying to pour something down my throat. Brandy or whisky, I don't really know, but it went all over my face. I sat up quickly.

"A fat lot of good you are," Len told me. "I don't know what you'd have been like with Clare. That was ten times worse. There was the dog's blood as well, and she was in terrible, terrible agony. There can't be a God, to allow so much pain. It ought to be proportioned out to people. You needn't worry about this one." He jerked a thumb over his shoulder at Leonie. "She's gone out on a cloud of booze. Probably didn't even feel it. There's an empty bottle of something here. She had a packet of pills, as well."

He helped himself from one of Leonie's decanters. His hands were shaking so much he hit the glass with the top of the decanter, and his face was the most dreadful colour. He wasn't as unaffected as he wanted to sound, but it was

Clare he went prattling on about. It had broken his memories of Clare's death.

"Well," he said, gurgling a drink from the neck of the decanter, "poor old Protheroe! If she'd been murdered it would have let Brother George out."

"Len," I said dizzily, "it's *got* to let George out. This has got to *look* like murder."

In my defence it was said afterwards that the strain I was under made me irresponsible for my actions. But it was nothing of the sort. All I thought was that, as no one could help poor Leonie any more, she might as well help George.

I went mad. I threw things all over the place. "Make it seem like a fight," I shouted at Len. "Make it look as if someone's come in and she's tried to defend herself. Break everything!"

Poor old Len tried to stop me. Drunk as he was, he did his best. That was the fight that people heard. He chased after me, knocking into even more things than I was throwing about.

"Here! Wynne!" he yelled. "You must be mad. They'll see through this! You'll make things worse! You'll go to prison! They'll have you up—this is criminal, what you're doing. You're bonkers."

I knocked down a lovely little lacquered chest. There was a leather jewel-box inside. I opened it, and stuffed most of the things in my pockets and down my front—motive for murder—robbery! I didn't really see what the jewellery was —necklaces, bracelets, costume or real jewellery—I didn't care.

I tried to drag poor Leonie to the door. I didn't think it looked right that she'd have died in bed. I wanted to have it look as if she'd been trying to get to the telephone. I can still retch when I think of the mess I made.

Blood sort of squelched unwillingly at me out of her throat when I tried to move her. The wound, where she'd cut it with the piece of china, opened up like a pair of lips.

I shouldn't have been surprised if they'd spoken to me, in the thick and terrible voice she'd used on the phone before she died.

I was too sick and faint to do more than pull her over the side of the bed.

It wasn't hard to understand what they said about me afterwards. I was a vicious teenager drugged into blood-lust. I was a jealous sex-fiend at fourteen, so resentful of George's friendship with her that I wanted to desecrate the body. I was a product of a brutal and disgusting age, and I had corrupted poor Corinne into seeking her death.

I upset and broke things in every room, because I thought that would make it look as if Leonie had been running away from her murderer, and not just lain in bed waiting for him to come at her.

Len, good and drunk by now, was just sitting on the end of that sad and terrible bed, shouting at me that I'd have us both in gaol.

He was far nearer the truth than I was getting. The people downstairs had already sent for the police.

The only room I hadn't done any damage in was the one Leonie had stopped me going into. The one she told me George wanted to be kept secret.

I went into it, snapped on the light, and stood quite still.

It was a little, turret-shaped room. Leonie must have used it as a store-room. There was everything in it, from bottles of drink to rolls of lavatory paper. But that wasn't what I was staring at. On the table, which was covered over with felt, was a model, about a foot high, of Number 3 Collins Wood. It wasn't quite finished. On another table there were tools and paints, and some drawings with writing on them, in George's hand.

Somebody was banging on the door. "Come out! We've sent for the police. Mrs. Protheroe! Are you all right?"

It was surprising they hadn't come up before, really. But I suppose they were used to noises in Leonie's flat.

"Len!" I squeaked. "Look at this! Whatever can it mean? Come and look at it."

Len pulled me out of the doorway. "Can't you hear the racket, you little twit? We've got to get out."

I was standing staring at the model of Number 3 Collins Wood. The whole front opened up. It was perfect inside.

Len grabbed my shoulders and dragged me back. He ran me to the door and pulled it open so suddenly that a man who'd been trying to force it fell on his face, which would have been funny if we'd been in the mood. There was another man with him. There were also two women. Len shoved me through them so fast I hardly had time to 'see.

I suppose it was shock that made them lose a few seconds before going for us. We were a nasty, bloody sight, and I shed pieces of Leonie's jewellery as I ran.

A woman called, "Oh, the hooligans! The vicious little *hooligans!*"

A man had run into Leonie's flat, and very soon there were shouts of "Murdered! It's murder!"—"She's dead! She's been killed!"

Len and I fled down those twisting stairs like drops of hot grease down a corkscrew. Len stopped to push back one of the men, and I went crashing out into the garden. It was dark outside, except for the light from the porch that shone over the drive.

I plunged into the rhododendrons. It was a huge garden, and full of big shrubs. I lay waiting for Len to catch me up. But he didn't. There were people searching the garden, so I thought he must have gone another way, and I'd better get home at all costs.

I managed to scramble over a wall. Every bit of Leonie's jewellery had dropped off me by then.

I could hear shouts and see torches flickering about in the grounds behind me. There were sirens, and cars drawing up. Police, I supposed.

I waited, breathless and sore from my scramble over the

wall, for Len. But there was nothing except the shouts in the distance. So I ran on.

It gets quite countrified between Harrowvane and Dalstead, to use a word that George hated. He always said, "How can country be 'fied'? Either it's country or it isn't."

It was lonely enough at that time of night, and even though I went the short cut and the back way across Harrowvane Park, I was nearly collapsing by the time I got near home.

If only I hadn't panicked and run with Len! If only I'd called those people downstairs and told them we'd found Léonie murdered! After all, that's what I wanted to prove! I'd mucked things good and proper. Still, we could always say we'd run because we thought they'd think we'd done it. As long as they thought she was murdered while George was safely inside the police station, it didn't matter to me. Nothing mattered to me except that.

To make sure that Len had got home before me, I thought I'd ring him from the box on the corner, just before you get to our block of flats. If he wasn't at home already, I'd wait in the bicycle sheds and catch him before he went home.

There were some terrible slums all round our flats, and the telephone-box was in the middle of them.

I got straight through to Grandad and tried to disguise my voice. "Is Mr. Leonard Kinch in, please?"

"No, he's *not*. Is that *you*, Wynne? Where the 'ell are you? Wynne! *Wynne!*"

I hung up in fright. I'd have to wait by the bicycle sheds. It was black, raining, and cold. The only light came from the windows of our block of flats. The lower landing shone out past the bicycle sheds, and I saw a man sort of slink, hurrying, round the corner.

I called out from my hiding-place, "Len, come here."

I turned to get back into the space between the bicycle sheds and the Comprehensive School, so that we could talk without being seen, when he sprang at me.

I would have screamed, but a hand slapped hard down over my mouth.

I couldn't even count out loud. The hand was hurting my gums against my teeth.

Somewhere in the back of my head I started to pray.

**25** ❖ I WAS UNCONSCIOUS when they found me. The police had traced my call from the local telephone-box, and they'd discovered me in the space between the bicycle sheds and the Comprehensive School.

When I came round in hospital, Detective Superintendent Ranville and Sergeant Dowley were sitting by my bed. My throat was hurting and so was my jaw.

I thought, "Oh Lord, there's Sandy's Whiting again, and the one who'd have clouted me if I'd been his daughter." They made me feel strangely uneasy.

I quickly remembered that there were some important lies I must be sure to tell. I must be terribly careful not to get muddled. Oh yes! Leonie Protheroe had been murdered. She hadn't killed herself—because if she had been murdered, George couldn't have done it. That was it!

But almost right away they told me they knew that the "murder" of Leonie was a cock-and-bull story and that I'd tried to make it look like murder to protect George.

I said nothing, because I was terribly worried about something else. My memory felt as if it was stuck all over my brain with different bits of sticking-plaster. It just didn't seem to join up. But one thought was troubling me badly. It was clear for a bit, and then stopped. I was in a dark, wet place, waiting for Len, and when I called out something horrible happened and somebody's hand wouldn't let me scream.

Whose hand, if George was safely down at the police station?

Could I remember who attacked me, they wanted to know? I said no one attacked me. They said, what about those marks round my throat? I said, what marks? They brought me a mirror and showed me. No wonder my throat hurt, and I'd been clipped on the jaw as well, it seemed.

I said I must have tripped in the dark and fallen over something.

They even brought George to see me. But I nearly died of embarrassment. What do you say to someone you love, when you've thought he was a strangler and smashed up his girl-friend's flat? I put my face in my pillow and wouldn't speak to him. The doctor said I must be allowed to rest, so everyone went away. But they came back again.

They told me I was a very lucky girl. If they hadn't turned up after Grandad reported my call, whoever it was might not have run off. Some other poor girl might not be so lucky, so hadn't I better tell them anything I knew?

They asked me if I was sure I couldn't remember what happened that night? I could only remember that I was waiting for Len, and that I called out to him, and that someone tried to strangle me. But what I couldn't forget was how extraordinarily calm Len had been when he saw Leonie's body. He wasn't put out at all. Almost as if he'd seen lots of bodies. Not just Clare's, of long ago.

It made me think that I must be very careful about what I remembered in front of the police. There was something about a dog. But I couldn't recall what it was. Len wouldn't have had a dog, so that bit would be all right to tell them.

"I think he had a dog," I offered. "I think he said he had a dog."

They both sat forward. "Oh, so there was a 'he' to have a dog, was there? We've remembered that much, have we?"

"What sort of dog?" Sergeant Dowley enquired.

"I don't know. I just think somebody said something about a dog."

When they told me they had nabbed Len at Leonie's flat, and he admitted what I had tried to do, I thought they were tricking me. I thought it best to say nothing, and that was what I hoped I'd said.

Detective Superintendent Ranville and Sergeant Dowley kept up being nice. But I shouldn't have blamed them if they'd wanted to murder me themselves. After all, I'd been destroying clues and lying all over the place, which doesn't exactly make you a policeman's pin-up.

But even though I thought I was saying nothing, they got it out of me that my final scare was that the man in the bicycle shelter was Len.

How they did it, I don't know. They didn't *ask* me if, now that I was sure it wasn't George, I thought it might be Len. Just like the last time, they didn't seem to be asking questions along those lines at all.

They said, not to worry, dear. Not only did they have George down at the station at the time I was attacked, but they had Len, too. They nabbed him at Leonie's flat, remember?

Apparently I was right in thinking that the other tenants would have sent for the police much earlier if they hadn't been used to rows and violence coming from Leonie's flat. They were saving their complaints for the landlord again, until one of them thought things had gone too far.

It wasn't until the police brought Len to see me that I really believed that both my brothers were in the clear.

"Wynne," Len told me, "you're daft not to see George. You surely can't still think he did it?"

"No, I don't still think it was him. But he knows I thought it was, and what must he think of me for that?"

"Well, just now you thought *I* did it. But I haven't taken offence! He wasn't all that flattered that we were so certain he was the stuff that stranglers are made of. But he admits he did act a bit rummy. He wanted to keep that model a surprise for you, so he acted like he didn't know about the measurements on the wall at Collins Wood that you rubbed off—and you can't blame him over the sweater and things.

Nobody wants the family to know his current bird is a wrist-slashing old booze pot. That's where he got the blood on him from."

"He acted rummier than *that*," I said.

"Yes, well, we set each other off. He thought I might be mixed up in it somehow. Or know the chap who did it. I kept reading that *Hatter's Ghosts* to see if there was anything in it that would give a clue to the Dalstead crimes. But there wasn't. It was completely different."

"I know," I said. "I read it too. It was completely different, except that it was about a town where women were getting strangled."

"Yeah," said Len. "Well, then, of course me suspecting him put my nerves on edge, and got me onto booze and pills, and he suspected me even more. It was a ruddy vicious circle of sheer suspicion, and then you come in and run round and round it. Can't you see?" he shouted, as nervy as he'd ever been before. "Wynne, you must've bumped into the genuine article. They think he must've known where you lived, and been waiting for you—so maybe it's someone you know. They think he was afraid Corinne got in touch with you and gave him away. Now anyone that knows you could be in danger—Hélène—or any of your friends."

"But, Len, I'm not holding out any more. I was waiting for you. I called out from the shelter. Then there was a hand over my mouth, and everything went black. But I *think* there was something about a dog."

"What kind of dog?"

"I don't know—I don't remember seeing one. But I've got this feeling about a dog. Wait a minute, something's coming back. It—somebody *said* something about a dog. Right into my ear, with their hand over my mouth. They said I really must be very fond of walking on such a dreadful night, and it really was a waste I didn't have a dog. No, I'm daft—that was the conductor."

"What conductor?"

"The one on the 32A Collins Wood 'bus. The one that used to make poor Corry mad because he gave me more looks than her. Yes. It was him that said that. I must have got mixed up."

*They* were already on their way to see if *he* could "help them with their enquiries," while I was still struggling to remember. It transpired later that someone had seen him meet Corinne at a cinema. And they had traced someone else who had seen him drive her off in his car.

His name was Mr. Bright. I didn't know that.

Len was allowed to go home, but they told him that the facts were being considered and he might be charged later. I came up before the court as being "in need of care or protection."

I've already said how Mum carried on—but they wouldn't alter that decision. I was taken to the Remand Home and both Len and I had to wait and see what the Director of Public Prosecutions decided.

Len shouldn't have burned the sweater, of course, but he hadn't muddled everybody up quite as badly as I had, and he did try to stop me in Leonie's flat.

But I, although I only knew Mr. Bright to speak to, and had nearly come to grief through him, was in danger of being accused of "assisting and comforting a murderer," and charged with being "an accessory after the fact to murder."

That's what you get for destroying evidence, apparently.

When Matron told me that George was going to visit me, I said, "No. Please don't let him come. I don't want to see him." Matron said not to be silly. I'd have to see him, wouldn't I? Besides, it might help to "have everything out."

Matron and Father Murphy wanted my conscience eased in some ways, and certain things hammered home to me in others, such as the folly of telling lies, jumping to silly conclusions, harbouring false suspicions, and destroying evidence, never mind tampering with dead bodies. Doesn't it

sound extraordinary! Tampering with dead bodies! *Me!*
Who got quite sick if I had to pick one of Grandad's poor
little mice out of its box when it died.

They had recovered most of Leonie's jewellery. But one
or two bits had been trodden into the earth and damaged.

My worst fear was that George might think it was
jealousy. He might think I'd done all that to poor Leonie
out of jealousy and spite.

I'd been waking people up by counting out loud in my
sleep, apparently, and Matron said there were going to be a
lot of things I would have to take out of the back of my head
and put them in front of it, and George might help me to
see them properly. I think she knew I'd feel better if I knew
I had his forgiveness, too. But would I have it? The reason
I couldn't bear to see him was because I knew him so well.
If he hadn't really forgiven me, I'd know it, and I didn't
want to know.

Father Murphy argued that George would know that,
whatever I'd done, I'd done for his sake, and surely I knew
what he'd feel about that.

"But, Father," I said, "George was 'off' me in any case—
not just because of this. He was definitely cool, and kept
out of my way."

"You're growing up," said Father Murphy. "He must've
known your feelings for him, and he wouldn't want to encourage them. You're not the baby any more that he used
to coddle and pet—and there's a pretty big gap between
your ages. He couldn't ignore that."

George wrote to me, but I made Matron open the letter.
It started off with, "You'll be delighted to hear that Aunt
Rene Tindall says it all comes from allowing a great big
girl like Wynne to sleep 'in wi' George.'" I did laugh at that
bit. But I didn't laugh at the next. He said, "When you come
home, Grandad thinks Mother could do with the house to
herself for a bit. The rest of us might take a holiday.

Jimmie Wells can carry on for a bit. We might have a trip
to the Lakes. Sandy sends love."

I burst into tears at the Lakes part. "Oh, Matron, he must
have put that in on purpose, to make me feel awful. It was
in the Lake District that I set my dreadful made-up story
to Corinne—the one that made her try and get off with
someone to pay me out. George must have said that to bring
it home to me."

Matron said, "Nonsense." She said that well. You thought
things really were nonsense if Matron said so. "You, of all
people, should know where misplaced suspicion can lead
you. If he minded what you'd made up about the Lake
District, he wouldn't have mentioned it. And about Corinne,
you think that you caused her death because of your constant visits to Collins Wood."

"Well, he'd never have seen her if I hadn't taken her out
on that 'bus so often."

"The other poor souls that he murdered had never been
out on that 'bus. They were killed on the common. He met
them in town, and on the outskirts. He met Corinne in the
town, as well. He was the sort of man who would take an
interest in any young girl, and—we might just as well face
facts—Corinne was the sort of girl who would have re-
sponded to any man. The tales she made up about marriage were quite likely invented for your sake, but she'd
have done that with any man willing to notice her. All you
did was possibly to determine the place of her death. He'd
followed you to your empty house, and he must've thought
it a safer place to kill poor little Corinne. You influenced
only the *place* of her death. You might say that Corinne
nearly caused yours. He was after you, because of her."

"George doesn't even know I'm going home," I sobbed.
"I may get sent somewhere else from here."

"Well, he's hoping you won't, and looking forward to having you back, isn't he?" Matron asked patiently. "There's a
P.S. Do you want to hear it?"

"Yes, please."

Matron read out, "You probably know that they are going to use the model of Number 3 I made you at the Bright trial. I think in view of what happened I'd better tell them not to return it, don't you? Sandy sends more love."

"Oh, Matron," I said, "I want to keep it. It was so marvellous of George to make it for me. He had such sad memories of it himself."

"I think you should write and tell George all that."

It was a terribly hard letter to write. I knew that I shouldn't have wanted to keep the model. But I did! I did! Not just because George had made it, but because of the house itself. The thought of it being knocked down made my throat go tight. It was like someone dying. I couldn't believe it, although I knew that it had to happen. The model would keep it alive. And in some peculiar way I felt that it would be disloyal to Corry not to keep it. As if I wanted to destroy the memory of where she died, to try and forget my part in it.

I wrote, "Dear George, Thank you for your letter. I would like to keep the model, please. Give my love to Sandy. Wynne."

It was a dismal, pale grey morning when my wonderful news came through.

Of all the people to bring it, it was Sandy's Whiting and the sergeant who had wanted to belt me one.

They said that the D.P.P. had recommended that no further action should be taken against Len and me.

Even the sergeant couldn't keep a bit of a smile off his face when they told me, and Sandy's Whiting looked really pleased. He said, surprised though I might be, it was a great treat for them to carry good news for a change. They had enough of bringing bad, and at home he had a kiddy of my age. He hadn't told me that at the police station! I suppose he didn't want me to think he could be sympathetic.

The D.P.P.'s recommendation was due to lots of things;

not wasting public money by bringing me in front of a jury, which would be likely to be sympathetic because of my impressionable age and my motives. Also because my actions had led them to the murderer.

I was a very lucky girl, because the D.P.P. might not have taken that attitude, might he?

I said no, he might not, and I was so nervous that I giggled out that my aunt Rene Tindall would always think the worst of me, never mind what the D.P.P. had decided.

The sergeant said well, we all had our crosses, hadn't we? I had my aunty and they had daft little girls that went about destroying evidence and making police work four times as hard as—

Sandy's Whiting gave him a look and he broke off to say well, maybe I'd been punished enough, but if I'd been his daughter—

Sandy's Whiting gave him another look. Obviously if anyone was going to have a go at me it was going to be Sandy's Whiting.

He said I must realise that every honest citizen's responsibility was to the community, and not to the individual. It didn't matter how much you thought of one person, you had no right to put his welfare before others who could be harmed by it. Did I see how wrong I'd been in trying to cover up for George? I said yes, but I meant no. I'd have done exactly the same if it happened again.

Sandy's Whiting said it was no light thing I had done. Not something to joke about at the expense of my aunty. My aunty would be right to take a serious view.

Those footsteps I had cleared up were Mr. Bright's. I knew that, didn't I? I said yes. Well, said Sandy's Whiting, destroyed some pretty important evidence, hadn't I? I said yes—and like a dafty reminded them I'd cleared up the tramp's as well.

The sergeant said that that made no difference, and I saw him go right back to wanting to belt me if I'd been his

daughter. He'd only been on the brink of wanting to forgive me, anyhow.

Sandy's Whiting said the tramp had proved not quite
right in the head. But he was harmless. He'd certainly been
there that night I was hidden in the cupboard. He often
slept at Collins Wood. He'd also seen the strangler. That's
what scared him off. But you couldn't blame him for not
coming forward. The poor old man thought he was a bird
and could only answer "Cuckoo" or "Tweet-tweet" if you
spoke to him. Sandy's Whiting made the noises so well, and
I got such a picture of the tramp answering questions in
court ("Do you solemnly swear to tell the truth, the whole
truth and nothing but the truth?"—"Tweet-tweet, cuckoo!
cuckoo!") that I went off into a shocking attack of the
giggles.

The sergeant said very funny but I *could* be blamed for
not coming forward. I *was* right in the head, or supposed
to be. If I'd come forward I might have saved my little
friend from getting murdered, mightn't I? If I'd reported
her telephone call to the police instead of trying to shield
George they might have got there in time to save her life,
mightn't they? Maybe I hadn't thought of that!

I said I had, and got the shakes. Matron had to be sent
for.

She said it was my remorse over not taking Corinne's
telephone call seriously that kept both her and me awake
at nights.

Sandy's Whiting said well, perhaps that was another reason why the D.P.P. had recommended no further action.
But of course I'd have to come up before the court again.
However, not to worry—the whole family would be there to
support me and George had agreed to stand surety for my
good behaviour.

I said I couldn't face him. I'd rather stay in the Remand
Home.

Matron said thanks, but she was running out of tea, and

the sergeant said if I refused to go home I could be sent somewhere else indefinitely where I might not get any tea at all.

Both Matron and Sandy's Whiting gave him a look, and he said well, maybe, like he'd said already, I'd had my punishment.

I wasn't afraid of the court any more. I was only scared of George. He was the only person I was really conscious of in court, and the one I was trying not to look at.

Mum, Grandad, and the twins were there. Mum was in tears and Grandad was obviously telling her to pull herself together. I could positively *see* him reeking of embrocation.

Len was making rude signs with his fingers to cheer me up, and taking off Aunt Rene Tindall praying for light. Hélène was trying to make him stop it, but she was crying too.

The only person who wasn't doing anything was George. He was neither smiling nor looking upset. He was just looking everyday George, as if nothing terrible had ever happened.

But I couldn't meet his eyes—not for a long time. And when I did, in spite of myself I started to count out loud; one, two, three, four, five, six, seven . . .